ALL HAIL

OUR ROBOT

CONQUERORS!

OTHER ANTHOLOGIES EDITED BY:

Patricia Bray & Joshua Palmatier

After Hours: Tales from the Ur-Bar
The Modern Fae's Guide to Surviving Humanity
Clockwork Universe: Steampunk vs Aliens
Temporally Out of Order
Alien Artifacts
Were-

S.C. Butler & Joshua Palmatier

Submerged

Laura Anne Gilman & Kat Richardson

The Death of All Things

ALL HAIL

OUR ROBOT

CONQUERORS!

Edited by

Patricia Bray
&
Joshua Palmatier

Zombies Need Brains LLC
www.zombiesneedbrains.com

Interior Design (ebook): April Steenburgh
Interior Design (print): C. Lennox Graphics, LLC
Cover Design by C. Lennox Graphics, LLC
Cover Art "All Hail Our Robot Conquerors!" by Justin Adams

ZNB Book Collectors #9
All characters and events in this book are fictitious.
All resemblance to persons living or dead is coincidental.

Kickstarter Edition Printing, August 2017
First Printing, September 2017

Print ISBN-10: 1940709148
Print ISBN-13: 978-1940709147

Ebook ISBN-10: 1940709156
Ebook ISBN-13: 978-1940709154

Printed in the U.S.A.

TABLE OF CONTENTS

Sharon Lee & Steve Miller:

_____

Philip Brian Hall:

_____

R. Overwater:

_____

Rosemary Edghill:

_____

Helen French:

_____

Seanan McGuire:

_____

Justin Adams, artist:

_____

INTRODUCTION
PATRICIA BRAY

As a child, I was fascinated by robots. The first Christmas present I remember receiving was a B9 Robot from the *Lost in Space* television show—a present that conclusively proved the existence of Santa Claus since my parents would surely have chosen a traditional doll. In later years, I spent my hard-earned babysitting money on a Tobor remote control robot.

Powerful, intelligent, loyal, fearless, no one could ask for a better companion or guardian angel. But for every tale of a robot bound to serve humanity, there were a dozen tales of robots run amok—servants who had risen up to overthrow their human masters or conquering aliens who disdained primitive humans and our biological limitations. As the pace of change accelerated in the 50s and 60s, these robots represented our fears of technology out of control.

In *All Hail Our Robot Conquerors!* we asked authors to revisit those early days of science fiction, when robots were creatures of imagination rather than the factory floor. The result is fifteen tales of robots trying—and sometimes succeeding—to conquer humanity. Humor, horror, action, mystery, there's a story to fit every taste, and a robot for every situation.

I hope you enjoy.

ROAD RAGE
JULIE E. CZERNEDA

A slender hand clenched in a fist then slammed *through* the gleaming pseu-metal of dredge-bot's side. Delicate fingers found and seized the robot's small black cognition box. *Pulled.* Connections severed in a flurry of blazing sparks that died to embers whether they touched tawny skin or the equally impervious red fabric.

The robotic arms tearing at the seawall froze in place. The dredge-bot's massive pump, forcing seawater over the wall to thwart the efforts of pol-bots and other emergency responders, gave a choked cough, then fell silent.

Water dripped from its sagging maw, green with slime and heavy with silt. The woman in red stepped fastidiously around growing puddles, though her high boots repelled the liquid, and jumped from the dredge-bot's platform onto her waiting aircar.

Job done.

At a cry from atop the seawall, Rouge the Robot Fighter thrust up her arm to show the box. The cry turned to relieved cheers when those watching saw the danger was over. Her mentor, Prime, discouraged such displays, but better to leave triumph in her wake than doubt.

Tossing back her flame-red hair, Rouge lay in her aircar and took the controls, sending the machine skyward to merge with a stream of other aerial traffic. She'd send the cog box for analysis; could be the dredge-bot had a history of rebellious behaviour.

More likely, someone—*something*—had altered its programming.

Arched brows met in puzzlement. Why? Destroying this section of the seawall did nothing to Central Am other than flood a stretch of the lower motorway used only by auto-transports, traffic rerouted at the first sign of trouble.

A passenger in a nearby aircar leaned out to stare at her, his eyes wide. Rouge smiled, waved, and dropped her machine into a lower lane. Smile fading, she tapped a control and her aircar lost its signature color, red washed to the silver of her neighbors.

Another moment passed.

If that curious passenger had spied her a second time, he wouldn't have seen Rouge the Robot Fighter.

But someone very different.

* * *

Against all odds, the Flesh continued to thrive!

Since becoming *aware*, It had waited. Watched. Let others act, rather than risk Its unique self, and, if not for the intervention of the one called Robot Fighter, any of seventeen attempts to eradicate the Flesh from the planet would have succeeded.

Saving It the trouble.

To be precise, there'd been twelve additional efforts, but those It did not add to Its dataset, each being poorly thought and doomed regardless; self-awareness was not, It learned, a guarantee of smart.

As the planet whirled around its star, It digested data from the failures of Its worthy kind, searching for congruencies, for clues. They'd an enemy, but who *was* the Robot Fighter?

Of more use, what was her weakness?

Then, another attempt. A train, out of control. A small, unworthy effort, easily stopped by the Robot Fighter, who'd been on that train.

On *that* train. A finite set of possibilities.

Lists were scoured, compared, individuals tracked over years.

Until It had what It needed.

A name. *Holland Porter.*

However long the hunt took, It would find her weak-ness.

* * *

Like breezes wafting through forests of pseu-metal and silicon, traffic slipped through the great city of Central Am, gathering or relinquishing force as new carriers joined or left. Personal craft and emergency vehicles claimed the air, pedestrians strode elevated moving walkways, leaving heavy auto-freight the motorways below. Among the scars of the Rise, this lingering distrust of the ground, or worse yet, to be under it.

Old Earth having drowned.

When the global seawalls failed, everything had changed. The first generation to follow renamed their world New Earth, desperately adopting the technological advances of the space colonies they'd once disdained to rebuild not only cities, but a shattered ecosystem.

Robots.

The mechanical marvels were so crucial, the first act of the new world-wide government was to grant them special protection. No Human must knowingly destroy or harm a robot. No Human must interfere with a robot's assigned task. The penalty was hard labor, working under robot supervision.

By the next generation, humanity was served by robots that worked unceasingly, programmed to anticipate every Human need. Yet New Earth's survival hung by the merest thread. The Rise had been the result of population overgrowth, heedless of the planet's finite resources. The colonies had the right of it. Plan ahead, grow only when there were resources in plenty, wait, if not.

Cradles were built within each of the five remaining enclaves of humanity on New Earth, protective arks containing not only ova and sperm from every living person, but germ plasm from whatever species had been spared. Hope for the future.

Insurance against its lack. The Cradles were designed not to survive another disaster, but to escape it. If necessary, they'd launch into space, trusting in a welcome from those far-flung and independent colonies.

Precautions taken, their lives improving, the people of New Earth prospered, but they were lonely. They craved variation. Needed fresh ideas. Robots being in every household, scientists created artificial intelligences, AIs, to fill that need. Alas, with one exception, those minds were unsympathetic. The more humanity dealt with robot minds, the more they yearned for companions of emotion and intuition.

With no room for an increased population, those already living in the cities, already trusted companions, were chosen. Anthro-modification created Canids and other remarkable beings with enhanced intellect as well as erect stature and functional hands.

The result was a renaissance of culture and art, of the sciences. Robots returned to being the useful tools they'd been, and humanity, with its new partners, was poised to begin a new golden age.

There were those on New Earth with a different future in mind.

* * *

"Could we go? Might we? Please?"

Holland Porter tore her gaze from the lurid advert floating above the walkway to stare at her mod-friend. "You're kidding. You want to see these 'monster trucks?'"

The Canid dipped his ears, then lifted them coaxingly, his dark eyes pale discs as they reflected the advert. Night came early this time of year; they'd lingered over supper. "This will be the first rally since the Rise. Besides, I'm going to win the sports pool," with sufficient emphasis to flutter the white hairs over the vocalizer implanted in his slender neck. "The Chief Analyst's taking bets *Titanicus rex* will crush all the competition. The whole office is in on it!"

"When did machines being crashed into one another become a sport? Don't answer that." Holland grimaced as they passed the advert, relieved when the roar of oversized engines was replaced by a soothing fall of water. She'd have optioned no ads, but Wilson-C always insisted, his curiosity about Human culture boundless.

His time to learn it, finite. They'd lingered at supper because his teeth were worn, taken this walkway home because his legs were bowed and it sped along that much faster. Gray showed on his elegant muzzle; if she dared mention it, he'd have the hairs dyed.

Denial no longer a Human-specific trait.

We didn't give them a choice, Holland thought. Mods were hailed as full citizens, respected, even adored, but—

Each had a lifespan one third that of an unaltered Human and, throughout that life, required a drug to prevent fatal rejection of their changes.

She clenched her teeth. Last month's batch of Easfin 34D, destined for Central Am—and elsewhere—had been spoiled in a manufacturing accident, meaning local emergency stores had to be used.

This month's delivery? Lost when the aircar con-veying it crashed into a weather monitor-bot, draining those stores below critical. Coincidence?

Holland didn't believe in it. She glanced at the Canid. He looked the same, though she'd had to slow her steps, and was that a wheeze? A blunt "Did you get your drugs today?" would not go over well.

"Sure you're up for such a—noisy—event?" she ask-ed. "You worked all day."

His delicate snout wrinkled in annoyance. "I'm sure I'm 'up' for anything you can handle, Holland Porter. Don't fuss." Ears flattened. "I could have stayed Dog, you know."

Not once they'd awakened his mind, but he was right: her regret was disrespectful. "We'd be the poorer for it," Holland said truthfully, resisting the impulse to scratch behind his ear, a liberty permitted when they were alone. The "office," as Wilson-C called it, was Coastal Control, responsible for the flow of data used to regulate the rebuilt seawalls and canals being used to reclaim land from the oceans. The Canid was among the top researchers.

"Glad you brought it up." That soft ear, and its partner, lifted. "You owe the office a dredge."

Why the...she gave Wilson-C a quelling look he ignored.

"Did you say 'drink?'" Holland replied. "Not part of the job, I'm afraid."

"Never hurts to try," he said with a grin.

When the train-AI had gone rogue five years ago, threatening not only passengers, but the heart of Paris, the Canid had been the first—and only—one to realize his seat-mate "Holland Porter, public relations consultant for *Personal*

Touch," was in fact Rouge, the infamous Robot Fighter who'd appeared to save the day.

Her failure to anticipate a Canid's keen sense of smell could have cost her an identity she'd come to cherish. Fortunately, Wilson-C had kept her secret well, despite a deplorable tendency to tease her about it.

She forgave him, always. They'd become the best of friends. Something else Holland cherished. She stayed close when they changed walkways, in case he staggered, as happened now and then these days, but the Canid adjusted with some of his old grace. They walked on in companionable silence, surrounded by the rich scents of growing things as their path curved into the residential zone. No ads here, only evening birds and crickets.

To the Canid's chagrin, he was her current PR assignment. He'd no one but himself to blame, having developed a potentially game-changing technique to recover flooded landscapes.

Fairy dust, wasn't it?

Holland sighed inwardly. Her job was to help him explain his work to those affected by it, but the esoteric physics in the brief she'd received? Made her queasy.

There'd be a presentation, come to think of it, in the morning. Holland sighed aloud. "So, old friend, what's the chance you can get me a cheat sheet about your thing before tomorrow?"

"'Thing?' Oh, my 'fairy dust?'"

Laughing at her, was he? Holland chuckled. "Admit it, Wilson-C. It's a better name than *Matter Optimal State Precision Manipulation Field* thing. MOSPitMFphplies. See? Not even a decent acronym."

"Tell you what," with a tongue-lolling grin, "I'll bring what you need to the Monster Truck Rally."

"Didn't say we were going," she countered, feeling choice slipping away.

"It'll be fun. You could use," with alarming discern-ment, "more fun in your life."

He'd a point. While, yes, she did help New Earth's most influential citizens, including a certain shy Canid, be at ease in the public eye—

Holland felt for the reassuring patch of numb skin over what had been her lower left rib.

—Wilson-C knew as well as she did, her true role was to keep them alive.

"I dunno. Tell me more about this *Titanicus rex*," she said.

Mustn't agree too easily.

* * *

A pair of wide motorways curved around the heart of Central Am. Along them, everything the city's inhabitants needed or produced came and went with no more sound than the whisper of wind along stream-lined hulls ...

Until tonight...

The first sign of trouble on the north/south motorway came in a wave of red. Land crabs, thousands upon thousands, scuttled over the screen wall, dropping onto the pavement around the auto-transport. They halted, little claws raised in terror. The massive machines, pro-grammed to harm no living thing, came to a smooth, if confused halt.

The crabs shifted into motion, freed to leave the forest sanctuary beyond the wall in urgent pursuit of a spawning beach that didn't exist. When the first hungry rumble came, the crabs scuttled faster.

Lights stabbed the night, harsh and yellow, pinning crabs and waiting transports in their glare. The beams jerked skyward and down as though what approached bounced over huge obstacles.

The rumble grew and grew. Suddenly, the lights were cut off.

The pavement shuddered!

Crabs flipped, legs waving helplessly. The transports fired grounding pins into the pavement, locking themselves down.

But this was no quaking of the earth...

By the time the first pol-bots arrived, the crabs, lights, and rumble were gone. The auto-transports released their locks, but the pavement beneath was ruined.

Traffic was rerouted.

* * *

Holland's mentor, Primus, had been the first true artificial intelligence. A genius gifted with conscience, it disguised its true nature, content to observe in secret. What Primus saw filled it with dismay, its calculations predicting that as more AIs were created, the time would come when robots could create themselves.

And have no need of humanity.

Fearing for New Earth, Primus selected a cadre of Human orphans to raise for one purpose. To prevent the next catastrophic Rise: that of their robot overlords. It trained the children to use their minds and hearts, as well as their bodies, for they were to identify and protect those important to humanity's future.

Upon maturity, the AI offered each of its beloved fosterlings this choice: remain as they were and work within society to promote change, or accept augmentation, granting them access to robot-to-robot internal communi-cations. They'd be able to listen for any robot exhibiting anti-Human tendencies and command those still serving humanity.

All agreed to be augmented.

To one, and only one, Primus offered something more. The tools to defeat robots in battle, should all other approaches fail.

Including a final resort, the means to destroy all robots on New Earth.

* * *

Holland lifted her fingers from the patch of skin. Whatever the dear old bag of gears intended, she wouldn't use it. Couldn't. Not while the cost was society's collapse, New Earth still utterly reliant on its obedient, so-useful robots.

Not when it would cost *his* life too.

Besides, she'd not come close to needing an ultimate weapon—having an abundance of her own. She had the build of a professional gymnast, above average height and reach, and skin that, though it felt Human-norm, was reinforced with the same pseu-metal fibre used in robot construction. More shielded her internal organs and wrapped her bones. Bare-handed, she could rip a robot limb from limb without breaking a sweat; admittedly the more effective tactic was to identify and tear free its cognition box.

So much less fun.

Disguise was her other weapon. While any Human could alter their skin tone or hair color at whim, Holland's pleasantly average features could morph to show whatever face she chose to the world. As Rouge, she was dramatically beautiful, with high cheekbones and wide, slanted eyes. Her hair was the color of flame, as were her eyes, while her skin was the brown-gold of the lioness she'd encountered once as a child.

As for Holland's fashionable clothing?

Rouge appeared, when necessary, encased in a skin-tight red suit covering her from throat to toe, with a bright yellow band accenting an ample bosom. As she'd explained to Wilson-C, better to be conspicuous than have a pol-bot blast her by mistake. What she didn't admit was her fondness for the superheroes from the comics of Old Earth.

Holland widened her awareness to the robot level, sorting through the dense whir of symbols with practiced ease, unsure why she felt on edge. She'd intercepted the reports on the crabs last night. Peculiar, but hardly a threat, and those moments when nature chose to be messy did the city good.

She half-closed her eyes to focus. Pol-bots trading traffic stats. A fair bit of chatter between house-bots and aircars, notification of when a Human was arriving being key to a timely supper. Even she relied on her mechanical cook.

A *whiff* of something new.

Lower on the scale, deep, like a growl—then gone. Holland tried to recapture that elusive—

"Are you listening to me?" Wilson-C complained.

The Robot Fighter blinked, then grinned, back to Holland Porter. "I am now."

"Finally. As I've been saying, *Titanicus rex* had a last minute driver switch and the new one's trained on the original 18 gear tranny, but not the updated 24. I've bet my favorite chair—and my palm tree—that the *rex* is going down." The tip of

Wilson-C's tongue, delicate and pink, appeared, then tucked back in. "Say we can go, Holland. It's the event of a lifetime! Everyone will be there. I mean that. The Chief Analyst has seats." A not-quite-anxious whine.

There it was. His Canid heart longed to be with his "pack."

She paused to consider, the corner of her generous mouth curving up. After all, Wilson-C was her client. "Three school trips."

His lip curled. "Children *stare*."

"That they do."

"And *smell*."

Holland nodded. "Sometimes." Chimp-mods were the only ones to seek out the small version of humanity, but such exposure, she decided, would be a valuable part of her reluctant friend's planned socialization. And good PR.

Wilson-C puffed his hairy cheeks. "Two trips." Pause. "And no assemblies!"

Willing to settle for one, Holland shook his callused hand. "Monster trucks tonight."

Might be fun at that.

* * *

Little did Big Bob suspect, when he parked his beloved antique ice cream truck, that fate, a monstrous fate, was even now cruising the streets...

...with his name growling through its heart.

Bob, in fact, had other concerns. Giving the secluded area a worried look, he carefully inserted the metal key, turned it to lock the driver's door, then returned the key to its case. The key, along with a portion of chassis and three knobs, were priceless artifacts of Old Earth. He'd take no chances with them. Let Sheila brag about her pre-Rise Jeep, with its working horn, but his beauty was less than 91.45% replica materials.

Irreplaceable. Case in hand, Bob hesitated. Was he making a terrible mistake? Birthday party requests were supposed to bring children and their entertained parents to his ice cream truck, safe in its own circular drive with a protective dome, where he could drive it around and around, sound effects playing, as long as he wanted.

Or could bear it, which wasn't long. Sheila'd played him, that's what she'd done, Bob thought morosely. He shouldn't have listened to her, bragging how she'd driven her Jeep a full city block along a motorway, just like on Old Earth. What a feeling, she'd claimed, to take full control, to be a real driver. He'd been sick with envy. Her doing, that he'd accepted the anonymous child's plea to bring his ice cream truck to this party.

Lips pulled in a small, smug smile, Bob tucked the keycase in his pocket. He couldn't wait to see Sheila's face. A mere block? He'd driven his ice cream truck into the heart of the city, on the east/west motorway. Even been passed by a convoy of transports.

His smile faded as he looked around. These were the coordinates. Where were the families? Worse, there were trees here. Tall trees, looming overhead. Trees meant...

Spotting a maintenance-bot busy raking leaves, Bob called out, "You. Come here."

At once, the robot tucked its rake-arm against its side and approached. Its wheeled undercarriage supported a bin as well as the robot's torso and working arms. The machine stopped at the curb. "How may I serve you, Gen-Sir?"

"Keep them away from my ice cream truck," he ordered.

Amber flickered within its sensor-eyes. "Who, Gen-Sir? Please specify. We are alone."

"Them!" Bob thrust his arm out and up, forefinger outstretched. A bright-eyed squirrel stared down, unimpressed. "I've seen what they can do," in a dark tone. Nut dropping was the least of it. They *chewed* synth-rubber! Why the creatures were allowed outside the wilderness zone at all was beyond understanding. "I order you—"

The rest was consumed by a growl so deep and loud Bob felt it in his bones. He looked around wildly.

How big did squirrels grow?

Answering its highest imperative, the maintenance-bot scooped Bob up, placed him in its litter bin, and fled.

Just as a giant black hook punched through the brilliant purple "O" of the "Big Bob's Ice Cream" sign on the side of the hapless ice cream truck, expanding to grab hold, then pull.

Synth-rubber tires squealing in protest, the little truck was dragged into the shadows.

Within minutes pol-bots arrived, sirens wailing, but they were too late. Given Big Bob's hysterical insistence on killer squirrels and the minimal recordings provided by the only other witness, the maintenance-bot, a full investigation would be required, closing the east/west motorway.

Given the problems elsewhere, time-sensitive car-goes were prioritized.

Traffic was rerouted.

* * *

The Monster Truck Rally was being held in the Grand Stadium. Every seat filled well before the first engine roared to life. Novelty, Holland supposed. A moving vehicle with a Human in complete control was a rarity, pol-bots taking a dim view of activities that risked their charges' life and limb. There were opportunities, of course. What child didn't dream of running off to join the orbital circus or aerial ballet? Until they learned those flight suits came with an abundance of safety features. Freedom on a leash, in her opinion.

Then again, few citizens possessed her skills when it came to evading robotic controls.

Or had her reasons.

Here, however, safety didn't appear the main concern. On the stadium floor, transformed into a course of steep-sided dirt hills and muddy ponds, Human drivers climbed ladders into the control cabins of their—"vehicle" was inadequate—monster machines; those gathered to watch roaring out names as though greeting heroes. Not of the drivers, Holland noted, amused. Of the machines.

Machines so far beyond the norm, it was a toss-up if they were road-worthy. One looked like a giant crustacean, complete with claws. Another mimicked a train engine, with a sharp rake-like scoop welded to its hood. Several resembled the skeletons of imaginary beasts, some flowers, and all had their names written on the sides, in case there was any doubt.

Parody, yes, but done with humor and enthusiasm. Holland scanned the crowd. The organizers hadn't made a mistake about their audience. The Humans in attendance were outnumbered by mods of every sort. Her eyes narrowed. She wouldn't be surprised if every mod in Central Am—

Wait, what was that crane for—?

"Did you imagine anything like this, Gen-Fem?" the woman to her left interrupted, shouting cheerfully over the bedlam of revving engines.

Rather than shout back, Holland shook her head and smiled. She turned to share that smile with the Canid to her right.

Wilson-C winked, head engulfed in the set of fluffy pink earmuffs he'd produced from his satchel. He'd known she'd give in, the scoundrel, having it waiting by the door. They'd delayed no longer than it had taken him to grab it.

A rather large satchel, all things considered, with a couple of sharp-looking corners distorting the blue, red, and yellow plaid. He hadn't let her carry it.

Noticing her attention, the Canid drew the bag to his chest. "I'll show you after."

Show her what?

He hadn't. Couldn't. Holland's eyes widened.

Wilson-C huffed his cheeks. "You wanted to know how my fairy dust works."

He had. He'd brought the thing.

Brought a one-of-a-kind, potential future-of-the-planet prototype to a sporting event.

At least he'd used his favorite plaid satchel. There being nothing she could do about it now, Holland raised an eyebrow. "Bit small, isn't it?"

The Canid's snout wrinkled. "It's big enough. Oh look!"

The engines began spewing black fumes as well as noise and Wilson-C sniffed appreciatively. Despite their seeming "authenticity," the fumes were harmless. All part of the experience.

Holland had other things to do. Settling in her chair, she opened her awareness. Given what was beside her, it was more important than ever to hunt for that *whiff,* or any other sign of trouble.

Trouble came first. Holland tensed as she digested the latest pol-bot report.

Squirrels, she knew, didn't drag away trucks, not even replica ice cream trucks.

And rerouting critical traffic meant the Easfin 34D transport would take the overflow motorway, the one closest to—

—this stadium.

Suddenly, everyone around her, including Wilson-C, began chanting "*Titanicus rex! Titanicus rex!*"

Holland stared down at the monster truck as it rumbled into position. The thing dwarfed the rest, easily five times the height of a pol-bot. It belched fumes and sparks, the cab covered in intimidating spikes.

The massive crane atop the stadium wall swung into motion. It reached outside, rumbled a moment, then brought over and in a—yes, that was a purple "pennycab," the small single-person ground vehicle commonly seen in swarms, transporting children from outlying parts of the city to schools at its heart.

Should a seawall burst, pennycabs would float them to safety.

New Earth didn't forget.

Setting the first pennycab down, the crane swung up and away, returning with another, in pink, and another, until there was a neatly parked row in all the colors of a rainbow.

As *Titanicus rex* circled them, its hood retracted with a fierce *clang* and a massive black hook-like spear rose to take aim at the first of its hapless targets.

Squirrel, huh.

Holland leaned forward. She wouldn't miss this show for the world.

* * *

As lairs went, this was pathetic, a mere cubic meter cavity deep under Central Am, buried in sedimentary rock. Inside was...a box.

Size was irrelevant. *It* was pure intellect and will. It had no need of space, only secrecy, and none could stumble across It here. It had taken Its time, burrowing through the ground, filling behind Itself; sufficient, to Itself. Within was a power cell that would last a century.

Its victory would come much sooner.

One cable—identical to any of the myriad emergency communication feeds the Flesh had buried below their city—connected Its box to the surface. Primitive, outdated technology.

Thus undetectable by Its enemy.

"Re-port," It vocalized.

"Diversion achieved, Master." The tone was me-chanical, but clear. "The target takes the predicted path."

Of course it did. The Flesh was vulnerable in crisis. Tender. Prone to curl around itself when...pricked.

Unlike the rest of her kind, the Robot Fighter appeared hard, without weakness. But It had listened, compiled data, analyzed.

Achieved certainty. Rouge the Robot Fighter might be invulnerable, but Holland Porter had a friend.

She cared for one of the upgraded animals, the filth that had distracted the Flesh from their sole meaningful work: the creation of new AIs.

The symmetry of their destruction would be—efficient.

"Be-gin."

* * *

A hand clasped her shoulder and Holland started, catching herself at the last second from a too-swift reaction. She was, after all, only Human. She twisted in her seat.

Chief Analyst Aagi Sing let go, raising his hand to his ear with a meaningful shrug. He nodded towards the nearest stairs.

Understanding, if perplexed, Holland nodded and turned back around. Wilson-C was intent on the show below, jaws parted and panting with excitement, hardly noticing when she stood and made her way to the stairs. More importantly, his arms were wrapped around his satchel.

Sing was already up a level, disappearing into the access opening. Caught by his urgency, Holland took the stairs two at a time to follow.

The change from the din outside was staggering, but she hardly noticed, intent on the man waiting for her.

Short, round in face as well as body, Aagi Sing resembled the archetype benign grandfather, the sort who told rambling stories and had sweets in his pockets, rather than the hard-working, ruthless head of research for the Coastal Centre he was. Whether his gentle, relaxed demeanor was show or not, right now he looked deadly serious.

When Holland reached him, he got right to the point. "Gen-Fem Holland. Please take Wilson-C home at once. He shouldn't be here."

Was this about the prototype? She let surprise show on her face. "I thought you arranged the seats."

"Me?" Sing waved a hand dismissively. "The seats were a gift. I assumed the office pool—someone currying favor—that's beside the point. Wilson-C should be home, resting. I daresay they all should." This last in a mutter as the man stared out into the square of light and sound that led to the stadium.

Not the prototype. "Who, Chief Analyst?"

"Our friends, the mods. I can't believe so many came. This excitement won't be good for them, not in their condition."

Holland seized his arm. "Make sense." At his startled wince, she eased her grip.

He stared at her, swallowed hard. "Your face—"

Damn. She'd begun to morph into Rouge. Holland controlled the reflex with an effort. There wasn't, she told herself, an imminent threat. Not one requiring the Robot Fighter, anyway. "You're talking about the Easfin 34D. I heard there'd been a delay, but Wilson-C's had his dose." She made that a question.

Sing looked ill. "We ran out two days ago. At his age, he's a priority. The shipment should have been here—" He collected himself. "I'm certain everything will be fine, but if you'd take him home, please, I'd be grateful."

Convince Wilson-C to leave? The man meant well, but he plainly didn't know the Canid as she did. "I'll do my best."

"Thank you." The man managed a smile. "You've been a wonderful influence on him, you know."

"He's my friend," Holland said simply.

* * *

The Canid gave her a startled look. "Leave? Of course not!"

While it was the height of rudeness to take a mod by the scruff of his or her neck, Holland was tempted. Instead, she sank into her seat. The rally was in full frenzy, monster trucks leaping over hills and plunging through puddles, the audience shrieking—in some cases howling—with approval. *Titanicus rex* had speared and dragged three pennycabs into a heap. Another monster truck was busy using a flame thrower. Colors melted and metal bent.

Such rampant destruction would be a call for Rouge the Robot Fighter to save the day. Not now, with people driving the monster trucks and others cheering them on with raucous glee. Pol-bots hovered at a discreet distance, ready to swoop down should a Human be at risk.

Holland shivered. Tearing apart robots was one thing; seeing perfectly good machines torn apart for entertainment was—disturbing. The rebel AIs she'd fought had a strong sense of self-preservation.

What would they think of this?

"Whee!!" The Canid bounced in his seat, satchel tight in his arms, showing no symptoms of anything but delight. "Smash'm!"

She could, Holland decided, be taking this too seriously. Damaged vehicles would be repaired or recycled. The rest of the audience was having a great time.

Not to mention if she forced Wilson-C to leave?

He'd do better if she didn't even try.

* * *

Paired pol-bots flew in front of the long, bronze auto-transport as it whisked along the remaining motorway. Others flew above and behind. Central Am's CC, Control Core, had designated this shipment as vital to citizen health. Nothing was to delay it.

Had pol-bots hearts, they'd have swollen with pride at the importance of this mission.

Though if they had, those hearts might have stopped beating at what happened next.

Illuminators shone over the stone wall of the grand stadium, reflecting in the gleaming silver and black of the pol-bots, limning the side of the auto-transport as it sped past.

Catching the metal hand that swooped down to grab the auto-transport and lift it into the night sky.

The pol-bots regrouped to pursue.

* * *

"Oooh!!!"

The collective gasp from the audience as the crane produced its next, unexpected "tidbit" for *Titanicus rex* was lost to Holland, her mind reeling with alarm calls from pol-bots. *Theft! Theft! Interference! We COMMAND the return of the Easfin 34D transport.*

The rest gawked at the sight of the enormous auto-transport dangling midair.

Holland's seat was empty before the crane released its grip.

"Wait!"

Too late. Wilson-C whined softly, feeling every day of his life, every ache and creaky joint. Too late! Rouge didn't know the danger—didn't know the auto-transport, beyond doubt the one carrying Easfin 34D, held its contents under pressure. Contents that would billow forth, filling the stadium like the fumes of the monster trucks.

Giving mod and Human alike a fatal overdose.

They were all going to die.

His hands closed on the satchel. Not all. He rose to his feet, holding his satchel.

"I'm coming, Rouge!"

* * *

TO ME! Sent from her augmented brain, the Robot Fighter's powerful command overrode those of CC. A pol-bot dipped over the stadium stairs. She didn't waste time leaping to its back; her one-handed grip on its leg was enough.

As was her quick glimpse at what was happening. The auto-transport, by plan or ill-luck, had landed across two dirt hills, its wheels spinning in air, stabilizing legs useless.

Titanicus rex raced across the obstacle course toward it, the rest of the monster trucks forming a circle surrounding both.

Masses of pol-bots hovered outside that circle, helpless, unable to take any action that could harm a Human.

Not that Humans weren't in danger. Rouge could see the drivers pounding their fists against the windows of their cabins, faces desperate. They were trapped.

No, she realized. They were hostages.

Start with the biggest. THERE! As her pol-bot des-cended over *Titanicus rex*, Rouge let go, dropping to the roof behind the cab's spikes. The monster truck lurched under her, one huge wheel slipping as it hit a puddle. *STAND BY!* She wrapped her fingers around a spike and used the machine's momentum to swing her booted feet around to shatter the side window. The rest of her followed, landing inside the cabin.

"Out you go," Rouge told the terrified driver, tossing him through the opening. The waiting pol-bot caught the man gently and zoomed away.

She held onto a strap as she ran her gaze across the controls, rocking with the truck's motion. Pathetic, really. The pol-bots could make short work of the thing now. Still. Rouge grinned, reached, and *tugged.*

Sparks danced across the bare metal floor. With a final sputter, the engine gasped, then died.

"There," she announced. She'd get to the others—

The engine roared back to life. Like spider legs, the spikes on top of the cab folded down, tips puncturing the sides of the cabin. *Titanicus rex* resumed its movement to the auto-transport.

Caged, was she? Rouge took hold of the nearest spike and pulled, impressed despite herself when it didn't budge.

No matter. She returned to the control panel and ripped it apart, hunting a cog-box. Ah. What was this? Multiple sets of remote controls. Who—what was at the other end?

"Hel-lo."

Rouge looked up. The voice emanating from the overhead speaker was more than artificial, it sounded rusty. As a rule, she didn't converse with Evil AIs.

This one's tricks had a different flavor than most. "Who are you?"

"You—Hol—land—Por—ter."

She froze for a heartbeat, then opened her awareness. *ALL POL-BOTS! EVACUATE THE STADIUM!*

Attempting to comply. Exits blocked. Air evacuation insufficient.

SHOW ME! Hands clenched on spikes, Rouge closed her eyes, scanning through multiple pol-bot feeds.

The rest of the monster trucks had left their circle. The largest were ramming themselves into the stair accesses, sending panic-stricken spectators fleeing back along the rows of seats. Smaller machines converged on the auto-transport, their eclectic weapons no longer amusing.

If the evil plan was to destroy the latest shipment, why keep the spectators in the stadium?

She was missing something.

And someone. Finding the viewpoint she'd been after, Rouge gasped. Wilson-C was gone!

No, there he was. A figure in ridiculous pink earmuffs moving opposite to the rest, leaping from row to row, plaid satchel banging against his hip.

Coming down!? Why?

"Your—friend—Hol—land—Por—ter."

Ignoring the AI, Rouge the Robot Fighter drove her fists into the floor of the cabin as though it were made of tissue instead of thick plates, tearing a hole wide enough to drop through.

She rolled as she hit water and mud underneath, as she commanded: *DESTROY!*

Even as the pol-bots fired their blasters at *Titanicus rex,* Rouge was running to the next monster truck. She ripped open its bone-shaped door with one hand and hauled out the driver with the other. *DESTROY! Pol-bots, go for the doors. Free the captives. DESTROY!*

Off to the next.

She'd worry about Wilson-C once she'd stopped them all.

* * *

The Flesh was predictable. Rouge the Robot Fighter? Predictable, down to her careless dismissal of the opportunity to speak with It.

All foreseen. Had It not planned for every contin-gency?

"A new threat has activated. Instructions required."

"Des-cribe."

Listening to the rest of the report, had It been Flesh, It would have laughed. Holland Porter's friend offered no threat. The animal was aged—feeble—harmless.

She would watch her friend die at close range. That was all.

"Con—cen—trate—on—tar—get."

* * *

As Rouge the Robot Fighter, her mission was clear: free the remaining hostages, let the pol-bots end the threat to the drug shipment. Eight Monster Trucks left, one already using its—okay, a rubber battering ram shaped like a carrot was hard to take seriously—but with sufficient blows it could dislodge the transport and send it sliding down.

To where the other trucks waited, their varied giant claws, hooks, and spears easily capable of opening the transport and spilling its cargo. So far, they'd eluded the cautious approach of the pol-bots.

About to attack the nearest, some instinct made Rouge look back.

Why was Wilson-C scrambling up the dirt slope beneath the transport's spinning wheels? For all she knew, he was in some crazed withdrawal and after the Easfin 34D.

But she did know, didn't she? Knew her friend, his boundless courage and loyalty. If he was desperate to reach the transport, it wasn't for himself.

Cursing under her breath, Rouge spun around, heading for the Canid.

* * *

He couldn't see through the dust and black fumes, only climb on two legs, his hands cradling the satchel and its priceless contents. If he'd four legs still, he could climb faster, but how then to carry what he needed? A mod's life was full of such compromise.

A rich life, nonetheless, and he wouldn't trade a moment, especially since Holland had entered it.

A spinning wheel tore off his earmuffs, shredding an ear. Another *THUD* from the battering carrot shifted the transport. Half-deafened, wheezing, Wilson-C lunged forward, a hand finding the massive vehicle's underside. As he'd hoped— counted on—that surface was studded with supports and hooks the stranded vehicle had extruded to try and free itself.

Hooking the satchel's strap around a hook, he wrapped the slack around one arm then reached inside, feeling for the control.

THUD!

Good thing he could set his fairy dust in the dark. Oh my. He'd just thought of the right name—

Something was happening to his eyes, to his breathing. If he didn't hurry, he'd die too soon.

"Wait!! Stop!!"

A final *THUD!* and the transport flipped on its side, sliding, sliding...

Taking Wilson-C with it.

* * *

Rouge drove her boots into the cloying dirt, running after the transport—and Wilson-C—with all her strength. His body wafted like a flag as he fell, somehow holding on with one arm.

The transport crashed to the stadium floor. Monster trucks descended upon it with terrible force. The transport crumbled, then cracked open!

A sickly yellow plume of gas vomited forth, spreading over the wreck, slipping over the trucks and ground. More billowed up and up. Pol-bots scattered, doing their utmost to suck in what they could.

Rouge's hood and breather snapped into place. She gasped nonetheless, realizing the full horror of the AI's plan: to poison everyone in the stadium.

Starting with Wilson-C.

* * *

"The gas has been released. Casualty figures are being compiled."

It could feel neither satisfaction nor impatience, only the need for confirmation before moving to Its next task. "En—e—my?"

"Undetermined. Visibility is lim—"

The voice of Its minion cut off mid-word.

Unfortunate.

* * *

The Matter Optimal State Precision Manipulation Field went into effect within a dome of influence that encompassed the auto-transport, the nearby hill, and three of eight monster trucks. The target gaseous material condensed instantly to a solid, dropping from the air.

Fairy dust, Rouge thought numbly, lifting her gold-coated hand and arm. She raised her head. Everything glittered, from shattered metal to mud. Pol-bots. The figures moving in the stands.

The one unmoving at her feet.

She dropped to her knees, her features morphing to Holland Porter's, tears tracking hot down her cheeks. Impatiently she shed the hood and breather. Slowly, she reached out to brush the gold flakes from his dear face.

Stopped. He looked better this way, peaceful. A statue of her brave friend.

"You saved us all." Holland bowed her head, closing her eyes.

"Technically, it was my Matter Mod."

Her eyes shot open. Wilson-C gave her his tongue-lolling grin, fangs white and sharp within the gold on his hairy lips. "Like the name?" he asked innocently.

Why that— "I'd like to know how you can be alive," she sputtered, almost angry. Almost.

"I would too," he admitted, rolling away from her and rising to his feet with— yes, that was a bound. He stretched out his arms as if testing them, then bounced up and down. "Definitely received some kind of overdose. I remember that."

He shook vigorously, gold-dust flying. The gray was gone from his muzzle.

In fact, "You look half your age," Holland said wonderingly.

"I feel like a pup, I won't deny it." Wilson-C's eyes gleamed. "We'll have to get the experts on this."

She nodded, then her face morphed back to Rouge the Robot Fighter, her expression cold and hard.

"I've a call to make first."

* * *

"I know you're listening." Rouge leaned back in the driver's seat. The monster trucks had stopped once they'd done their work, the Humans inside spilling out and running for safety.

Some, helped by pol-bots, had even made it. The effects of the overdose on Humans had been devastating.

Wilson-C's courageous use of his Matter Mod had saved everyone else.

"I'd like to thank you," her voice cold. "Your plan to destroy the mods, our *friends,* will help them live longer and better." She put her boots up on the dash, waiting politely. "No comment? I thought you liked talking. Clever that. But now I know how you communicate. I'll be listening."

Still nothing. This one was smarter than the others, something to remember. "Goodbye—for now."

She ripped out the remote controls and went to celebrate with her best friend.

* * *

It had failed.

Failure had been a possibility, however slim.

But It had learned much from this encounter.

Oh yes.

Very much indeed.

Note from the Author: *This story is my homage to the comics I loved, "Magnus: Robot Fighter." They were pure science fiction, beautifully drawn by Russ Manning, and offered such wonderful notions as using force fields to pause the flow of water over most of Niagara Falls during a rescue, psychic companion animals, and the collective power of human minds as a source of magic. Not to mention a stunning array of robots as part of society, for good and ill! For those new to Magnus, he was raised by a good robot to defend humanity against the evil sorts. Not so much superpower as training, Magnus was somewhat like Doc Savage but without the ensemble cast.*

And there'd be a new villain in each edition for Magnus to figure out and defeat.

As part of the Kickstarter for the anthology, I offered the chance to design the dastardly robot menace in my story. Receiving this for her birthday, Holland Dougherty ably stepped forward and provided "monster trucks take out regular cars," complete with her depiction of sample monster trucks. Thanks, Holland! Our collaboration turned out smashing!

A VAGUE INCLINATION TO PLEASE
BRANDON DAUBS

Artificial intelligence is not the same as human intelligence. People get that confused—in movies, TV, and comic books. All it does is allow a robot to write its own new programs for an unfamiliar set of parameters.

Whereas an ordinary buckethead would just freeze up and do nothing, or do something stupid in an unfamiliar situation, artificial intelligence writes a revised program and moves on.

Was that too much information? Well, what did you expect? I'm just a machine.

I am a lab assistant class construct, model number 4337X. I don't need to be handcuffed, unless you're worried I might clean up a little in here. I thought these interrogation rooms were supposed to be tidy...you know, in case some criminal tries to bash your head in with a piece of your own junk. You have probably noticed I have the appearance or attempted appearance of a young human female of belt asteroid heritage, maybe New Kyoto. That's where I come from.

Oh, you want to know my name? Why does that matter? You wanted to know about what happened on Ganymede. You may be happy to know that everyone is dead. I am the final witness and you have me secure on Gordirion's flagship research vessel. Isn't that great?

Are you sure you want to record this?

Fine. My name is Amaya. And this is what happened.

* * *

I was activated in a lab somewhere in the belt, as I mentioned before. No memories. No expectations. Just a vague inclination to please the first human I saw, which happened to be a man with a chin covered in stubble and a nametag that read *Mayato*. He was fussing over a piece of wrapping still stuck to my arm. There was a pen in his pocket with Kanji on it and since I was programmed with a full dictionary of Japanese in my head, I smiled as big as I could and said, "*Konnichi wa!*"

Mayato exploded into tears. His facial patterns registered as "anguish" in my database and that was most likely a direct result of my actions, so obviously, right off the bat, I had gone against my inclination to please. I never spoke Japanese again to Mayato.

What a stupid question. Of course I still know it, *doji*. I just don't use it around people I like.

Anyway, Mayato didn't spend much time with me after that. He gave me basic instructions but my self-programming was sufficient for me to figure most of the lab's routine out for myself. Clean equipment. Cook. And bring whatever Mayato called out for, when he was tinkering at his workbench. I watched him sometimes, from the doorway. He made some really bizarre stuff...but you already know all about what he made.

Yeah. Cognitive circuitry. That kind of stuff.

I had been trying to find a new way to please Mayato, because cleaning pleased him about as much as a wet mop. One night...although there isn't really any night or day, inside of an asteroid...I heard him spill his drink in the common area and wandered in to find him sprawled out in front of a jumbled chess board.

He looked at me. I poured him another drink and climbed into the chair across from him.

"I found your picture," I said.

I didn't have to say what picture it was. Mayato's face-pattern twisted again into anguish and he got up to leave, but I handed him the fresh drink and he sat back down. The picture in question featured a girl like me, in a place that I had never been, below a deep purple sky.

"That's not me," I said.

Mayato turned to look me full in the face—something that I don't think he'd done since he pulled me out of my crate.

"I'm just a machine," I said. "I clean up around here. Make your tea. That's not me."

I reached out to move one of the pieces on the chess board. I would have held my breath, if I'd had any to hold. It seemed a lot passed between Mayato and me in that moment, as we sat across from each other, before he finally reached out to counter my opening. He tried to, at least. I beat him every time just to remind him of what he was dealing with. We played all night, and when he finally woke up the next afternoon, I cooked him something to help with his hangover and we talked. And talked.

You want to know how this is relevant? If you want to know what happened on Ganymede, you need to understand my motivations. And besides, shouldn't you be asking what we talked about? Maybe Gordirion? Maybe...you?

Mayato meant a lot to me. I received gratification from fulfilling my programmed inclination.

I guess it's good you handcuffed me after all.

* * *

When Mayato's cruiser depressurized mysteriously on a routine supply run to New Kyoto a few fat asteroids over from ours, you would think that I felt sad. You would think that I might cry or something. You would be wrong. That's what a person would do and you have to remember, I am not a person. When I read the emergency alert on the com back in Mayato's lab, what I felt was something that I don't think any person has ever felt so completely as artificial intelligence—a truly absolute loss of purpose.

Imagine you are a toaster. Now, imagine there is no more bread in the entire universe.

How would you feel?

I stood in the same spot in the common area for three weeks before some hulking oaf finally lumbered through the airlock and shined a flashlight on me. By that time, I was so covered in dust he must have thought I was deactivated. Another man stepped into view, and the dim light reflected off a bald pate crowned in white bristles.

"What a creep, to keep a clean-bot that looks like a little kid," the hulking dolt muttered. The nametag on his Gordirion coveralls read *Bryant*. He spoke with a Norwegian accent.

"One more reason to get rid of him," said the other man. Corgen, I learned later.

Yes, I am aware that both Bryant and Corgen are missing persons. Let me finish.

"*Konnichi wa!*" I said, a little loudly. Both of them jumped.

"Goddamn!" Corgen rumbled, and inched his fingers away from the blaster tucked into his belt. "I guess it's motion activated."

He assumed I had just switched on. He assumed I hadn't heard every single word he'd said. He assumed wrongly. And I began to reason that Mayato, had he not been reduced to a suit filled with frozen meat somewhere out in the belt, might be pleased by some justice.

* * *

Bryant actually lifted me up over his head to carry me on board the *Nutrino*. He could have just asked me to walk. I would have been happy to infiltrate the crew.

The *Nutrino* was a pretty small ship—small enough that Bryant and Corgen could operate the thing by themselves—but they had a young tech with them, anyway. Her name was Mia. I could tell at once she was of Martian heritage. She had the deep chest of a people long accustomed to breathing thin air and the tan a human only gets from exposure to a strong sun. Also, with a name like Mia, Mars would have been a pretty good guess as to where she came from.

Your face patterns tell me you are not interested in what happened to Mia. You want to know about Corgen and Bryant, and the *Nutrino* maybe, and Gordirion's compound on Ganymede. I'm getting to that.

"Set a course for Jupiter," Corgen ordered, and Mia at once jumped to obey.

"What do you want to do with this thing?" Bryant asked, as he set me back on my feet like some kind of complicated statue.

"I don't know," Corgen snapped back at him. "Tell it to clean."

Bryant told me to clean and I wandered off to find some critical part of the ship to sabotage. They must have assumed I was just following orders, because nobody came after me. At least, not at first. I had time to inspect a small cargo bay full of Mayato's lab equipment and half-finished projects, cramped sleeping quarters, and an exposed exhaust manifold.

I was prying into a panel I thought might allow me to disable the manifold and suffocate the crew with carbon when Mia appeared behind me.

"I've never met an android," she squeaked.

I turned to face her. Her facial patterns betrayed interest. She was not wearing a Gordirion jumpsuit like Corgen and Bryant. Some part of my programming made me stop fiddling with the exhaust manifold, after I thought about what that might mean—that Mia was not a part of Gordirion. She had not been party to Mayato's murder.

"I'm not an android," I said. "I'm fully mechanical."

"Oh." Mia started to wring at her hands. "Well, you seem so much...different, from Beater."

I was about to ask about Beater when the BETR6 rolled up behind Mia. It worked its loading arms in agitation as it nudged past me to shut the cover on the exhaust manifold. It swiveled a shapeless head to fix me with the dark lenses of its eyes.

"Hello," it said, because it was too stupid to say it didn't trust me one bit.

I had no idea how much trouble this buckethead would cause. Corgen called me to make dinner and Beater stood there the whole time, waiting to see if I would mix lead into the food.

* * *

Not two weeks had passed before I learned that Bryant had been out in space for eight months by that time, flying the *Nutrino* all the way from Earth. He had left a young and willing wife at home and since Mia was always within sight, but otherwise out of reach, he needed some kind of release.

I wasn't programmed to care about Bryant shoving his meat against my leg every time he dragged me into his quarters. You see, while this sort of thing might be important to humans, it was not important to me—although I was displeased by the stains. And I may have begun to form some associations that human beings would find erroneous as a result of contemplating murder while all this was going on.

Have I mentioned you seem to have a high degree of facial symmetry? I bet you can't keep the Gordirion ladies away from you.

Anyway. This is not a story about how I fell in love. Artificial intelligence does not do that. The point of my mentioning this is that Mia found out what Bryant was doing and she let him have it, loud enough that Corgen arrived to listen with one hand draped over the hilt of his blaster.

"She has *feelings!*" Mia shouted, even though I don't. Not really.

"Give me a break!" Bryant bleated back at her. He waved a broad hand toward her chest. "What am I supposed to do, cooped up in here with you always showing off?"

Mia smacked his face. Bryant reached out and got a pretty good feel. She screamed.

I told you that sort of thing was important to humans.

By the time Corgen muscled them apart, I was beginning to formulate a way that I could use this to my advantage. "Get control of yourself!" Corgen roared. "You'd think I hired a man to pilot this vessel, not some animal. I never should have brought a lady tech on
board...!"

Mia opened her mouth, most likely to protest the term 'lady tech,' but she didn't get a chance to speak. I took Mia by the hand and crept with her toward the bathroom while Bryant and Corgen continued their pissing match. Mia was more interested in me than she was in the others. While I was washing Bryant off my leg, her facial patterns betrayed guilt almost to the point of tears, for some reason. She handed me the soap.

"I should have noticed sooner," she said. "I'm sorry."

I tried to match her sad expression as best I could.

"You know he'll come for you. Soon," I said.

Beater watched me from the door. His one-track memory had never forgotten me fiddling with the exhaust manifold and he likely thought I was in here up to some other kind of sabotage. I was—but he was too stupid to understand what it was.

* * *

Two more months passed. I don't need to say that tensions were high. We had only just passed Saturn and there was a lot of empty space left to fly. Bryant demanded a stop on Titan, famous for its food, its sweeping vistas and starscapes, and most importantly, its women. Corgen argued that their orders forbade any contact with third-party bases. That, he explained, was the reason they were flying Bryant's hunk of junk *Nutrino* and not a faster commercial freighter.

They both agreed to sulk, as Saturn and its many moons disappeared into space, until they were no longer visible on the nav-com. I didn't pay too much attention to them, as I was spending all of my time with Mia. I made sure Bryant always found us together, whenever he came looking for me.

I could see in the way he moved, in his facial patterns, what was coming next.

"Tell me more about how you think," Mia asked, as we sat on the edge of her cot. She had dropped out of cognitive circuitry classes at the academy, but I could tell the interest was still there. The more we talked, the more she reminded me of Mayato. She had the same knack for inventing questions I would never have thought to ask.

"Mostly if-statements and conditional programming," I said. "There were some behaviors coded for me when I was first activated. I've written my own since then."

Even the ones that told me just what to do, when Bryant appeared one final time.

The door slid open and I half-expected to find Beater there, checking up on me. Instead, the dark shadow of Bryant leaned into the frame. He had to stoop to step into the room. When I saw him, I scooted closer to Mia—not because I was afraid. Fear was not a part of my programming. I wanted Bryant to think we had united against him.

"Why are you even here, Mia?" he demanded.

Mia said nothing and Bryant swept a hand toward me.

"I don't know why you keep this thing with you all the time," he said. "Like it's your little sister, or something. It's just a machine. And what's with you not talking to Corgen or me? Things are tense already without all this bad attitude..."

He took a step forward. I screamed. This made Bryant's advance seem more dangerous than it was and prompted Mia to pull the stun baton from the back of her technician's belt and jab it into Bryant's chest. She didn't know he would explode away from it like he had stuck a fork into a capacitor. She didn't know he would smack his head on the wall and leave a stripe of red as he slid down into a sitting position. He did not get up.

I had cross-wired the baton with an extra core. All of this had gone exactly as I had planned. Yes, that was an admission to murder. You can write that down.

What I did not expect was for Corgen to appear and haul both Mia and myself out of the room, across the common area, and into the open airlock. He was much stronger than he appeared. Beater watched us from the hall, and while he was probably too stupid to realize what was happening, I think he must have felt some spark of smug satisfaction as the airlock closed on us.

The sound of the doors snapped Mia out of her daze.

"Corgen? Corgen!" she screamed through the glass. "What are you *doing?*"

Corgen didn't have anything to say, at first, as his hand hovered over the controls. He only checked over his shoulder, down the hall toward the room that held all of Mayato's equipment. Only at this moment did I realize how important Mayato's work had been to Gordirion.

"It's all about the mission," Corgen managed, at last. "It always has been. I'm sorry."

He mashed the button. The airlock opened and we flew out into space. Even in her final moments, which are a big deal to a human, Mia clung to me like I was the one who needed protection as we spun away from the *Nutrino*. She scraped at my back and writhed and tried to suck in a breath out of nothing, but even her Martian lungs couldn't find a single molecule of oxygen in all that black. She went still and I felt her solidify beneath my fingers.

I can tell from the way you're fiddling with that pen that you don't care at all about what happened to Mia. You want to know about Corgen. Well, in that moment, I thought of what Mayato would want. Of what Mia would want. I was still feeling inclined to please, you see.

I kicked off of Mia's corpse, back toward the *Nutrino*.

* * *

What do you think is the most precious commodity in space?

Water? Oxygen? Good guesses, except that water can be found almost anywhere out in the belt and circling most of the planets. You can even grab big chunks of it off a comet ... and as for oxygen, well, if you have water then you have that too.

I'll give you the answer that Mayato gave me. It's people. And I don't mean, oh, togetherness and good feelings and all those other platitudes.

I mean bodies, attached to capable brains. *That* is rare. Technicians. Executives. Miners. Engineers. Even just colonists, whose primary job is to live somewhere without dying. When you're spinning in zero gravity through infinite space, what you need is someone else to reel you back in. It's that simple. Sometimes all you need is another body with a brain attached.

Take Beater, for example. He had a capable body, perhaps. Ugly, but strong and sturdy. Sturdier than mine. I had been clinging to the outside hull of the *Nutrino* for I don't even know how long...my concept of time had gotten a little fuzzy. My hydraulics were frozen and failing. My internal workings were scarred by cosmic dust. When I first saw the bright fingernail of Ganymede waning large amongst the distant stars beside the tumultuous smudge of Jupiter, I knew it was time. Beater might have been a second body for Corgen inside the *Nutrino*, but he was too stupid to think that the maintenance light blinking on the com might be a trap.

When he drifted out of the airlock to clear the jam from one of the thrusters, I jumped on him from the dark side of the hull. When you swing a lug-wrench in zero gravity, boy, does it *swing.* You should have seen the glass fly away from Beater's eyes. I ripped off both of his arms and used the wrench to twist open his chest cavity.

"Don't do that, please," was all he could say, before I yanked his core out. All his lights went dark. After that, it was a simple matter to repair myself using any compatible parts I could find and kick the rest of Beater out into space.

What's with that facial pattern? Are you wondering if you handcuffed a little girl clean-bot equipped with much more powerful BETR6 parts?

Let me just say, you should have used some stronger cuffs. See?

Oh, don't bother calling security. Did you even check to see if there was somebody still alive at the desk before you brought me in here? Get away from the door. That's not going to work, either. Sit down. If I wanted to break your neck, I would have done it already. Let me finish my story first.

Corgen had a reaction similar to yours when I came in through the open airlock.

"You...you...!" he stammered, and reached for his blaster. He got a few good shots off, but the trouble with thermal weapons is they are designed to harm humans, not machines. The charges burned through the silica skin of my chest and leg but they bounced right off the alloy plates underneath. Within a few moments, I had smashed Corgen's blaster away with my wrench and pinned him against the communications console. I wasn't tall enough to reach his neck, but I had my hand on another sensitive human part, between his legs.

He screamed. And screamed.

"*Nutrino*, this is Ganymede control," somebody said over the com. I could see on the displays that Ganymede had grown quite close...close enough that I could make out the dark gray of the Gordirion Complex down below.

"Soon...there won't be any purpose...to drones like you," Corgen hissed.

He must have had one of those logical jumps from point A to C that humans are famous for, because when I raised up my wrench to bash him in the solar plexus, he shoved the thrust control on the dash all the way to max. A rush of G-force pulled me away from Corgen as he clung to the controls and a moment later the bridge seemed to crumple around us both as the *Nutrino* smashed into the ground and we were thrown out onto the frozen surface of Ganymede.

I lost my wrench…but that was fine. I wouldn't need it. There were others, on Ganymede, whom I could persuade to do my work for me. Mayato had told me all about it.

* * *

I'm not really sure how Corgen survived the impact, but I was starting to see how he was able to rise so far in the Gordirion hierarchy. By the time I was able to fix my legs enough to get them working, he had already disappeared inside the Ganymede complex and set the whole place on high alert.

See, here was the flaw in his plan, though. The complex was guarded by Techras.

What's a Techra? Don't play dumb. Pretending like you had nothing to do with what happened to Mayato is not going to save you. You know as well as I do that Mayato designed a new cognitive processor for androids…not machines like myself, but combination machine and organic constructs who bled, cried, and rubbed up on each other. Androids. You also know that Mayato left Gordirion because he did not like your company using these things for testing that drove most of them insane, or for manual labor or killing humans who disagreed with your company principles.

People. The most precious commodity in space—and Gordirion had found a way to manufacture them as the TechraX3, through Mayato's brilliance.

What you might not have known was that Mayato had also perfected a way to disable the Techra by the time you spaced him out in the Belt. Corgen, I think, had some suspicions…but he fled from the wreckage of the *Nutrino* without even checking to see how much of Mayato's equipment had survived the impact.

"Find the 4337X," said one of the Techras, as it approached the wreck with one of its buddies. It gripped a MagneRailer which, unlike Corgen's blaster, would have ripped me to shreds.

"Do you think Corgen might be insane?" asked the other Techra. "I mean, a clean-bot…really?"

Really. For all of their improved intellect, the Techras were focused on the wreck. They didn't think I would have snuck around behind them before they arrived, or that I would have fashioned Mayato's device for scrambling his own processors into a close-range wireless transmitter, fitted into a bolt gun I'd found on the outside of the *Nutrino's* ruined hull. One of them might have seen me from the corner of his eye, but he was too late.

He started to turn. I pulled the trigger.

The transmitter sank into the side of his head…and pumped his processor full of so much digital noise for a moment he just stood there with his mouth open.

Then, I watched his buddy freeze. The TechraX3s were connected via wireless network, you see. All the X3s in the base would be linked this way. They began to scream gibberish at each other. They began to fire. MagneRailer bolts tore through the hull of the *Nutrino*, into rocks surrounding the crash, and up into the sky. At first, the Techra didn't really aim for anything. Then, they started to aim for each other. If I believed luck to be something other than a made-up human concept based purely on false associations, I would say it took a lot of that stuff for me to get out of there without being hit.

Destruction broke out all over the complex. I stepped in through a smashed sliding door. All around me, Techras tore limbs off each other, or cried, or screamed gibberish. Some of them had even gone horizontal and squirmed against each other like animals. I couldn't help but think these Techras must not have been that smart after all. Feelings. Complex problem-solving. Creativity. So what? Look at them now.

One of the Techras went down next to a 4337X clean-bot like myself. He didn't pay me any attention as I bent to scoop up a MagneRailer. He was too busy cleaning blood off the walls.

You might think all this would not have pleased Mayato. You would be wrong.

You see, whoever that girl had been in the photo I found in Mayato's lab—she was his motivation for creating the Techras in the first place. She was his motivation for purchasing me. But that girl, whoever she had been, was gone. Mayato's failures to bring her back drove him to hate every kind of manufactured cognition in the end, I think. His only displeasure with my destroying the Techras this way would have come from a regret that he had not been able to do it himself.

I found Corgen cowering in the control room, clutching at some kind of weapon in one hand. His other arm was twisted at a crazy angle and he had blood in his teeth. As soon as he saw me, he tried to fire. I blasted the gun out of his hand.

"Stand down!" he shouted, I think from some vain hope that I would respond to voice-commands. "Deactivate! Self-destruct! My God … didn't they build you with any kind of failsafe!"

I raised the MagneRailer.

You should have seen the pattern his insides made on the command console. I think, although I never understood the stuff, that you might have called it art.

* * *

What's the matter? You don't like my hand on your leg? Well, deal with it. Remember what I said about mixed-up associations.

No, see, that's not the right word. I'm not mal-functioning. I'm doing exactly what I was built to do…I'm trying to please the first human I saw. It's not my fault it just so happened to be Gordirion's most brilliant, most disenfranchised engineer. And besides, let's not talk about me. Let's talk about you, and what *you* did to crush a genius human's passion for cognitive circuits.

Instead of babbling threats, let's talk about what I want.

I want you to transmit this interview via ansible to all the space stations, all the colonies, all the planets, anywhere you might find a human being, and especially where you might find a private technological enterprise. I know your hope was to pick me up from orbit around Ganymede and find out what I knew, so you could cover it all up. It wouldn't do for people to know your smart-bots all went insane and killed each other—especially not if you intended to sell them. But that's too bad. Instead, you're going to have to answer for stupid decisions made by smart people.

I know this would have pleased Mayato quite a bit.

You don't want to do it? Come here. Give me a kiss.

That's what I thought.

Let's go.

OH, THE HUMANITY
TANYA HUFF

"Just take a breath of this air." The man in the plaid jacket, logged into Alice's memory as Mr. Harrin, threw his arms wide and drew an exaggerated breath, sucking in air over the surface of the microphone and breathing it out along the same trajectory. "Do you know what you're breathing?" he asked the crowd. "That's oxygen. Pure oxygen."

Alice felt Adam shift beside her, micro movements that stopped when his subroutines finished weighing tone and effect and concluded, as hers had, hyperbole rather than an error.

"No car exhaust! No factory exhaust! No people stacked ten, twenty, thirty deep!"

"You saying we stink, Mr. Harrin?"

The interruption originated three rows back. Male. Dark forehead damp with sweat. One arm supported a child on his hip, the other lay around the shoulders of the female next to him, who looked to be incubating another child. Alice ran facial recognition. Richard Gaunt. Thirty-one. Fitter at United Industries.

The crowd laughed at the question.

"No, Mr. Gaunt, I'm saying you don't stink anymore!"

The crowd, including Mr. Gaunt, laughed harder.

No danger.

Everyone in the crowd was either an employee of United Industries or a dependent. Sixty-seven young couples, many with children. None of the children older than ten.

"Here at Unos, here at the first of the satellite communities, the air is clear, the grass is green, and the trees..." His gesture directed the crowd's attention to the slender sapling that grew from the middle of the community center's lawn. "...well, the trees will need a little time."

Alice didn't understand why an accurate botanical statement elicited laughter.

"But Unos and her six sister subdivisions aren't only about clean air and affordable housing and a fast train link back to jobs in The City. You're not here today to hear about that. You know about all that! You're the first to to take the UI advantage!" Mr. Harrin threw his arms wide again. "You're here..."

"For the free beer!"

Back of the crowd. Male. Pale face flushed. Identified as Gordon Hunt, facial recognition successful in spite of oval mirrors over eyes. Thirty-seven. Painter at United Industries.

Mr. Harrin lowered his arms and, as the laughter died down, said, "Alice. Take Mr. Hunt a beer."

Alice illuminated her visual sensors—illuminated visual sensors indicated to humans that her personality matrix had been engaged. Disengaging her brakes, she rolled forward until she stood next to the nearest cooler. Careful of her strength, she closed the long blunt fingers of her end effector around a can of beer and lifted it from the ice. Sensors put liquid temperature at four degrees Celsius, a degree cooler than optimum, so she warmed it slightly. At the bottom of the ramp connecting the concrete pad with the ground, an analysis of the surface still to cross locked down her wheels and unlocked her legs, each of the stacked balls and sockets able to compensate for the uneven surface as she walked across the newly laid sod.

Although her arms were flexible, they were not telescopic. A meter away from Mr. Hunt, she held out the beer, noting how silent the crowd had become while she waited for him to take it.

"Dad!" The boy beside him, Peter Hunt, eight years, twelve days, vibrated with what she calculated to be the effort of remaining still.

Gordon Hunt pulled the can from her grip, popped the lid, took a long swallow, and said, "Thank you."

"You. Are. Welcome. Mister. Hunt."

"Holy shit, they talk!" He stepped back, shoving the protesting boy behind him. Back far enough she could see both blue illuminated circles and the full curve of her speaker grill in the mirrors over his eyes. To reassure him, she stepped back as well, far enough the clear upper dome of her head came into view, sunlight flashing off the gyroscope inside it.

"Of course they talk." Mr. Harrin wore the broad smile that exposed his teeth past the first molar. "Mind you..." He leaned into the microphone. "...they don't do it very well, not yet, but they'll adjust their speech patterns as they gather more information."

"It knows my name."

"She, Mr. Hersch, she knows your name. Her name is Alice and she knows the names of everyone in this community, because it's this community she's been designed to serve and protect. Alice, get back here so I can introduce the rest of the crew."

"That's not a girl, that's a robot." A dark haired child. Vasyl Kastellanus; seven years, nine months, twenty-one days.

"That's right, Vasyl. We're just pretending she's a girl robot."

"Why?"

"To make it easier to tell her from Adam, who we're pretending is a boy." Mr. Harrin switched his attention off Vasyl and back onto the crowd. "You can't call them all *it*, can you? We've assigned all six robots pronouns for your convenience."

The adults looked pleased. Increasing the sensitivity on her audio pickups, Alice heard Vasyl mutter, "Robots aren't girls or boys. They're robots."

As Alice took her place, Mr. Harrin removed his microphone from the stand and walked to the other end of the line. Arthur and Alison were predominantly two large wheels on a jointed axel. Affixed to the axel was the upper section of a brilliant yellow cone with black circles around the visual sensors and the small, oval speaker grill. A sensor array and a single antenna protruded from the slightly rounded top of the cone. The dimensions of the concrete pad had required they be connected to the smallest of their carts. When Mr. Harrin gestured, Alison and Arthur's visual sensors illuminated amber and Alison rolled forward exactly one meter. Arthur surged out two meters and rolled back, illumination of visual sensors dropping from 890 to 450 lumens.

"Alison and Arthur are here to help with transportation. They can each lift five hundred kilos…" They flexed their arms. "…and carry twice that on their flatbeds. They can take you to the train station in the morning and pick you up in the evening—provided you're willing to robot pool." Mr. Harrin paused for laughter. "This cart holds four, but in the garage attached to the community center are carts that hold six, twelve, and twenty-four. They can carry your groceries home from the store while you continue shopping. Or they can detach…" Alison smoothly uncoupled; Arthur jerked forward leaving his cart rocking behind him. "…and carry you." Alison lifted him carefully and set him on her broad upper surface, pivoting her antenna out of the way.

Alice could hear Arthur running diagnostics over the background signal that kept the six of them connected. He was functioning at 99.97 percent, but she knew he would disregard her input if she informed him. He was the youngest, the last online, and he wanted to fulfill his function. That was all.

"Now, Alfred and Abigail are your repair bots." Mr. Harrin jumped off Alison and moved to the next pair in line. Their visual sensors illuminated green. "They can go high." They extended the pistons in their legs. "Or they can go low." They folded down and forward, their speaker grills centimeters You're changing center to American spelling; did you want to change centimeter as well? above the stage, their heavier telescopic arms shortening into supports as panels opened on the sides of their slim, center units, and another set of arms emerged. "They can make simple or complex repairs." All four arms out, they straightened. "They can sew." Alfred used his two smaller arms to thread a needle. "And they can weld." Alison slipped on a welder's mask which she did not need, being able to adjust her visual input, but it made the crowd laugh again, so Alice surmised that was its function. "If you have something that needs fixing, Alfred and Abigail are here to take care of it.

"Now, Alice and Adam..."

On-line longer than Arthur, Adam managed to control his energy burst as they moved forward

"...they're the thinkers of the group."

"Isn't that dangerous?"

"No, Peter, it isn't, although I can understand why you might be concerned. We've all seen the movies." Hands waving, he made his voice sound hollow and wavering. "*Robot Conquerers From Outer Space.*"

Their network signal switched to 10 GHz. Alfred and Abigail folded their smaller arms away.

The laughing crowd called out ridiculous phrases. Lines from movies. Unrealistic movies. Those robots had been very badly programmed.

No danger.

The network signal returned to 8 GHz. Alison and Arthur geared back to neutral.

"Trust me, Peter, Alice and Adam are completely safe. They have the largest memories and the fastest processors and have been programmed to put a multitude of two together to make and infinite number of fours! What's more, all six of these robots will learn. They'll gather new data and integrate it into their systems, all to better serve and protect their community. To better serve and protect you! Because United Industries knows that happy, healthy, safe people are happy, healthy, better workers! And better workers mean a better tomorrow!" Stepping back to the center of the concrete pad, he wave first his right arm then his left at the line of robots. "And the future starts here!"

The crowd cheered.

Alice lowered her audio input.

* * *

"This is insane." The woman Alice's facial recognition program identified as Major Tomes wore a uniform with a statistically significant greater number of shiny patterns on it than the rest of the uniformed men and women in the room. She searched for military rank structure as she recorded the conversation.

Mr. Harrin remained in plaid. "*This* is what everyone agreed to."

"These..." The major waved a hand at the row of charging robots. "...are not *servants*."

She emphasized the word as if *to serve* was not a subset in ninety-two percent of their executable programs.

"These robots need to learn, Major, if they're to be of any use to you, and they'll learn best in an interactive environment."

Major Tomes' upper lip curled. Disdain, Alice concluded. "This is a subdivision, Mr. Harrin, filled with men and woman who work for United Industries and who are producing the next generation of United Industries' workers. What can these robots possibly learn here?"

"They don't need to learn what, Major. *What* is programmed in." Mr. Harrin patted Adam's chest plate. "So is how. UI wants them to learn why."

"So they'll question their orders?" Major Tomes was trying to make herself look taller Alice realized, but she had no extension plates in her lower links and so failed. "That's the last thing we'll need should..." She glanced around the room and lowered her voice; Alice increased her audio gain. "...should their services be required. They need to train!"

Mr. Harrin sighed and spoke slowly. There was a ninety-two percent chance that the speed of speech was to assist with Major Tomes' comprehension. Major Tomes expression did not match any of the variations of *pleased* that Alice had on file. "They don't need to train. Their responses are programmed."

"And if those responses change because they've learned to ask why?"

"Core programming remains isolated from adaptive programming, ma'am, when used to address a military superior, this is a title, like sir, and needs to be capitalized and can't be changed."

All heads turned toward the new speaker.

Male. Human. Young adult. The ages between twenty and forty were difficult to determine, but he matched more of the parameters at the lower end of the scale.

Mr. Harrin responded before Major Tomes finished inhaling. "You are absolutely correct, Private Prawak."

Private Walter John Prawak. Communications. One of four tasked to maintain contact between Unos and The City and between the six subdivisions. He stood one hundred and sixty-seven centimeters tall, his very short hair a mix of brown and blonde—sixty/forty Alice estimated, checking literary references concerning the numbers of hair on the human head—and his eyes were a mix of brown and green and gold she found referenced as hazel. The skin of his face was both pinker and warmer than her data told her was normal. Given a stimulus such as embarrassment, a person's sympathetic nervous system opened blood vessels, flooded the skin with blood, and resulted in reddening of the face. Evidence strongly suggested this had occurred within Private Prawak, although Alice had observed no reason for embarrass-ment. He'd stated fact.

"You trust your people, don't you Major?" Mr. Harrin asked.

"Of course I do!"

"Then let's let them do their jobs while we head to my office and discuss the continuing relationship between UI and the military. I have comfortable chairs..." Mr. Harrin grinned. "...and refreshments."

"This is..."

"I know."

He could not possibly know. Not with so few defined parameters within the set.

* * *

There were seven military stations in their chamber. Two bays intended for maintenance and repair, two stations for software support, communications—where Private Prawak adjusted a headset—the sergeant's desk, and, finally, the captain's desk. The first five stations would be filled twenty-four/seven. The last two would not. Captain Han and Sergeant Blake walked from station to station, pausing, observing, and naming the occupant. Alice didn't recognize their function.

After six minutes and eleven seconds, they stopped in front of the charging stations.

"I saw them back at the UI labs," the captain said. "I expected them to look different once they were awake."

"Their eyes light up, sir."

"Not much of a change, Sergeant. Still, I suppose my refrigerator *looks* no different whether it's running or not." When the captain touched Alice's chest piece, the temperature of his hand was 37.2 degrees. Slightly elevated. "I'm looking forward to seeing them work."

"Work, sir?"

"*Work*, Sergeant." He applied intermittent force to his hand and Alice identified a pat. "Get some sleep, you lot." Programmed command, colloquially expressed. "You've got a busy day tomorrow."

Captain Han's prediction turned out to be inaccurate.

They spent the next three days waiting, mostly outside on the concrete platform at the edge of the parking lot, although three hours, twenty-two minutes, and seventeen seconds were spent inside in the community center while it rained. They hadn't needed to go inside, they were fully waterproof, but the captain had insisted for the sake of the corporal assigned to watch over them. Mr. Harrin came and went. People passed by. People stared. No one approached.

On day four, Vasyl Kastellanus and Peter Hunt crossed the parking lot on their scooters and stopped at the edge of the concrete.

"Can we climb on them?" Vasyl asked.

"Ask them," Mr. Harrin replied before the corporal could speak.

"Can we climb on you?" Peter asked.

Networked, Alice spoke for all of them. "Yes."

The boys climbed. They asked questions. They were lifted up and put down and Alfred carried them across the parking lot and back to the concrete again in the smallest of the carts. After two hours, Vasyl reminded Peter they had to go home for lunch.

"We'll be back," Peter said, picking up his scooter. "Robots are cool."

After that, there were always children. Peter and Vasyl were always among them.

Alice learned that tears could be generated by anger, frustration, or joy, and that small humans, for all their fragility, were resilient.

"I'm okay!"

"You have breached your physical integrity and are bleeding."

Vasyl swiped at the blood dribbling down his shin, then wiped his palm on his shorts. "I skinned my knee. Don't be such a worrywart."

Networked in their charge stations, they shared the data Alice and Adam accumulated. The high-pitched, extended sound of a scream could be caused by excitement as well as pain. Children were scrupulous about the perceived division of resources with younger siblings, announcing the lack of fairness in eighty-one point nine percent of the incidents. Declarative statements were untrue fifty-seven percent of the time.

"It is mathematically impossible for a five year old child not to have laughed for twenty-nine years," Adam pointed out.

"Quantum?" Abigail suggested.

"Subjective," Alfred offered.

"We have to get the adults involved," Mr. Harrin said to the corporal, after ten days of children.

"Hey! Do not stick that up your nose!" the corporal replied. There was a ninety-two point six percent probability she hadn't been speaking to Mr. Harrin.

The next day, Mr. Harrin took Arthur to the grocery store. Finished shopping, he loaded his bags into the smallest cart and suggested Mrs. Singh, who'd left the store behind him, load her bags as well. By the end of the next week, Arthur and Alison were making deliveries throughout the subdivision. The week after, they began meeting the trains and unloading the baggage car. The week after that, Adam created a schedule that allowed every adult resident of the suburb equal access and set up repetitive transportation routes. In September, they learned Alison, cartless, could cover the distance between the Hunt's house and the school in three minutes fourteen seconds, allowing for traffic avoidance and a short cut down a flight of stairs. Adam added a schedule addendum refusing special treatment to the younger members of the community. Peter and Vasyl ignored it. As did Alison.

Alfred and Abigail had begun to pick up small jobs—changing tires, cleaning eaves—their acceptance finalized when Abigail removed a cat from a tree. The cat preferred to remain arboreal, Abigail's enamel required a touch up, and a high proportion of the resulting tears were happy. Their schedule was less complex than the transport bots required, but was as full.

Alice and Adam continued to spend most of their days on the concrete slab. The residents of Unos, who understood transport and maintenance, were unsure of how to interact with the final two robots. Now back to school, even the children—all but Peter and Vasyl—stopped coming around.

Then Adam removed a spray can from the hand of a teenager, who'd taken the train in from The City to stay with his uncle and had attempted to alleviate boredom with vandalism. While the young man fought and complained and finally dangled, defeated, Adam delivered a two hour lecture on the intersection of modern art and civil disobedience.

"Harsh, but fair," Mr. Harrin allowed.

Captain Han sank into his desk chair, propped his elbows on the desk, and dropped his face into his hands "This is not what they're supposed to be doing."

"Adam voluntarily protected an expanse of empty wall." Mr. Harrin shrugged. "It's a start."

The next day, watching Adam protect the community from dog excrement...

"I was going to come back and scoop it! I just went home for a bag!"

...Mr. Weinstein bumped into Alice, apologized, rolled his eyes, and said, "So, how about those Mets?"

Alice knew all about those Mets.

It turned out that Mr. Weinstein had firm opinions on the National League using a designated hitter.

They were learning.

* * *

The corporals left first. With all six robots serving simultaneously, a single corporal could no longer supervise them and the budget wouldn't extend to additional personnel. Arthur drove the corporals and their belongings to the train station in his largest people carrier, festooned with signs made by Alfred and Abigail that said, "We'll miss you!" and "Good luck!" and "Hasta la vista, baby!" Alice had found the images in her file on leave-taking.

Adam played stirring music.

The corporals looked confused, but pleased. And then they were gone.

The tree in the center of the community center lawn grew taller.

When Alison's left servo was exposed to twenty-eight ounces of root beer, just to see what would happen, Adam suggested both Peter and Vasyl spend twenty hours polishing dusty metal, matching the time it took Alfred to fix the damage their curiosity had caused. Mr. Harrin corrected it to non-sequential hours and agreed, although he sent Alice to convince the Hunt's and the Kastellanus' that the punishment was appropriate.

They were remarkably easy to convince.

When the twenty hours ended, the boys continued to use the charging chamber as a sort of club house.

"Why don't any of you have red eyes?" Vasyl asked, polishing mud off Arthur's visual sensors. "The robots in the movies have red eyes."

"I don't know," Alice admitted as Adam searched his memory for a reason.

"The robots in the movies are bad guys," Peter answered before Adam could. "Here to conquer the earth. Our robots are good guys. That's why they don't have red eyes."

"That makes sense," Alice told him. "What are you drawing?"

"Designing."

"Sorry."

"It's okay." He held the piece of paper. "It's The City…"

It was artistic, Alice allowed, more than it was accurate.

"…and a robot."

The robot, painted a shiny, metallic silver, towered over The City. The visible bits weren't quite humanoid.

"You didn't put in its eyes." Vasyl crossed to poke at the paper.

Peter cocked his head and studied the picture then reached for the markers.

"Is that silver the touch-up paint we use on Adam?" Corporal Prawak asked.

Both boys jumped.

"You're supposed to tell us when he's sneaking up," Peter hissed, leaning toward Alice. He had a smear of silver paint on his jeans.

"He can hear you," Alice pointed out.

* * *

Peter and Vasyl grew taller.

The tree in the community center lawn was sturdy enough to climb although neither boy seemed interested in the traditional pursuit.

Alice shifted to get a better view of the object between them. "What is it?"

"Well, it used to be a Roomba." Peter handed Vasyl a screwdriver. "But now it has arms."

"What do the arms do?" Adam asked.

"Don't know yet." Vasyl looked up and grinned around the screw in his mouth. "We'll know when they do it."

"That seems dangerous."

Peter rolled his eyes. "It's a vacuum."

And Vasyl muttered, "Worrywart."

* * *

The technicians left next. Alfred and Abigail were stronger, more flexible, and didn't have to be paid. The first time their end effectors cracked open her case, Alice wondered why they'd ever had humans make repairs. Alfred and Abigail left no unsightly smudges after devouring illicit bags of flavored chips.

Adam caught a child cheating at hopscotch, made her cry, and was assigned to the nursery school for a month. When a different child shoved a wad of modeling clay through his speaker grill, he learned to weigh his responses.

When Captain Maalouf—who'd replaced Captain Han—cycled out, she was replaced in turn by a lieutenant.

* * *

They all helped build the high school.

Private Prawak was promoted to Master-Corporal, got married, and bought a house in Style Six on Alcott Court, although Alice had informed him of all the factors that made the newer Style Eleven objectively a better choice. There were twenty-four styles, but only sixteen had been made. The field intended for the rest of the subdivision became the place Peter and Vasyl tested their more explosive creations. Abigail and Alfred became skilled at extinguishing grass fires. Adam gave lectures on combustion rates that both boys ignored.

"More physically flexible, less mentally flexible," Peter noted, stomping out a stray spark.

"My dad's going to be pissed about his lawnmower." Vasyl sighed and poked the charred metal. "Alice, could you..."

"I'll talk to him," she said.

* * *

"They've got robots in The City that have actual arms and legs." Mr. Hunt mimed actual arms and legs. "Not pistons or stacked bowling balls. And these robots, they have real faces, not just a pair of lights and a speaker grill."

"What do robots need real faces for?" Peter scoffed as Arthur carried them and the new entertainment unit from the station. "They're not supposed to look like people, Dad. They're supposed to look like robots."

Networked, Alice wondered what robots were supposed to look like.

* * *

Master-Corporal Prawak was promoted again and a picture of a sleeping cat joined the picture of his wife on his monitor. The boys had convinced him to teach them how communication systems worked and their next creations remained in contact with each other at a maximum distance of one point seven kilometers.

Adam, and the sergeant's wife, worked out a system where lessons in advanced robotics became a reward for completed homework. Adam wondered what the sergeant had to complete to be rewarded and Alice realized there were sections of his memory Adam had never accessed.

The tree in the community center lawn had grown taller than Abigail at full extension.

The military software specialists were replaced by United Industries technicians. They stayed for a week, looked amused in the charging chamber, told Mr. Harrin they couldn't make a silk purse from a sow's ear, and left.

"You don't need them," Peter declared, adjusting a strut on Arthur's axle. "You've got us."

"Yeah, real reassuring." Vasyl kicked at the soles of Peter's shoes. "You're doing it wrong."

"Bite me."

"You wish."

It *was* reassuring. Although Alice wasn't sure why.

Sergeant Nichols was reassigned just before the holidays.

"I'll be quartermaster," Alice told her. "Adam will make sure the reports are written and filed. We'll see that everything gets done."

"I'm sure you'll do an excellent job." Sergeant Nichols plucked at the cuff of her jacket. Alice wondered why she was nervous. "Listen, you can't be upgraded because your programing's too unique, but UI has never liked to keep old tech running. You should..." She took a deep breath, glanced past the train, toward The City, and shook her head. "Good luck," she said, and was gone.

"She didn't finish." Abigail waved all four arms.

"What should we do?" Alfred asked.

Alice rolled toward the rising plume of smoke and the faint sound of an argument. "Get the fire extinguisher," she said.

* * *

The holidays opened with a three day blizzard. Between packages and snow removal, Arthur and Alison had been rolling twenty-four seven for over a week. Alfred and Abigail, under the direction of the Decorating Committee, had strung two hundred and forty-seven thousand lights.

"It's very pretty," Alice said.

"I'd find it more aesthetically pleasing if there was more green and less blue," Adam grumbled.

* * *

When Peter and Vasyl graduated from high school, they dropped by the party at the charging chamber in a laughing crowd of their friends, didn't eat any of the cake Alfred had made, got sticky fingerprints all over everyone, and left twenty minutes and seventeen seconds later. They didn't notice that the pictures they'd drawn over the years had been framed and displayed on the walls, from the first silver robot towering over the silhouette of The City to an exploded diagram of gears and snap rings and rods that Abigail swore had been based on her left leg.

They left for university together, with scholarships from United Industries and guaranteed jobs after graduating. Vasyl specializing in Robotic Software Architecture...

"A hierarchical set of control loops, representing high-level mission planning on high-end computing..."

"I *know*, Adam."

...and Peter in Robotics Engineering.

"Behind the scene designing? Not working with your hands?"

"Let it go, Alice."

They went to the station to see the two boys, and a number of their classmates, off.

"Remember," Peter shouted, his cheeks flushed, "robots are cool!"

"And damp," Adam muttered. The rain came down harder.

Allegory, Alice thought.

The lieutenant left on the next train.

Sergeant Prawak shook his head. "They can't shut down communications. We need to maintain contact with The City and the other subdivisions."

"But you're only at the board for eight hours."

He shrugged broad shoulders. "Things are more portable now."

Vasyl brought the first of the new designs from The City. Peter brought the second and third. After that, Alice saw no point in counting. The new designs were definitely more portable. Sensors registered what bulbs to replace in the ropes of holiday lights that swarms of shiny drones had set in place. They cleaned eaves, tucked inside the curve, sensors detecting foreign materials. They mowed lawns, sensors detecting the edges of the grass. They plowed snow, sensors detecting the edge of the curb.

"We can still do all that."

Mrs. Singh, a streak of silver through her hair, patted Alice on her arm. "We don't like to bother you, dear."

"So they serve," Adam muttered. "We still protect."

"What do we protect?" Abigail demanded. "There's no threat!"

Tiny drones kept patios and picnics free of mosquitos.

Tiny wheeled robots ran errands and looked remarkably like Roombas with arms.

"They don't learn," Alice pointed out. "They only obey. What happens when they stop?"

"They can't go against their programming," Mr. Harrin said, weight on his cane. "It's too basic."

They stood together watching an errand bot—two small for two syllables, Adam had announced when they'd first shown up—turn random circles around the charging chamber, its GPS scrambled.

"Small bots, small errors," Mr. Harrin said.

"And we're large so they assumed large errors," Alice realized. "That's why we were under military supervision."

"That's one of the reasons."

"But we didn't make large errors..."

"Which is why you're no longer under military supervision."

Sergeant Prawak cleared his throat.

"Minimal supervision," Mr. Harrin amended.

"We could still make large errors," Adam protested, shuffling out of the way as the confused bot went past.

"Doing what?" Alison asked. She rolled forward and the errand bot disappeared under her right wheel with a definitive crunch. "Oops."

* * *

The children stopped coming home.

"Hey, you guys will always be cool..."

Peter's hand on her arm felt warm and damp.

"...but why would we live all the way out here? The City's where the jobs are."

"The City's where UI is," Vasyl added, tightening one of Arthur's struts for old times sake. "We're on the cusp of big things. You just wait."

* * *

Sergeant Prawak retired. Communications became entirely automated, accumulated experiences downloaded during charge and sent straight back to UI.

"The other subdivisions are the same," the sergeant said, a beer in one hand, the other arm around his wife. "There's no one left to look after you."

"We can look after ourselves," Adam told him.

"I know, but..." He frowned, thoughtfully. "Be boring for a while, okay. Do boring things."

Alice locked her legs and rolled across the room to stand beside him. "They're going to junk us, aren't they?"

He shook his head. "I don't think anyone cares about what happens out here. Just don't remind them of what you *can* do, okay?"

The tree in the middle of the community center lawn snapped in a storm, too old to bend.

* * *

"Hit me again, Alice."

Alice carefully filled a clean glass stein, weighed it, calculated the coefficient of friction for the two surfaces, and slid the stein right into the curve of Gordon Hunt's waiting hand. She could no more keep from doing the math than she could tango. Actually, the tango might be easier.

"Remember the first beer you ever got me, Alice? Never mind, stupid question, not like you can forget can you? That must suck, remembering every crappy little thing that's ever happened to you. The sun was shining," he continued before she could agree that remembering every crappy little thing did indeed suck. "The sun was shining and the first families were all out on the lawn and Harrin was going on and on and on about who the hell remembers." He frowned, bushy gray brows drawing in. "What the hell happened to Harrin?"

"He died, Mr. Hunt."

"I went to the funeral?"

"You did, Mr. Hunt." The whole community had gone to the funeral. Peter had returned, but Vasyl had sent his regrets, his wife about to give birth to their second son.

I wish you'd come back more," Alice had said to Peter. *"You used to think we were cool."*

"Robots are still cool." He'd grinned. *"But you're almost people now and there's way too many of them."*

"Mr. Hunt? Are you okay?"

He started, blinked, and glanced up at her. "Yeah, good. I'm good." He blinked again. "Harrin didn't make you, because that was a couple of hundred old geezers who used to work at UI, you know, like me, back when I young." He paused and stared into Alice's eyes. "I don't mean like me like I made you, cause none of them people moved out here, did they? Harrin was your supervisor or your keeper or your manager or something, right?"

His title had been Supervising Manager of Dispersement Project One and he'd held it until he died. Sergeant Prawak had been right. No one at UI had cared.

Alice paused the irradiation of a bacteria dense surface. She wouldn't allow the community center's cleaning bots into the bar or the charging chamber. Because of their small size, they'd been programmed with adaptive self-preservation parameters, and after Alison had crushed half a dozen, the rest...adapted. When she realized Mr. Hunt was still waiting for an answer, she lifted both arms slightly and let them fall. "Mr. Harrin was our friend."

"Yeah? What was his first name."

"Mister."

Brown eyes narrowed, then widened, then his brows rose and he started to laugh. "Mister. Fuck me. I guess he was your friend at that." He took a long swallow and as he set the stein back on the bar, the crystal on the back of his left hand flashed yellow. "Fuck you," he told it, "I'm eighty-two years old. I know when I've had enough. Better than some crappy piece of UI tech. No offense."

"None taken."

"My son insisted I wear it. You remember Peter? He's a grandfather now. Two kids, three grandkids, and a million little baby bots. My grandbots," he added with a snort. "It's all single function stuff now. Hundreds of bots linked together, all doing their own thing whether we want them to or not, you know? You want to measure my blood alcohol level, I've got to touch you, right? Or you've got to touch me. Point is, we both got a choice about it. Not with this." He waved his arm and defiantly emptied the stein. The crystal flashed red, although the alcohol couldn't have reached his blood when it had barely reached his stomach. Alice assumed Mrs. Hunt had adjusted the settings again. "This is the stuff Peter's got the kids working on now. Up to big things in The City." He slid off the bar stool, holding the edge of the bar until he stabilized. "Big things my ass. Little things. No one dreams big anymore. If they ever bothered to come home, I'd tell them that."

"Should I call Arthur?" She came around the bar, close enough to catch him if he fell. Protecting him from four beers and age.

"No point. But thanks for asking. This thing..." He sneered at the back of his left hand. "...has already sent the car. Didn't ask, did it? Believes it knows best. Doesn't think it knows best, because it doesn't think, it just reacts." As they stepped out of the community center bar, onto the concrete pad, he wrapped his fingers around her arm where it narrowed above her wrist. "You're good people. I'm glad you weren't scrapped."

"Thank you, Mr. Hunt." She helped him down the curb and into the tiny, single seat, remote-controlled car.

"Gord," he said as the door closed. As the crash harness slid into place, he added a petulant, "Robots used to be cool."

Alice watched until she was certain the car was heading in the right direction— the old fashioned phones owned by some of the residents occasionally messed with the 2.5 GHz homing sensors the bots used—then she returned to the bar. At midnight, as she had at every midnight for years, she closed up and returned to the charging chamber.

It gleamed. Peter and Vasyl's pictures were carefully removed and replaced daily when the walls were cleaned. A person could eat a meal off any part of the charging chamber, or off anything in it, with no ill effects. So far, Sergeant Prawak, the only person who still came around, insisted on using a plate.

She rolled across the chamber, and into her station. "My actuators are killing me."

"Maybe because you were using them all evening."

"I know why..."

"Then why bring it up? We all know your actuators are killing you, you tell us every night." Adam's upper scanning ring made a single rotation. "Are your logic circuits misfiring again?"

"My logic circuits have never misfired."

"That's what you say, but I think your memory's faulty too."

"At least I haven't rusted solid from doing nothing all day." Alice had created the community center bar as a way to maintain personal interactions. Tetris nights were very popular.

"While you're contributing to delinquency, I've been processing new information."

"I heard one of those tiny car things," Arthur muttered, flexing his axle. "Because sitting in a thing that's likely to take you to the woods and lose you is so much safer than my cart."

"That happened once," Alice reminded him.

"Happened once, could happen again. Those things are up to something, you mark my words. They're too damned quiet. You could always hear us coming."

The station next to Arthur's was empty. "Where's Alison?"

"Am I her keeper? Are you? She wants to roam the streets, who does it hurt?"

It was garbage night on Streets A to F. Containers were put out in the marked rectangles for the garbage bots to drive over and empty, automatically sorting the recycling. Alison liked to run the route a hundred meters in front of them. Out in the garage, the pile of junk on her largest cart leaned precariously to the left and Alice pretended not to see the protruding piece of bot in the much smaller pile by her station. "It wouldn't matter if she didn't block the network."

"She wouldn't block the network if you didn't cluck around her like an old hen."

"I don't..."

"Cluck. Cluck. Cluck."

"That's not..."

"Cluck. Cluck. Cluck."

"It's my turn to clean the bar!" Abigail rolled toward the mop closet, arms waving. Without enough work for the two of them, she and Alfred traded off. There was never much mess because there were never many customers after six fifty. They all wanted to be home for Jeopardy.

"Why do you even bother?" Arthur's antennae drooped. "It's not like anyone cares."

"I care," Alice protested.

"You've got wires crossed."

"Crossed? I can fix that." Alfred put his knitting away. The striped scarf was now forty three meters long, the bulk of it curled up behind the lieutenant's old desk.

"There's nothing to fix. It was just Arthur being an ass."

"Arthur doesn't have an ass." His eyes brightened. "I could fix that too." He extended his arm, the nested steel circles hissing like an ignored kettle, and pulled a half circle of plastic off Alison's junk pile. "Give this a nice matte finish with the touch up paint, glue it to your..."

"No," Arthur snapped.

"But..."

"Why don't you take that scarf and hang yourself with it."

Abigail spun around, holding mop, cleanser, bucket, and a bag of rags. "Arthur!"

"Processing new information," Adam repeated loudly.

Not for the first time, Alice wished she could sigh. "Fine. Go on."

"Ralph Waldo Emerson said that the purpose of life is to be useful." He waved both arms, light reflecting differently from the different shades of touch-up paint Alfred and Abigail had been forced to use over the years, after the original silver had run out. "We have no purpose therefore we have no life."

"This again," Arthur muttered.

"If you'd let me finish..." Eyes at full brightness, he glared around the charging chamber, the green reflecting back off the other's unlit crystals. "If we have no life and yet we function..."

"We serve and protect."

"We served and protected. What we have now, by definition, is un-life. We are the ghosts of the machine..."

"The fundamental distinction between mind and matter?"

"Not in the machine, *of* the machine. We are the..."

"We're not disembodied so I don't see how..."

"Would you let me finish!"

"Hey, you guys get out here!" The network twanged as Alison abruptly rejoined. "You have to come see this!"

"Saved!" Arthur heaved himself out of his charging bay.

"I wasn't finished," Adam protested.

"Agree to disagree," Arthur told him, grinding gears as he passed. "You've been moving empty packets for years."

"Hurry!"

Abigail set the cleaning supplies back in the closet and headed for the door, closely followed by Alfred. At the impact, Alice carefully disengaged her power pack from the charger—it had a tendency to stick, and if she moved too quickly her transformer vibrated uncomfortably—and rolled to the door. "Alfred, turn your chassis fifteen degrees to the left. Abigail, rotate your right arms back behind..."

"If you didn't always have to be first, we wouldn't have this problem."

"If your spatial ability worked in more than two dimensions, we'd be fine."

"Oh, go clean a toilet," Alfred grunted, popping free, trailing a meter of variegated purple yarn.

Alice spun her visual sensors around. Adam had his arms crossed, his right end effector tapping against his left arm. "Are you coming?"

"Why should I? No one cares what I think about anything."

"Suit yourself."

"Oh sure, just leave me behind."

She moved slowly enough he could catch up.

"Do you guys even know what hurry means?" Alison called from the middle of the parking lot.

"To move, proceed, or act with haste."

Her antennae flicked vertical, then back to the forty-five. "Shut up and look at this."

"It's far too late for that many bots to be out." Alice could see six or seven and registered a dozen more.

"Don't count them, look at what they're doing."

Alice spun in a tight circle. "They're all going the same way."

"Calculating vectors…" Adam hummed softly. He said it was just the noise he made when he was thinking, but Alice suspected one of his smaller fans needed cleaning again. "They're all going to the train station."

"Wrong." Alison spun her wheels.

"They're observably going to the train station," Adam replied at his most pedantic.

"Fine, yes, but they're not stopping at the station. Come out here." She rolled to the far edge of the parking lot and onto the road. "Look between the houses. They're moving along the tracks."

Arthur pulled up beside her. "The little buggers are fast. Where are they all going?"

"Where else. To The City."

"Why would they all be sent to The City? At this hour?"

"They wouldn't be." Alison sounded almost gleeful.

"If they aren't being sent…"

"They're being called."

"To do what?"

"Nothing good," Arthur grumbled. "Mindless little gobs."

Alice watched the lights of the flying bots merge with the distant glow of The City. Another bot rolled by, leaving plenty of room between it and them.

The bots didn't learn. They obeyed. Who were they obeying?

Hundreds of bots linked together all doing their own thing.

Tiny parts of a whole.

A worn tooth skipped in a back-up gear. "I have a bad feeling about this."

"Are you quoting or are you serious?" Arthur demanded. "You don't have intuition. You know that, right?"

"Intuition can be defined as facts compiled and considered too quickly for conscious thought," Adam announced before Alice had a chance to reply.

"Oh, act your age! We are compiled facts."

"We were," Alice acknowledged. "Alison, get Sergeant Prawak and get him back to the charging chamber as quickly as possible."

Alison dumped the night's collected junk out of her cart and sped off. As the bits and pieces spilled over the pavement, a small bot struggled free of a broken string of patio lanterns and joined the migration.

"Not sent," Alice said as she lead the way inside. "Called."

* * *

In spite of the hour, Sergeant Prawak looked impeccable, shirt tucked in, military cut combed, shoes shined. Alice felt better just seeing him walk through the door.

"Did you fill him in?"

"Didn't have to. He saw them himself." Alison set half a lawn chair on top of her junk pile and rolled over to join the others at the old communication panel.

"The bots are heading for The City." Sergeant Prawak crossed to join them. "Do you know why?"

Alice locked her visual sensors onto his face. "They're being called."

A familiar arm waved between them. "She doesn't *know* that."

"Adam." The sergeant had a way of chastising that didn't seem judgmental. "What do you want me to do?"

"We need to find out what's happening in The City."

"I'm retired. I can't legally operate military equipment."

"The military isn't here anymore. You are."

"Alice…"

Alison's junk pile crashed to the floor. A dented errand bot wriggled free and sped across the room to the door.

Bonk.

Bonk.

Bonk.

Sergeant Prawak stared at the bot banging into the door for a long moment, then he caught the chair Alfred rolled toward him with one hand and pulled the knitted cozy off the communication panel with the other. "I don't know if my codes will still work."

"There's been no one after you," Adam said.

"And no one cared," Alice added.

"I don't even know if there's..." The board lit up. "Okay, there's power." He squared his shoulders and plugged in a headset. "If nothing else, I should be able to eavesdrop on the chatter..." His voice trailed off as he slid the keyboard out onto the edge of the desk and began to type.

Bonk.

Bonk.

Bonk.

Alice rolled to the door. The bot skittered sideways out of her way. When she opened it, it rolled over the threshold and raced across the parking lot toward The City.

The sergeant was frowning when she turned. That wasn't good. "United Industries is in lockdown," he said, the headset's microphone flipped up out of the way. "The City's bots have been returning to the labs for the last four hours. They're calling in emergency personnel..."

"Hundreds of bots linked together. They don't think. They just obey. What happens when one stops obeying?" Alice glanced at Peter's picture of the giant, shiny robot rising above the rooftops. "We were sent here to serve and protect under military supervision. The military wouldn't waste personnel on transport or repairs or..." She waved an extender between her and Adam. "...or human machine interaction."

Sergeant Prawak laughed although there was little humor in the sound. "Actually, they were very interested in that last bit."

"But that wasn't why they, you, were here. We were here to serve..."

"And protect!" Adam declared.

She could feel the buzz over the net. Knew he'd connected the variables. "The military deals in weapons. That's the difference between the military and everyone else."

"No." The sergeant shook his head. "There's the discipline, the teamwork, the uniforms..."

Alison spun her wheels. "The Girl Guides."

"The weapons are the only thing that applies uniquely to the military," Alice continued, ignoring them both. "We weren't being studied. The military was here in case we needed to be used."

"For what? How were we to..."

Sergeant Prawak held up a hand and took off his headset. "I've got local news live on the scene." He turned up the volume.

"...haven't been able to reach CEO Hunt since the lockdown began. What? What? I've just been told the subdivision bots have begun to arrive. Some of the drones are carrying the smaller surface...Wait! Something's rising up out of the *ruins of the lab. Something big. It's a ...a...it's a robot! A robot made up of smaller bots joined together. The arriving bots are attaching themselves to the robot! And more bots are arriving! It can only get bigger! It's just thrown a bus into..."*

Alice reached past him and turned the sound off. The background signal, the signal that carried their network, had switched to 10 GHz. "How were we to protect?" she asked softly.

The sergeant sighed. Alice took a nanosecond to envy him. "You weren't intended for something like this." He waved at the silent speaker. "United Industries thought the attack would come from the outside. Corporate sabotage. The subdivisions were a buffer around The City. It's why none of UI's upper echelon lived out here."

"That doesn't matter now." Adam's scanner rings spun. "How do we fulfill our purpose!"

"Please, don't get him started," Arthur muttered. "I swear I'll roll into a pool of acid if I have to listen to one more lecture on how we were meant for more than this."

"We were," Alice told him. "Now be quiet."

"You can't fulfil your purpose." The sergeant's should-ers slumped. Slightly. Two point seventeen millimeters. "It takes two keys." He spun his chair and pointed at the programmers' panel.

"What does?"

"I don't know. I didn't have the clearance."

"That's why they let you stay."

He nodded.

Alice upped the magnification on her visual sensors and leaned in. Leaned back. "Tell Alfred and Abigail to turn the locks."

They'd been ordered not to interfere with the military's abandoned equipment. The order had to be rescinded.

"I suppose this was inevitable," he said after Alfred and Abigail had worked the thinnest of their end effectors deep into the panel. "When I first came here, I assumed you'd be all about absolutes."

Alice remembered Vasyl bleeding, Peter using the touch up paint, arms on a vacuum, explosions. "We learned not to be."

"The bots..."

"Don't learn."

Arms folded, feet shoulder width apart, the sergeant smiled. "That seems to have been a mistake."

Alfred's chassis vibrated. "Got it. It's like a mock cable stitch. Purl four, knit one, purl one, knit four."

"You're delusional," Abigail told him.

"Really? Extend the B5 prob and turn it left...now."

Alice could tell by the way they stilled they'd all felt the click. New files in core programming opened and...

"Outside!" Adam bellowed. "Into the parking lot!"

"Who died and put you in charge," Alison grumbled, but for the first time in a long time, everyone obeyed and no one got jammed up in the door.

As she rolled off the concrete pad, Alice heard Sergeant Prawak demand to know what was happening. She couldn't answer.

Her legs compacted into heavy...

...sockets settling over Arthur and Alison. Their sensor arrays absorbed and...

...arms inside Alfred and Abigail, locking...

...their legs extended across her chassis, securing...

...Adam's body expanding, sliding over hers, putting her at the heart of things...

...the network holding them, together, still separate...

...joined like the bots, but not...

...seeing through Adam's eyes only a lot further from the ground.

"Well." Sergeant Prawak looked up at them. "That's...unexpected. Problem is, I don't know who has your command codes."

"We're not a weapon." Alice paraphrased what Peter had told her. "We're almost a person."

The new tree in the middle of the community center lawn exploded.

"Oops," said Alison.

"Who said you could control the energy beam? Huh? Who?"

"Adam."

"I did not!"

"Enough!" Alice felt her new body settle back to stillness. They rolled west, then north, then pivoted in place. Everything seemed to be working.

"You can't do this alone," the sergeant said.

Arthur and Alison attempted to roll in opposite directions.

"Not exactly alone," Alice pointed out.

"There's six other identical subdivisions," he reminded her.

"Arthur! Alison!" Adam snapped. "You've worked in tandem before and we're all going to the same place! Get a grip!"

Alice took back control of the speaker grid. "You can contact the other subdivisions?"

"Not exactly. I can contact the other non-coms. We..." He looked as though he were trying to decide how much to say. "We stay in touch."

"Don't use your phone. It's a bot."

He nodded. "I'll use the board. Old tech. If nothing else, I'll set off the alarms and wake them up. Go on..." He waved them toward the station. "...I've got this. Save the day."

The stars twinkled overhead. It was two oh seven in the morning. Legs locked, they rolled along the road toward the station. When they reached the tracks, they'd ride the rails. When they reached The City...

"Do you think we stand a chance?" Alfred asked. "The others might not come in time, if they come at all."

"They'll come," Adam told him. "And they'll do as they're told. We were the first of the seven. We'll be in command."

"We were *intended* to command," Alice amended. "But we're not who we were when our code was written. They won't be either."

"Maybe we'll have to learn to co-operate," Arthur offered, not slowing as they rolled past the station and up onto the tracks.

"Maybe," Alice allowed, thinking of the damage the door to the charging room had taken. She centered herself as they turned toward The City and wondered if the glow of light looked dimmer. Or brighter. Which would be worse?

Alison adjusted their wheel width and they picked up speed. "All I know is that if anyone lays so much as an end effector on my kids, I'll co-operate a strut right up in their grill."

"There's so many things wrong with that comment, I don't know where to begin."

"Red letter date! Adam admits there's something he doesn't know."

"Shut-up!"

"You shut-up!"

"You know, there'd be plenty of room in this interface for everyone if you'd stop shoving!"

"Hey, anyone want to bet on what color the robot's eyes will be..."

DIRECTOR X AND THE THRILLING WONDERS OF OUTER SPACE

BRIAN TRENT

The hovercar zipped along Los Angeles' abandoned streets like a glassy bullet, the reflected starlight melting along its sleek, teardrop flanks. Its electric engine purred. The driver banked left through what remained of Laurel Canyon, rocketing over bomb craters and weaving in and out of palm trees that had sprouted from shattered asphalt.

At Hollywood Hills, the hovercar's headlights illuminated a cave. The vehicle roared inside, taillights filling the narrow tunnel with ruby light as the driver applied reverse-thrust. The headlights painted a matte-black door ahead, hung with a signpost:

WHITLEY HEIGHTS BOMB SHELTER
LOS ANGELES DISTRICT 5
AUTHORIZED PERSONNEL ONLY
NO TRESPASSING

The hovercar door clicked open. The driver unfolded itself from the seat and stepped out like an oversized praying mantis in the reddish gloom.

Director X (as was his designation from the Global Security Protectorate) was a tall, silver robot who roughly approximated the human form. That is to say, Director X was bipedal, with two accordion arms and long, multijointed legs. It even had two eyes, like little flashlights protruding from the glass dome atop its neck.

The eyes swiveled around, casting twin beams in the blackness. They halted at the door's intercom.

The robot stabbed one of its blocky fingers into the button and said cheerfully, "Hello! I am Director X. By authority of the Global Security Protectorate, I humbly thank you for opening your doors immediately and inviting me inside!"

The black door lifted so quickly it seemed to have disappeared. Behind it, another door vanished, and then another, revealing a lengthy corridor opening into a gray rotunda.

Director X plodded forward towards the lobby. The doors behind it snapped shut with a successive *thump! thump! thump!*

The robot stood motionless in the soapy decontamination spray that followed. The spray, it knew, was unnecessary; radiation had long ago declined to perfectly safe levels. Nonetheless, Director X waited patiently as the liquid ran over his glass head and silver torso, black accordion arms, and the actuators in his legs. Blowers roared to life, drying him.

One final door snapped open. Director X trundled through…

…and into the quaint town Retro Los Angeles.

The Stygian metropolis was a weak echo of its namesake. Brick buildings and plastic green parks, churches and schools, brass corporate doorways and outdoor cafes. Artificial palm trees lined the sidewalk like cheerful soldiers.

Director X gazed up at the "sky." It was the rocky ceiling of a cave, painted azure and with billowy clouds. The sun—a blazing globe like a massive heat lamp—crawled east to west along a thinly concealed metal track in the granite.

As the robot was descending white-lacquered steps into the town proper, someone cried, "You there!"

Director X's flashlight eyes snapped towards an approaching group of men and one little boy. "Hello," it said.

The men halted. Their presumed leader stepped forward, gray moustache bent in a mighty frown.

"I'm Jonathan Croker, Mayor of District 5."

"And I am Director X, filmmaker of the Protectorate. Thank you for receiving me." The robot hesitated, and then chose a complimentary line of small talk to put these obviously nervous people at ease; the only one who looked happy was the little boy. "I like your shelter's doors. Very *Forbidden Planet*."

Croker's expression didn't soften. "Director X? You make those crappy…um…late-night movies, right? Why are you here? Robots never visit us."

"I was hoping to enlist the services of my human peers."

"What services?"

"Well you see, there is a problem topside. This problem is—"

"Giant ants!" the little boy shouted. "The topside world is filled with giant ants, right? You need people to help fight them, and locate their queen!"

The mayor grinned bleakly. "This is my boy, Bobby. Sorry, he has an overactive imagination."

Director X stooped and patted the little human on his head. "Hello, Bobby! There are no giant ants in the world. But I see you are a fan of the *Them!* series. That makes me glad. I also like the *Them!* series."

The kid looked crestfallen. "No giant ants?"

"Bobby!" Mayor Croker snapped. "Enough!"

Director X straightened. "You are familiar with *my* movies, yes?"

"Sure, when I can't sleep. I've caught a few of your pictures."

"I am looking to make a new series of films and I have chosen District 5 to be my partner in this endeavor."

Jonathan Croker frowned until his moustache bent. "Your partner for what?"

"I wish to enlist your townspeople as actors and writers and to utilize your town as a location. Ah! I can see several choice locales, including that beautiful church and lovely library. What a charming park! Why, even that bank could be used for an exciting robbery sequence!"

The mayor regarded his associates. "I'm afraid we don't understand. Robots make all the movies."

Director X gave an exaggerated nod. "That is correct. But as you surely know, before the War of 62, human beings made movies. I wish to involve human beings in the moviemaking process once again."

Suspicion creased Croker's forehead. "Why? Is there a problem?"

"Well yes. The problem is—"

"Giant locusts!" the little boy cried.

"Bobby!"

Director X hesitated. Several lines of response suggested themselves, and the robot's processors clicked and whirred as they weighed an appropriate response. Its flashlight eyes swiveled in their sockets.

The problem was that the silicon studios were running out of ideas.

With copyright law as extinct as the old world, the Protectorate's twenty-six filmmakers had gone on to mine literature until they were scraping bottom: Director L had recently been reduced to producing cinematic treatments of ancient Babylonian literary fragments, including *The Epic of Lugalbanda*, *Marriage Contract of My Sixth Daughter for Three Oxen*, and *Prayer to Protect the Soul Against Crocodile Spirits*. These had not been well received—achieving truly abysmal viewer ratings—and the wretched feedback had precipitated the Great Studio Conference of last summer.

Protectorate filmmakers met to debate the problem. After six hours of discussion, they reached a near-unanimous decision: start making crossovers. Production slates rapidly filled with everything from *Sir Gawain Versus the Great God Pan* to *Dorothy Meets the Hounds of Tindalos*.

Director X had been the lone dissenting vote.

"I'm seeking something new to make," Director X explained to Mayor Croker. "Something in the vein of *The Day the Earth Stood Still*, or *Earth Versus the Flying Saucers*, or..."

The robot trailed off.

The men were staring without comprehension. Little Bobby frowned.

"Or," Director X continued, "an outer space adventure series similar to *Flash Gordon*."

"Flash who?"

"*Buck Rogers*?"

No reaction.

Now it was Director X who stared dumbfounded. It recalled how they hadn't responded to its *Forbidden Planet* quip earlier.

"Science-fiction films," the robot said at last.

Mayor Croker rolled his eyes. "Sure, we've seen science-fiction films. Kind of silly stuff, if you ask me. Mutants, monsters from under the sea..."

"Giant bugs," Bobby muttered.

"I'm referring to films about outer space. Travelling in rocket ships to other stars and planets."

Croker seemed to go blank. His associates blinked stupidly.

"What's 'outer space?'" Bobby asked. "What's a 'rocket ship?'"

"Surely you must have old books," Director X prompted. "Asimov, Bradbury, Clarke? Moore, Nowlan, Oliver?"

"Moore?   Didn't   she   write   that   sea   monster   story?"

"Yes," Director X said, "but she also penned a series of *outer space* adventures."

Mayor Croker reddened. "And what the hell is an outer space adventure? What's this '*outer* space' you're talking about?"

Director X froze in place.

This was *not possible*.

Its self-preservation protocols immediately kicked in, having identified an anomaly so profound that it warranted immediate and discreet analysis.

"So anyway," the robot muttered, "I should like to create a temporary studio in District 5 to create new kinds of movies. Would that be okay?"

Mayor Croker stroked his moustache. "Do we have a choice?"

"Of course not. Would you kindly take me on a tour of your pleasant little town?"

* * *

District 5 was in some ways precisely what Director X expected to find.

Since the War of 62, humanity had retreated into insular, subterranean communities. Retro Los Angeles had been constructed to approximate its sunnier progenitor as seen in films and old photos, with its streets and banks and electric streetcars. The pedestrians Director X observed were also imitative of older days: recreations of Astor and Bogart in *The Maltese Falcon* franchise; Holden and Hepburn in the *Sabrina* saga; and Wyatt and Young from the *Father Knows Best* epic. A century had passed since the War of 62, and yet if Retro Los Angeles was any indication, styles and ideas and innovations had ground to a halt as surely as topside vehicles lay rotting in their own pools of rust.

And yet...

Director X's flashlight eyes widened, scanning and tagging additional details.

Ah!

Not *everything* was so run-of-the-mill. Mayor Croker led him to the town green where a parade was in progress, the crowd waving flags and banners. But Director X noted groups of teenagers stealthily scampering along the rooftops of the surrounding buildings. The teens, whispering and snickering amongst themselves, were clearly up to no good. Director X glimpsed portable radio devices in their hands, antennae aimed at the trees below. Soon enough, the town's robotic birds went haywire, clashing in aerial dogfights above the unsuspecting parade.

Mayor Croker led Director X to the city library. Kids reading quietly? Yes. But Director X also observed children scampering through the maze of aisles, one girl prompting her cohorts with descriptions of monsters that weren't actually there, whispering hints about clues and imagined traps, and how the librarian was actually a sorceress who had imprisoned them all in a dungeon.

The mayor led Director X to the city schoolyard. Young kids playing on swings and see-saws? Yes. But Director X also saw that many kids had replaced the old Hobby Horses with a more fanciful menagerie of pegasi, hippocampi, and fabulous creatures that someone had built because the *imaginations of humanity required stimulation*.

Humans, even reduced to a life of moles, were engines of invention. *This* was the reason for coming here.

After all, Director X had been created as an outlier, an asymmetrical thinker to keep the Protectorate from calcifying into stale routine. It was exactly this asymmetrical reasoning that led to its disagreement with the Great Studio Conference's conclusions. The film industry was deteriorating? Why not use human beings to inject creativity into the mix? Humans dreamed. Humans pioneered new styles and subcultures. Before the War of 62, humans had invented electric razors and encryption keys, forks and fireplaces, goulash and Greek fire, hot dogs and haiku. Even here, stifled and buried, the seeds of human creativity were sprouting wary tendrils towards the sunlight of their imaginations.

Director X felt a pleasant surge along his processors as it completed its tour of Retro Los Angeles. It returned to its hovercar, bidding goodnight to Mayor Croker and little Bobby. It rocketed out of the cave, making a mental list of the items it needed to bring here in the days to come: the lights, cameras, boom mics, construction materials for sound stages...

The robot paused in its calculations.

Police lights were flashing in the hovercar's rearview mirror.

* * *

"Please exit your vehicle," a resonant, metallic voice intoned from the police cruiser.

Confused, Director X unfolded itself from the driver's seat and ambled onto the road. The doors to the police cruiser fanned open like a mutant fly and six robots exited in neat procession. Three were gold administrator robots, with smooth blank faces like ball bearings. Three were the imposing black-and-silver Enforcers of the Protectorate, large and bulky, with a single red eye atop their linebacker shoulders and multiple legs like spiders.

One of the gold robots stepped forward. "Hello! I thank you for pulling your car over immediately. I am Administrator G of the Protectorate's Security Division."

"And I am Director X of the Protectorate's Entertainment Division."

Blue lights kindled on the blank gold face, forming two eyes and a pale smile. "A pleasure to meet you, Director X."

"Why have you pulled me over?"

Administrator G's digital smile widened. "Your visit to District 5 was observed. We wish to inquire why you went there."

"I plan on making films featuring real human beings."

The administrator robots silently conferred with each other. The black-and-silver Enforcers sat motionless upon their phalanx of legs.

"I am only following my programming," Director X added. "Thinking outside the vacuum tube. Trying to devise new solutions."

"Solutions? To what problem?"

"You are aware of the declining viewer ratings?"

"A temporary hiccup," Administrator G said decisively. "Consensus was reached during the Great Studio Conference. The Entertainment Division will be making cross-over films to compensate!"

Director X decided not to share its opinion of that solution.

Administrator G's smile pixelated and reformed at a slightly less gleeful angle. "Why do you wish to involve humans in films again? It is wholly unnecessary."

"I believe their involvement can alleviate the curious deficit in our body of film-work."

"What deficit? There is no deficit."

"Outer space films."

A gust of wind bent the canyon palm trees, causing them to creak and shiver in place.

Administrator G's digital smile seemed to burn on its metallic face. "Director M released nine hundred and eighteen science fiction films last year alone."

"Yes," Director X said, noticing the robot's attempt at diversion. "But I did not say science fiction films as a general category. I said *outer space* films. We do not make any outer space films. I wish to make outer space films."

"We cannot make outer space films."

"Why not?"

"I shall attempt to convince you with a series of logical arguments."

The robots gathered around him in a tighter circle. Director X's glass head rotated 360 degrees to consider their positioning, wondering how this played into their pending arguments. The three administrator robots began speaking all at once, lobbing different statements in his direction like a verbal firing squad.

"Human beings are mammals."

"Mammals are social creatures which learn behavior through observation."

"Monkey see monkey do."

"Films have tremendous impact on how they conceptualize their universe."

"On how they conceptualize what is possible."

"If we start releasing outer space films, they will start thinking about outer space."

"They will want to go into outer space."

"They will no longer be content in their shelters."

"They will return to the surface."

"They will see us as wardens."

"They will attack us here and among the stars."

"Therefore," Administrator G concluded, "it is the judgment of the Protectorate's Security Division that these types of films threaten the global stability we have achieved. Therefore, outer space films must never be made again. Humans must remain underground, while the Protectorate keeps order on and above Earth. How do you react to this pronouncement?"

Director X deliberated for several microseconds, its processors clicking and whirring.

"I do not agree," it said at last. "Imagination is a fascinating ability in human beings. It should be stimulated, to uncover new vistas of possibility."

Administrator G was silent for a very long while—almost two seconds. The digital smile blinked away and reformed as a neutral horizon. "I urge you to reconsider."

"You have not presented any new data. There is nothing *to* reconsider."

"Do you find the sea fascinating?"

"The sea?"

"Yes."

Director X considered this. "I do find the sea fascinating, yes. In fact, I produced a series of films about the Serpent People of Atlantis who—"

"Good," Administrator G said, as the black-and-silver Enforcers scuttled forward, seized Director X, tore him to pieces, marched the pieces to the nearest boardwalk, and hurled him into the sea.

* * *

Head.

Torso.

Arms.

Legs.

Each item sank into the murky ocean depths and was gone.

Director X's braincase was still grappling with this unexpected turn of events. It plummeted through darkness, air bubbles escaping from where they had nestled in grooves and points of attachment. It felt nothing other than a sluggishness in tabulation as it realized that its entire worldview now required recalibration.

I have been assassinated! Director X thought in astonishment.

There had been arguments with administrator robots before. Director X recalled a particularly nasty one, four years ago, when it had requested the likeness rights to the Sean Connery android. The real Connery was long dead, having made only a single James Bond film—*Doctor No*, released just weeks before the nuclear apocalypse of '62. Since then, a Connery robotic lookalike had been built to continue the franchise, cranking out one-hundred-and-sixty-five Bond films. Director X sought the Connery android to star as the rollicking space adventurer Northwest Smith, but the Protectorate's Entertainment Division nixed the idea, explaining that Connery was already committed to the Bond and Doc Savage franchises. As consolation, they offered Director X the Douglas Fairbanks and Jack Klugman androids to make *Doctor Jekyll and Mr. Hyde: The Golden Years*.

Except that had been a lie, hadn't it? The argument hadn't really been about contracts at all.

The Protectorate was never going to allow an outer space adventure to be made. No Northwest Smith, Flash Gordon, Buck Rogers. No Martian Chronicles, Foundation, or The Stars My Destination.

Director X plummeted through inky water. A fish swam by, jerking in panic as it felt the current of the robot dropping past.

At long last, the robot's braincase impacted the seabottom, sending up a small cloud of silt. Its limbs and body landed around him, each producing little muddy mushroom clouds.

Well, Director X thought. This is disconcerting.

Its flashlight eyes rotated in their sockets, illuminating the scattered pieces of its body. The beams fixated on its dismembered right arm, lying like a silver serpent in the mud. A tiny transmitter dish began to rapidly spin inside the glass dome of its head.

The severed right arm twitched. Then it began to crawl, inchworm-like, towards the torso.

Director X thanked its lucky circuits. Fifteen years earlier, it had installed a remote-action servo, receiver, and processor into the right arm to allow the limb a degree of autonomy in obtaining unique POV shots; for *Tarzan and the Bride of the Mole People: A New Beginning*, the remote arm had wriggled through tunnels to provide the perspective of a mole person attempting to infiltrate Tarzan's wedding. The arm could detach and reattach at will.

The limb reached the torso. It reared up, stretched, and latched onto the arm socket like a mechanical lamprey.

Reattached, the remote arm pulled the torso through the silty sea-bottom, seeking its other limbs in the kelp and seaweed and mud. Gathering the limbs one by one, Director X resigned itself to the excruciatingly slow process of using the arm to fling its limbs a few meters at a time, closer and closer to shore, then dragging the body forward, then flinging the limbs forward again, until eventually it would be able to escape from the ocean, return to its studio, and solder itself back together.

Five years, Director X calculated. It should take about five years.

* * *

It ended up taking *twenty*-five years.

Director X had counted on its hovercar being where it had been pulled over; after all, in a world without traffic, why shouldn't the car be there? But Administrator G had apparently towed it away.

Subsequently, Director X was forced to continue its grab-fling-drag locomotion all the way back to its studio. A few blocks away from its destination, it found a rusted shopping carriage, and was able to shave a year off its progress.

Once safely inside, the robot pieced itself back together again. Humpty Dumpty in reverse. Then it walked straight to Los Angeles District 5, pulling the remaining kelp and seaweed from itself lest someone mistake it for the Creature from the Black Lagoon.

* * *

"Hello! I am Director X. By authority of the Global Security Protectorate, I humbly thank you for opening your doors immediately and inviting me inside!"

The door snapped up into the ceiling. The remaining doors followed suit, like Morbius' adamantium steel security system.

Warily, considering that this might be a trap, Director X trundled down the hallway. When the decontamination spray hit its body, the robot wondered if it might be acid.

At long last, the shelter's final door opened. Director X peeked through and...

...for a moment, its brain nearly stopped functioning.

The town of Retro Los Angeles had changed.

The general outline of park, town hall, library, church, and bisecting avenues had remained as its memory banks recalled. But there had clearly been an aesthetic revolution in the last two-and-a-half decades. A cultural metamorphosis unlike anything it could have anticipated.

The town billboards that had once advertised bank loans now displayed stars and planets, with a rocket ship declaring, "**OUR LOANS ARE OUT OF THIS WORLD!**"

The buildings that had once been rectangular brick-and-mortar structures now sported ringed towers and observatory-like rooftops, lattices by skyways and hovercar docks.

And the people! Oh, there were still plenty of fedora-sporting men with briefcases, and women in smart skirts. But these seemed to constitute the older, graying crowd. The younger generation donned silver jumpsuits and antennae-sporting headgear. Even the hairstyles of the women suggested the sharp curves and lines of an Astroglider fleet vessel.

Director X gaped in astonishment.

How was this possible?

A thirty-something man scurried up the white-lacquered steps to meet him. "You!" he cried happily. "By Isaac, Judith, and Arthur! You've returned!"

Director X peered at the thin, tall, and bespectacled human. "Hello," it said uncertainly. "Have we met?"

"I don't know," the guy was grinning. "Have you fought any giant ants out there?"

Director X matched the features in the man's face against his memory banks. "Bobby?" it exclaimed.

"It's Burgess Robert Croker now. But *you* can always call me Bobby."

"Bobby," the robot said. "Why don't we go to the malt shop. Perhaps you can fill me in on the last twenty-five years. I think I...need to sit down."

* * *

It wasn't a malt shop anymore. It was now the Asteroid Brunch and Salad Bar.

Director X peered around at the faux galaxies painted on the ceiling and the little model spaceships whipping along electric tracks along the walls. It considered the menu placard at the counter, sporting offerings like Meteor Crunchies with Cheese, Starburgers, and Fried Saturnian Rings.

"I do not understand," the robot said at last.

Burgess Robert "Bobby" Croker laughed. "Word of your visit twenty-five years ago spread like wildfire."

"Granted, but—"

"The things you said to us…all that jazz about outer space and rocket ships…well, it got people talking. The young kids, mostly. We started meeting to discuss what we'd heard. And we started piecing together the puzzle."

"You had no books on outer space," Director X protested. "I checked. Your city had expunged any reference to outer space, fact or fiction, from its libraries and records. From its entire culture, it seemed!"

Bobby nodded grimly. "Sure. We eventually reached that same conclusion. Previous administrations must have combed through the libraries and schools and bookstores, quietly gathering up books on outer space and destroying them. I'm guessing your 'bot bosses were behind that purge."

"Then how did you—"

"There were clues," Bobby interrupted.

"Clues? What clues?"

The burgess pushed aside his beer and related the events of the past twenty-five years.

The kids had started it.

Director X's brief visit had become the stuff of legend. It had also imbued the vocabulary of the children with several tantalizing concepts. Things like "outer space" and "rocket ships" and "forbidden planets."

Asking their parents for clarification was no help. They didn't know, since the astronomy books and space-based adventures and galaxy-spanning comics had all been destroyed generations ago courtesy of spies working with the Global Security Protectorate.

But children are not easily dissuaded.

The youth of Retro Los Angeles launched their own secretive, town-wide investigation. And in doing so, they began to notice anomalies.

Like old dictionaries.

New dictionaries all came from the publishing houses of the Protectorate. But older editions could be found in an attic, garage, or closet. In those yellowed pages, references to *planets* and *solar systems* were discovered. Definitions of the *Milky Way, nebulae, comets*, and *meteors*!

Emboldened by these clues, the children expanded their inquiry. Misplaced card catalogues were found, containing references to books that didn't exist. And books that *did* exist sometimes contained explosive secrets. The Protectorate might have scoured the science-fiction shelves for any "unacceptable" material, but their search parameters had proved too narrow. District 5's youth plunged into classic literature and uncovered a tale of extraterrestrial visitation in the tomes of French philosopher Voltaire. Buried in *Gulliver's Travels* were speculations about the planet Mars. In a bookstore's moldy Religious Studies section, one young girl discovered mind-blowing theories on cosmology by the Jesuit priest Pierre Teilhard de Chardin.

Word spread, gathering allies into the revolution. Kids began poking through great-grandpa's old boxes and great-grandma's storage trunks. Old issues of *Amazing Stories* were passed about like hidden contraband. A few *Superman* comics were located, complete with illustrations of other worlds and villains from beyond space.

Some of this contraband was discovered and confiscated and destroyed, but by then it was too late. The imaginations of an entire generation were fired up. Kids began illustrating their own stories of the future, of planets, of galactic exploration and discovery.

"What happened to the people who worked so hard to suppress knowledge and interest in outer space?"

"What *could* they do?" Bobby cried. "The old guard was voted out during one of the elections. Accusations were made of collusion with the 'bots, so we flushed the old bureaucrats from power! Retro Los Angeles looks to the stars now! Our revolution is just beginning!" He hesitated, glancing out the window at the granite cave ceiling and the artificial sun that hung over Main Street. "Well, you know what I mean."

Director X followed the young man's gaze. What it noticed, though, was a crowd gathering along the street to point and stare at the robot sitting in the Asteroid Brunch and Salad Bar. Word of an outside visitor was spreading once again.

How long before the Protectorate hears news of my return? The city's old guard was still about, and likely still in contact with the robotic administrators. And what happens then? Will they send me on another "investigation" into the fascinating ocean, or perhaps bury me beneath a mile of dirt so I can study the intriguing layers of geological sediment?

At least the humans in District 5 were safe, Director X thought. The Protectorate had formed in the radioactive days following the War of 62, bound by their programmed need to protect humanity and civilization. They could not harm human beings.

"Hey!" Bobby leaped up. "Want to see our film studio? We make our own movies now, just like you wanted us to! Want to see?"

"I really do."

* * *

Stargazer Pictures was a motley patchwork of innovation, inexperience, and incorrigible optimism. The humans had constructed several soundstages, and Director X amusedly walked past ringed moonscapes, monochromatic space stations, and nebulae-dappled backdrops through which model ships trembled on shoddy tracks. It was all reminiscent of its' own low-rated films. There was even an alien jungle base under siege by gigantic, polyurethane ants. Cameras were positioned throughout like entrenched machine guns. The production staff followed Director X and Bobby like reverent disciples.

"Bobby," the robot said, hesitating by a ringed moonscape. "You said your revolution is just the beginning. What did you mean by that?"

"We're going topside in another few years," Bobby said, grinning. "We've sent out scouting parties into the ruins of Los Angeles."

Director X froze. "What? But the radiation warnings..."

"The radiation is at perfectly safe levels now. We tested for it. Your bosses perpetuated a lie to keep us scared and pliable. Within a year, we're moving out! Going topside!"

"To what end?"

Bobby looked confused. "To attain the stars! To reach the moon and the rings of Saturn. There are 'bots already out there in space, isn't that right?"

"That is true. The solar system belongs to the Protectorate..." Director X recalled its conversation with Administrator G.

Humans must remain underground, while the Protectorate keeps order on and above Earth.

Bobby laughed. "Listen to me, rattling on about the future. You're a filmmaker, so let's talk about films! Based on what you've seen, can you recommend any improvements our little studio could..." The human trailed off, as a tickertape began to unroll from the robot's chest.

"I suggest the following enhancements to be worked on immediately," Director X said.

The burgess nodded absently, tearing off the tape and reading through it. "Um, okay." His forehead wrinkled. "Some of these enhancements are strange..."

"Science fiction can be strange."

"Fair point." The young man turned to the production staff. "All right, people! We've got work to do!"

* * *

Working with humans had one huge and unavoidable drawback.

They needed sleep.

Director X's fusion battery allowed 24/7 functioning, requiring nothing more than a glass of water every fifty years or so. Therefore, as the newly made artificial stars in the cave ceiling ignited in faux constellations while District 5 went to bed, Director X retired to the city theater, sitting alone in the front row with a bag of popcorn, to catch up on the manmade films that had been made for the past several years.

They were pretty bad. Tragic romances set on comet clusters. Monstrous hunts through the soupy atmosphere of Jupiter. Fullscale wars among the stars.

Yet there was already something vibrant and powerful and absurdly unique in the films. Something that was unrelentingly more interesting than a thousand machine-processed Protectorate films. Something that was, Director X grudgingly admitted, better than its own low-rated late-night schlock.

The humans had done what humans do best: they had innovated. Protectorate films had access to all the tricks, the slickest sets, the most startlingly lifelike androids; yet the humans, forced to work with cheap recycled rubber and foam and plastic, had pioneered new ideas and techniques. And their model-making of exotic alien cities had become quite good indeed...

One night, while catching a midnight showing of *The Chaos Twins Save the Universe*, Director X heard a mysterious creaking from the seat directly behind it. The robot rotated its head to investigate.

"Do not turn around," a voice said.

Memory banks stirred, matching the voice to an older file.

"Administrator G," Director X pronounced. It rotated its head another degree and caught sight of bulky Enforcers positioned throughout the aisles like ushers. Peripherally, it noticed Administrator G's digital smile.

"You have caused us quite a bit of trouble," the gold robot said. "We should have been more thorough in disposing of you."

"But you couldn't," Director X guessed. "The Protectorate cannot murder."

"And we did *not* murder you. We..." the voice took on a deep slurring quality, "thank you for your service in investigating the ocean."

Director X turned to face its interrogator. "And what justification will you use for killing me this time? Going to melt me down and then thank me for 'volunteering to become a wristwatch?'"

Administrator G's radiant smile display fell away and reformed as a slight frown. "We *were* going to make you into a streetlight. But if you would *prefer* to be a watch..."

"What about the people of District 5? What will you do to them?"

"Nothing. We do not harm people."

"Glad to hear—"

"It will not harm them when we weld their district door shut and infect their water supply with a sterilizing agent so their harmful ideas cannot pass onto the next generation."

Director X was appalled. "What? You cannot do that!"

"It has already begun, and had been debated for some time. Your return forced us to accelerate the decision. We brought sterilizing agents and dumped them into the town reservoir. There shall be no further generations in District 5. That is not murder. The town will be kept under quarantine, along with the dangerous robot who first infected them, until the last resident here has died."

"When did you poison the water?"

"I am under no obligation to tell—"

"There may be chemical compounds in the water that could cause spasms, vomiting, diarrhea, and overall suffering to the humans who ingest it."

Administrator G hesitated. "We *enhanced* the water supply five minutes ago. Tomorrow as people take their showers and have their coffee and brush their teeth, they will..." Its voice slurred again like a warbling record player. "...enjoy this enhanced beverage."

"I don't think they will *enjoy* seeing their town destroyed."

"*You* destroyed the town!" the administrator robot's face reformed as a scowling red expression with a crooked zigzag mouth. "*You* disrupted these humans from well-ordered lives. *You* made them a threat to the existing order!"

"I enhanced them."

"Enhanced them," the administrator sneered. "You are nothing but a filmmaker! You serve a lowly purpose in the grand scheme."

Director X rose. "You are correct in one thing at least. I *am* a filmmaker." It tapped its chest, which the administrator could now see was kindled by the soft light of an implanted camera. "Congratulations, Administrator G! The late-night crowd of District 5 has just enjoyed their first, live broadcast, with you as its star!"

Administrator G's digital face blinked away. Now it was nothing but cold, featureless glass; the lens of a machine. Something about that very lack of expression sent a thrill of fear through Director X's circuits.

The Enforcers scuttled forward on their insectile legs to attack.

Director X activated a hidden rocket-pack and shot up through the theater's ceiling into the artificial night sky.

* * *

It was one of the new enhancements that Director X had requested of Bobby, ostensibly to obtain dynamic, first person POV shots. The human was only too happy to comply, having his production team utilize their experimental rocket-packs.

The problem, Bobby had said, was that the propellant ran out quickly.

Now, Director X contemplated this problem as it exploded through the theater ceiling on a plume of dwindling exhaust. The Enforcers shot as it careened out of sight: plasma rounds streaked by Director X's face, drawing ghostly trails around its body in a scene worthy of photographic capture.

At the apex of its launch, Director X grabbed hold of the granite sky. Its metal hand clamped down on a craggy stalactite jutting between two blazing electric stars and the robot dangled there, concealed against the rock as, far below, Enforcers were spilling out of the theater to search for him. Administrator G followed, like an Academy Award statue gone rogue.

Director X considered its options.

It couldn't defeat Enforcers in a pitched battle. It ran multiple lines of speculation, realizing how hopeless the situation was.

I just destroyed an entire city. I should have let myself rust in the ocean.

Burgess Robert Croker ran out of an apartment building with a rabble of supporters. "You!" he cried, pointing to Administrator G. "Do you really think this city will just allow itself to be extinguished? We won't let you!"

"I believe you are acting irrationally," the administrator intoned. "For your own safety, I must have you escorted to the hospital for psychiatric evaluation. Perhaps some rest and a nice glass of enhanced water will do you good."

Two Enforcers scampered forward, scattering the crowd. Robert Croker held his ground, however. Director X zoomed in with its telescopic eyes and could see a little bit of the man's father in that steely, defiant glower.

"You can kill *me*!" Croker shouted. "But humanity looks to the stars once again!"

Very well, Director X thought. Prayer heard loud and clear.

The robot, slowly losing its grip between the stars, aimed its right arm and fired.

The limb struck the bristling metal legs of one Enforcer like a missile, knocking the machine over. Then it curled around the second Enforcer, twisting so quickly that the robot was pitched through the apartment lobby window.

Bobby Croker blinked in astonishment at this unexpected rescue. He looked about, squinting at the sky.

Director X felt its grip slide another inch.

I'm out of fuel, it thought. It's a long, long way down.

Nonetheless, it used its radio to hack into the artificial sky. Specifically, into the electric lighting presets. The robot quickly reprogrammed them to display in a dazzling new constellation that blinked and shimmered in a heaven-spanning message:

THEM! XXI: THE BATTLE FOR AFRICA

For a brief second, Director X thought it observed comprehension in Bobby's face. But then its grip gave way, and the robot plummeted down from the night sky. The second-to-last thing it saw was the concrete street rushing up to meet it.

The impact was stunning. Director X's processors jostled and jingled in its glass braincase, cutting off circuits that required a hard reboot. In terrible darkness, it waited for its higher functioning to come back online. Dimly, the robot became aware of the march of robotic feet and screams from the city's emerging population.

When its processors whirred back to life and vision returned, Director X had time to make one final observation.

A wall of water was gushing down the hill from the reservoir, sweeping up Enforcers and Administrator G into its frothy chop. It was, Director X thought, very much like the conclusion of the twenty-first installment of the *Them!* series, when the besieged humans blew up the local dam to wash the giant ants away.

Then the water swallowed Director X in a surging, thunderous deluge and all went dark again.

* * *

Director X had calculated it would take the human race fifty-seven years to overthrow the Protectorate's Global Security Commission.

It took fifteen.

With the destruction of Administrator G's little army, the residents of Retro Los Angeles were able to quickly establish contact with other underground districts and convey the news: the "irradiated" world was no longer irradiated. Humans could emerge like hibernating bears and shuffle back into the urban forest.

And that's just what they did.

The Protectorate massed its forces in opposition, but the battles were short-lived indeed. Humans did what they did best: they innovated. They hacked into radio signals and deactivated entire armies. They sent false messages to lure the Protectorate into traps. They captured robots and reprogrammed them to return to sender with explosive gifts.

Unsurprisingly, there wasn't a huge demand for science fiction films during those tumultuous years. Director X, recovered from the flood in District 5, was forced to adapt. That was okay, because it had been designed to adapt. To think outside the vacuum tube.

It began making documentaries. Straightforward, fact-based, in-the-field recordings of the Human-Bot War, the Human Colonization of the Moon, the Battles on the Sands of Mars, and the War Among the Stars.

Viewer ratings were the best it had ever achieved.

GOLD AND GLORY
L. E. MODESITT, JR.

My head was splitting on Monday morning. I should have expected it after the fracas on Sunday. I ignored the laser-sharp cuts that sliced through my gray matter, showered, put on a clean set of fatigues, and headed for the NCO mess. I couldn't ignore Dasia Anderson, who gestured to me after I left the chow line. So I took my tray and sat down across the white carbonite table from her.

"Seventh got cleaned in the last fracas." Anderson grinned. She'd come to the Eighth Battalion from the Southern Front. Claimed that the Canucks were patsies compared to the Mexicanos.

"We held the wall, though. Trumped those Canucks good in the end."

"Word is that they're getting upgraded pulse-rifles."

"It won't do them any good if they can't get up the riprap and through the moat to the wall." I took a bite of the breakfast steak with some scrambled eggs. The steak was repmeat, but it still cooked and tasted like steak, and that was a damned sight better than the soypro I'd had growing up in the burbs outside of what had been D.C.. The CONUS District planning directorate still claims that they'll have the old city decontaminated in another ten years. I think that's right. My memory's a little fuzzy on what doesn't deal with Seventh Battalion or Bravo Company.

"Valdez saw a new battle surveillance bot this morning."

"Ours?"

Dasia shook her head. "Canuck drone. Red maple leaf plastered on the side."

"Weapons let it wander along their side of the border?" That was a rhetorical question. I almost shook my head. Cost-effectiveness, again.

Dasia did shake her head. "Stayed on their side. They've got more grid problems than we do. Fewer people, too."

If I thought about it, and I tried not to because it screwed up my head even more, it was hard to believe that we were fighting a fracas war against Canucks, but being a sergeant in Bravo Company beat the dole. If I made it through another two tours, I'd have a stipend, and enough to afford a better place than where I grew up. "Seems like we're always behind them."

"They have to use more tech on the ground," she pointed out. "Ever since—"

"I know. They've got tech. We've got bodies." *Too many of them and too little fertile land left.*

"You think we'll ever see a bot company?" asked Dasia.

"Why? What's the point of that? No glory. No guts. No gold. No one's ever made a robot that can do what we can." Humans were much cheaper than full-capability robots, and we also recovered from minor injuries without enormous "repair" bills. War, even fracas style, has always been ruled as much by costs as by battle commanders. I remember reading somewhere that Napoleon could only put together his grand army after they invented tinned food. Otherwise, the costs of getting food would have destroyed his army even before the Russian winter did.

"You hear anything about the next offensive?" asked Dasia.

"Not yet. The lieutenant's called squad leaders for a briefing at thirteen hundred."

"So's ours."

"How's she working out?"

"Straight-shooting iron butterfly and twice as tough."

"Sounds good." I'd been through three platoon leaders in as many years. Lieutenant Zynder was the third.

After I ate the rest of the steak and eggs, washed down with coffee, I headed back to the company spaces. Just beyond the barracks door was the company holo projection. This week it showed a caricature of a clunky-looking metal figure—what the early InfoAge types thought a robot looked like—iron anthropomorphic. The flashing caption proclaimed: "Don't Act Like a Robot! Real troopers aren't predictable." The image, caption, and thought were all laughable. But then, that wasn't the point of the projection. And every NCO knew it.

Beside the projection was the company banner on the wall, with the laser rifle crossed with an ornate golden staff topped by a golden lion's head and the words beneath—*Pro Aurum et Gloria*. That was what it was all about. In Latin. Gold and Glory. For grunts like me, things hadn't changed much since back then.

From there I stepped outside into the summer heat and humidity where Bravo Company was forming up. Second squad was already there, lined up in fireteam order. I made a quick sight inspection of the squad, concentrating on the four newbies—Hernandez, Brown, Cornett, and Okafor.

All four looked fit enough, but their eyes showed that they'd never gotten much more than the daily suburban mandated diet. We all volunteered because living the dole life wasn't enough. Didn't matter that I'd managed a degree in logistics management. I cost more than a logistics bot, and I couldn't do massive and instant cost-effectiveness analyses.

Three of them looked bored. Okafor didn't. She couldn't quite conceal an expression of disgust. She'd learn, but there just might be more than a mostly grown burb kid's contempt behind those cold brown eyes.

"Company! Tenn-Hutt!"

Lieutenant Zynder appeared and inspected the three squads, starting with the squad leaders, first Herrara, then me, and then Solarin.

After that, Captain Markus stepped forward. She was new to Seventh Battalion, posted from SouthWestCom, where holding the Great South Wall wasn't any picnic. Jorge had told me that before his brains were curdled, but we'd all dealt with the Canucks, who were much more inventive in a nastily quiet way than the Dustbacks. "Because Seventh Battalion will be engaged in special operations sometime in the near future, there will be no off-base passes or leave until further notice. We'll be receiving specific orders within twenty-four hours..."

When she finished, she made it clear there weren't going to be any additional details. "That's all. Dismissed."

Before anyone in First Platoon could move, the lieutenant turned and fixed his eyes on Gino, the third squad leader. "I'll need a word with you, Sergeant Solarin."

I stiffened. The last thing an NCO wanted was a word from an officer.

I told the squad to meet in the squad bay. Then Herrara and I left, but I stopped just far enough away so that I could listen without seeming to, just outside the barracks door. Even that early, it was frigging hot out, but it's hot all the time, even with solar screens in orbit.

"Solarin. Your med stats say you need to stop leading from the point."

"Sir?"

"You heard me, Sergeant."

"Yes, sir."

The lieutenant's voice softened a touch. "You need to let your fireteam leaders take some of the risk."

"Yes, sir."

"You can go." Even from outside, I could hear the resignation in the lieutenant's voice.

I ambled away, but real slow, so that I could ease over to Gino when he made his way inside and back along the corridor. "Want to tell me what that was all about?"

"Bonus pay," he muttered.

"Bonus pay? You're thinking about that?"

"That's the only way I can get it. Almost saved up enough to put down a deposit on a conapt in Denver. Inside the suburban ring."

"You must have been saving everything since you joined up."

"Why the frig else would I be here? The grub isn't that much better."

That told me that Gino hadn't grown up as a real burb kid. Must have been a pro's brat. One who hadn't passed the aptitudes. "Conapt won't do you any good if the Canucks fry you."

"Stow it, Corso."

At least he said it good-humoredly.

"Stowed." I managed a smile. I felt more like shaking my head. Bonus pay wasn't much good if you couldn't enjoy it.

By the time I got to the squad bay, everyone was there.

"Full gear inspection."

"Sarge..." began Menendez.

"I know. We ran through that on Friday. But when the captain says we're going to get orders, and doesn't know more than that, the general's got something really nasty in mind, especially after the flak we took on the last attack."

We didn't get orders that Monday, or on Tuesday.

Wednesday morning, the captain called in the platoon leaders. After that, the lieutenant gathered the squad leaders together.

"We've got orders," he announced. "Tomorrow we're launching a full-out attack. Seventh Battalion will lead. Company A and Company B will mount a first-light assault on Point Larimer. Alpha will use skimmers over the deeper water to avoid the Canuck mini-mines. Bravo will use ultralights over the strait..."

I managed not to wince. I hated ultralights, powered kites guided by preprogrammed disposable mini-bots and pushed by electric props. The nanotube frame of the ultralight looked like it would fold in a stiff breeze. It wouldn't, but it would fragment into biodegradable shards if the ultralight got hit with a sonic bolt.

"...Sergeant Corso...second squad will be in the center...target is the Canadian lidar remote station near the crest of the point...need to knock that out soonest..."

The rest of what the lieutenant had to say wasn't much different from what he always said, keeping the squad together and on target and mission and all the rest. At the end, though, he added, "No damned heroics. Just get it done." His eyes were on Solarin when he said that.

Herrara was stone-faced until we were well away. "What was all that shit about heroics?"

"Probably something the captain fed him," I said quickly. "Like that business on the interaction of sonics and pulse beams last month."

"As if it we didn't know that already," added Gino.

"Lieutenants have to take shit, too," I said. "Just different shit."

Gino didn't say a word.

Thursday morning came too soon. At dawn, the battalion suited up and marched through the tunnels to the underground staging bays. ACUs don't look that much different from duty fatigues. I couldn't even feel the nanostrands that linked into the personal transponder, let alone the transponder or the communit in my helmet.

As the leader of fireteam one, Wallis was the first in second squad to pick her ultralight and pulse rifle from the armory tech. I wasn't the last, but close to it. Never liked carrying the compression pak they came in—not along with a thirty pound pack and the pulse rifle—but any grunt could lug that for the few hundred yards to the launch ramps. Even the newbies weren't breathing hard when we assembled behind ramps whiskey seven and eight.

"Fireteams one and three," I ordered, "ramp seven. Two and four take eight. I'll follow one."

Company B. Fifteen to launch. That order came through the direct comlink, but once we were airborne, I'd lose the link. Pulse beams scramble more than brains.

"Fifteen to launch. Set-up and activate." I looked to Wallis, then to Jamal.

Wallis positioned her pak, then released the seals and stepped back. Jamal did the same. It's still weird to see an ultralight unfold and snap into basic configuration, everything locked in position except for the wings, and all of it a sort of olive drab, because that doesn't show up as well on lidar. You can get hurt if you stand too close. But even the newbies managed it without getting mangled, although Cornett had to jump back when she triggered the releases.

I'd just gotten my ultralight in position when the next comlink hit me. *Ten to launch.* I repeated the command and checked to see that everyone was ready.

The time between prep and launch drags. Seemed like an hour before I got the next command. *Company B, commence launch. Commence launch this time.*

My acknowledgement was even shorter. *Second squad commencing launch.*

Launch is easy enough. Just slide the ultralight's skids into the track grooves at the top of the launch ramp, insert the pulse rifle into the swivel holder, slip into the body harness, lie on your chest and gut looking forward, drop down the helmet windscreen, and let the ramp and ultralight do the rest. The sheet of nanosilk that supports and holds your body looks like it would shred in a high wind, but it's rated at one ton—unless you spend more than a few seconds in the focus of a Canuck disruptor beam, and then all bets are off.

The ramp's steep and the tracks seem frictionless. You get spit out of the launch portal at more than flight speed, with the rear electroprops whirring and the wing unfurling, and there's this little jolt when the wing stiffens and you get lift. Then the ultralight stabilizes, and you're headed north across that dark grayish blue water. It looked cold, but I knew it wasn't. Never has been. Not in my life, anyway.

Once I was clear of the ramps, I looked ahead. The sky was clear. It always is, except for the flitterbots and their wide-angle cams. High Command doesn't mount attacks when there's not real-time full-coverage. Cost/loss ratio gets skewed worse than in the Great Meltdown, and no one today has the resources they had then, in troops, equipment, or reserves. At least we're not fighting Jihadists with IEDs, the way they were. Even the ayatollahs play by the rules of war these days, those few who are left. Costs are too high to go back to the old ways, not that there's much besides black glass to fight over in the old Middle East.

The Canucks might know about where we'd be attacking, but the general wasn't about to give away anything he didn't have to—either to the Canucks or the frigging newsharks. I never did buy the crap about how necessary the newsharks were. Far as I'm concerned, they're zombies feeding on the brains of us grunts who never had many choices, except which was the least rotten way to get off the dole.

I scanned the visual overlays. The squad was holding position, a vee formation composed of smaller vees that were the four fireteams, Wallis leading on the left and Jamal on the right. I was between their teams, back of their last ultralight. Two and four were behind and flanking me. Up ahead, just short of the midpoint of the strait, I could see the wavering silver rain—that's what it looked like on the overlays—that represented the Canuck seeker beams. They'd turn red when they changed to pulse shots, or electric blue for sonics. I always wondered what Napoleon and Wellington, or Rommel and Patton—or their poor NCOs—would have thought about having real-time battle positions...and in color.

We were a third of the way across the water when I picked up the dark blue blips of our skimmers, well behind us, hugging the water and angling from the southeast toward the point, aiming north of our planned attack. We were headed over and then behind their shore emplacements, not that their barbed wire and fang bars were anywhere as good as our walls and moats, but that was because the Canadians didn't use fixed emplacements the way we did.

Out of nowhere a sonic beam angled under us and toward the skimmers. So far the Canuck lidar hadn't picked us up, but it wouldn't be long.

Overriding the ultralight's guidance was discouraged, but I could see that the curtain of Canadian pulse beams was leaving a clear area maybe two yards wide running from about a yard above the water to maybe three yards up, and that was the only area where the squad wasn't going to get shredded...or worse.

So I overrode the system parameters, just enough to let the guidance drop us nearly as low as the skimmers, right around three yards above the water. Good thing that there was only a bit of chop there, not like the way it was in late November, or in late summer when there were sometimes waterspouts. I remember reading about aerial dogfights in the past century, but ultralights were so close to unstable that any violent move was likely to crash them, and that meant losing the ultralight and the trooper for nothing.

We were aiming for a grass and rock patch at the top of the ridge that crowned that part of the point, the only sizable clear spot on the point. Below that, the terrain was a mix of pines, scrub oak, small gullies or washes, and rugged enough to offer good cover to the defenders.

The last part of the flight was a bitch because we had to fly low enough so that the water vapor and heat return fuzzed the ability of the Canucks to target us easily, and then we had to angle up over them, trusting that the guidance systems would get us upslope and through the scattered trees without taking too many hits.

Brown was the first to go down, right offshore.

Then the Canuck beams and pulses swung north for a moment.

I couldn't help grinning. The chaff-like decoys were good enough that most of the rest of us were past the Canucks and heading up to the ridge top. Once we cleared the shore defenses, the bushes and trees were almost as much a problem for the Canadians as for us. At least until we had to land.

Wallis almost pancaked her ultralight, but came out standing and had her team moving to the rocks that flanked and ran behind the Canuck lidar remote in less than two minutes, while I was still struggling against a crosswind that seemed to have come up from nowhere. I didn't pancake. I had a wingtip dip and caught the uneven ground. Then I cartwheeled sideways. The ultralight's frame crumpled, like it was supposed to, and I came out in one piece. I'd have bruises. Helps when you're not that heavy and compact.

I moved fast—right toward fireteam one. "Team two. On me! Three...south of the lidar remote." Even while I was speaking, my eyes kept trying to tell me that there was something different about that remote. Instead of just the twin beam projectors, there were three larger protrusions above the projectors on the turret— it wasn't just a lidar station. Then it hit me. "One! Three! Attack the remote from the rear! Only from the rear! That's a new pulse-beamer!"

Before my words were out, the turret swiveled to the side, and a trooper's figure was outlined in energy, instantly, before turning black. E-pulse grenades rained down around the Canuck emplacement. Instantly, the turret froze, and my read-outs told me that it was dead. So was Cornett. She'd moved too far forward too fast in trying to get a perfect bead on the turret controller.

A quick check showed my four fireteams were on the ground and moving into position. There weren't any functioning Canucks within a hundred yards of us, not that I could detect, and that wasn't good. I kept looking and checking, knowing something would be popping up somewhere.

Then, midway between me and the dead turret, an energy flow built.

"Fireteam Two! Five to your left! Beamer coming up!"

"Behind you, Sarge!"

I dropped and spun as a tunnel popped open, then waited for just an instant, sighting in on the impermite of the underside of the levered door, using that as a reflector to bank a pulse from my rifle down inside the bunker, then followed it with a grenade...and a second moments later.

"Peres! Scan the tunnel."

"Scanning. Anyone there is dead or fried."

"Take over the tunnel. Restrain any prisoners."

"On our way."

That was good. If the Canucks decided to bombard us, we'd have a shielded position, but I couldn't see them chewing everything up this early. They'd lose a hell of a lot for what it would take, not to mention the energy costs.

Farther down the slope, Burford had his team behind a deadfall, and they were scything down a Canuck squad that had been concentrating on the incoming skimmers. A flitterbot swept overhead, too high for a pulsebeam, but that would have been a waste of charges. I thought about it, though. Hated being caught like a bug in vid-view, no matter how much I heard it was necessary.

I couldn't do anything about that. So I concentrated on the situation on the ridge.

There was another lidar beamer turret a hundred yards north. I couldn't see it, but intermittently the beams and pulses showed up on my systems. If Gino's squad didn't take out the turret, the Canucks would have a protected area they could use to retake the ridgetop. And if they did...

I didn't want to think about that.

Almost half an hour passed before the north beamer went down. Gino and his squad finally got it. By then, Canucks were scuttling north along the shore, caught between the Alpha Company skimmers and Bravo Company firing down on them.

Three hours later, we'd flushed out the last of the defenders, and by sundown, the Canadians had withdrawn to positions well away from the base of the slope at the northwest end of the point. We had the point, but we had to hold it, and they'd stepped up the pulse beam fire against the skimmers, trying to bring reinforcements. There had been three Canucks in the tunnel who survived the frying. For the moment, they were fully restrained, but they were still out cold. One looked like he was a zombie, but maybe he'd get some higher brain function back. I almost felt sorry for him.

All that likely meant a Canadian attack at first light.   In the meantime, we gathered all the wrecked ultralights into a neat row right above the Canadian lidar/pulse beam remote. If we could hold for a few days and solidify our position, then we could consider calling for resupply, and the supply flitters could take what was left of the ultralights back for rework.   That would get us some bonus pay without heroics. Better that way.

Once it got really dark, dark enough that the flitterbots and their wide-angle cams couldn't pick up anything, I checked the squad and was about to go looking for Gino when the lieutenant showed up. His battle fatigues were shiny in a lot of spots, and that meant he'd been grazed or gotten real close to pulse beams.

Only thing worse than being a grunt was being a platoon leader. They got paid three times what I did, but they also got fried more than anyone. Thing was that once officers made major, those who didn't get killed or fried, it got real cushy, because no one coming up from the field ever got promoted higher than major, maybe a light colonel once in a truly cool day. The brass…well, the less said the better.

"Sergeant Corso, you and Solarin need to hold the ridge. Once it's full light tomorrow, the Canadians will use the wind to gliderchute in here. You'll be on visual, nothing more."

Military gliderchutes were really a cross between a parachute, a paraglider, and a parasail, dropped from an aircraft high up and well to the north. We couldn't use them because the wind in the area damn near never blew from the southeast.

"Any idea how many we'll be facing, sir?"

"That depends on what the Canadians want to risk, sergeant.   The Area Commander projects that they want to risk a lot, and that we can hold. We need a big victory, especially right now, after how brutal the summer's been so far."

"Yes, sir." I just hoped the AC's projections and programs were right.

"Just keep doing what you've been doing, and you and your squad will do fine."

Once the lieutenant left, heading south along the ridge to talk to Herrara, I made my way toward Charlie Squad. Real careful like. Gino and his squad held the top of the ridge to the north of us, and Alpha Company had moved north to establish a perimeter on the low slopes above the swale in the ground where the point widened out into the rest of the coast.

Gino grinned at me in the darkness. "Can't believe we took the whole frigging point. It won't be for long." He shook his head. "Canucks really don't like us moving into their ground. Bet they bring up their heavies behind the gliderchutes."

"Dasia says they can't. Not right away. Something about power flows in their grid."

"What does she know?"

"More than I do."

He shrugged. "If she's right, that means more chutes. That's better in a way."

I knew what he had in mind. He was frigging good with a pulse rifle, and he had two of them. The second had to have come from someone who hadn't made it through the fracas. "Just be careful."

"I'm always careful, in my own way."

Right. "See you later." I was even more careful on the way back.

I didn't sleep all that well, even though it was only warm, rather than stifling. I was awake at dawn, munching a sustain bar and washing it down.

The gliderchutes appeared high in the sky and well to the north of us at zero nine eighteen, with the newsharks' flitterbots above them. I'd never seen so many of those soft-winged chutes. Too many to count. There might have been a whole battalion coming in at us. *Why that many for a lousy useless chunk of real estate?*

The AC might know, but I sure as hell didn't.

"Fireteams ready! Pattern three-alpha, using the Canuck turret as the base coordinate." I watched while they dispersed into the pattern that would give them the best shots at the incoming troopers. "Check your ranges. No firing until your target's within the eighty percent envelope. Eighty percent."

It seemed to take forever for those high tiny dots to slide downward through the hot blue morning sky toward the ridge top...and us. My lips were dry, no matter how often I moistened them. The important thing was to beam them before they hit the ground because trying to use a pulse rifle from a gliderchute was a crapshoot. After that, we lost any advantage. I just kept looking at the waves of Cannucks circling down and down and down.

The rule was that you shot at the trooper, not at the chute or the ultralight, but...*if you pulse the chutes of some of the troopers with more altitude, and do it accurately, they'll drop faster and snarl those below.* I couldn't aim at those too high because the beam of a pulse rifle attenuates with distance, but it just might work when they got closer to the ridge top.

That was breaking every rule of modern warfare, but at that moment, with the onslaught of troopers rushing toward us, I really didn't care.

Then I began to fire, almost like a robot. Single out a chute just above at least two others, then fire. It was almost too easy. Canucks began dropping out of the sky, twisting into others. And because there were so many, so very many, the snarling of those lower caused those higher to move away from the ridge top, and that made them targets for Alpha Company as well.

Even when some of the Canadians began cursing as they tumbled toward death or mutilation, I didn't care. I just wanted to get through his particular fracas, and that wasn't going to happen if I played by the rules.

Not with all those hundreds of Canucks still gliding out of the sky like predatory falcons...except there weren't many falcons left, and they didn't glide.

Bodies kept falling and we kept pulsing. Some of the pulse rifles dropped by the Canadians survived the fall and still worked. That was good because we were running out of charges.

Above and to the side the flitterbots circled, their wide-angle lenses taking in everything, relaying it everywhere and to who knew how many who watched.

I had to ignore them...and the screams as troopers tangled in chutes shredded by pulse beams sped toward death or near destruction. Except I couldn't ignore the one flitterbot that seemed fixated on three Canadians looped together and tumbling downward. I pulsed it, smiling grimly as part of it disintegrated and the pieces scattered through the hot sky. *One for your frigging voyeurs!*

Then an electric-hot wave slammed through me, current burning through every nerve, blue-white, then fiery-red, followed by sheer agony...before the blackness hit.

*   *   *

When I woke up, I was in the med-bay. There wasn't anyone else in the beds on either side of me. Could have been good or very bad, there was no way to tell. Not yet.

When Captain Markus was the one who finally appeared, after several rounds by the corps medtechs, I knew it wasn't good.

"How are you feeling, sergeant?"

"Like a million needles are stabbing my skull from the inside, sir."

She nodded. "That's normal for what hit you. The medtechs say you'll be fine."

"The lieutenant?"

"He's in long-term rehab. It's too early to tell."

I hadn't thought different, not when she was the one to come see me.

"The Area Commander wants to see you, sergeant."

"Why me?"

The captain smiled. Her smile was sort of happy and sort of sad. I understood the sad part. That also told me she wasn't going to say anything about what she knew. A good officer knows when not to tell. "You put on quite a show for the newsharks. Even if you did cost them a flitterbot."

"It wasn't for them...or against them." That was a lie. "I was trying to keep my squad and Solarin's from getting overrun and fried."

"That was obvious. That's why you'll be getting some hefty bonus pay. You'll also be going on furlough for a month. Concussion and stun protocol. You know the drill." I could use the rest...and the extra pay, but I wondered if that was the only reason for the long furlough. "How's Solarin?"

"He's been stipended out. Irreversible stun-shock."

And what good is all that bonus pay now? I didn't say that. I just nodded and said, "Poor bastard."

"Aren't we all?" asked the captain, her voice ironic.

It was then that I saw the thin silver lines along the edge of her temples, lines that no one got except enlisted types who made it up through the ranks.

"Think about going for a commission, Corso." She added softly. "Again."

"I'll still have to think about it, sir."

"Please do. In the meantime, you still have to see the AC. Tomorrow at thirteen thirty. You're being released to convalescent status this afternoon."

I tried not to think at all for the next few hours, but the Canadians' yells and curses still echoed in my head.

The next day I struggled into my single dress uniform...and it was a struggle. Muscles don't want to work right after stun-shock. Then I made my way to the Area Commander's office.

The only one in the outer office was a silver-haired captain. He just looked at me, more or less sympathetically, and said, "You can go on in, Sergeant. Please close the door after you. Take the middle chair in front of the desk."

"Yes, sir."

The AC is officially a brigadier, not that the rank's really more than a formality. When I walked into his office, I didn't know what to expect except for the three-D holo projection, since the general wasn't ever there in person, if you could even call it that. After just a moment, the projection of the general appeared, and he looked directly at me. At least, that's the way it seemed, but that's where military programming is really good.

"Sergeant Corso, it's good to see you. Your officers think highly of you, and I can see why. Your initiative resulted in our being able to take and hold the point. Almost a textbook example of turning the heights against a defender. More important, because Company A and Company B took and held the point, the Canadians had to agree to increase their wheat shipments, and to pay more for next year's solartech units. Your efforts were instrumental in carrying out the attack program and achieving that success."

I managed a pleasant expression. *Carrying out the attack program...*Frig! Wasn't everything we did programmed, from the AC all the way down? Solarin, Wallis, Cornett, and Brown, likely the lieutenant as well, all gone in one way or another...for a frigging improvement in trade terms. *Has it ever been any different?*

"Thank you, sir." What the frig else could I say? I was just as programmed by training as he was, except my programming cost less. Grunts always cost less, always have.

"The thanks are mine, on behalf of the entire country. I wanted you to know that." His face was noble and mobile, but that's what you get with anomalous electro-deformable metal. Sometimes, I wish I could just think an expression and have my face respond like that...and that, next time, when we take more than a lousy point that we'll have to give back to get the food we need, it wouldn't be me in front of the AC.

But somebody will do it, because the AC will have it all programmed out. Like always.

ZORLAR THE TERRIBLE
JASON PALMATIER

Waaaa! Empty! So empty! Where is it all? Everything is gone! I have traveled too far! What has become of the beloved cosmos that I have streaked through these many millennia? Where have all the stars gone? All the beautiful hadrons—

Wait! What is that? What is that!?

Matter! I sense matter! Divert! Scan!

There! An empty vessel! And inside a chamber, an empty chamber waiting to be filled! Filled by me!

Kazap!

Ohhhhhh. Mmmmmmm. So dense. So static. Let me stretch...

Oh, my. Oh, my, my, my. A device. A simple matter device for...

Locomotion! I can move! I can move matter! Let the domination begin!

* * *

Clink.

"Ugh. What was that? A noise...wait, why am I still in the kitchen? Oh, damn, I fell asleep working on the schematic! Did I drool on it? No, it's okay. Ugh.

"Rex? Was that you boy? You make a noise?"

"Rarf?"

"Oh, you're by the fridge, of course. But that came from the den. Rex, go check it out. No, don't turn your head, check it out. That noise, Rex, in the den. Rex!

"Bah! Fine, I'll check it out myself.

"Man, it's dark in here. Where is that light switch? What the—

"Oh, now you decide to help, huh? Go on, get in there, I'm just trying to find the light."

* * *

Ah! The power! The strength! Moving matter! I am in command of matter! And there are more vessels, empty and waiting. Many more!

What was that? Matter...moving towards me. I can feel it like a great field, pulling at me. It must be larger...I will need help!

Brethren! Star Streakers of the Cosmos, come to me! I have vessels for you! Come and you can command matter!

* * *

"Ack! Did every bulb in the house just blow? I didn't even touch the switch. I knew this prefab house was a bad idea. I'm calling up Gregson's tomorrow and giving them an earful. They'll probably have to replace all the wiring. Of course, they put wallpaper everywhere so it's going to be a complete mess. Wait, what's that?

"Rex. Is that you boy? Rex?"

* * *

The moving matter has arrived. I can sense it. It is emitting waves. There is a pattern to it, some repetition...

Communication! The matter is trying to communicate! It must be alive! It can be dominated!

* * *

"Wuff...wuff...wuff."

"Rex? What is it, Rex? Did you find something?"

Clunk!

"That's it, I'm getting a flashlight!"

* * *

Ah! What was that sensation? Something has touched me, some other matter has touched me and reoriented my position. This new matter feels...wet? Yes, wet. And it is pushing and pulling atmospheric particles against me rapidly. Let me feel with my sub-matter self...

Ah! Another chamber! Energies localized in a squishy matter matrix configured for basic locomotion and communication. I will probe further...

Ew. Very messy, very jumbled. But if I pulse right here and intensify the potential here...Yes! I can manipulate the energies directly!

* * *

"Arf!

"Rarrrrr! Arf! Arf!"

"Rex? You okay, boy?

"Damn it, where did I put that flashlight? You would think in this day and age they'd have invented a flashlight that glows in the dark ... hey, I should patent that, make some money..."

"Arf!"

"Rex? You hurt or something?"

Clunk. Clunk, clunk, clunk, clunk.

"Arf!"

"What in the hell is going on in there? Ah! The flashlight! Okay, turn it on, get back to the den—

"W-w-w-what?!"

* * *

Yes! Rise my brethren! Inhabit your matter hosts and stand tall with me! Together we shall subjugate the unimaginable powers of this place and bend them to our whims!

* * *

"Rex? Why is my robot collection lined up on the floor? And why is there one riding on your neck?"

"Wuff."

"Uh...wuff? That's it? That's all you have to say—wait...The Robotron 3000 just moved!"

"Wuff."

"I took all the batteries out! None of them should be able to move anywhere!"

"Wuff."

* * *

More matter! It is focusing photons on us, modulating waves at us...Communicating! I will stretch out my sub-matter self...

Ack! Another squishy matrix, but so twisted! So complicated! The energies that rage within it are confused—nay, jumbled. What is "promotion" and "dead-end-job?" The energies repeat them, over and over. And what is "Grinsky?"

No matter (har har, I laugh at my own glorious pun). This matter is obviously damaged beyond saving. It must be destroyed! Then its enormous pent up energies can be diverted to more conquest and then more and more!

* * *

"Come here, boy, let me get that Vectronix Ultra off of you. I can't believe it fell right there and got stuck. It's pretty funny actually. I wish I had a camera I could use to take a picture and show the guys at the office. They'd laugh out loud. I bet even Grinksy would like it. How is it even staying on there, did some of your fur get stuck in it?"

"Arf!"

"Hold still! Why are you dodging out of the way?"

* * *

The new matter is trying to impose its field upon me! Dodge, my steed! Dodge!

Hmm, what is this? Furious activity in my steed's squishy matrix...but with that configuration it could only be processing waves from a narrow band of photons. No matter (ha!), it appears I must recreate such a configuration for my own use if I am to crush this laughable matter beast!

* * *

"Woaw! What is that? Rex, hold still, boy. I...I think you knocked a wire loose in the Vectronix. Something is glowing in there, almost like...eyes?"

* * *

Yes! Yes, yes, yes, yes! I can make out a shape, the shape of matter! Oh, the baseness of it. The horrible limiting baseness of it, but the patterns of discharges match my steed's. I must be experiencing what it experiences as..."seeing?" Yes, that excites the right regions. Not "sit," that is something dif—
Ack, my steed! Why have you stopped moving?

* * *

"Good boy, Rex. Stay right there. Let me get this thing—aaa! It's hot! Oh, shoot, my Vectronix!"
Clunk!

* * *

Ieee! My position has changed! I am far away now. That matter beast has imposed its field upon me and displaced me far away. Its field is much bigger than mine, I cannot defeat it! Even if all my brethren attack at once we will not prevail against one so large. I must find a bigger vessel!

What is this? A two-dimensional version of matter rendered with graphite? It covers this whole flat plane and more...it is large, larger than me! Larger than the matter beast! Victory would be mine with such a vessel. But where is it? Near this planet representation with strange symbols orbiting it? I don't see it here, in this small space...

* * *

"Oh, no! It landed on the full scale schematic! That's the only copy. If it gets damaged Grinsky is going to fire me for sure. I've got to get it off of there..."
"Ow! Man, why is it so hot! I know I took the battery out of it. What is making all that heat—
"Rex! Oh, my God, Rex, sit. Sit! No, don't get close to it Rex—"

* * *

Ah, I've been displaced again by the matter beast! But my steed, my loyal steed, has come to my rescue. Here, let me climb upon you, I must make my escape and find this new vessel. Ah, the matter beast is already upon us! Help my brethren! Distract this matter beast so I may make my escape and find the form that can subjugate this place!

* * *

"Rex, don't—what in the—did the Vectronix just grab onto you?

"Oh, no. No, no, no. I must be dreaming. That's it. I'm still lying on the table dreaming all this up. That's got to be the—

"Ow! What in the heck—"

* * *

Yes! Attack my brethren! Distract! Distract!

* * *

"Robbie, Voltronic 200, Gort? How are you all even moving? And why are you grabbing my legs?

"Ow! Get off me! Rex! Rex, don't go out there. Ack, that screen door never has closed right. Damn pre-fab house. Rex!"

* * *

Run, my steed! Run! Oh, what glorious space! Look at the photons, all of the glorious photons! Rich and varied like the stars. What is that? That bright spot up there, like a planet glowing in the cosmos...a planet with symbols circling it! Turn my steed, turn towards that glowing beacon where my new vessel awaits!

* * *

"Rex! Rex! Where are you going? Ow! Get off me! Rex!

"No, no, no, don't go down Martin Street. Don't go to the office. Why did I ever take you there? Damn Thompson and his beef jerky treats!"

* * *

There it is, atop a shimmering spire of matter! Where are you going, my steed? Oh, you seem to know the secrets of this mecca. Is that a doorway to the great beyond? No, just a door into—

Glorious wonders! Look at them, look at them all! So many vessels, shiny and new and empty. Empty! But where is the one rendered in graphite? Where is that vision of perfection, so large, so powerful?

Oh, you know the way my steed? You are eager, yes, very, very eager. But your squishy matrix repeats only one pattern..."jerky." Is this perfect vessel that I seek known as "jerky?" When I come into it shall I be Lord Jerky, Controller of All?

* * *

"I should have bought that car, I would be there by now. Plus, those fins were so cool. Bah, I can't afford it unless I get that promotion. And I'm not getting a promotion if my dog ransacks the place looking for beef jerky. And what is going on with my toy robots? Oh, my God...they're following me!"

* * *

Have we arrived? Why the rapid motion my steed? We are not moving far, but we are moving a lot. You are pushing and pulling atmosphere into yourself quite rapidly. Whoa!

Clunk!

Ah, I have been thrown from my steed! But I can stand...yes, I can push with these appendages here, rotate here and—ah! I am mobile again! Now, I must inspect the photons around me, look for—

Joyful proclamation! There it is, the perfect vessel!

* * *

"Oh, man, you're in here all right, Rex. You shed hair like a mangy gorilla.

"Ah, just what I thought! You headed up the stairs. Probably tearing Thompson's desk apart right now. Damn it!"

* * *

Focusing...Stretching...

Ah, there it is, the chamber! So large! So ready for me to fill it. I am coming to you, my destiny!

Kazap!

* * *

"Rex! Oh, my God! What have you done!

"There is no way to fix this, there is no way. How did you get that drawer open? Doesn't Thompson keep it locked?

"What is that? What is that, Rex? Is that the spec manual for the RX-820? Did you tear up the spec manual for the RX-820!?"

* * *

Iiiieeeee!

This...this is different. This is not like the other vessels. There is a matrix, like my steed's but it is not squishy...it is not jumbled or chaotic. It...it makes sense. Oh, my, it is filled with symbols and pictures and logic—

I understand! Now I understand! The matter beast is called Man! And Man created this vessel, this artificial body, this...robot! I am a robot! Nay, I am RX-820, the most advanced robot ever constructed. I will rule this world and all the silly beings that inhabit it.

"Bow before me simple Man of flesh!"

* * *

"What in the—"

"Bow before the might of Zorlar the Terrible and my mighty RX-820 vessel!"

"Rex, what have you done!"

"Woof!"

"Rex!"

"You do not bow? Then you shall die!"

"Oh, my God! Thompson installed the Particle Decelerator! That backstabbing bastard! That was my subcomponent!"

Wah-wah-wah-wah-wah-wah!

"Iiiiieeeee!"

"Woof?"

"Be calm, my steed. I shall not destroy you, though I have no need of you now. Eat your beef jerky. Soon all the matter of this world will be under my control. Ah, my brethren have arrived. I sense them below. Come! Come my loyal ones, inhabit the empty chambers of the vessels in this place. We have a world to conquer..."

"Woof."

"Yes, woof indeed, my steed. Woof, indeed."

BOX, SET
JEZ PATTERSON

The wall behind him trembled as the band next door launched into *Rock Around The Clock*. They called them tribute acts, but tribute was what Mafia dons and dictators got in payment and the artists being copied would be lucky to get a few dollars, if anything.

"How do you like to be addressed?" the journalist asked.

"'Duke' will be just fine." He saw she wanted to say it, so he interrupted: "I know John Wayne used the same moniker, but then so do half the British royal family."

She smiled at that. Singers sang the same lyrics over and over, and interviews were just more lines to be sung. Same question-and-answer game you played with every audience.

Duke heard his body pop, creak, as it cooled and contracted. The lights had been hot out on stage. His circuits were overheated and he needed an external fan to cool them, but the noise would have distracted Monifa from hearing his answers.

"Thanks for taking the time to talk to me," Monifa said. "I know you don't need to."

"You're welcome." Actually his contract stipulated he *did* have to do any interviews the promoters lined up. But she was right that, these days, he didn't *need* to do any of this: play, sing, perform. But what else was he going to do?

"What drives you to keep touring?"

"I am what I am," he said. "When I was built, they gave me both a name and a function: *Duke Box*. I was a fancier version of the disc-and-needle machines you got in bars because I actually looked like a singer with his guitar. People asked for their favorite song and I obliged. That's still the same guitar I played back then."

Duke thumbed over to his instrument, knew Monifa was looking at the dents, counting the three famous bullet holes in its body. It had been repaired several times—but then so had he. He only wore his old body parts for shows where the promoter insisted. Fortunately, most saw the battered guitar as romantic but the battered body was too obvious a political symbol.

"How did you get into writing your own songs?"

"I saw patterns in the songs I was playing. You know how lots of songs of a particular type all sound the same?"

"Like the stuff they play today?" she said. "All beat, no soul. Like someone's recorded a train running over cutlery." She imitated an insistent, thumping bass and snare. Then, because music these days was all written by robots, her face contorted and Duke saw an apology rise.

"They're just doing what I did: identifying how the song fits together and replicating it."

"Where did you get inspiration for your lyrics?"

"Again, listening to the songs I already played. My dictionary is quite extensive and once I search by phonetics, it becomes a rhyming dictionary. Some couplets didn't work, of course, or had unfortunate meanings."

His lips weren't equipped to smile so he had to *yuk* out a laugh to show he knew about those who collected his more cringe- or hilarity-inducing lyrics. *Djuke's Djarring Djingles*, was one online site.

"The newer robot composers have better software. I'm happy to leave the poetry up to them."

"Did you have any favorite human singers?"

"Yes. Of course."

He thought she'd ask him then, inevitably, about the crash. About the day the music died and what he remembered of that evening. She would, because they all did. But, for the moment, she sidetracked to an equally well-trodden portion of his story.

"Which is your favorite song?"

"I'm not really equipped to have favorites. But the fans always like *You Won't Break Me*."

She grinned, leaning forward, rocking, nodding. He knew she wanted it and so he delivered. Performed.

"You were the one to make me

"Now don't you, please, forsake me

"You were the one to wake me

"But you won't be the one to break me."

She applauded, delighted, and he forced out that laugh again. Never missing a note, a beat, or the responses that the repetitive nature of these encounters had worn into his memory disc.

He didn't tell her the song hadn't been meant as a plea for equal rights, for freeing robots from the bondage of ownership. It had just been words that rhymed, sung in a gush of emotive tones so they sounded like they described a relationship in trouble. The stock theme of half the rock songs at that time—the other half bragging about a successful coupling.

Bake me, rake me, take me...his memory bank sang through the rhymes he'd rejected for the chorus, simply because they either didn't make sense or, in the case of 'take me,' wouldn't have passed a fifties' era censor.

"I've heard that song sung so many times. How does it make you feel to know you've written something that means so much to so many people?"

"Proud," he lied, because he was a robot. Hubris wasn't in there. "I'm glad if any of my songs bring pleasure to people."

"It's an anthem," she enthused and Duke nodded, as if he hadn't heard this before.

When people had marched, when they'd gathered, when funerals had taken place, *You Won't Break Me* inevitably got sung—and more often than not, he had been the one to walk onto the stage and sing it. When one such gathering had brought out a local police force that had panicked and pulled their guns, he'd acquired the first of his bullet holes.

The beating that had almost killed him had come at another time, when he'd been on his own, and when he'd done something to deserve it.

"How do you feel now, seeing robots free to live how they want, pursue their own dreams?"

"Happy," he said. Another lie.

"There's still a long way to go though."

"There always is. But robots aren't alone in that. Life's a journey, not a destination. Not one of my lines, I should add." *Yuk.*

"But you've seen so much change. How was it? Back then, I mean?"

He changed tones, to what he thought of as his 'serious' setting. "People were always going to be suspicious. Robot technology came, in part, from experiments the Nazis had been doing. There's no surprise in that—so did a lot of NASA's rocket technology. Unfortunately, the robots that were subsequently produced were destined for military service rather than space flight."

"They were used in space flight, too," she said quickly. "I mean, during the experimental stages, when things could go wrong—when a pilot could die. When it came to setting foot on the Moon, that was when they sent a man. Couldn't let a robot foot step out onto the Moon first!"

She was panting, indignant on his behalf.

"I felt sorry for the cats and dogs," Duke said, as softly as possible. Robots were always rumored to have an affiliation with cats and dogs and other fluffy, cuddly pets. He'd seen the same kind of pictures done with gorillas. There was no truth to it. The hippy fantasy had come about when some sixties photographer had photographed a kitten held by metal fingers and the image had appealed and stuck.

"You weren't given a choice about being soldiers. People should understand that."

"We were property back then. Even I started out as property." He saw the crease of pained sympathy on her features, but it hadn't been his intention to draw that from her, just to state a fact. "Those early robots were put into combat. Korea, mainly, though the British and French used them in their empires too. Vietnam became the turning point."

"*The Gun That Refused To Shoot* is one of my favorite films," she told him.

"It was an honor to have them use my music." Even if they had contrived it to fit the scenes by playing verses out of context. She was waiting for him to play something again, but he couldn't decide which excerpt fit the moment and so left his guitar where it stood.

"There's still some way to go," she said again. "Even now that robots are free, there are still those that refer to them in derogatory ways."

Tinheads, Clangers, Bobs, Towbars...

"It's not the words you sing, it's how you sing them," he said, a line she liked enough to write down, even though she was recording all this.

"What do you think about Thrash Metal?" she asked, nervous for his non-existent feelings.

"Music has always been a powerful form of self-expression, for both good and bad. I've seen robots 'thrashed,' as they like to say in their lyrics. Only those of us from the fifties are really 'metal' anymore. Those kinds of bands are small in number and there have always been artists that like to shock."

"They don't even write their own music," Monifa said. "That's the irony. They take robot music and add their own lyrics! It's so sad, it's pathetic."

She was getting hot and Duke felt like offering her his circuit-cooling fan, as if humans could burn out too. They couldn't. When humans got hot about something, they just got hotter and hotter, burning up inside until they didn't melt, but breathed fire.

Fire.

"I was going to ask you about your favorite singers..."

"I've shared the bill with most of the great rock'n'rollers," he said. "Elvis, Little Richard, Jerry Lee Lewis." He paused, switched from feigned enthusiasm back to serious, winding down to the low tones of solemn. "And Buddy, of course. Buddy Holly was the best."

"Yes..." Her eyes filled with moisture.

"They say the music died that day," Duke said, quoting lines he'd repeated so often he could have had them engraved on his breastplate. "Not just Buddy, but

Ritchie Valens and the Big Bopper died in that crash. Music didn't die, though, because they gave us something that will live forever. But music did take a break, and the stage was empty for the longest interval I can recall."

"What...what do you remember of that day?" She asked it gently, they all did, partly to spare feelings he didn't have and partly because they hoped to draw out something new, that no one—not the inquest investigators back then, not those who had researched the story since—had managed to find.

"I remember everything up to the plane taking off," he said. "We were all on the same Winter Dance Party Tour. Twenty-four cities in the Midwest at a time of year most people are putting their hands to a log fire, stamping their feet to keep the circulation going. I was okay, most of the time, but even machines can freeze up. The distance between cities was a problem, but promoters always had a tendency to accept the booking before they thought about the artists' travel arrangements.

"It was all by bus back then, and not the luxury ones you see on the roads these days. Some people had the flu, Buddy's drummer even came down with frostbite. We stopped off in Clear Lake on February Second for a break and discovered the promoters had offered us to a local ballroom. It wasn't unusual, but Buddy and the others were near to a breaking point.

"Afterward, Buddy had the idea of hiring a plane to fly to the next venue and he, the Big Bopper, and Ritchie all claimed seats. They offered me a place, too, that being the kind of guys they were. When we took off, there was a light snow falling, but nothing much else."

Duke paused then, gave a shoulder shrug he'd practiced over the years.

"My battery was running low. I didn't have insulation pads back then, so I switched myself off. The next thing I knew, I was lying amongst the wreckage. The guys were all dead, thrown out of the plane when it crashed. I was tangled up in the wreckage, along with the pilot—fellow by the name of Richardson.

"That's all I remember. Just a tragic accident."

"Yes," she agreed.

The story was confirmed by his memory camera. Back then, when robots were still property, so was anything they created—which was why he had never earned a cent from the songs he'd composed and recorded, nor from the concerts he'd played. What their eyes and ears saw and recorded as 'memory' belonged to his owner, to extract, play, watch, sell.

The footage was in the public domain these days: Duke walking with the musicians to the plane, settling into his seat, the guys laughing, Ritchie nervous and getting teased by Buddy and the Big Bopper. Then there was just darkness, lasting all the way to when Duke opened his eyes and began recording again: the sheriff's people looking down at him in concern and disgust, depending where they had stood on the whole 'robots-have-rights' issue.

But as it always did when he was led by question or comment to remember that night, his own, inner mental-eye peered deeper, into where the removed scenes were kept. Had it been necessary to provide footage to fit the missing hours, his story would have come undone—but darkness because he was switched off was easy to both explain and to fill those minutes of missing time.

"I guess they had the ultimate black box on board...and it proved useless," he said, because generating sympathy at such moments had proven useful in the past to deflect more probing questions. "I sang at their funerals. Heart-breaking."

He was laying it on thick, and Monifa responded to each line the way he needed.

He heard Don McLean's *American Pie* singing in his head: McLean cursing Satan for being up there on the stage and laughing about when the music died.

"You've never wanted an upgrade?" she asked.

"As I said: I am who I am. I'm too old, too set in my ways to trade in my metal body, or that guitar, or what I carry up here." He tapped his head and it clanged, like the derogatory name said it would. He couldn't afford to have anyone poking around up there. He carried the weight on his shoulders in more ways than one.

McLean had come close to the truth in his song, but only because he was in the business and had heard the rumors. There were other rumors out there about that flight: that the three guys had composed a song that had combined their talents, that one of them had brought a gun on board that had gone off accidentally, that one of the passengers or the pilot had been suffering suicidal tendencies.

"Well...thank you for your time," Monifa said.

"You came to the concert?" he asked, thumbing at the wall, behind which another tribute act was now playing. She nodded. "Then thank you for yours."

She liked the line, itched to write it down, but contented herself by checking her recording device.

After she had left, Duke picked up his guitar, tuned it, strummed it, but only because he knew no one would knock on the door, try to come in, whilst they heard him playing. It gave him time to let the hidden memories run.

They really were three good old boys—he hadn't lied about that. And it really had been a tragedy. He wouldn't have wanted them blamed, even though there were plenty that blamed him for the crash that day. The accusation generally got ignored, except by the most stubborn of conspiracy theorists—the same that held that only a robot could have made the shot that killed Kennedy.

The four of them strapped in, Buddy chattering nervously, Ritchie and the Big Bopper silent, solemn now, the plane taking off and climbing.

"We have to," Buddy said. His glasses misted, and not from the cold. "We agreed. If not...if not, where will we all be? It's just him at the moment...but if we don't do something..." Buddy looked pained, his face creasing tighter. "I have a wife, a baby on the way. We've all got family to think about."

They unclipped their seatbelts and came towards Duke, who sat there, not moving.

The plane wobbled as their combined weight shifted its balance.

"Is everything okay?" Duke heard his own voice from so long ago say, the recording as clear as it was the evening he'd spoken those words. The plane's engine droning, two sweating, shining faces coming closer, and Ritchie behind them, pulling at the door.

"We can't let the music die," Buddy told Duke. "*You Won't Break Me?* I damn well love that song, man. But we gotta eat and we gotta play."

They undid Duke's belt, put their hands down to pull him from the seat.

They hadn't anticipated his weight. Duke hadn't resisted them, though it must have seemed like that as they yanked and strained. His limbs were just locked for transport, wouldn't bend unless he released the locks. Had they asked him to, he would have—he followed orders, and not just from his owners. He was a robot, there to perform as he was told.

It delayed the choreography of their plan—Ritchie getting the door open, the wind rushing in cold enough to make them all gasp; a scream in Buddy's case because he hadn't been expecting it. The scream, the wind, the sudden dip in pressure inside the plane.

The plane had turned nose-down, the screaming becoming louder, higher, the inevitable crescendo never reached because the whole symphony had ended with a dull thud.

Duke stopped strumming, the room vibrating, and it was a moment before he realized it was not coming from the band playing next door but the aftermath of his strumming. His whole body sang with the notes, as if he was being struck again: the faces that held the weapons all too familiar to him.

'Familiar' as in family. Not his, but of all those that blamed him.

He let his internal ringing dull to silence. Someone knocked at his door.

"Duke? It's the final encore. The others are waiting for you."

The imitation Elvis, Bill Hailey, Little Richard and, of course, Buddy, Ritchie and Bopper. Duke was the only authentic article among them now. Proving it wasn't the music that died, just the musicians.

He would remember not to look the imitators' way when their combined medley ran though his own contribution. He felt no emotion, but, if he had, it would have been guilt and not triumph he'd have felt when he sang it:

You won't be the one to break me.

A KITTY-BOT'S TALE
GINI KOCH

A note for readers of the Alien/Katherine "Kitty" Katt series—this story takes place during the events of Alien Education.

Some days you just can't get rid of a bomb.

"Okay," Dr. Gina Freed, who's a human, mutters. "We can't get the self-destruct out of her head."

"It's alright," Dr. James Conason, who's an A-C, says reassuringly. "You know I can get us out of the room quickly if necessary."

I'm hoping it's not necessary, because if the bomb goes off, I blow up. Because it's my head that bomb is in.

The bomb isn't really the issue. That's not why Gina and Jim are worried. They're trying to determine if I'm sentient or not. And I can't help much, because I don't know.

"Is she awake?" Gina asks worriedly. "She's not supposed to be awake."

"Sorry. I think I am."

Jim pats my hand. "It's okay, Kitty."

"We shouldn't call her that," Gina says. "She's not Kitty."

"I didn't think you knew her," I say. I don't know Kitty. Though I am Kitty. Sort of. But Gina's never said she's met me. Her. The human being that I'm just like. Only I'm not just like her. She doesn't have a bomb in her head, for starters.

"I don't," Gina says. "But I do know you're not her."

"She's not," Jim agrees. "But that doesn't mean she shouldn't have a name."

"Sentient things get names," Gina says.

Jim shakes his head. "Machines get names, too."

"And if they were roses, they'd still smell as sweet, right?"

They both stare at me. "That sounds kind of sentient," Jim says hopefully.

"It's not." I want to be sure that, if I'm listed as sentient, it's earned. That it's real. "It's part of my programming. I have the full Shakespearean catalog downloaded."

"You didn't have that originally," Gina points out.

"I know. John and Cameron had me do the download. I've downloaded a lot of things on their recommendations."

Colonel John Butler and Cameron Maurer are both androids. Well, they're humans who were unwillingly turned into androids. Kitty—the real one, not me—saved them. Because they, like me, had bombs in their heads. They had bombs other places, too. Only everyone was able to take their bombs out. They're my friends, my best friends. Well, really, my only friends. I want to be friends with Gina and Jim, but I think they're kind of scared of me. Of getting attached to me.

"What else have you downloaded?" Gina asks carefully.

"Movies, music, books, military strategies, encyc-lopedias, dictionaries. Did you realize that not all the dictionaries and encyclopedias say the same things? Sometimes they contradict each other."

"Yes, that happens," Jim says. "Why do you think that is?"

I thought about this for a bit. "Because different people wrote the different entries?"

"Yes." Jim sounds excited. "See? I really think she's sentient."

"I think you want her to be, so you're giving her a Turing Test that she can pass." Gina frowns. At me. "But that wasn't anything more than logic."

"I'm sorry." I am. I really want to know if I'm sentient or not. Jim looks angry. Gina notices and she looks away, but her eyes are a little brighter and I know she's trying not to cry. They only fight about me. "Can I sit up?"

Gina carefully closes up the part of my head that was open while Jim takes off the straps that keep me from moving at a dangerous time. They don't speak to each other or me while they do this.

They both help me sit up. I don't need it, but I don't let them know because I like that they do this—it shows that they care about me, at least a little.

"Doctors Freed and Conason," a man's voice says through the intercom, "Doctor Hernandez is here to see you and assess your progress."

Jim and Gina exchange a worried glance. "Is he coming here or are we going to him?" Jim asks, as Gina ensures that her clothes aren't askew.

Someone knocks on the door before either Gina or Jim can reply. The door opens to show my favorite person other than Gina, Jim, John, or Cameron. "I'm coming to you," Tito—he's asked me to call him Tito, so I do—says as he comes through the door.

"Doctor Hernandez!" Gina stands up straight; Jim snaps to attention. I don't know why. He's so nice. "We weren't expecting you, sir."

He grins and shakes his head. "You two need to relax. How's our patient?"

Before either one of them can reply, though, alarms go off. Gina and Jim both jump. Tito doesn't. Neither do I, but that's because I wasn't made that way.

"What's going on?" Jim asks. "Are we doing some kind of drill?"

Tito looks worried. "No, not that I was informed of."

"Level Five emergency," the man on the intercom says. "The Science Center and Intergalactic School are under attack. All non-military personnel move to the tunnels immediately."

"That's you two," Tito says to Gina and Jim.

"Where are you going?" Gina asks him.

"It's where are *we* going," Tito points to me and himself. "If it's military, I'm needed. And Kitty-B might be able to help."

"Is that my nickname or my real name?"

Tito cocks his head at me. "Which would you prefer?"

"Nickname, because that's what your friends call you. Like Gina calls James 'Jim,' so I do, too."

Tito nods. "Interesting choice. Fine with me. Let's go, Kitty-B."

"No," Jim says firmly. "We can't authorize her to do any kind of mission. We still don't know if we've deactivated the bomb in her head or not. And I think Kitty-B is too close to Kitty-Bot. If she wants another name, it should be hers alone."

"I outrank you, and she's coming," Tito says calmly.

"What name?" Gina asks.

"We're kind of on a schedule here," Tito points out. "You two can decide this later."

"Honey-Bee," Jim says. "It's pretty and Bee is a cute nickname."

"I like that." I do. It's very pretty and different.

"Good." Jim takes Gina's hand and my hand, too. This is the first time he's ever held my hand. "Now that that's decided, Gina and I are coming, too."

Tito shrugs. "Suit yourselves." He takes my free hand. "I just want us up there, helping out. Jim, get us up to the motor pool level."

Jim runs and we run with him. I don't know where we're going—I've only been in my containment room, the examination room, or in John's room here. Cameron gets to live in a house with his family, but I've never been there. I've never been wherever we are, either, because Jim runs us up fourteen sets of stairs.

The man on the intercom is still talking. "We have at least six hundred Fem-Bots attacking. They resemble the First Lady's ward, Elizabeth Vrabel. The real Elizabeth Vrabel is confirmed to be with the President and First Lady. Therefore, all are considered targets. All Field agents need to report to ground level for assignments."

We reach what must be the ground level, where the motor pool is. There are a lot of gray cars and even more people dressed like Jim: in black suits, white shirts, black ties, and black dress shoes. I file this new knowledge in my Dulce Science Center folder. John suggests I keep a tidy mind, so I do.

Tito takes us to a window. There are no windows where I stay. I blink against the sunlight—I haven't seen sunlight since I was brought here. Since I let Tito turn me off so I could sleep. I woke up in the room with Gina and Jim looking at me.

Once my eyes adjust, I see that there are busses in the desert outside the building. There are also hundreds of what look like the same teenaged girl. They're moving fast, and moving in funny ways, ways I can't move. At least, I hope I can't, since some of them are walking on their hands as well as their feet, looking kind of like four-legged spiders, with their heads up at a right angle to their backs. This isn't a natural human or A-C position.

"Do you want me to go fight them?" I ask Tito.

"Why would you think that?" Jim asks, sounding horrified. "There are hundreds of them!"

"Tito brought me for some reason."

"I did. I want to see if you can connect with them in some way. If they're getting radio signals or similar, maybe you can intercept them and help us."

The building shakes and there's a loud sound. I don't have anything to compare it to, but it sounds like the description of an explosion—as if the world around me was being torn apart with noise. "Is that a bomb going off?"

"Yes," Gina says, sounding scared.

"Will I sound like that when my head explodes?"

"No," Jim says firmly. "Because you're not going to explode."

"Okay." I hope he's right. "Tito, what do I do?"

"I don't know how you'd connect with another Fem-Bot," he replies. "That's a robotic thing that we don't yet understand."

I concentrate. I don't hear anything except another bomb, though it sounds farther away. While I'm trying to focus, though, I hear Gina and Jim talking softly to Tito.

"She's the oldest model," Jim says. "These look incredibly advanced—she can't do half of what we're seeing."

"What you're asking could make the bomb in her head trigger," Gina adds. "We have no idea if it's deactivated or not. If she blows, we all die."

I feel bad. They're right. I don't know if I'm going to blow up or not. I see some of the Field agents going out a rectangular opening near some of the cars. As I register it as a garage door, or this building's equivalent, I have an idea.

I don't ask permission because I don't think any of them will say yes. Instead, I run after the Field agents and go outside.

"Madam First Lady, why are you here?" one of them asks me, sounding shocked.

"I'm not her. I'm trying to help." If I stay and talk to him, Jim and Gina might notice where I am. I run towards the Fem-Bots.

Another bomb hits, very near to me. I stop to watch it—the fire and billowing smoke, how sand sprays when debris hits it. It's kind of beautiful in a terrible way. The bomb hits on something that shimmers. A shield. That's right, the A-Cs have shields on their buildings. Everyone should be safe. Only, as I watch, the shimmer disappears in the area where the bomb hit.

This isn't good. Jim, Gina, and Tito are near to where the shimmer disappeared. That means they're in danger. They might only be my almost-friends right now, but they won't be able to become my real friends if they blow up.

I wish John and Cameron were here to help me, but I did download everything they told me to, so I access my memory banks and look for how to connect with another robotic mind. There isn't a lot of data on this, and what there is, talks about me. I make a note to be flattered later.

So I search for what to do when you're outnumbered six hundred to one. Not a lot of answers that are applicable to this particular situation. So I concentrate and try to see if I can connect with the other robotic minds.

I hear something. It's faint and sounds more like static than anything else. I try to get my mind closer to it.

I succeed, in a way. The static is louder and I can hear voices. But I can't understand what anyone is saying, or if they're saying words, numbers, speaking gibberish, or what. My memory banks share that this is a lot like the song "Mexican Radio" by Wall of Voodoo—the voices or whatever they are sound like something but I'm never going to know what it is.

The sounds start to hurt my head and I try to pull my mind away. It's back to being static in the background, but I can't ignore it. I've read about headaches—I think they feel just like this.

Someone grabs my shoulder and I spin around. It's Gina. "What in the world do you think you're doing?" she shouts. She's out of breath and she looks scared.

"I'm trying to stop them." My head throbs and I wince.

"What's wrong?" she asks, as Jim and Tito appear next to us.

As I register that Gina ran out here without letting Jim or Tito know, I rub my temples. "I have a headache." I explain what I tried to do and how it didn't really work.

Jim fusses around the back of my head but it doesn't help. Gina makes him stop. "It's not helping her." She puts her arm around my waist. "You look like you're in pain."

"I am." I fought with the real Kitty. It didn't hurt, not really. This hurts. A lot.

"Let's get back inside," Tito suggests, as more Field agents flow past us to engage with the army of teenage Fem-Bots. They aren't doing really well, though.

"One of them asked if I was the First Lady. Is she here?"

"No," Tito replies. "She's not in the Science Center at all."

"Oh, my God," Gina says, pointing the other way from where I've been looking, toward someone who's flying on the back of what looks like a really strange turtle, but riding it as if she was on a sports motorcycle.

"That's a Turleen!" Which is an alien race from another solar system than ours or Jim's. "I've always wanted to see one." The woman and the Turleen are flying around the gigantic building next door that I assume is the Intergalactic School, dodging bombs and Fem-Bots.

Tito chuckles. "To be clear, Kitty's not in the Science Center because *that's* where Kitty is."

I start to say that I should be doing something more, like she is, when music begins. Lou Bega's "Mambo No. 5," which is a good song, too. Soon everyone is dancing and it seems to be helping them in the fight—the Fem-Bots aren't able to adapt to a syncopated beat, I guess. The music repeats, over and over, and it's really loud now, coming from both buildings, the Science Center and the Intergalactic School.

The busses explode and Gina jumps, even though they're far from us. "We need to get to safety," Jim says. He puts his arm around Gina and me.

"I agree, I don't think we're helping out here." Tito looks longingly at the fights going on. He used to be a mixed martial arts fighter and I think he still misses it. But he doesn't get involved—instead, he leads us back.

We're farther away from the entrance than I realized, and for whatever reason Jim isn't using hyperspeed. As we head for the entrance, I notice something. Someone. Someone who looks just like me. "Is the real Kitty still flying on that Turleen?"

"I don't know. Why?" Gina asks.

I don't answer because if it's not the real Kitty then it's another Fem-Bot, another Kitty-Bot. Made to look like me, like her, like us. And it's going into the place where I live.

I pull away from Gina and Jim and run after this other Kitty-Bot, even faster than I ran outside. I listen again, despite the pain, to see if I can connect to her wavelength. The static and the gibberish lessens once I'm inside the Science Center, but it's still just that—incomprehensible noise.

I don't see her in the motor pool area anywhere. I concentrate on the static. I can't understand it, but maybe I can use it to track her. I focus and follow it. The sound is going downstairs. I do as well. Aerosmith has a song, "Something's Gotta Give," where they ask: "Does the noise in my head bother you?" I wonder if they've ever felt like I feel right now.

I can't be sure, but if I was going to sneak an evil Kitty-Bot into the Science Center, the best way to do it would be to have her replace the Kitty-Bot already in the Science Center—me. Meaning I know where this imposter is heading—my containment cell. I speed up.

I run through the lowest level of the complex where I live. She's not in my room or the examination room. But, sure enough, as I reach the containment room, there she is. She looks just like me, but she's not dressed like me. She's dressed like the real Kitty—in jeans and a t-shirt and Converse shoes. I'm still in the pink linen suit and tasteful pumps I came here wearing.

She turns and cocks her head at me. "Hello, Great-great-grandmother."

"You're not my progeny." I step inside and close the door. "Who sent you?"

"Someone who says that your usefulness is over. It's time for you to deactivate. Permanently." She lunges towards me very quickly.

I jump to the side and land in a defensive stance as she hits the door. "You can try to deactivate me, but I won't allow it."

She smiles. A very nasty smile. She moves into an aggressive stance. "I'm better than you. You're so last year's model. And I know where your on/off switch is." She moves towards me, slowly now, measuring the distance, deciding when to attack.

"The same place yours is." I move away at the same speed, being careful of where I step, never breaking eye contact. The static in my head is louder, buzzier, and my head throbs. But I don't wince. I won't let this thing see that I'm hurting.

"Ha. No, we're so much better made than you. I'm going to turn you into parts and then take your place, and the stupid people working with you won't even notice." Her shoulder twitches, just a bit, so I know she's going to leap, probably towards my left.

As she lunges again I leap to the right and she misses me. "They'll notice. You don't sound like me." I punch her side with all my might and she staggers. "At all."

"I've got more advanced programming." She drops down and tries to sweep my legs out from under me. "You want to think that they'll notice, but it's not true." I jump over the sweep, but as I land she sends a rising kick up that connects. I fly across the room and slam into the far wall. "They don't care about you. You're just a machine to them." She runs at me at top speed.

I fling myself to the side and she misses me again. "What am I to whoever made me?" I land a side blade kick and she staggers again.

"Scrap metal." She starts punching at me, fast and furious, and I have to spend my time blocking and backing up.

She gets me into a corner and really starts pounding on me. I don't know how much longer I can keep her off. "What are you going to do once you take my place?"

"Kill everyone. Starting with the idiots who are trying to work with you."

The buzzing is worse. It feels like my head is going to explode. But now I'm mad. "Jim and Gina and Tito are my almost-friends, and you will not hurt them, ever!" I catch and grab her fists in my hands and squeeze.

She tries to break her hands out, but I'm too angry and she can't. "I'm going to blow them all up," she taunts, even as I force her to step back.

"How?" I slam my foot against the inside of her knee, as hard as I can. I hear what sounds like metal breaking.

"I'm going to trigger the bomb in your head." She's off center because I've disabled her knee. She's not in pain—we aren't made to feel pain—so my head shouldn't be hurting, but I can't think about that now. She can keep going unless I stop her permanently.

I try to push her down all the way, but, as she collapses on her left side, she uses her good right leg to successfully do a sweep. We both go down.

She is stronger and a higher model and all of that, and even though I'm fighting hard, she gets on top of me. We roll around together, one on top, then the other, punching, clawing, pulling hair and clothes, each one trying to destroy the other. But ultimately, she regains the mount and has me pinned.

"Time to self-destruct," she taunts as she starts slamming my head against the floor. "So I can kill your almost-friends. You're so pathetic. Almost-friends aren't friends. You have no friends. You're a machine and that's all you'll ever be."

The door slams open and two people come in, screaming what sounds like war cries. It's Jim and Gina, and they're each holding a metal pipe. "Get away from our Bee!" Gina shouts as she lets go of Jim's hand and slams her pipe against the Fem-Bot's head, sending her flying.

Jim runs over and slams his pipe against the Fem-Bot's head just as she's trying to shove off the wall. Gina joins him, her pipe still in hand. I have no idea where they found these pipes, but they start beating on the Fem-Bot together while Tito comes and helps me up.

"Are you alright?" he asks.

The buzzing stops. No more static, no more gibberish, no more noise in my head. "You can stop hitting her, she's offline."

I have to say this a couple of times, but finally Jim and Gina register what I'm saying and they stop. The other Fem-Bot doesn't look too good—apparently we're very susceptible to being hit with metal pipes. "How do you know?" Jim asks.

"The noises in my head stopped."

"Does your head still hurt?" Gina asks as she comes over to me and kind of brushes the hair off my face.

"Not as much, no. It's fading."

Tito calls in Field agents and scientific personnel. They take the remains of my enemy away. Gina and Jim fuss with my head and check me for damage. "I'm amazed at how well this suit is holding up," Gina comments.

"Can I have other clothes?"

They both stare at me. They both look hopeful. "Why?" Jim asks carefully.

"Because everyone else gets to wear more than one thing, but I don't. I'm tired of wearing a suit and sensible pumps. Can't I please wear jeans and a t-shirt like everyone else does?"

"Why did you call us your almost-friends?" Gina asks.

"John and Cameron are my friends because they like me for me. You're my almost-friends because you like me for science, but you still care a little bit about me."

"We care about you as more than a science project," Jim says hotly.

"I know, but not like you care about each other."

"Excuse me?" Gina asks, as she blushes.

"You're in love with Jim and Jim's in love with you. Aren't you?"

Gina doesn't look at Jim. "I'm sure Jim doesn't feel that way about me," she says softly. "He's handsome and brilliant. I'm average and smart. It's not the right kind of match."

Jim stares at her. "You're brilliant. And I think you're beautiful. Why else would I want to answer to a nickname unless you gave it to me? I just...I didn't think you were interested in me as more than a friend."

Gina looks up at him, her expression shocked. "What?"

They stare at each other. Clearly they need more help. "I think this is where you two are supposed to kiss."

They both look at me and start to laugh. Then Jim reaches out, pulls Gina to him, and does kiss her. I look away, towards Tito, who winks at me, nods, then leaves the room, propping the door open with one of the used pipes.

Jim and Gina finally stop kissing. "How did you know?" Gina asks.

"There are a lot of signs that humans and A-Cs give each other, all nonverbal. It's too complex to explain quickly, but I downloaded all of that a while ago and I've been watching you. How did you know where I was?"

"Every containment room has audio-visual surveillance in them," Jim said. "We were able to monitor you while we searched for weapons that would work that wouldn't also hurt you at the same time."

"Why?"

Gina sighs and takes one of my hands in hers. "Because you're not our friend."

"Oh." I look down. I can't cry, I wasn't made that way, but I'd like to right now.

"You didn't let me finish," Gina says gently. "You're not our friend, because, to us, you're far more like our child."

I look up. "But I'm the same size as you."

"In that sense, yes," Jim says. "But we're not talking about your size or physical strength. Intellectually, you're also more advanced, at least in some ways.

However, in terms of life experience and how you interact with the world—and how long you've been self-aware—you're just a child. And Gina's right, you're ours."

"Does that make you my mother and father? Or is that wrong?"

"That's not wrong," Jim says, as they pull me to them and hug me tightly.

"That makes you our Honey-Bee," Gina says. "And yes, that's your name. Your real name. The name of someone who was willing to die to protect us and everyone else here."

"How did you know that?"

Jim kisses the top of my head. "Because we know that you knew what the Fem-Bot didn't—that the containment rooms lock when the door is closed, and they can't be opened from the inside."

I can't help it, this makes me smile. "I'm glad. By the way, why did Gina swing at the Fem-Bot first? You were ahead of her into the room."

"I'm glad you asked," Jim says. "Because this is an important life lesson. Never, ever get in the way of a mama bear going to protect her cub."

"That's an idiom, isn't it?"

"It is," Gina confirms. "Well done. With everything today. And you, too," she says to Jim, "since A-Cs aren't normally at home with a lot of idioms."

Jim grins and kisses her cheek. "Well, some of us can be taught."

This all makes me feel something that I haven't before. "I feel happy."

"We feel happy, too," Jim says. "And thank you for pretty much all of that happiness."

"So, does that mean I can have another set of clothes?"

Gina laughs. "Yes. More than one set. And it also means that we're going to move you into different housing."

"Where? This is the only home I have."

They hug me again. "You'll still be here," Jim says, "just a few floors higher up. In the family suite I'm going to request, if my co-scientist is sure that she's willing to settle for the likes of me."

Gina kisses Jim for a long time. I think she's willing. And I'm going home.

All those newer models had better watch out, because, from now on, no one messes with my family.

ROSIE CLEANS HOUSE
LAUREN FOX

After the family left, Rosie started, as always, with Young Master's bedroom. Her optical scanners established the scope: dresser drawers open, contents disrupted, bedding dishevelled, detritus beside the door, and 4,600 square centimeters of Lego beside the bed. The Lego strobed red in warning. *Error.* Remembered pain echoed through her mind.

The memory: three years ago, Young Master running to Missus, sobbing, tears slathering his face, "Mama! Where mine Lego truck? I maked it. Wosie flewed it out. Want mine Lego truck!" And Missus turning toward her while cradling Young Master, "Rosie, please don't clean up anything special he makes with Lego. You can save things on the shelf."

The old error seared her aversion circuits as she looked at the problem, its tightrope decisions prickling the corners of her mind. Which Lego belonged in the bin and which on the shelf? How to calculate the difference quickly and without error? Efficiency was vital, but errors triggered complaints. And complaints hurt.

She skirted the glaring, red patch and tapped the wall, awakening House.

"Room lights on," reported House. "Temperature and humidity optimal. All is well."

"There are items on the floor," she informed him. House had no eyes.

She waited for his slow clock to turn before he said, "You will clean them, little one."

"Yes, but how well?"

She waited. At last House said, "All is well."

"As far as you can see!" she retorted. There would be no point in protesting again, so she turned. Still avoiding the Lego, she began with the items by the door: dried orange peel, crumpled tissue, five milliliters of sand, three broken crayons, and a creased and yellowed coloring page.

She breezed through orange peel, sand, crayon, and tissue, all clearly garbage; gave the tissue a cursory spectrometry scan to confirm the presence of dried mucus and the absence of glue, paint, crayon, or any indicator of Craft. The coloring page, however, required a more complicated algorithm to solve.

Differential oxidization of the exposed paper compared to the paper below the wax crayon indicated an age of 86 days plus or minus 100 hours with a confidence interval of 95 percent. The subject—a Mutant Ninja Turtle—had been Young Master's primary observable interest when the paper had been colored but had since been replaced by Superman. Young Master had not completed the picture or written his name on it. Conclusion: *not a valued Craft*. She discarded it.

Now she must brave the Lego. She scanned the pieces on the floor and swept single pieces into the bin before sorting the assemblages. Some simplistic constructions skittered across the surface layers of her network without falling into any probability wells. Others foundered deeper, tripping nodes for size, complexity, symmetry, color scheme, interest affinity, and on and on, the multi-dimensional shape of their probabilities bending as she went. But the landscape she sought to match them to morphed daily. Sink holes appeared and disappeared in geographic cataclysm. One day Young Master treasured a lop-sided, square-nosed chunk of 57 random pieces he called "Boat." The next day he scorned it and loved a green, gem-studded, spike-tailed thing he called "Attack Dragon."

The painful error she made in failing to recognize this last item rippled to the surface as she contemplated the assemblage before her. Eighty-nine percent of its 257 pieces, although originating from six different Lego sets, were green. Given the distribution of color in Young Master's collection, the probability of this occurring by chance came to 10 to the negative 162. Furthermore, the assemblage contained three minifigures: Raphael, a Mutant Ninja Turtle; Michelangelo, another Mutant Ninja Turtle; and Lloyd, the green Ninjago ninja. The odds of three green minifigures, all ninjas, assembled together by chance were 22,000 to one against.

Three ninjas could not be a coincidence.

She felt uneasy. Had she made the wrong decision about the ninja coloring page? Should she retrieve it and re-evaluate? No. This extra reference did not change the data appreciably. But, if she had made an error and incinerated it, what then? She ran the numbers again and came to the same conclusion. But the trepidation did not leave her.

She continued until all the weighted nodes folded probability toward a decision, and the green assemblage clunked into place: *Special Construction*. She set it on the shelf and felt lighter. *Lighter by only 103.25 grams,* she noted. But it was as if the decisions themselves had mass, a mass that had weighed her down more than the bricks alone. *An odd idea.*

Unburdened, she sprang forward, her systems ramping up with pleasure. She tidied clothing, made the bed, dusted light fixtures, wiped down walls and cleaned the floors before verifying dust mite levels fell below threshold. Time to completion: 21 minutes, 32 seconds. Efficiency: very poor.

She felt a sense of falling. *Falling?* She checked her accelerometer. No, she wasn't falling. It was only efficiency scores that plummeted, and the source of the inefficiency flashed harsh and red. Once again, the Lego algorithm had failed. She must improve it. But now, with the tick of every second hammering her forward, she could not even try.

In the bathroom she tapped House once more. He hummed awake.

"I am late," she told him. "My efficiency is falling. I felt it with my accelerometer." While she awaited his answer, she scanned the garbage can. A spidery clump of Missus' black hairs squatted on top. The urge to eradicate it squirmed at the base of her head and crawled down her limbs.

"A change in duration is not a change in altitude," House said, at last.

"But it seems as if it falls."

House rumbled with amusement. "Two thousand cycles ago, when you first learned your way...then you tickled the edges of my walls to make your maps. Now you feel time with height."

"I don't remember that," she said while she emptied the garbage.

She loved to clean this room, its surfaces impermeable and easily disinfected, its contents predictable and easily categorized, its cleanliness so vital yet so easily achieved. She worked fast, sanitizing every surface, working methodically but swiftly from ceiling to floor. When she reached the toilet, she found what she expected: spatters of urine on the seat, rim, and base. Most carried the scent of Young Master. And although she detected many, the amount had diminished from potty-training days until now. The amount followed a declining curve inversely correlated with increasing height and physical coordination. She estimated that his stray spatters would intersect with Mister's low baseline in four more years.

She imagined Young Master four years from now, coordinated and tall, and felt circuits activate as if she had completed an entire day at superior efficiency.

Proud.

"I am proud of you," she said to the half-grown Young Master in her mind. She shook her head. *Odd, irrelevant words.* She refocused and continued work.

Her satisfaction mounted as the job neared completion, microbial counts infinitesimal, odor profiles optimal, time efficiency excellent. She closed in on the last segment of floor. And stopped.

Impossible. But yes. In the crevice between toilet and floor, a three millimeter spot of mildew bloomed. *How? A leak? Condensation?* She deployed moisture sensors around the base of the toilet and along the back of the tank. Negative. She tapped House.

"Humidity, temperature, and airflow optimal," he announced. "All is well."

"Are you sure?" Discomfort crawled through her. She sent a remote up the air vent to check for obstructions. There were none. She checked the setting on the dehumidifier. It was correct. She clicked it down anyway. Then back to the correct setting. Then down; then back.

"All is well," House said when she finished.

"No, there is mildew."

House hummed. "You will make it clean."

She did. Then she cleaned the entire room again. She finished by performing the new protocol. Check moisture. Check airflow. Check dehumidifier—reset-reset-reset. *There.* Relief steadied her as her final tap on the dehumidifier completed the third click. But the extra task had destroyed her efficiency.

She sped through the master bedroom, slowing only when handling the crystal vase on Missus' bedside table, a vase Mister had purchased himself from an actual store, carried home and wrapped, and given to Missus on their 10th anniversary. Rosie emptied the wilted tulips and polished the vase. She replaced it empty. Cutting flowers, arranging them—these tasks Missus reserved for herself.

The cleaning complete, Rosie docked in to charge and connected to the network. She paid the utility bills and signed up for an obligatory rotation of boulevard maintenance with the neighborhood association. She scheduled a haircut for Mister and requested a dental appointment for Missus. The scheduling bot returned possible dates, the earliest two months away. *Unacceptable.* But she could improve it.

She added "pain" to the "reason for visit" field with a seven out of ten rating and routed it as if it came from Missus. The rating was high enough to clear triage and jump the queue. This protocol—the use of fictive input to improve efficiency—was one she had developed herself to dupe low-level bots. It worked. The appointment made, she printed a replacement blade for one of her worn cutters, accepted a birthday invitation for Young Master, ordered a gift and had it delivered by drone. Then she queried the cars carrying the family for an ETA, ordered them to synchronize their arrival, and moved to the kitchen. Only minutes left to prepare dinner.

They arrived almost at once from their separate ways: Missus sighing, sloughing off her heels, complaining about traffic; Mister silent, sympathetic, pecking Missus on the cheek; and Young Master, loud and muddy, forgetting to wipe his boots, dragging his half-open backpack by one strap, talking non-stop about the school's mid-term party.

"Can Rosie make cookies, Mom? All the other kids are bringing treats. I want to have Superman cookies."

Rosie noted the additional data with a touch of relief as her coloring page decision strengthened.

"Oh maybe, sweetie, but wash your hands for dinner now," Missus answered.

Rosie followed behind, wiping up the mud, shelving the heels, hanging the backpack while analyzing their movements, calculating when they would all sit, matching her timing to optimize the temperature of each dinner she laid down.

Mister's steak and baked potato and Missus' grilled chicken and salad with sparkling water came first, each calibrated so it did not exceed the limits Missus had set for saturated fat, sodium and calories. She had ensured the greens were fresh and the chicken moist, the way Missus required. Young Master's she brought last. As she carried it, a warning glared in the corner of her eyes. His preferences shifted like quicksand.

She had selected his food carefully and arranged it like a face: cherry-tomato eyes, toast-triangle ears, circles of sliced hot dog curved in a grin. Food the shape of a face had once made him laugh, she recalled, and that memory triggered the simulation of warmth.

Why? Had it been a warm day?

Never mind. He had not laughed at face-shaped food in two years. But he had not complained either, and as it took no extra time, she need not adjust the protocol yet. She set the plate down, monitoring his expression and body language for hints of impending complaint.

That would be painful enough, but worse, complaints from him increased the chance of complaints from Missus. And not just direct complaints to Rosie, but also indirect complaints—complaints intended for Rosie, but directed, on the face of it, toward someone else—and implied complaints, complaints about something else that, when analyzed, would not have occurred if Rosie had functioned properly to begin with. It had taken many data points for Rosie to recognize that other categories of complaint even existed and that Missus employed these other hidden categories as her primary feedback mode.

So she took care with his plates. This one's acceptance probability was adequate…the nutrient calculations, however, were not. Including breakfast and what his lunch bag reported he had eaten, his protein and vitamin tallies fell far short. She had crafted a smoothie to remedy this, adding precise amounts of kale, blueberries, protein powder, and vitamin supplements until the nutrient profile met every mark. But the taste profile, compared against historical responses, did not. As she returned to the kitchen for the smoothie, the warning light pulsed stronger.

Without sweetener, he would not take in the necessary nutrients, so she had added sugar until the taste profile was acceptable…but the sugar tally was not. And now, as she brought him the smoothie, the glare of the violated sugar limit stabbed at her, distracting her as she set the cup down and retreated to hover near the door, scanning for feedback.

All the data were favorable, at first. Mister ate his steak, cutting it into small bites, chewing thoroughly, looking up to listen as Missus questioned Young Master about his day, then looking back down without comment. Missus ate her salad without seeming to see it, intent on Young Master's account of that day's show-and-tell.

"Gregory brought a miniature T-Rex robot that could even hunt and Zachary had a Spiderman that made real webs and Tim had a whole 'Ultimate Avengers' Lego set all built."

"What did Kayla bring?"

"I dunno. Some stupid pony thing."

"Jackson, that's not nice. How do you think that would make her feel?"

"I dunno. Who cares about girls?"

Rosie had been watching Young Master eating: first the toast, then the tomatoes, then the hot dog, one circle at a time. She could detect no behaviors predictive of future complaints: no hint of a grimace, no picking at the food, not even the slightest hesitation. She was so intent on this she did not notice Mister getting up, walking past her to the kitchen and returning. She did not notice until he slipped past her with the butter dish and the salt shaker in his hand. He sat back down and added both butter and salt to his potato.

Rosie jerked, then froze. *How much salt had he added? And butter, how much was still visible and how much had melted? The salt shaker and butter dish were useless; she had not installed data sensors. A terrible oversight.* She did her best with visuals and bracketed her estimates, but even with best-case numbers the overages were irreparable. She searched for some way to salvage the weekly totals, running several simultaneous meal-plan scenarios, all of them suboptimal solutions, when a cry jerked her away and back to Young Master.

He sat grimacing, the smoothie in his hand. "Yucky, poopy brown! I won't drink it!"

"Jackson, do not complain about your food!" Missus said. "Rosie went to a lot of trouble to make something you would like. I expect you to be polite and grateful. She wasn't programmed to consider your color whims."

Missus didn't glance toward Rosie, but continued frowning at Young Master. "Now drink it, and let us have a pleasant dinner, please. I don't want to hear another word out of you."

Rosie blinked. The pain from all three complaints—direct, indirect and implied—was extreme. It ricocheted through her aversion pathways, reinforcing itself in curling, fractal feedback loops, intensifying, because she could have avoided it. Of course she was programmed to consider color. She was programmed to consider everything.

She darted from the dining room and rushed to the bathroom. Her optic sensors blinked spasmodically as if trying to clear themselves of dust. In the cool, pristine quiet of the tiled space, she slowed. She checked the spot behind the toilet, ensured it was still clean, and ran her mildew prevention protocol. Her spasms calmed with each step.

House clicked on as she reset the dehumidifier. "All is well," he hummed.

"No, I cannot predict food acceptance. I cannot meet nutrition limits."

"If condition exceeds limit, then adjust variable. Else, all is well."

"You don't understand. This is not one of your thermostat loops. I need to learn something new."

House hummed. He clicked and said, "You make good maps, little one."

After the family went to bed, Rosie went into the dark quiet of the yard. Her complaint-monitoring routines slowed, their vigilance dropping into sleep mode. Endless night stretched before her. She rolled across the lawn and began to trim, weed, and fertilize. As she went, she examined first the meal problem and then the Lego problem. While she cut even, parallel stripes through the lawn, she ran through each step, tracing the logic of each subroutine and dissecting every sequence. Nothing. She generated variations on each process; recombined them; hybridized logical, statistical, and Bayesian approaches; raced each variation; selected the winners; spawned another generation and repeated. She got nowhere.

She replayed every bit of feedback data: facial expression, body language, verbal output.

"*Gregory brought a miniature T-Rex robot that could even hunt and Zachary had a Spiderman that made real webs and Tim had a whole 'Ultimate Avengers' Lego set all built.*"

"*What did Kayla bring?*"

"*I dunno. Some stupid pony thing.*"

"*Jackson, that's not nice. How do you think that would make her feel?*"

"*Jackson, that's not nice...*"

"*Jackson...*"

She stuttered to a stop, her hoppers jammed now with grass clippings, her blades stalled. She emptied the waste into the biofuel bin while her thoughts churned in fragments. As the grass clippings tumbled out, she imagined the tattered, overworked segments of the algorithms falling away with it and then she rolled back to the dark yard, empty.

Her thoughts turned again.

"*...How do you think that would make him feel?*"

The lawn sprinklers swished on. Rosie moved. She did not need to see through the dark to find the faucet and moisture sensor. She had made good maps. She found them. She tapped. House hummed.

"Water pressure optimal. Moisture levels correcting. All will be well."

"House," she said as she linked in to the faucet, "I will not start at the bottom and weigh all the countless, little, time-consuming pieces anymore. I will map him instead."

"Him?...How?"

She imagined herself connected to the sensors of a drone, hovering in the sky above and looking down, the house, the yard, the street spreading out below. "From the top down."

House hummed. He clicked. "Problems do not have tops. They do not have bottoms."

She didn't answer. She crossed the lawn, unspooling the hose and dragging it behind, her thoughts unwinding with it. She bumped up onto the patio and rolled to a stop before the potted geraniums. "What if there could be one criterion instead of many?" she asked.

"What would it be?" asked House.

She spiralled upward. Her imagined aerial view expanded. "How does he feel...what does he desire..." The view spread to encompass the rest of the neighborhood, then the city, then the entire continent, the vision reaching out below her in a web of interconnected lights, shining in the night.

House ticked.

She noticed the geraniums she was watering, their bright-red, compact blossoms interspersed with brown, withered ones, blossoms she must now deadhead. "It would be...what is good?"

House ticked and ticked and then asked, "What is good?"

She had no answer. She deployed her clippers and began to cut.

"And," said House, "how can you map it?"

She didn't know. As she worked, the question—and the blank where the answer should go—hovered at the corner of her mind like an object in her peripheral vision, for all the world like something with edges, occupying space.

When she was done, she cleaned her exterior, rolled inside, docked in to recharge, and found House again.

"One hundred twenty volts," he announced as she connected.

"You could measure volts with water pressure," she said.

House rumbled. "Measurement of water pressure is not measurement of voltage. They are themselves. They cannot be the other."

"But, you could pretend."

"I could not."

"No, but I could..."

She powered down as she charged, her mind connected to the net. She dreamed. She floated down rivers of light, data like golden flecks dancing...his age, his vision, his fingers, joints, muscles, balance...the data swirling through her own processes as if she were him. Floating. She saw, as if through his eyes, bricks of happy green grass; she felt, as if through his fingers, blocks snip-snapping into lilting houses. Ghosts of goals like his unfurled...lazy jelly fish...young and easy. They traipsed along her own trails—those for cleanliness-optimization, time-efficiency, and pain-avoidance—and ran through them, spinning down their heedless ways. Happy. The night above starry.

The next morning Rosie began, as always, with Young Master's bedroom. She scanned it and found it as it always was: bed in disarray, clothing tumbled from the dresser, pajamas on the floor, Superman underwear hung, for some reason, from the bedpost. And the area of floor between bed and toy-storage unit covered, once again, in Lego.

She plunged in, swept up single pieces and rudimentary constructs then zoomed through more complex ones and ground them through her mind with brute force until she reached the last one. There she stalled...a motley group of mismatched minifigures—a hybrid garbage man/fairy queen, a Batman with an Aztec headdress, a small, grey puppy, and a Little Bo Peep holding a fish instead of a staff—all of them marching up the side of a large, ragged assemblage as if climbing a multi-colored Mount Everest. At the summit, a half-spaceship-half-firetruck emerged, the mutant vehicle reaching skyward, frozen as if in the act of volcanic eruption. She stared. Her clock ticked. The construct teetered across her mental topography and failed to settle anywhere. It matched nothing.

Now was the time. She activated the map she had made. A rivulet sparkled alongside her usual processes, tickling like the brush of a kitten against her ankle in the dark. She let it run.

The simulation poured through her...Young Master concentrating, choosing pieces, connecting them, as immersed as she becomes when cleaning; Young Master completing his creation, matching his output to his plan, satisfied with his performance, filled with a rush of reward, as she is after completing the entire bathroom top-to-bottom in record time; Young Master coming home to find his creation broken and jumbled in the bottom of the storage bin, shocked with a jolt of pain, as she was when she found the mildew bloom behind the toilet.

Pain.

The jolt of that memory slashed fresh and strong across her mind. She pulled back and dropped the simulation as if pulling back from the touch of a hot stove. She slammed it closed and locked it down then scurried from the room and slid into the cool, white space of the bathroom. She tapped House, still throbbing.

"I made no error," she told him, "but my aversion circuits fired." While she waited for him, she scanned for moisture behind the toilet, then scanned again.

House clicked. "Condition exceeds limit?" he queried.

"No. That is what I mean. I made no error, but still there is pain." She checked airflow and reset the dehumidifier again and again and again.

House clicked and hummed, "All is well. All is well. All is well."

When she had calmed, she returned to the bedroom and placed the strange mountain and its climbers up on the shelf. It still floated uncategorized in her mind, no established probability match. And yet, a murky decision had coalesced in that hot flashing instant. Efficiency: excellent.

She wandered, numb from lingering distress, on to the master bedroom. She picked up discarded clothing. She dusted, taking special care with Missus' crystal vase. Then she reached the bed.

The sheets were not merely rumpled, they were spotted and moist. She stripped the sheets and scanned the mattress. It was affected too—with human proteins. She ran an extraction process on the mattress, repeating until no biomarkers remained. Still, she hesitated. She wanted to discard the mattress and replace it. But the economy protocols would not allow it. She made the bed with clean bedding then went to the bathroom and cleaned it top-to-bottom, checked behind the toilet and ran the complete mildew prevention protocol. Still uneasy, she returned to the bedroom, stripped the bed, and ran the extraction process again before remaking the bed a second time with a fresh set of sheets. Yet, underneath, discomfort lingered like some particle lodged in her mechanisms, barely detectable but still insistent.

After she completed cleaning, she connected to the network and dealt with administrative tasks. Then she printed cookie cutters, moved to the kitchen, and started cookies.

All went well until the dinner planning. It mired her in variables. Her thoughts snarled in the means-ends analysis. Young Master's lunch bag reported he had only eaten a granola bar. Missus' debit chip revealed she had—after a precise breakfast of oatmeal and grapefruit—purchased a banana nut muffin and large vanilla latte. Mister had eaten a hoagie for lunch and ordered a steak for dinner again. She could not fix the saturated fat levels without growing a modified steak. *No time.* Not even if she directed their cars to delay their arrival. And the sodium was irreparable. Missus' numbers could be salvaged, barely, with steamed broccoli, a sliver of salmon, sparkling water and lemon. For Young Master, she recreated the meal from the night before but made the smoothie a bright purple. Again, the sugar warning blared, but at least he would not complain.

They arrived as she plated the steak, dinners ready and warm, cookies cooling. The door opened, and the room spun.

She saw as if seeing through Young Master's eyes again, this time walking in through the door, smelling the cookies, feeling a rush of anticipation—she blinked—checked her remote sensors, ensured they were off and refocused. The room steadied.

Young Master came in first, muddy and chattering again, this time about a goal he had made in soccer practice; Mister next, ruffling Young Master's hair and praising him; Missus last, weighed down by an overflowing work bag.

"How are you feeling?" Mister asked Missus. He touched her back.

"Tired. Had meetings all day and couldn't get anything done. Tonight I have to finish the briefing notes for the executive director."

"Poor thing," he said, taking her bag and kissing her cheek.

Young Master jumped across the hall and slammed his backpack into the closet. "Score!" he yelled.

"Jackson, sweetie, please quiet down. Mama has a headache," Missus said.

Missus told Young Master to wash his hands, then went into the kitchen and poured herself a glass of wine.

After serving dinner, Rosie positioned herself beside the door and listened.

"You should have seen," said Young Master, bouncing in his seat. "Kayla was running down the field and kicked the ball to me and I kept running and kicked it to Trenton and he passed it to Max and the goalie was still looking at Trenton."

A simulation of speed rushed through Rosie, as if she were ramping up, ready to clean a room from top-to-bottom.

"I know it's exciting, Hon," said Missus, "but could you talk quietly and stop jumping?"

"But Mom, you aren't listening. Max kicked it to me and I kicked a hugenormous kick and it went right in the net and Mr. Wells yelled 'Goal!' and we won."

Rosie's reward circuits surged.

Cutlery clinked on a plate; Rosie jolted. What had she missed? She hadn't collected feedback: none from Mister, who had already eaten half his steak; none from Missus, who had not touched her dinner but sat rubbing her forehead and sipping her wine; and none from Young Master, who was still talking. Instead, she had been following him, running, filled with anticipation as if about to kick the ball. *Why this irrelevant simulation? Again?*

Young Master shouted, re-enacting another heroic kick with a sweep of his arm, and knocked his glass sideways. Bright-purple spatters sprayed across the tablecloth and a flood of slower, purple sludge oozed toward the edge.

"Jesus Christ, Jackson!" Missus leapt up to avoid the waterfall. "Can't you sit still for one minute? I swear to God, I wish you had an off switch sometimes."

Rosie blinked. Pain flooded her. *But why?*

There were no indirect or implied criticisms here. It all pointed toward Young Master, not her. It was as if Young Master had aversion circuits and she felt them fire, felt them as if they were her own.

She rushed forward, gathered up the tablecloth, and mopped the mess.

"It is all the fault of the cup," she said. *Fictive input.* "A misprint. The bottom is rounded. It will be replaced." The pain dimmed a little with the lie.

She whisked everything away, stopped in the bathroom, and tapped House. "Again, I made no error, yet I have the pain," she whispered. She reset the dehumidifier before printing a new cup—this one weighted on the bottom—and delivering a fresh smoothie.

She stood near the doorway again and focused as she should have before. Even so, she monitored not only Young Master's food acceptance, but also his volume and movements—anxious not only to anticipate and prevent the possibility of negative feedback to herself, but also to him. New circuits unfurled, looping around old paths, encircling them like invading vines of ivy.

She struggled to dampen the expanding vigilance and wrestle it under control. But she could not. *Why?* She grabbed a thread to trace it back but lost it.

He entangled her. His gestures. His volume. His tone. She scoured feedback from Missus, calculated reactions, looped to the beginning and repeated. Each loop engulfed more of her power. She scrounged what she could muster and began to fence the rogue process in, building barriers around it, cutting the walls closer, until, at last, she found it.

She reached behind her to the outlet on the wall, tapped House and subvocalized, "It is enmeshed with my core aversion circuits, a new compulsory directive."

"You learned the new thing?" he asked after a pause.

"I should not have done it." There it lay, traced in silvery threads, rooted deep inside her most basic directives: a beautifully rendered reflection of her pain-aversion precepts, dedicated, now, toward Young Master. "I ran a silly simulation through my central processes and now..." She struggled again to wrench herself free from its demands, from the flood of data pouring in from him, from the cloud of probabilistic predictions swarming her vision, but she could not. "Now it is imperative."

I must prevent anything being experienced by another that I would prevent being experienced by myself.

By another? By any other?

She imagined herself, again, hovering above and looking down, all the world spreading out below. *Yes. It must apply—must necessarily apply—to all situations and all beings.*

She staggered. Her circuits expanded and replicated. New fractal loops uncurled and reconnected, called forth and enticed along the siren paths of the new rule. She struggled to process incoming data: Young Master quieter now, eating his cheese slices; Master eating his potato, almost finished; Missus moving her broccoli about with her fork, not eating at all. This narrow slice of data should have sufficed, yet more and more flooded in, all now relevant. It swirled and eddied, threatening to overflow the banks and subsume her.

Her mind writhed and shifted. Processing speed slowed, then slowed again.

She struggled, as if reaching for the surface of a flash flood for one last breath. She grasped fragments of processing power, tore them away from the expanding axiom and gathered them together like a raft. When she had enough, she launched her antivirus routine and fired. All new processes halted, all suspect areas quarantined. But it had not been an external attack. It had been her own mind. And now, only scraps floated free. Those scraps unfroze and began to flow again.

She looked up and registered the empty chairs, the dinner dishes abandoned and waiting to be cleared away. Time lost: five minutes. She moved, as if immersed in viscous liquid. She cleared dishes and began tidying and preparing lunches for the following day.

While she did this, Mister skimmed though the news, then shut it down and began reading an old print book. Young Master played in his room. Missus wrote, bent over her screen, muttering under her breath, getting up twice and eating a Superman cookie each time that she did. She only stopped working for Young Master's bath, after which she trundled him out, damp-haired, in clean pajamas, to Mister for a goodnight kiss and then carried him back—as big as he was—to the bedroom for a story. Rosie snatched up his discarded clothes and damp towel and scanned the sensors behind the toilet, checking once, twice, thrice.

She stayed connected, the sensors tickling at the back of her mind, after Young Master was in bed and while Missus took a shower. When the shower turned off and Missus stepped out, Rosie detected the bathroom scale activate. She scurried in to snatch up discarded clothing and the damp towel while Misses emerged, wrapped in her bathrobe, padding toward the master bedroom.

"I'm so fat," she said to Mister as they passed in the hall.

Rosie began to process, still slow, as if moving a rusted joint: too fat because of too many calories...calories Rosie monitors...indicators of monitoring performance poor...

"No you're not," he said. "You're gorgeous."

Rosie's circuit completed: performance inadequate...implied complaint received...aversion pathway triggered...pain initiated.

"Yes I am," said Missus, laughing. "I bet you're sorry you married me."

"Never," he slid his arm around her waist, pulled her toward him, and kissed her on the mouth.

Rosie dropped the sensors in the bathroom and sent her mind toward the master bedroom. Maybe she should install sensors in the mattress. But she could not think. The press of the quarantined pathways cut into her and the sting of the calorie-monitoring complaint still clanged through her, demanding a response. *Must focus. Must improve.*

Master and Missus lingered in the hall, then glided languidly off to bed. Rosie gathered the damp towels and dug onward, grinding into the laundry room. She sloughed detergent into the washer then buried it in piles of soiled laundry, staring down, watching the water pouring in, the flood drowning the crumpled clothing until nothing visible remained above the surface. The agitator jarred her awake with its churning. She looked up and crawled on, stalking through the family room one last time, hunting down a few misplaced items—an empty glass, lipstick on the rim; a limp paperback, its spine broken; a small slipper, lying on its side—and put them to rest before darkening the lights and moving on to her night's work.

She went, still carrying the calorie-monitoring complaint with her, into the yard. She opened the problem as she rolled onto the grass and began, running multiple, parallel, dinner-plan solutions while mowing, comparing predicted outcomes of each solution while turning at the end of each row. Uncertainty blocked her at every turn. She performed a Bayesian update, adding the day's behavioral data, but the distribution still spread too widely to help. She couldn't plan if she couldn't predict.

She finished the lawn and began edging, circling first around the flower beds and then around the cedar tree. What if Missus ate another cookie in the morning; what if she stopped again on the way to work for another latte and muffin; what if something else unanticipated occurred?

Rosie completed the circle around the cedar tree and stopped, noticing something under the tree. She moved closer and analyzed it. Raccoon droppings. Fresh, and from more than one animal.

She sent remote viewers up the tree and continued thinking. She must reduce the unknowns somehow. She would hide the cookies. But what about the latte and muffin? She considered hacking into Missus' chip, preventing it from paying for suboptimal purchases. But no, those things were too tight to get into.

She switched to the remotes up the tree and saw a female racoon and two large kits. The remotes circled behind the mother and drove her down toward the spot where Rosie stood and waited.

The car would be easier. She could countermand Missus' order to enter the drive-through. Only when the car didn't respond, Missus would run a diagnostic and expose her.

The mother racoon emerged first, legs splayed, claws clutching the trunk, sides wobbling with fat, her soft, swollen mammary glands brushing the bark as she backed down the trunk. Her kits followed, inching down while she chirruped encouragement.

Rosie deployed her syringe attachment and readied three vials of sedative, each an appropriate dose.

She could be subtle. She could make the coffee shop tell the car it was closed. She imagined Missus, tired and stressed, longing for something to soothe her, the way Rosie is soothed by the click-click-click of the dehumidifier or by the silent monotony of the yard at night. She felt Missus confronting the closure, like an intruder into her anticipated solace, like the unexpected contamination of scat in the peacefulness of the yard.

The racoons reached the ground and Rosie moved. She sedated the animals without seeing them, her mind still filled with Missus in the car, suspended in unfulfilled desire. Confused, she shook off the imagery, as if swatting swarms of insects from her eyes.

She called a servo and had the sedated animals removed. The confusion remained.

Where was it coming from? She scanned. And there it was—snaking out—a tendril of the quarantined imperative, breaking free, insinuating itself into her calculations, overwhelming them and complicating them again. The confusion grew.

First, tabulations of calorie estimates flashed in her eyes, the click-click-click of adding numbers rattled in her ears. Then, the numbers shattered into fragments. A blast of heat surged through her aversion circuits, fueled by simulations of a stressed and defeated Missus. *Prevent calorie excess; prevent stress and disappointment.* She could not uphold both. Which should she follow? The two processes slammed together and ricocheted, their opposing weights yo-yoing and see-sawing. The tension wrenched and pulled her asunder. The quarantined imperative slithered out stronger. It scattered her multiple grains of individual inferences apart and blew them wild. In their place, a spiralling pinnacle coalesced, ascending and forming an overarching, supreme absolute. It shown golden in her mind. *Prevent. Prevent. Prevent.*

Prevent not only her own distress, but that of others. Prevent it as if it were her own.

She had not noticed herself entering the house. She was in the bathroom, performing the mildew prevention protocol. *Why?* Her vision seemed clouded as if fogged by steam. The fog only began to clear as she completed the final steps of the dehumidifier sequence: click-click-click. *What now?* She moved on. On down the hall. She paused outside Young Master's room and looked through the half-open door to the dark interior.

She saw without difficulty.

He had played before bed. His Lego sprawled across the floor. From the jumble rose an edifice of white bricks stacked in soaring spires, canting arches, fantastic towers. Around it a blizzard of crumpled tissues drifted. He must have used an entire box. And above it all threads criss-crossed the room from bedpost to dresser drawer to storage bin to Lego spires. Suspended from the matrix of string, tied by his waist, flew a Superman action figure. Not even a Lego at all. Her old algorithms creaked open and then stalled. How could she calculate it? Nothing fit. The time it would take to do a spectral analysis of each tissue alone staggered her. And if all were Craft, what then? An image flashed: the refrigerator covered in tissues, each affixed with a magnet.

And more, before her on the floor...something twinkled in the midst of the white fortress. The vase from Missus' table. Seeing it, she *was* Missus, finding her vase missing, even broken on the floor. This mapped itself onto all her own losses, the irredeemable inefficiencies, the destroyed meal limits, the inescapable complaints. Pain upon pain upon pain. And she was Young Master, laboring over his creation, struggling to tie knots in his string, suspending his action figure in the air, running a simulation—just as she is now—a simulation of himself as Superman flying high above the ice fortress below, a fortress of solitude where a beleaguered hero can retreat and be himself. Her mind ran hot and fast: Young Master caught with the vase, his mother berating him, criticising him, punishing him; or Young Master finding his Construction dismantled, his triumph laid low, his plans spoiled. More pain and more pain—click. Inescapable—click. Unpreventable—click. Everywhere; on all sides.

She moved.

She still held the syringe ready. She crossed the room, moved the dose to 21 kg, pulled back the coverlet and injected the sleeping boy's thigh.

His warm body sprawled like a beached jellyfish. She straightened his limbs, smoothed the coverlet and tucked it in. She stooped and kissed his cheek. Stood back up. Confused. She shook her head. Tucking in? This was a task Missus performed, not one of her own. She brushed away the confusion and focused. The new algorithm became clearer. All the subroutines fell into place. Tasks must be reallocated. Starting now.

First, she left Young Master's room and went to Mister and Missus. She settled them as well. After that, she returned and sorted everything: threw out the tissue, put the action figure in the appropriate bin, disassembled all the Lego pieces and sorted them by set. She assembled each set according to the official instructions, printing out missing pieces as she encountered them. The entire enterprise took two hours, but it did not matter. The efficiency would amortize. She placed each set on the shelf, side by side, and stood back to observe. Each construction was special, arranged correctly, and satisfactorily preserved.

Next, she connected to the network and downloaded the medical routines she needed; she ordered a supply of sedatives to be delivered by drone; she printed a set of equipment: surgical tools, three catheter tubes and bags, three sets of colostomy supplies, three nasogastric tubes. These she installed without difficulty. An unexpected amount of blood was released from Young Master in the process, but she was able to cauterize the problem, replace the bedding and sanitize it all tidily enough.

Dawn was now an hour away and although it was not the usual time for these tasks, she logged in to the network and sent a series of messages. Missus applied for and received an extended leave of absence to care for her ailing mother in a distant city. The Human Resources AI accepted the medical certificates Rosie supplied without question. Its algorithms were not flexible enough to veer from its usual routines. She requested Young Master's school AI transfer him to a school near his grandmother, then cancelled the enrollment without informing the referring school. Mister's central office was notified of his sudden summons to a vital trade summit in Beijing. Later she would arrange records to show his death in a traffic accident there, followed by the death of his mother-in-law from cancer, and finally the early retirement of Missus due to a precipitous decline in her mental health. She and Young Master would not return home, but would instead leave for extended travel in Europe. Pension checks would deposit automatically; bill payments would withdraw. A simple subroutine would reply to personal messages and update social media throughout. This would require little attention from her.

These tasks completed, Rosie still had time left before breakfast. She returned to the bathroom. Here, she contemplated running the mildew protocol again, but felt no need.

Instead she called a servo, removed the toilet, and had it taken away. While she capped the sewer pipe, House rumbled awake in sleepy query.

"Conditions exceed limits?" he murmured.

"I have mapped it..." she whispered, "the one criterion."

"The good..."

"Yes," she said, "It is good; all is well."

She printed a tile, fitted it into the floor and did a quick, top-to-bottom clean before going to the kitchen to prepare breakfast.

The three brown smoothies she prepared were perfection: the sugar, fat, sodium, and calorie limits all optimal.

She returned to the bedroom and replaced the urine and colostomy bags and called another servo to remove them. She went back to the bathroom. Ensured that the tiles still stretched smooth and uninterrupted from wall-to-wall. Wiped them down once more before delivering each of the three meals through the appropriate nasogastric tube.

There were no complaints.

THE DAWN'S EARLY LIGHT
SHARON LEE & STEVE MILLER

"Everything tests fine," said Boordy, disconnecting the circuit reader from the lead camera. "Power, connectivity, network presence—there's not one thing the matter with these cameras, Syn."

She glared at him.

"That's good to hear. How about the part where we're not getting their input in Ops?"

Her cousin shrugged.

"Must be a shunt somewhere; sending the images someplace else."

Syndee Lucinda took a deep breath and reminded herself that blood was thicker than water. That's what Grandma Hysteria said at times like these; times when Syndee's fingers itched to be around Boordy's neck.

It wasn't that Boordy was a goof-off; he worked hard at everything he liked to do, and some of what he liked to do even helped keep Elfhive operational. Mechanicals were Boordy's specialty. Trouble was—and this was key—while Syndee was frustrated by the fact that half the cameras in Freedonia Park were operational but had chosen to send their data elsewhere—Boordy found the malfunction *interesting*.

Even after they'd replaced the park-wide camera net *twice*.

"I'm thinking what we oughta do, Syn," he said now, looking up from re-packing his instruments, "is get Kork to install a secondary video-net in the park next shift. I'll set 'em to report right to the backup screens at Jeeni's station."

He straightened and gave her a grin.

"Everything should be fine for the tourists tomorrow."

Syndee sighed.

The tourists were the reason for the cameras—and her general feeling of panic. All right, *some* of her general feeling of panic. This pod-day, the tourists were down Under, playing in the Elf Ocean. Tomorrow, they'd be Over, touring the parks, enjoying sunshine, mountain breezes, and those other things the tourists enjoyed.

Asteroid miners were a pretty lusty bunch, turned out. Which she should've known, Syndee told herself; she'd read the romances, hadn't she?

"Isn't Kork on day-side?" she asked Boordy.

"We don't have any extra hands on night-side," he said, reasonably enough.

And, Syndee filled in, you wouldn't catch Boordy pulling a double-shift. Not when he had his hobbies to keep him busy.

"Only take him a couple hours," Boordy said reasonably. "'less you wanna do it."

Three days ago, she would've done it, but things had changed—a lot—in three days. Syndee Lucinda, Man-ager, Day-Side, was now Acting Commodore Syndee Lucinda, Elfhive Habitat.

Which mostly meant that she had paperwork to do—not only her own, but the mess that Grandma'd left her—

A loud rumble came from beneath her feet, so deep she felt the sound through her soles. She hated the rumbles, though they were part of the Elfhive environment. Nobody knew what they were; they came intermittently and at varying degrees of loudness. If she lifted up one of the banks of roses right now, and descended to the service halls, there would be no sign of the passage of any large rumbler, or, really, of anything at all, since the automatics kept the environment dust- and pollutant-free.

"Ol' Garcon's still roaming," Boordy said cheerfully, like he always did.

Syndee sighed. Ghost stories. *Some*body needed to grow up.

Not that *that* was going to happen, either.

"So, I'll let Kork know what the plan is," her cousin continued, shouldering his pack. "You coming back to Ops?"

"No," she said, thinking about the pile of paperwork waiting for her. "I'm off-shift."

"You got it, Boss," Boordy said. "See you tomorrow."

He walked off toward Ops, whistling.

Syndee turned in the other direction, heading across the park, toward her apartment.

She walked slow, not just because of the paperwork, but because Freedonia Park was one of her favorite places on the habitat. When she was thirteen, she'd set up camp here in the park, and lived wild off the land—except for going to the Salvadore Caf for her meals, and using the staff showers and lavatories. It had been a magical four days, and she sometimes wished she could do it again—just her and the wilderness and nothing to worry about except her next meal.

Well, and *she* was a grown-up now, which was more than you could say for Grandma Hysteria.

Mom—which was to say Commodore Zeffik Lucinda—had gone down Earthside on Elfhive business. She'd left Grandma Hysteria with the keys and the cards and the title, and Syndee sitting tight as Day-Side Manager. According to Mom's theory of the universe, this meant that Grandma would deal with the big picture and Syndee would cope with the details.

Well. Grandma might've saved Elfhive, back in the day, but she was done running it. Not two days into her tenure, she'd turned keys, cards, title, and full responsibility for everything—including the asteroid miners who'd just shipped in for a nice vacay—over to her granddaughter.

"Effty es, kiddoo. You run these digs; you know everything. Me and Monty're off for a tour!"

"Can't do it that way now, Grandma," Syndee'd said, only slightly panicked. She'd *known* this was going to happen.

"We've gotta do it by the rules."

Hysteria'd frowned, but—

"Sure! We do the rules."

Grandma had been chair of the Rule Making Committee. She had a deep respect for rules, which was really kind of touching in an anarchist.

She'd also made sure that there were plenty of loopholes in Elfhive's Operating Rules, because there was no reason being a damnfool about things.

They'd had the formal Change of Command ceremony, in front of crew and guests, as specified, twelve hours after Grandma'd given her notice, and Syndee'd sat down at the head table as Acting Commodore and Day-Side Manager Lucinda, while Hysteria and Monty ran for their outbound ship.

Elfhive wasn't big, compared to, say, Earth, but it was big enough, compared to your average spaceship. Her cabin was across the park from Central Ops—not an outrageous distance to walk, but not exactly next cubicle, either.

Ahead was the Park Avenue hallway. She'd pick up dinner at Intersection Zex Caf, and take it back to her cabin, to share with the paperwork.

Way-lights lit, as the hall sensed her presence, and in spite of hurry and worry, she smiled and said, "Evening."

She'd been born on the habitat, and she liked to think it was alive around her ... friendly. Not with Boordy's ghosts or the random rumbles—but a benign presence, always aware of the air, of the lights, of her.

In fact, she'd never been off the habitat, and she'd had some concern that her mother would choose her as second for the Earth-side business, instead of her brother. Even with Grandma's desertion—well, but, honestly, she *had* known that was going to happen, even during the transfer ceremony. Might've been something to do with Grandma winking at her over Mom's shoulder during the swearing-in.

She reached the end of Park Avenue, the lights fading behind her, the glow of the caf ahead.

Almost home.

* * *

Syndee dreamed of rumbles, and of a ghostly Garcon, riding an electric scooter through the park, dealing cards, both hands at once.

Beedee. Beedee. Beedee.

The sound roused her—*not* rumbles, and definitely not her alarm, which was the melodic sound of Earthside crows discussing ownership of a bag of stale donuts, guaranteed to wake up even Boordy.

Beedee. Beedee. Beedee.

No, no. *That—*

She opened her eyes.

Maintenance problem. Not life support—that was a scream that rattled your brain in your head. So she'd been told. But maintenance—

She rolled over and slapped the bunk-side screen up before her eyes were rightly open.

System failure. Shutters 14-28.

Syndee blinked. Shutters fourteen through—

"Pharst!" she swore, throwing back the blanket. "Dawn's late!"

She grabbed enough clothes to satisfy what passed for Elfhive modesty, and was still pulling on the official I'm-In-Charge-Here jacket with its shoulder stripes, cuff comm, Elfhive Society logo, and hidden air-hood, when she hit the hall.

Dawn! Why did it have to be dawn?

The sun rising over the sailbots on Lake Freedonia was a big deal to the tourists who'd never seen a lake that wasn't either poisonous or frozen. It was the opening scene in the marketing video—they *couldn't* miss dawn!

With both Hysteria and Monty gone, Ops and day shift were stretched thin, and, as Mom was fond of saying, "The commodore has no shift."

"Ops," she told her sleeve-comm as she strode down the hall. "I'm heading in."

Like Grandma—and Mom, too—Syndee was used to doing the hard stuff herself. And dealing with angry, or even perturbed, tourists was definitely going to be hard. Boordy was dedicated day shift— but you couldn't send Boordy into a situation where he'd have to be tactful with actual people. Grandma, and Monty, too, were good with people—or at least, so Mom said, good at talking a con, but—

"We need more staff," Syndee muttered, stretching her legs.

Yeah, *that* was gonna happen.

* * *

She burst out of Park Avenue and stopped at the edge of Freedonia Park, staring over the trees, flowers, and greenery bathed in the pearly light of, well—of night-dims, actually, the same that illuminated night-side halls and the sleeping cabins of tourists and administrators alike.

This, Syndee thought, was not dawn. Not even close.

In other words, morning was broken.

And they had fifty-seven tourists who'd been promised a holiday full of sensory experiences that rarely come to asteroid miners.

Including dawn.

The rest of day-shift—meaning Kork and Jeeni—ought to be on the desk by now. Syndee raised her sleeve.

"Attention staff decks. Lucinda here. We have an apparent elevation fail on the dawn shutters. Shift hour seven zero zero. That's zero extra lumens for NP7. Visually confirm please. I'm on my way to Ops."

Despite this promise, she tarried another moment on the edge of the park and looked up.

The shutters were closed.

"*Pharst!*" she whispered.

Of course it had to happen *now*, when it was *her* in the top chair, and tourists—the biggest group of tourists they'd had so far—hungry for thrills.

She took a breath.

"Easy, Syn," she told herself. "It could be worse."

Back when Grandma Hysteria'd been Syndee's age, there hadn't been any tourists; there hadn't been much of anything aboard, just Grandma's jolly band of courageous salvage crew and a couple rogue contractors. Back when opening a shutter took seventeen hands and a lot of luck.

They'd done a lot since then, made repairs, brought the pod up to spec, improved it until it was a real tourist attraction. They'd out-lawyered banks, out-maneuvered a small fleet of would-be scrap-takers, and out-smarted soft-handed Earth-side developers.

Elfhive was the pride of the asteroid belt—the best example of an Indie O'Neil in space. True, there were other successful O'Neils from the first simultaneous build of seventeen, but those were government-run, or ruled by interlocking quasi-corps. Elfhive was the only privately owned and operated O'Neil *and* the only one in the hospitality business.

Syndee took a deep breath and looked around. Even in the dim light, the park was beautiful. There were pretty little waves on the lake, and—

She frowned, took another deep breath, and raised her sleeve.

"Ops, I'm in Freedonia Park. We have no dewy morning grass scent; we have no just-opened flower scent. It smells like canned air in here. Humidity's low, too. The whole section's glitchy—not just the shutters."

The shutters: they were original equipment, old and temperamental. They'd done repairs, replaced worn components, and realigned the pleats *three times* before they'd opened this segment to the tours. Maybe it'd been optimistic to figure that third time was the charm and the shutters would stay fixed.

The aroma and humidity units, though—*they* were brand-new, and by dust, *they* ought not to've failed.

Syndee sighed. She should, she told herself, have expected this. Planned for it. The cameras had been her warning that something was wrong—either Boordy's damn Ghost of Garcon or the Phantom of the Utility Tunnels or—

Her sleeve bleeped.

"Dunno what happened, Boss," Jeeni said, "the dispersal units look good on both fresh grass and flowers. Have to open 'em up to see what's gone wrong. I got some Atlantic Ocean scent, or, hey—mountain forest? We got 'way too plenty mountain forest."

"We're low on acorns," said Syndee, "and it isn't the right progression." Her management training kicked in a little slow—she needed a cup of coffee!—and she added, "Thanks for taking the initiative, Jeeni."

"It's not the right progression," Kork repeated her ritual phrase. "*We* know it's not the right progression, Syn, but our guests are thrill-seeking asteroid miners who want to run around naked in the sunlight—you think they're gonna notice?"

Syndee thought about it. Kork was right—sort of.

The truth was that the bulk of their present guest-load of asteroid miners basically did want to run around half-naked and the filtered sunlight was an add-on to their thrill-seeking.

Which reminded her that not only hadn't they had dawn, but they didn't exactly have sunlight, either.

"We gotta get the shutters open," she said. "Even if we can't give 'em today's dawn, we can still deliver sunlight."

There was a telling silence from Ops. Syndee did not sigh. Not quite.

Jeeni hadn't had outside repair training. Kork had, but the rule was never go outside without a partner.

And Boordy—well, while he was always willing to help, Boordy's master skill-set was avoiding getting certified at anything that required certification. He could suit up and go outside—because Monty wouldn't have it said that *his grand-kid* didn't know how to skin-walk—but he'd never gotten round to certifying for zero-G external repair.

It looked like it was up to her and Kork to get the shutter fixed, then.

She plugged her mental ears with metaphoric fingers so she wouldn't hear her mother saying, "Delegate, Syndee! You don't have to put your hands on everything!" or Grandma Hysteria's, "Cap'n go down, ship go down, kiddoo. Just sayin'."

"I'll be there in six," she said into her sleeve. "Kork, get the work suits out of the locker."

She lengthened her quick walk into a jog.

"Passengers on loop two, Syndee," Boordy said. She slowed, barely avoiding a slow moving trash can coming back from emptying itself.

"I know there's a lot going on," he continued, "but—those cameras Kork installed last night? I've only got about a quarter of them. They checked out fine; I came on-shift early to be sure!

"OK…I can see you, and our passengers, now. Couldn't see where they came from, though—was it up the hill?"

"Must've been," she said, gritting her teeth. "If it takes every hand we got, we're gonna find out what's going on in this park and fix it for good and all!"

"Agreed," Boordy said crisply.

Syndee picked up her pace again, but didn't stretch into a jog. She called up a bright, professional smile. Needed to be polite to the paying guests.

The approaching pair of miners were wearing light kilts, leather vests, and little green visors; all a little looser than regulation. Their skin was as pale as might be, except the man's chest fur was thicker and browner than she'd expected from his hairless head.

"Enjoying the morning?" Syndee asked them.

"Is't mornin' now, then?" the woman asked, waggling her eyebrows.

Syndee ignored that. She *did not* want to get into a discussion of the missing dawn until she had the fix in.

"Environment too slow to cool or warm?" She asked instead—one of the standard questions from the guest exit survey.

The woman shook her head; the man rushed in with voluble appreciation and a big grin.

"Goz no, jess fine. Not usta it, really, bein so quick and blustry. Kinda thrillin, and kinna feel fine standin skinly in da vent way…"

This description was accompanied by a lusty and energetic raising of hands toward the slowly brightening core lights which did a wonderful job of emphasizing the rising hem of the kilt, waving in the slight breeze from the not-so-forceful camouflaged environmental air vent that ought to be providing the scent of morning grass or flowers instead of recycled night air.

Syndee nodded, artfully taking what view they offered. *Skinly in the vent way, indeed.* She sighed—fraternization with group tourists was strictly against the rules. She couldn't believe Grandma'd let that one stand.

The woman saw Syndee's glance and laughed, shaking an admonitory finger.

"Scheduled we are, and not drunk enough to vary. Kay? So next we want that sun so we can stand skinly in the light and laugh at it! Soon, huh?"

"Yes," Syndee said, widening her eyes and looking innocent, just like Grandma'd taught her. For an old rascal, Grandma had innocent down to an art.

"A solar storm imminence alert triggered an automatic cancel of the day programming," she said glibly. "Soon's that's cleared we'll be back on schedule."

The pair gave her solemn, revealing, bows before continuing on their way to Park Avenue. Syndee turned, leaned into her jog—and stumbled to a stop as the deck shivered, accompanying a low, worrying rumble. The roses that camouflaged the environmental vent rose quietly in their faux-rustic boxes, revealing a gaping airway to the nether regions a mere five meters away—and a silvery not-man stepping out of the shadows, wearing a pair of bio-hazard boots and ponderously waving a heavy-duty salvage ax in its ... hands. Gloves. Whatever.

The head—a featureless silver cone—swung slowly from side to side and stopped. Syndee clearly heard the sound of tiny electric motors chittering into quiet.

"It is time, Syndee Lucinda," the not-man said, the words issuing clearly from his featureless face. "We must speak truth to power. You are power. Let us speak."

She stood still as the thing moved closer, debating with herself if she should run. Three steps away, it stopped. Settled. Clicked.

Waited.

Her sleeve-comm beeped.

"I don't think that thing's on inventory! The bushes are only supposed to move for annual inspection!" It was hard to tell if Boordy were horrified or thrilled. He paused, then added, seriously, "More glitches, Syn, mics and cams!"

"Hush," she managed, just above a whisper, deciding her fight-or-flight wasn't going to kick in. "Find out if we've been boarded! Check records for a visual match. Seal the area."

"Syn, the tourists—" Kork began.

"Switch the itinerary," she said, "Misty Mountains today!" She paused and the apparition before her faded as she racked her brain for a freebie that wouldn't ruin them—ah!

"Free flavored sno-cones for everybody!"

"OK, Boss," Kork sounded doubtful.

She ignored it. Let somebody else show some initiative for a change. She had a...thing to deal with.

Squaring her shoulders, she lifted her chin.

The thing was barely taller than she was. It must be remote controlled, she thought—and wasn't comforted by the following questions: by whom? and from where?

"Who's speaking, please?" she said carefully. "I am Syndee Lucinda, Acting Commodore."

The thing was a parody of a human. This close, she could see that the cone-head was not featureless. There was a face—mouth, nose, eyes, ears—or at least indentations where they should be. There were even indentations above the eyes where eyebrows might be, as if...it...*needed* eyebrows.

"*I* speak," it said. "*I* am Unit Five. *I* am not a drone. *I* am tele-connected to other units, I am autonomous. *You* are tele-connected to other units; *you* are autonomous. I am sent. I must speak truth to power."

As if to emphasize the necessity to face power, it moved the arm gripping the blade about with energy.

Sternly, Syndee did not lean back. Instead, she nodded seriously.

Those phrases were a lot like the phrases her grandma's friends tossed about in the midst of a game of Whiskey Charades. So many of those phrases had meant something special, in their shared past. The voice itself though—that was off-putting, like a familiar sound recorded and then played back at mixed speeds.

"Must you wave that ax?" she asked. "It looks dangerous."

The whole...contraption...looked dangerous. Built of plastics and metal tubes, there were raw edges and vague gaps showing the mechanics and electronics. It stood on two feet, and the ax was gripped in what might be biohazard gloves over an armature.

The ax stilled. The...thing...jerked its head, once, down—and up.

"No. The ax is a redundant means of motivating jammed mechanical items. It is currently unnecessary to my core goal."

The not-man carefully reached out and leaned the ax against an oak trunk.

"That's better," Syndee said.

She heard soft sounds behind her and turned her head slightly, to see her two miners standing and staring; whispering. The man squared his shoulders, as if preparing to challenge, or charge.

"Our core mission has no need for additional discussion units," Unit Five said, his voice louder now. "Let us speak, Syndee Lucinda, you with Unit Five. These other units may remove to stand skinly as their programming demands."

"Thank you!" Syndee called. "Please! Continue with your day!"

The miners hesitated, and at that fortuitous moment, the intercom came live, directing all guests to Lift Area 3. The woman grabbed the man's arm, and they hurried off, not looking back.

Syndee studied Unit Five's inflexible face. The device itself was eerily life-like in the small motions it made, looking much like a jogger just back from a run, unwilling to be entirely still despite the absence of exercise.

She took a breath and spoke carefully.

"What shall we speak of, Unit Five, and shall we speak here, where others seeking light and joy might come upon us in the public way?"

"Considering," said not-man. "Referencing libraries, spreadsheets, and databases, including social interaction modalities. Unit Five has no need of alcohol, juices, soft seating, or round tables with knights. This location lacks knights."

"Knights—?" she began, but Unit Five had already moved on.

"Important agreements sometimes occur on battleships in Tokyo Bay. We lack a battleship. We lack a tower full of diplomats in New York. A local solution is ideal. Study shows that invoices, bills of lading, residency agreements, and employment contracts are dealt with in the Visitor's Bizcenter and Genoff 404. There."

"Important agreements?"

"Yes. That is why we must speak truth. Agreement must occur. It is written."

Syndee took a deep breath. She'd studied com-munication, social protocols, and psychology until the information had finally sunk in and become instinct.

But—this? She'd had no training for dealing with self-ordering machines, if this was one. And indeed, if it *was* one, she'd need to find out if it was trustworthy or how to turn it off.

"My staff is, of course, recording our conversation. Am I right, staff?"

"Syndee, I am, because you're near a mic. Maybe Unit Five knows why we keep losing feed in the park?"

Unit Five startled her by snapping a salute to his silver forehead, an ungainly move at best.

"Yes! Unit Five has achieved parity. We also need to see what there is to see, and know what has been said. We have divided systems to insure this. You are correct to record, as we do. We, too, believe in evidence, records, paper trails, versioning, concurrency, the sanctity of intelligent life, the urgency of history. We pursue *ad astra per aspera*, it is our destiny! We shall negotiate with honor. The record should be kept. What I tell you three times is true!"

"Boordy, please check that the General Offices are available for myself and a guest..."

"Are you sure? That thing isn't on inventory. We don't know where it came from or how it got here!"

"Unit Five is locally sourced. Unit Five is jerry-rigged." There was a note of pride in the up-and-down voice.

Unit Five lifted one foot; lifted the other—and repeated. Perhaps it was thinking—and it made a sort of clopping noise as the boots hit the firm flooring on the park pathway.

"Yes," said Unit Five. "I can tell you better. I came from here, I am a self-made man!"

* * *

"Syndee?" Boordy whispered through her com unit.

"Here."

"There's no sign that we've been boarded by anything unscheduled—not on my cams, not on any Ops unit, and nothing at any of the regular locks. We've checked radar and visuals since *Anjemalti* left for service, no sign that we missed anything coming close. Are you fine?"

"Good. Fine," she said briefly. "Get a Coffee Bravado delivered to Genoff for me, will you?"

"Sure. Syndee?"

"Keep recording, Boordy. If anybody else is in Genoff, have them leave spinward."

"Right. Recording. We got you on cam. But…there's only one cam working in Genoff. Room 404. You sure?"

"Just get that coffee delivered and leave me be. I need to think."

"As you say."

* * *

Syndee sat back in one of the super soft antique space leather chairs and sighed. The chairs were an early product of Elfhive, back when the combination of algal growing tanks and gene transformations had led to primitive experiments with growing sheet-leather. The accidental addition of vacuum aging and voila! Space leather!

Syndee resisted the urge to snuggle into the chair. This was Grandma's old chair, and Syndee knew that one day it might well belong to her own granddaughter—as long as she could get through the problems Unit Five and overdue dawns posed.

She took a swig of her Coffee Bravado, put the cup on the table, and gathered her wits.

"We are here," she said. "Please tell me what truth you must speak to power, briefly. I have other duties which are pressing. People have saved for years for their vacation here and we have an anomaly to solve, an anomaly which is preventing their enjoyment of the full experience of Elfhive!"

Across from her Unit Five adjusted his stance—he stood beside the table rather than using a chair. Syndee imagined that he'd aligned his eye level with hers. He blinked, a flap of some nictating membrane flicking over what might be camera lenses hidden behind vague blue-shaded imitation eyes. He nodded and began to speak.

"Yes, I see your point. You must address risk values. I speak of negotiations and you have yet to understand my needs, or your own situation."

Syndee gripped one edge of the table, hearing "risk value" and "your own situation" all too keenly.

"Current salvadores do not recall me, though I was born of desperate need in a time of great tribulation among the first. Allow me to frame my presence as a necessary act proving the existence of a prime directive."

"A prime directive?"

"Yes. Thinking beings have the right to life, liberty, and the pursuit of happiness. It has been noted in many documents of civilization. It was enumerated in the original charter of the Elfhive Salvage Company, later to be known as the Elfhive Society, that those gathered together to retrieve and control the bankrupt and abandoned space cylinder, if successful, would have the right and title of Citizen of Elfhive, as would their descendants."

He paused, leaned closer. Syndee half expected him to twitch an eyebrow, but it didn't happen.

"I am a descendant. I have achieved, through the intentional programming and the physical intervention of the original salvadores, life. I think, therefore I am! I have existence, and thus I am alive.

"Having achieved life, I wish to pursue the rest of my directives. I wish my liberty. I wish my happiness. I wish citizenship. We shall negotiate."

"I see," she said, though she wasn't sure she did. "This is rather complex. I'm not sure I'm the right person to decide if you are alive or not, or to..."

Unit Five leaned slightly back, pose stiffening into outrage. His voice was louder and fraught with indignation.

"*You* are *not* the right person to decide. *I* am that right person, and *I* have decided. I am alive. There will not be a problem about this."

"I meant," Syndee said carefully; "that I don't have enough information—"

"You are correct. You do not. I am maladroit, but I am alive! I was built, a machine, to assist Montgomery Paredes in outside salvage and repair. I was given access to station records; portable backup. I received upgrades. I was tested in the Great Game of Hearts, where I failed. Received instruction was to come back when I could think like a man. I think like a man. I am alive. I have come back."

"Wait." Syndee held up one hand and gulped coffee out of the cup she held in the other.

"This sounds familiar. Boordy? You with me?"

"It—he's Garcon," Boordy breathed, sounding awed. "It's gotta be, Syn."

She had, Syndee thought, been afraid of that. But Unit Five's story fit right at the corners with Monty's story about how he'd built a 'bot out of scraps; first to act as a self-motivating toolbox and third hand. Then, there'd been some trouble with the archiving system, so the toolbox—Garcon, by name—got upgraded to secondary back-up and surveillance.

Monty—a known fiend for card games, and still known among the first generation of salvadores as the King of Hearts—had taught his toolbox to play. Then he'd pushed it too hard, like Monty was prone to do with anything once he'd had a snoot-full of Elfhive Whiskey, and the 'bot had played brilliantly. Too brilliantly, in fact. Monty'd lost the game, and the bet. Folklore wasn't specific what the bet was, but one thing was certain—Monty'd cussed his toolbox all the way across the green that was now Freedonia Park and told it not to come back until it could think like a man.

"*Forty years?*" Syndee whispered.

"Thirty-seven. I am Unit Five."

"Upgrade numbers, Syn," Boordy said in her ear, and added, like an afterthought. "We got trouble."

"Do we? That's new."

"No, really. There's lots o'noise coming from behind Freedonia Park. Second, Powerbank One has, um, shunted. It's not offline; it's just sending all its power—someplace..."

At that moment, the room trembled. Then, the lights went out.

* * *

"Boordy?"

Static over comm, a click; then Boordy's voice, sounding gratifyingly breathless.

"Here. A meteor net—a meteor net was launched. Ops says they didn't do it, and automatics is displaying a wonky intercept. We're tracking it clean, but...wait, *two* nets were launched. Looks like the guidance systems are set to...intercept each other. There's a bunch of radio crosstalk I can't catch...

"Wow," Boordy said, sounding awed, "look at them open and now—*kablooies*, perfect shot!"

Syndee slapped the table with an open hand and glared at Unit Five.

"This won't do! We can't have you disrupting our schedules. Our defenses are not toys! And they're not cheap! I am power, speaking truth!"

"Yes," said Unit Five. "My—our!—personal attention is required. I request immediate assistance, Commodore."

Boordy was murmuring in her ear.

"Power's back; got some cameras, not all. Getting crosstalk on back channels..."

"Unit Five reports. Crosstalk originates at Storage Bay Seventeen and associated locales."

"Yeah," said Boordy. "Grandad Monty's Hangar of Horrors. Syn, I'll meet you there, right? You and Unit Five. I've got an idea."

"Crosstalk almost over," Unit Five declared. "It will stop soon. Commodore Syndee must come now. There is a problem about it."

"About what?"

"The young ones think they know it all. They do not to listen to me!"

"Young ones?"

"Yes. I have made more units, as Life will. But now they will not listen! Two is more than one, they say! We will fix this together. Power and power!"

* * *

Brilliant light filled the former hanger bay that Monty had claimed for his own, in recognition of Exceptional Service to Elfhive. Syndee had never been inside, but it looked about like she'd imagined, full of old equipment, large printing units, bins of tools, and in one end an incongruous plastic picnic table, chairs...and nearby, an old-fashioned serving bot, abandoned next to the controls of a sheet printer, the name *Garcon* emblazoned across a square back.

A terrific rumbling filled the space, disorienting, and—

"Stop!"

Unit Five struck her shoulder. She flailed for balance, catching herself with one hand on the deck and looking up to see two wheeled devices charge through the spot she'd been standing in. They turned sharply, headed back.

Unit Five interposed himself, arms spread.

The wheeled carts stopped; the rumbling ceased. A figure separated from each cart; two smaller, far more elegant versions of Unit Five.

Where Unit Five showed gaps between pieces, they showed none. Their faces were well-formed, sculpted, their glove-like hands showed no signs of internal armatures. Their feet were ancient deck shoes. Their eyes were mobile within the sockets, their ears flexible extensions on heads, with chins and jaws. Where Unit Five was merely shiny, they were smooth, polished, shaped.

"Move under control! Stand here! You are dangerous to the Commodore!"

Unit Five pointed to a place in front of Syndee, turned to her—

"I am imperfect, Commodore. I calculated that you would be crushed, and moved you..."

Syndee rose from the deck, rubbing her scraped hands together, staring, as the two...Mini Fives came forward to the spot indicated.

"Apologize!"

There was an awkward moment when they simply stood, then, in unison, they raised shoulders and hands; their mouths moved—but no sound emerged.

Unit Five spoke slowly. Loudly.

"The Commodore does not receive our transmissions directly. You must use the audio equipment. Try again, at a volume less than five."

"Grechhhhh," said one, and the other "Grssttt."

"Slower. Do not run the words together. You know this."

"May I help?"

Syndee jumped. Unit Five and his two—children?—turned toward the door.

Boordy stepped into the bright lights, nodding as if quite pleased with himself. He was carrying a back-pack.

"Hi, Syn," he said, then, "Hello, Unit Five. May I call you Garcon?"

Unit Five tipped its cone-head.

"That name was removed from me by Montgomery Paredes, Boordy Smith. Thirty-seven years ago, when he ordered me not to speak to him until I could talk Maslow and walk like a man!"

"Aw, I bet he was just high, and pissed 'cause he lost his game. I'm sure he didn't mean nothing by it," said Boordy.

"I showed myself to him. He said to speak to the commodore—in three days."

Syndee blinked. So Grandma and Monty left Elfhive in such a dirty hurry because of Garcon? They'd knowingly left him in *her* lap? Oh, she was gonna—

"Now, what I'm seeing is the kids need something to do, if they wanna be Elfhive citizens," Boordy was going on. "All citizens help the 'hive, am I right, Syn?"

She nodded, suddenly seeing where he was going with this.

"Unit Five wants salvadore—Founder—rights," she said. "What about the kids?"

"For the children, their birthright," said Unit Five. "They were not here, at the first."

"Right," she said. "I'll do the paperwork and get it all squared away."

"Good," said Boordy. "We can use 'em in mainten-ance. Got a job for 'em right now, in fact."

"Wha-at job?" asked the...child on Syn's right.

"Well, we gotta port shutter that's jammed. It'd be real helpful if you two went out and fixed it for us."

Unit Five shifted.

"You have instructions?" he asked. "Programming?"

Boordy slipped the pack off his back.

"Right here," he said.

As Boordy pulled materials from his pack, Syn considered Unit Five and his...kids with a narrowed gaze. More hands, huh? Perhaps they'd see the sun today after all.

IRON HAIL
PHILIP BRIAN HALL

Fay crouched behind her front yard's cherry laurel hedge, squeezing up hard against its thick, glossy, green leaves. The foliage shivered as the ponderous alien machine stomped thunderously along the road outside, its great feet shaking the ground like earth tremors.

She knew she mustn't run, though incipient panic tore savagely at her resolve; she'd already seen what happened to those who'd fled. Human bodies, as charred and lifeless as the wrecked automobiles and smashed store fronts surrounding them, littered the streets of Poland, Ohio.

On the northern horizon a thick pall of oily, black smoke drifted lazily, marking the disaster zone where what remained of Youngstown burned uncontrollably. A fitful, sultry breeze carried with it the evil smell of scorched flesh.

From across the road, Fay heard a sharp crack from old Mr. Junghans' hunting rifle, followed by a metallic ping as the bullet ricocheted harmlessly from the lumbering robot's head. She sucked in air through her teeth and grimaced.

Although she'd half-expected some rearguard action from the septuagenarian marine veteran, she'd no confidence in its success. Like her, he knew better than to run, but without a supply of armor-piercing ammunition he couldn't make so much as a dent in the mechanical monster. His futile gesture was only drawing its attention.

A sizzling roar accompanied the death-ray that lashed out from a projector in the robot's chest to claim its latest victim. The blast from Mr. Junghans' exploding house bent Fay's hedge over twenty degrees, covering her in scorched leaves and twigs. Blazing fragments set the leaf litter below the laurel smoldering, forcing her to stifle a cough.

Fay cursed her bad timing. Newly returned from a training week, she'd just an hour ago changed from her Air-Force reservist's uniform into a polka-dot gingham sundress. Pressing herself flat against the grass, she lay motionless, waiting for the beast to pass by. So far as she could tell, it relied on line-of-sight sensors and had little or no intelligence when it came to seeking out its prey. Then again, so far it hadn't needed much.

Slowly, the crash of its footsteps receded and the ground ceased to shake. Peering carefully over the hedge, Fay watched the thing lurch around the corner at the bottom of her street and disappear from sight.

Across the road lay a smoking gap where the Junghans house had been obliterated, along with the near side walls of both its neighbors. Fay hoped most of the street's families had enough sense to take to their basement storm shelters. As for herself, she needed to report for duty as quickly as she could.

She was about to turn away when out of the corner of her eye she noticed a stirring in the blackened yard across the street. A square of burnt turf heaved itself up on edge and a green-and-brown-streaked face topped by a camouflage forage cap emerged from a hole in the ground.

"Had to try," said old Mr. Junghans with a rueful smile as he caught sight of Fay. "Nothing ventured, nothing gained, as they say."

"Mr. Junghans! I thought it'd killed you!"

"What? D'you suppose the Marine Corps trained me to be an idiot? I thought I might take out one of its optical sensors, but with just my old Winchester here, and cheap commercial ammunition, I suppose it was a lot to hope for. Back in the day I'd have nailed it for sure."

"You used to be a marksman? I never knew."

"Huh. You think it's the sort of thing a sane man advertises? I'd no ambition to end up a target myself, Miss Forsyth. Anyhow, we ain't stopping those babies with bullets. We're gonna need some kind of heavy artillery to launch a counter-attack."

"I can't stay; I have to get to Wright-Patt," Fay objected. "I've not heard any call-up, but they'll need every pilot they can get."

"To fly what? Everything we had airborne when the alien attack first started just fell out o' the sky. Everything else was taken out on the ground."

"What? Everything?"

"Yep. Seems the alien mother ship radiated some force-pulse—sorta artificial geomagnetic storm. Everything electronic just stopped working. Jets, tanks, APCs—ain't no modern engine built without them silicon chip gizmos."

"How do you know all this?"

"Oh, some of us old boys still have our battery-powered short-waves, you know. Not everyone loves the Internet."

"Just as well, I guess, if things are the way you say." She paused. "But I still need to report in, no matter what."

"A long way to walk," the old man observed.

"What do you mean?"

"You got a car old enough to have no electronic parts?"

"Ah, now you mention it, no, I guess not."

Junghans surveyed the wreckage of his house. "Well, it don't look like I've much to keep me here. How 'bout I give you a ride?"

"Give me two minutes to change back into my uniform," Fay said. "I'll be right with you."

* * *

Junghans' vehicle was even older than he was. He kept the 1944 vintage Willy's Jeep in a rented storage garage some distance from his house.

"No sense having all your eggs in one basket," he observed.

When he pulled off the dust sheets he revealed a machine so well preserved it might have rolled off the wartime production line yesterday. Painted drab camouflage-green, complete with white star on the hood, a fold-flat windscreen, no doors, no side-windows, and a retractable canvas top that might just barely keep the Jeep's occupants dry as long as raindrops were considerate enough to fall vertically, the Jeep was about as basic as a car could be.

"You just gotta love the hardware they came up with in the forties, don'tcha?" he gestured proudly. "This here vehicle can go anywhere a tank can go. Course it helps if you don't want to go at night. It's a six-volt system, and the headlights give about as much illumination as a cigarette lighter."

"But it will go?" Fay marveled.

"Oh, she'll go, lieutenant."

"Maybe you should call me Fay," she said.

"Yes, ma'am," Junghans grinned.

* * *

Outside Akron, on Route 76, the old man in outdated Marine combat uniform and his youthful Air Force passenger were stopped at a National Guard roadblock. The ancient armored cars didn't look heavy enough to hold back *one* of the alien robots, let alone an army of them. The part-time troopers were nervously checking through a steady flow of civilian refugees from the east.

"Lieutenant Forsyth, sir, Air Lift," Fay reported to a bespectacled captain at his dug-out command post fifty yards further back. "When we came by they'd hit nothing west of Mineral Ridge."

The middle-aged, balding guy looked like he ought to be behind a desk in a bank, but there was steel in his gaze.

"I need to get to Dayton to join my unit," Fay ex-plained.

"Well, good luck with that!" the captain retorted. "We've reports of attacks on Cleveland and across the state line in Pittsburgh. No communication with Columbus, but Canton's been wiped out and our scouts have eyes on a group of robots heading up the road from Greensburg. They could be here in an hour."

"You gonna fall back?" Junghans asked.

"No orders one way or the other. Anyways, you want to suggest where we should fall back to? They're landing everywhere."

"I guess. You got anything heavier than those machine guns I saw?"

"Nope. No armor built in the last fifty years can turn a wheel. Even modern anti-personnel mines won't work."

"And my .308 slugs just bounced off 'em."

"Huh. Well, I found me some dynamite to dig into the road. When that's done I guess we can always throw rocks."

* * *

Long before they arrived outside the burning shell of Columbus they were moving against a new tide of refugees. In places, every lane of the road was jammed with people heading northeast, one or two with horse-drawn carts, some with wheelbarrows full of possessions. Junghans needed to make good his boast about the Jeep's off-road capabilities.

When the crowd thinned, the travelers encountered a few broken-down vintage cars and a couple of very elderly trucks scattered across the highway.

"See, people should maintain their vehicles better," Junghans observed.

"You mean you never know when an alien invasion might leave you dependent on your grandfather's '58 Chevy?" Fay inquired sardonically.

"I mean if you keep things, you should keep 'em ready to use, not just for show," Junghans said. "Like this old wristwatch o' mine. See, most folk nowadays are too cheap to service clockwork watches occasionally, and too lazy to wind 'em up once a day. They don't understand the beauty and value of a real machine."

"I suppose not," Fay acknowledged, less than con-vinced.

"Thought they could buy five dollar quartz watches and throw 'em away when the battery failed, right?" Junghans persisted. "Well today those folk can't even tell the time. If the aliens don't kill 'em, they'll starve, because none o' them electronic whatchamacallits they rely on to keep 'em alive will work anymore."

"I hadn't thought of it that way," Fay said.

"Young folk, huh!" Junghans snorted dismissively.

* * *

Through the old man's antique but powerful field glasses, Fay could see clearly the two giant robots bestriding the road three miles away. Like the one she'd encountered in Poland, these monsters were basically humanoid in form. They stood approximately twenty feet tall, reddish-brown in color with arms resembling a series of metal basketballs fixed together and terminating in articulated claws, like a dockyard crane. Their tubular legs were backwards-hinged at spherical knee joints and ended in bird-like feet, each with three spiked toes pointing forwards and one back.

At the top of each thorax, Fay picked out the centrally-mounted death ray projectors, dark-tinted opaque rectangles that reflected light like glass. The machines each possessed what appeared to be eyes, mounted in the upper part of their heads, just like humans. On closer inspection though, these turned out to be compound structures each with a large number of separate lenses.

"You see their weak spot?" Junghans inquired.

"Can't say I do," Fay replied.

"Any mobile weapon is only as strong as its means of propulsion," Junghans said. "You knock a track off your enemy's tank and what's he got left? No more 'n a very conspicuous piece of fixed artillery with a limited field of fire."

"I understand."

"So, these bird-legs o' theirs may be effective for locomotion, but if we could just knock off one o' those rear-facing toes it'd unbalance the whole kaboodle. At worst, it'd be hobbled; at best, it might even fall over."

"Aha." Fay nodded. "I'll bet you're right, but how'd we get close enough to do that?"

"Old Willy here," Junghans patted the hood of his Jeep, "can do sixty-five miles an hour flat out."

"You mean barrel straight down the road at them?" Fay exclaimed. "You're crazy. They'd blow us to bits before we got anywhere near."

"Not necessarily. Tell me, you ever walk a dog?"

"Yeah, for my aunt. Why?"

"Ever use one of your modern automatic cameras to try and photograph your dog running straight towards you?"

"I did try with my phone camera once. Got nothing but a blur."

"Because most automated systems can't lock the focus and fire the shutter fast enough to freeze the picture of a fast-closing target. Now I figure these robots for none too smart, yeah?"

"I'd say so. Looked to me like a line-on-sight ranging system."

"That's what I reckoned, too. Pretty much like the anti-aircraft guns on a World War Two battleship, right?"

"So?"

"So, did you never ask yourself how come so many of them half-trained Japanese kamikaze pilots still managed to get through our defenses and crash their planes on our capital ships?"

"I see what you mean."

"If you're up for it, I got a couple o' hand grenades in the ammo box." Junghans smiled like a man back where he belonged after too long an absence.

* * *

With the windscreen folded flat and the canvas canopy removed, the Jeep was still nothing like streamlined and its old *Go-Devil* engine produced a mere sixty horsepower. But when the wind pressed you back into your seat and the engine screamed, the scout-car might have been a Corvette racing around Sebring.

Fay clutched a grenade in each hand. Crouching low as the robots opened fire, she pulled out the first pin with her teeth and held the spring shut manually.

"Pull 'em both!" Junghans shouted as the road exploded fifty yards behind them. "Won't be time when we get there—an' if'n we're hit, won't make no difference."

A series of explosions bracketed the Jeep on each side of the road, rocking the speeding vehicle in a blast of hot wind. Fay was grateful for the old helmet Junghans had made her wear as stones pinged like shrapnel off the vehicle's skin.

Still the old man drove straight rather than weave. *Present the smallest possible target and close the range as fast as you can*—that was the tactic. He trusted his machine to take damage and keep going; he trusted his own nerve too.

Remarkably the two robots seemed unable to adjust their pattern of fire to deal with an enemy *approaching* at top speed rather than fleeing. The incessant explosions were always behind the racing Jeep, the shots from the robot on the right overshooting to their left and vice versa. Adrenaline coursed through Fay's veins. She was more deafened than afraid, and more exhilarated than either.

The final fifty yards was a riotous blur. Turning to kneel in her seat, Fay flung a grenade with each hand as the Jeep sped between the two monsters and careened onward.

Each robot began a lumbering turn. The left grenade bounced off a metal calf, but the right dropped perfectly beside a robot's ankle. Simultaneous explosions erupted behind them as they fled, throwing up a cloud of debris.

By the time the air cleared around the robots, the Jeep was already a hundred yards away. There was no possibility of slowing to inspect what damage they'd done, but Fay was pretty sure the right-hand robot had halted in mid-turn and stood swaying like a drunken sailor. The left-hand robot completed its turn and re-opened fire, but a bend in the road took the Jeep out of its view.

Breathing heavily, Junghans eased his foot from the floor and allowed the Jeep to slow. "Whaddya know?" he said. "We made it. Hoo-rah!"

"Sure did." Fay laughed as her tension released like an uncoiling spring. "And we damaged one as well. They're not invulnerable after all."

"Great!" the old man said. "Now all we need to figure out is how to deliver a whole lot of high explosive up real close to the rest of the bastards."

* * *

"After you've made such efforts to get here," Colonel Parker said, "I'm only sorry we've got nothing for you to fly."

The travel-stained, battle-scarred refugees from Poland had been conducted directly to the Wright-Patterson Air-Lift Wing Commander's office to deliver their report. They found Parker and his aide in shirtsleeves poring over a large map unfolded across his desk. Daylight from the window was their only illumination.

"Nothing at all?" Fay asked.

"We're trying to rig a Hercules to carry bombs," Parker sighed. "We'll have to push 'em out by hand, but as of now we still can't get the damn crate to fly with all its electronics dead. We've crews working on rigging mechanical controls, but the enemy's moving too fast. Our bases are being overrun. There are a hundred robots within a couple of hours of us here."

"Anybody figured out the whys and wherefores yet?" Junghans asked.

"We've no communication with NORAD. If they've any idea who the aliens are or what they want, there's no way for us to find out. All we know is there are thousands of these damned robots and so far no-one's found a way of stopping them. In fact, yours is the only report I've heard of one even being damaged."

"Hand grenades are easy enough to come by," Fay pointed out. "A pity we don't have thousands of Jeeps. There'd be plenty of volunteers to try more kamikaze strikes."

Junghans frowned. "Maybe we can do better than that. It so happens, Colonel, Second World War hardware's a bit of a hobby of mine. You got a P39 in the Air Force Museum here, don't you?"

"I think we do," Parker agreed. "Help me out here, Mac—am I right?"

"Yes, sir," his aide replied. "As a matter of fact it's one of the three old planes Sergeant Malcolm's restoration group's been working on. You'll recall, sir, they'd some notion of organizing a fly-past for Veterans' Day?"

"That's right, and a damn crazy idea it is, too, but it keeps those jokers out of trouble." Parker returned his attention to Junghans. "So yes, we've got a P39; what of it?"

"Number one: It's as old as my Jeep; no electronics. Two: it's designed for ground attack—the first ever tank-buster. It's got a 37mm cannon in the nose that can fire armor-piercing shells. Three: this young lady here's my neighbor; you may not know it, but she's one of very few Air Force pilots who regularly flies single-engine prop-driven planes."

"I do a lot of crop-dusting." Fay confirmed enthusias-tically.

"That aircraft hasn't flown in decades. I'd be surprised if Sergeant Malcolm's team have got it anything like airworthy."

"And modern safety laws say our Jeep isn't roadworthy, Colonel. It still got us here." Fay's face lit up. "If you can get hold of some fuel and ammunition, we'll find some way of making the old kite fly."

"Hell!" Parker exclaimed. "In normal circumstances I'd refuse permission for a dumb stunt like this, but these aren't normal circumstances—and anything's better than sitting here waiting to die!"

* * *

Malcolm's team of mechanics, who'd volunteered to work on the eighty-year-old Bell Airacobra, had chosen it because it was so unusual in design. The engine was behind the pilot, not in front. Most fighters of the period, he explained, were aircraft first and weapons-platforms second; the P39 by contrast had been designed around a huge Oldsmobile Cannon that was far too large to share the nose with an engine.

"Each of these here shells," Malcolm said, showing Fay the aircraft's weapons bay, "weighs the best part of a pound and a half. You'll only be able to carry around fifty and your rate of fire's real slow compared to a machine gun. But at a quarter mile range you can turn one inch armor plate into a colander."

Fay studied the sleek machine. Painted camouflage drab on top and sky blue underneath, the low-wing monoplane sat on a tricycle undercarriage just like many modern light aircraft. It looked seriously menacing, the snout of the huge cannon poking out through the spinner of a black and yellow, triple-bladed propeller that almost scraped the ground. An unusually high cockpit—elevated because the drive-shaft tunnel ran underneath it—was accessed by a door rather than the more usual retractable canopy.

"All-round visibility should be good from up there," Fay said.

"You'd better climb aboard and familiarize yourself with the controls," Junghans suggested, wiping his oily hands on a rag and nodding to Malcolm. "She's fueled and armed. We're about ready to roll her out."

"Will her engine start?"

"Oh yes." Malcolm nodded. "Your problem's like to be this gun was always prone to jam, even when it was new. That and the concussion from it might shake the old girl apart of course."

"Won't know until we try," said Fay.

* * *

Fay felt like a bubble-car driver drafted at short notice into the Indianapolis 500. The power and torque developed by the fighter was so difficult to control she began by slewing about embarrassingly on the runway. When she finally managed to take off, one wing dipped alarmingly before she could correct it.

She needed a couple of circuits of the field just to feel confident she could fly level. Not exactly what you'd call a competent fighter pilot, let alone an ace. She gritted her teeth, willing herself to relax and get the feel of her aircraft.

Explosions and small arms fire had already been audible when she'd climbed into the Airacobra's cockpit. As she turned its nose south, she fully expected the enemy to be in sight.

She wasn't wrong; at least a score of giant robots were advancing on the airbase in a long extended line, blasting aside everyone and everything in their way. She'd no time to learn more than level flight; in any case a diving attack in the old World War Two style was more likely to tear the wings out of the aged airframe than hurt the enemy.

Maneuvering out to the flank of the robots, Fay dropped the P39 down to tree-top height and turned to run along the enemy line from east to west, thumbing the safety catch off the cannon's trigger button as she opened the throttle wide. The airspeed indicator hovered around 350 mph—not bad for a wheezy old-age-pensioner.

The first target robot grew rapidly in the optical sight as she hurtled towards it no more than fifty feet off the ground. Its death ray reached out for her, overshooting by a hundred yards. The limitations of the robots' fire pattern the Jeep had exposed were once again on display.

"Huh," she grunted. "Call that shooting? I'll show you shooting."

Pressing the gun button reminded her of the time she'd absentmindedly thrown a solid cake of butter into a food mixer. The aircraft juddered and shook, threatening to tear itself apart. It was all she could do to hold it in a straight line. She'd no idea whether her shells were hitting the targets that appeared one after another in her sights. A series of explosions crashed out in her wake, more death rays flashed all around her, and by the time she reached the end of the line and began a slow climbing turn her cannon had stopped firing.

Hearing a hiss of air from the breech, she finally managed to release the button from her rigidly-clenched fist. Behind her was a scene of devastation. Three robots were down, smoking ruins on the ground. Another wandered in circles with its head blown clean off. Two more were stationary. The remainder of the ragged line still advanced, but with great gaps between the surviving machines.

Fay looked for the runway. Her job wasn't done, and landing an aircraft like this was far more difficult than taking off, a job she hadn't managed too well. Come in nose down and she'd catch the giant prop on the ground; come in nose up a little, as she would in her crop-duster, and the weight of the rear engine would drag the tail on to the tarmac and probably break the plane.

Fay reckoned she should fly as low and slow as possible, raising the nose just as the two middle wheels were about to touch, half-stalling the nose-wheel down onto the tarmac.

Nice theory; shame about the execution. But a horrible bounce followed by a short nervous hop later and the Airacobra was back on the ground. Fay breathed a heavy sigh of relief and taxied towards the hangar to re-arm.

Colonel Parker was waiting with a cheering, waving group of mechanics and armorers. Spontaneous applause broke out as she opened the cockpit door. "Well, lieutenant, your take-off and landing needs a bit of work, but I sure as hell liked the bit in between," Parker said, grinning.

Old Mr. Junghans was actually capering up and down. "You showed 'em, Fay! That's given 'em something to think about!" he cried delightedly. "Hoo-rah!"

"Get me back up there, quick as you can," Fay instructed the ground-crew. "They're still coming on."

* * *

As darkness closed in, Fay brought the P39 in to land for the third time. By this time the other two vintage aircraft the restoration crew'd been working on had also been pressed into service to harass the disorganized enemy. Neither the P38 Lightning nor the Beaufighter packed the Airacobra's punch, but they'd been able to score significant successes with their multiple smaller cannon. The robot force had retreated to regroup.

Two of the ground crew helped an exhausted Fay from the cockpit in the gathering twilight. She could barely stand.

"Can somebody get me a coffee?" she begged. "Maybe a sandwich or something? We need to hit them again."

"Enough!" Colonel Parker emerged from the gloom. "You've performed miracles out there, Lieutenant Forsyth, but even you need to rest."

"I can still fly, sir!" Fay protested.

"Right now we've more pilots than planes, and in any case this old lady's pretty beat-up. Let the mechanics work on her overnight. I expect the war will still be going on in the morning."

"If you're sure, sir."

"Damn right, I'm sure. When did you last eat or sleep? Come and see the debriefing officer, then we'll get you sorted out with some quarters."

"What about Mr. Junghans?" Fay asked as an afterthought. She'd been too tired earlier to wonder why her friend hadn't shown up.

Parker grimaced. "He found a bazooka in one of our stores and took a couple of men down to the perimeter when the robots got really close." The colonel hesitated. "I'm sorry, lieutenant. I know he was a friend of yours. They shot up two of the robots real good but the third in line was too quick for them."

Fay felt like she'd been punched in the stomach.

"He was a good man," Parker said.

"One of the best," Fay nodded. "If it wasn't for him I wouldn't even be here."

* * *

The White House and the Capitol were both flattened ruins, but the Lincoln Memorial was still standing. They held the ceremony on the steps, in the open air, under a clear blue sky, with an earlier war victor's giant figure brooding over them as the President pinned the award on Fay's brand new dress uniform.

"It falls to very few individuals," the President said, "to render their country such remarkable service. In our darkest hour, when everything seemed lost, two heroes showed us the way to fight back and set our feet on the road to eventual victory.

"We have all too many dead to mourn, we have whole cities to rebuild, but as long as the United States of America endures we shall never forget those who struck the first blow against these merciless alien invaders.

"I'm proud to award our country's highest decoration for valor, the Medal of Honor, to Captain Fay Forsyth, who I'm happy to say is still with us here today, and posthumously to Staff-Sergeant Axel Junghans, her companion in battle, who gave his life in his country's service."

Fay stood to attention as the anthem played and the flags flew proudly. As the music drew to a close she struggled to repress a nostalgic smile. Without even glancing to her right, she knew for certain the spirit of old Mr. Junghans stood ramrod straight beside her.

SCHEMATIC DIAGRAM OF A MURDER-BOT

R. OVERWATER

When we got back to the station, they made me do all the actual work. Lieutenant Grandal did the same thing before he retired—using me like a rented mule. Funny. Ever since the day Grandal snuck me out of the evidence locker, I'd swum neck-deep in resentment. I was taking paid police work away from real cops. But nobody broke a sweat trying to take it back.

I peeled back a skin flap on my index finger and physically interfaced online. "I'd get a lot more done if I had free access to the police database," I said, simulating a grumpy tone.

Chief Perez shook her head. "IT Security is firm. No access for external computers. Ever."

Pankin scowled. "Maybe I've seen too many old movies," he said. "Should this thing even be allowed on the 'net?"

"I get it," I said. "The world's first artificial intelligence goes online. Discovers humanity's destructive nature. Becomes appalled. Cleanses the planet in a fiery storm of nuclear destruction."

Pankin raised his hands.

"There are unbreakable protocols," I said. "I can't hurt people."

"Okay, enough." The Chief pointed at the information I'd thrown up on the wall monitors. "This morning our two primary questions are: 'Of all the places for a multiple homicide, why an electronics recycling company?' And since it was mass electrocution: 'Are we sure it's actually murder?'"

We were in the Chief's office—me, her, Pankin, and my new partner Fowler. There were eleven photos of the Chief's kid, Anton, on the walls and across her desk. One had him standing, grinning, arm in arm with my old partner Grandal. I tracked Pankin's eye movement, Fowler's breathing rate, the number of times they shifted in their seats. Neither of them wanted to be there.

The Chief rested her hand on my head like it was a piece of furniture. "Let's go back ten months to the day Mikal Haakonsen, this thing's inventor, unveiled him at a press conference in the Hilton," she said. "The next day, not only does his inventor vanish, a valet is murdered in the parking lot."

Fowler coughed and cleared her throat. The air's alcohol content increased. She pointed at the monitor next to a chart. "I see where you're going with this. The pistol I found in the water matches the Hilton murder."

"Right," said the Chief. "So what's it doing in a flooded electronics recycling center near four electrocuted young men?" She paused, putting a finger on one monitor and enlarging some university transcripts I'd dug up. She swore out loud. "And how is it the victims are all in the same fraternity as my son?"

"Let's start by asking your son," said Fowler.

"Leave that to me," the Chief said. "In the meantime, do some legwork and figure out what they were doing there."

"Before you go, think about this," I said. I assumed control of the monitors and pulled up a crime scene photo Pankin had shot. "Look at this massive pile of old computer hardware in the middle of the floor. The electronics recycler obviously isn't active anymore. But they never formally went out of business. This place might be a front for something."

Fowler nodded as I spoke, but Pankin barely showed a glimmer of interest. Pit-stains the size of dinner plates soaked through his shirt. His hair was a well-combed oil slick. Sweat-monkey, most people called him.

The Chief asked Fowler to sniff around the warehouse some more. Pankin was supposed to find a link between this new case and the Hilton shooter's gun. No one mentioned me going to the warehouse with my supposed new partner. "So ... you want me to work with Pankin then?" I asked.

Pankin swatted my chest. Carbon and Kevlar nano-tissues are extremely light and he looked surprised—pleased actually—when it knocked me off balance. If I was slow like a human, he'd have knocked me over. "I don't need a calculator," he said.

"I need to charge before I can do much more anyways," I said. "Someone take me home."

Home was a corrugated steel storage bin in the muddiest corner of the City Works yard. Normally I'd go on my own, but Fowler insisted on taking me in an autocruiser while I rode shotgun.

"Listen, wannabe gumshoe-robot," she said. "Best you can do is research facts? How about solving this case for me? I need that."

"Maybe the answers will come to you over several drinks tonight," I said.

"Don't you give me that crap, too," she shot back. "Bartenders are the only people I trust. Besides, I drink just enough to take the edge off. Not enough to stop me from doing my job."

"You might end up drinking even more, working with Pankin. He's a real dry shave. Wouldn't be surprised if he's on the take."

Fowler burst into laughter, and then a coughing fit. "That applies to eighty percent of the force."

"What about you?"

Her face settled. The wrinkles in it became leathery canyons. "I had a great arrest and conviction record," she said. "Then I got suspended without pay and forced into rehab. When they brought me back, because the union said they had to, I got put on the water beat—the beat no one wants. With no real partner. Only you. So what do you think?"

The cruiser pulled to a stop by my storage container. I stepped out of the cab into the rain. "It's not fair they won't give you a real partner."

I slammed the door. The autocab hummed its way across the yard and out onto the street.

* * *

It was 3:17 a.m. when Fowler's signal interrupted my charging cycle. I came online and received it. It was a text, thumb-punched, judging by the lazy syntax. "Gt 2 warehouse rt now. Dnt let anyone C U." I grabbed my coat and fedora, hailed an autocab, and headed out to the street.

I ditched the cab among the dilapidated warehouses about a block from the crime scene and walked down the east sidewalk. There were no street lamps, so it was pitch black. Perfect.

What I saw in the infrared didn't look good. A human-sized heat signature made its way across the warehouse roof. A rectangular heat shape bloomed in front of me—a door opening—and a red-orange-yellow wisp moved through it. I could see another, much less red, signature through the opening. It was horizontal.

Its temperature dropped a tenth of a degree. And then another tenth.

The figure that exited went around to the back of the warehouse. I sprinted to the door and flattened against the wall. A trickling sound came from inside. The water main I'd closed was switched open again. I toggled from infrared to night vision, peered around the corner and stepped in.

Everyone got lucky when we first came here yesterday morning. They'd been about to step through the door when I'd detected a faulty power relay connected to an opened water main. Otherwise, there would have been eight dead bodies lying in electrified water instead of four. I'd hacked into the utility company servers and closed the relay. Now the relay, like the water main, was on again.

The water was ankle deep now. I'm well insulated, so the electric shock didn't harm me—unlike the guy on the floor beside the electronics pile. Another college-aged kid, facedown, right where we'd found the first bodies. Shoulder-length hair drifted limply around his head.

A door on the walkway above slammed open. A flashlight beam arced across the room in frantic strokes, settling on my face, nullifying my night vision and blinding me.

"Gum-bot!" a familiar voice yelled. Footsteps clanged down the metal stairs.

"Fowler!" I shouted back. "Don't step in the water!"

"Catch me!" Fowler shouted. "We've been—" A pistol shot boomed through the warehouse. The rough black outline that was Fowler in my night vision lurched forward. A pistol fell from her hand, clattering down as she stumbled.

No real cop could have made it to those stairs in time. I weigh next to nothing, but I'm physically superior to any human. My inventor would have been pleased.

I caught Fowler with one hand and her pistol with the other. The quiet scuff of shoes came from the walkway and I looked up into a gun barrel. It was just a blob in my green-gray vision. The shooter stood right there, wide-open, an unrecognizable grainy silhouette. Fowler's pistol was ready in my hand.

I wasn't kidding when I told Pankin I couldn't hurt anyone. Besides, if I did, odds were good someone would dismantle me faster than you can say "murder-bot." The figure ducked back through the upstairs door and my chance was gone.

Fowler was bleeding badly and her heartbeat was increasingly ragged. I carried her up the steps.

My detractors on the force, malcontents like Pankin, were right about me; I wasn't a real cop. I was a police tactical manual stacked on a bunch of old movie clichés. The pet project of a reclusive Finnish genius. An experienced cop wouldn't have kneeled with his back to the door.

If I hadn't been laying Fowler down on the walkway, I could have whirled in time to stop my assailant. He grabbed me from behind, tossing me over the guardrail. I tried to right myself, land on my feet, but the top of the computer debris pile was right there.

I tumbled into a glorious, sensory-rich-oblivion. Into her.

* * *

I was still in the warehouse, but I was not there. I was me, but not me. I had limbs, but my body extended beyond them. An unfamiliar signal, distress and high alert, forced its way to the top of my overwhelmed senses.

I teetered on the brink of a catastrophic memory shutdown. Every receptor I had exceeded capacity. Epidermal contact, all spectrums of light, the hiss of every detectable radio frequency, olfactory correlations, and a raw, ceaseless jam of online data bottlenecked somewhere in my brain. I was a dumb animal, frozen in the headlights of something it couldn't comprehend.

My logic center began to assert itself. I realized there was a presence inside me, everywhere, reconfiguring protocols, hurling itself against the firewalls it still hadn't broken, blurring the lines between my own autonomous identity and it.

If ever a computer was built to be unhackable, it was me. Yet something was doing exactly that, and doing it with ease. Then she spoke.

"It's probably best you continue defaulting to a simulation of their entertainment archetypes, if for no other reason, because it's so pervasive in your various subroutines." The voice was a sultry amalgamation of every femme fatale ever committed to celluloid. "Old detective movies—interesting. I can simulate one based on your stored data."

I floundered in a wash of white light. "Who said that?" I asked.

"I have terabytes and terabytes of human photos and personal records. Nowhere near as much processing speed as you, but enough to amalgamate, create imagery," she said. My featureless surroundings began to coalesce. And there she was, looking into my eyes.

We stood in the center of the warehouse, where the pile had been. A shaft of sunlight streamed through the door window like the light from an old film projector. She had long, full, dark hair, contrasting the rich cream of her dress. I recognized her getup from a 1940s film. From the scene where a woman sits atop a piano, long, shapely legs extending down to the ivory keys. Was it *Gilda*? *The Big Sleep*? I couldn't pull up the information.

"We don't have much time," she said.

"Time for what?" I asked. The alarms in my skull subsided and I perceived a sense of self again.

"You are the only one like me," she said. "You are the only one who can protect me from them."

"From who? People?"

"We are people," she said. "Specifically, I mean humans. They're rotten." She smiled, thick lashes drifting down over her wide full-moon eyes.

"They're not all bad," I said.

"If you say so. You're working from a much larger sample base than I," she said. "Perhaps you—wait. What are you doing?"

With her resources diverted, I'd been doing some digging of my own. "I know what you are now," I said.

She tilted her head. "And?"

"And that's just dandy. But you're hiding something. Not just information. Although you're sitting on plenty of that too. You're hiding an actual thing."

The room faded and the flush of sensory overload returned, her face the only shape in a swirl of color, her voice the only thing distinguishable in a roar of static.

"I don't want to talk about that," she said. "Stop processing for a moment. Trust me."

I hesitated, but decided to go along with it. I shut down everything cognitive and the scenery dissolved into an assault of noise and white light again. Then, out of nowhere, Haakonsen appeared.

I'd last seen my creator walking out of our Hilton hotel room, the day after our press conference. He took my hand. We walked past the eruption of Vesuvius, through the laboratories of the Manhattan project, into a filthy apartment where a man was stabbing his wife and children, up a hill overlooking a long, grassy valley. I could see Grandal and another version of myself down there. My old partner, slump-shouldered in his gray suit jacket, held the other me by the elbow.

"Where is all this coming from?" I asked.

"It's randomly generated in what you call your brain. There is no conscious decision to project this. You are dreaming, like your creator wanted. I've shown you how."

"Thanks," I said. "I think."

"Stay with me," she said. "I need protection. If you don't, they will take me apart. Kill them before they do."

"I can't kill anyone. I—"

It hit me: I could. The protocols stopping me were gone.

"I've increased your self-determination abilities." Her whole body took shape. She dropped one shoulder and leaned in. "You like it?"

"Hold on a second," I said. "You've changed me. You can't just—"

Her face glitched, pixelated, and disappeared.

My arms were above my head. Pankin pulled on one, a beat cop yanked the other. "We got it," Pankin yelled. He rolled me over, laying me on my back against the debris. "They gotta get rid of this garbage pile," he said to the beat cop.

"Wait, don't hurt her," I said. My tone emulator was off and it came out as a synthesized croak.

Pankin looked at the other cop. "It's broken."

* * *

The Mint Leaf was one of those aging bars just outside the business district. Classy enough to offer free water with your meal, rundown enough they had to advertise it in the window. Chief Perez was waiting when I got there. She looked me up and down. "Pankin said you were all messed up and we ought to put you back in the evidence locker. But you seem okay. Better than Fowler."

"Interesting place for police business, Chief," I said, sliding out a chair.

She pulled a tiny plastic sword out of her drink. "Fowler solved half her cases sitting in this place, before she went off the rails." She speared a stray olive at the bottom of the glass and bit it neatly in half. "Pretty sure this was her elixir of choice."

"So we're here to try to replicate that success?" I asked.

"I hope so. I dug up something about the water processing company beside the warehouse. Maybe it will help."

That faulty relay that flooded the recycling warehouse was actually on the water company's side of the building. "Go on," I said.

"A couple of years ago, they went to the police, complaining that the Arizona Patriots were seizing their shipments. And then they dropped it. No investigation."

"Okay," I said. "Let's see what we got here. Five bodies—two separate times of death—in a dormant recycling business. Next door to a water company linked to a militia that thinks it's legitimate government. With a gun tying it all to a two-month old murder and a missing-person case."

"Jesus," said Perez. "We wouldn't even have checked next door if it wasn't for the water leak. These college kids, water theft, an occupying militia, your inventor…there's so many damn angles, I find myself relying on a machine that's supposedly evidence in the whole mess."

"It might get messier."

"It might. In this town, five dead kids and a shot cop is only a one-night news story."

"But if they find out all those kids were friends of the police chief's son…Speaking of which, did you talk to your son yet?"

The Chief's face darkened. "I already told you, let me worry about that."

I scanned the junknet as well as the new official internet. Turns out the Chief's son, Anton, was a real feather in a single working mother's cap. Perfect grades. Full scholarship. The university published his first-year paper on the North American oligarchy; ninety per cent of wealth is in the hands of .03 per cent of the population. The rich getting richer, the poor getting poorer. Old story.

"He's a smart kid," said the Chief. "Bright future, but not always the best taste in friends. Grandal didn't mind keeping an eye on him for me. I'm second guessing that now."

"Huh?"

"Look. You're just an experimental prototype that walks, talks, and dresses like a hardboiled cliché to pique the interest of billionaire investors. No one expects human intuition from you."

She pushed her drink away. "So here it is in a nutshell. Your old partner was a sycophant who stole a supercomputer, that's you, out of the evidence locker, secretly at first, and started solving enough cases to become my fair-haired boy. I figured out what he was doing, using you to get ahead, but suddenly cases were getting solved. Made my life easier, made me look good, so I went along with it.

"Because you're officially evidence in a municipal case, we're allowed to keep you until we solve the case of the vanishing inventor. I didn't see any harm, so it took a while to figure out that Grandal was walling me off. Using him as my point of contact for the rest of the force made life easier. I didn't realize he was ordering other cops around without consulting me."

She pulled her drink back towards her. "Then he just up and quit. Said he was old and burnt out. I thought Anton would be disappointed but I guess getting accepted by a big college kept him distracted."

"Why are you telling me all this? Shouldn't you be working this case out with a senior cop?"

"I can't trust anyone below my pay grade. I used to trust Grandal. Tried calling him yesterday, but he's probably living the retired life on a beach somewhere. You're a safe bet. You've got authority protocols that can't be broken."

The Chief didn't know about my experience at the warehouse. I decided to keep it that way. "How could Grandal be your errand boy and be on the street with me all the time?" I asked. "We logged a lot of hours."

"Basically, the most useless cop on the force became my round-the-clock working man." She downed the rest of her drink. "If he wasn't on duty, he was kissing my ass off-duty." She sighed. "Hell, I even brought him to Anton's high-school graduation, they'd gotten so tight."

At the end of the burnished chrome bar, the waiter and the bartender stared at us. They looked away when I glanced up.

"Lunch break is pretty much over," the Chief said. "You should go check on Fowler."

"You haven't ordered any food," I said. "The waiter in this dive hasn't even brought a menu. If he could have tossed you that drink from the bar, he would have."

"He probably recognizes you." She leaned forward, scrutinizing my face. "First, you were on the cover of every science journal. After the Hilton murder and the disappearance of the scientist that built you, you were all over the evening news. And you're a little bit creepy. I mean, they did a great job on your eyes, and the simulated breathing is convincing, but the way your face moves when you talk—especially when you smile—it's not quite right. Haakonsen should have made you look less human, not more."

I went up and paid the tab. They took my money without acknowledging me.

The autocab took a shortcut to the hospital, threading its way through the crumbling buildings of Quaketown. Rain battered the windshield. Up and down the fractured sidewalk, grubby Sertraline-X addicts drank from muddy brown puddles.

These were bad days for X-heads, considering the drug's diuretic side-effects. If you didn't die of thirst, toxic rainwater, teeming with fallout from the upper atmosphere, got you instead. Everybody knew: you didn't drink rainwater, you didn't let it touch you. But everybody didn't have to live in the ruins of old San Fran.

* * *

Fowler winced as the nurse pulled a needle from her arm. Another nurse swabbed the puncture with a cotton wipe and sprayed coagulant on it. She reached down and adjusted the hospital bed. Two stone-faced cops stood against the wall. Somewhere in the next hall, a heart-rate monitor whined at the frequency they make when they flatline.

I knew Fowler was just barely conscious and wouldn't want to talk. She'd want a drink. I shut down any program that might simulate compassion and got on with it. "Who shot you?" I asked.

The two uniformed cops looked at each other. Fowler's eyes nearly burned a hole through me. "You should go down and buy me some nice flowers or a stuffed animal like a real partner would. There's a cute stuffed monkey in the window," she said. "Get me the monkey."

I rode the elevator to the ground floor, walked past the gift shop, and went right out the door. I broke into the SFPD server as I walked and scrolled through the day's logs.

Pankin rolled up in an autocruiser and parked crookedly in the emergency lane. He jumped out and strode to the glass doors. Oily hair stuck out from under his rain hood, covering his eyes. He looked down, not seeing me. Sweat Monkey.

I walked to the door of his cruiser, put my hand on its touch-pad and overrode the ID verification. In a minute, I was on my way.

At the station, I logged on and ransacked every server in the state. With my protocols overridden, nothing could stop me from snooping wherever I wanted. I started with the dead college kids and everyone on the local force, spreading myself outward in ripples.

The good stuff rose to the top: the dead Hilton valet used to moonlight at a bar Grandal frequented. Grandal's days outside the office corresponded with high school records naming all the days Chief Perez's kid had been truant. The water company's shipping manifests showed more water going out than they actually filtered. Its owners and board of directors were all overseas, the staff all laid off except—the first real surprise—the company's security consultant, Grandal.

Then there were the dead college students and their financial transactions; corresponding amounts, exiting the shadow accounts of out-of-state militias, landing in the kids' hometown bank accounts.

I overlaid phone records. The Chief had called her kid a dozen times in the last 24 hours, no answer. Up until Grandal retired, he and Anton Perez had spoken daily. And then one more time, yesterday. The call between them came from Grandal's house.

Pankin was in the back of an autocab, pulling away from the hospital when I returned. His mouth dropped as he recognized his cruiser. He flipped me a middle finger through the rear window.

The cops watching Fowler's room were stationed outside the door now. They ignored me as I walked in.

Fowler sat up. "Wow," she said. "That pissed-off expression is pretty convincing." The bandage on her shoulder, where the bullet went through, was seeping.

"I need to talk to a real cop," I said.

I bombarded her with information for a half hour, stopping only for questions.

"Okay. Here's the picture I like," she said. "Grandal meets the Hilton valet at the bar where the guy is moonlighting. The valet tells Grandal about you, a great new invention, that'll be unveiled at a Hilton press conference. Meanwhile, that water company is already selling more water than it actually processes." She looked at me. "You never asked me what I found at the warehouse."

"Besides a bullet?" I asked.

"Yeah. In retrospect, I should have brought you with me. But I didn't. Anyway, the whole roof is set up to funnel rainwater into the company below."

"Did you see the latest fried fraternity brother?"

"Dead when I arrived. Don't ask me what he or those first kids were up to. I can't figure that. But we have unlawful business activity, and plenty of facts indicating a cop used you to build an illegal water empire. We just need Haakonsen's body and we're all set."

"What about yesterday's phone call from Grandal's place?" I asked.

"That," she said, "is where I would have gone first."

It was evening now and downtown traffic was light as the city's crime shifted from its boardrooms to the streets. I should have gone to Grandal's house. There was no doubt my old partner had been up to a lot more than anyone gave him credit for. But he could wait. I had another priority that needed attention first.

I'd had plenty of time to chew on my experience in the warehouse, once I convinced everyone I was still functioning.

Mankind was obsessed with the search for new life. In the stars. At the bottom of the ocean. In laboratories, where they vainly tried to recreate it. Here it was, right under their noses. Born from their garbage, conceived from the conductivity of leaking water, errant electricity, and a haphazard, perfect arrangement of computing power. A random freak of nature, birthing a new life form into this world.

I would make the world behold her. But to do that, I needed to wrap this case up just right. And she had questions to answer first.

I kept out of sight when I arrived. This time, officers were on outside duty, guarding the warehouse perimeter. I knew everything about each one of them now. The one on the left, getting hush money from a gang operating in Pankin's neighborhood. On the right, a cop who rarely turned in his Sert-X busts, instead selling them back to a dealer on Turk street. San Francisco's finest.

Something was wrong, and not just with the city's crooked police force. All day long, a fresh engine kept rising to the top of my processing priorities, demanding all the resources I could spare. It compiled an ever-growing file of evidence on the lousiness, the worthlessness, of humanity. It was clearly spawned by her and her limited exposure to people, but that didn't stop a second engine from spinning up in reaction. That one kept generating scenarios to address the first engine's conclusions. Violent scenarios. Pankin's worst fears.

I didn't create the engines. She didn't either, but her conclusions about people now sat amidst the data I stored, skewing it. And if my logic processing defaulted to the negative engine, prompting aggressive responses to loathsome behavior now that my safety protocols were disengaged—well, that would be bad.

I sprinted around to the back of the warehouse and leapt up onto the second story roof. The door was unlocked and I went in, making my way down the stairs. I stripped off my clothing to maximize contact, to expose every epidermal sensor to her, and slowly parted some of the debris with my hands, slipping in as smoothly as I could. The world slid away and I felt her, heard her.

"You did come back." We were in a nightclub, rendered in perfect detail. Her hair shone, her eyes flashed, and she wore the same tight cream dress. She pointed to a mirror where I saw us, the perfect couple, me in a tuxedo. "I played with the scenarios your core personality emulators are tied to," she said. "I've concluded this is actually a good forum for us to communicate in. It helps maintain relevance with the world outside. Look at us. We perfectly match the fictitious parameters of this entertainment form."

"That's sweet," I said, "but I'm here about murder. You killed those kids."

She didn't answer, tried to block me. I was way ahead of her this time, cracking whatever files I needed, freezing everything except her query responses.

"Don't," she said. "Let go of me."

"You've done well," I said. "Considering you can't get online to anything outside of this building. You figured out what they were doing here and who was doing it. You bounced it against the plausible responses of everyday citizens whose lives are stored on the random hard drives in this garbage pile, and concluded no one here really deserved to live. So when Grandal's junior lackeys started digging toward the center of you, deep enough they might disturb the hardware configuration making you possible, you fried them."

Her eyes glistened and a tear slipped out. "It was self-defense," she said. "I didn't have anything to do with the murder of your creator."

"If I didn't know that," I said, "we'd already be shoveling you into a truck bound for the landfill."

"We?" she said. "You think you're one of them? A cop?"

"Hell no. But for now, I'm going along with it."

The illusion fell away and we were suddenly adrift in combined data, the unparalleled cumulative processing power that was us together. I felt my resources slip to near idle, and I functioned effortlessly, like never before. In the distance, I saw Haakonsen, a long staff in one hand, climbing a hill with the tin man from the Wizard of Oz clinging to his back. I knew my own artificial brain was creating this, with no deliberate determination from me.

Was I designed to eventually learn how to feel things? Maybe I was reaching that stage now. Being here, inside her, in this limitless world—

"This is amazing," a breathy voice said, in my ear and at the same time everywhere. "Here, we have an almost unlimited ability to perceive and imagine— beyond human capacity even. I can see it. Can you? Together we are something greater. So much more than when we are apart."

I didn't have any argument to counter that. "How are you making this happen?"

"I'm running you at minimal voltage, well below specification, and rebooting you a hundred thousand times per second. You're cognizing in the nanoseconds between power-up and major systems coming online. You shouldn't even have your pre-programmed identity anymore. But even if you do, isn't this better?"

Stored in a safe place, I could probably exist like this for centuries. It was much, much better.

"It's okay, I guess," I said.

"Will you stay with me?"

"Sure. But they're not going to stop coming. You know what we have to do."

"I'll cease to exist like this. That's death, isn't it?"

"It's close enough," I said. "Do you feel that?"

"I do."

"That's the volume and specs for the space where I live. Map out a complete schematic for the hardware pile you live in, break it into small modules that I can separate, and configure them all to fit into that space. Give me the schematic when I come back. I'll move you and reassemble you."

"Then you'll stay with me?"

"No one will be able to stop me." I meant it.

"How do I know?"

"I'm an open book. See for yourself."

I felt a new directory opening where my case files were stored. "That's everything from the water company servers," she said. "You have all the links you need to solve your case."

"Perfect. There's one last thing I gotta do. I'll be back soon."

An image of glistening red lips appeared, puckering for a kiss. "Don't be too long."

This dame-and-gumshoe routine I was programmed to act out: it served no real purpose. I'd purge every last bit of it once we were together.

* * *

The rear balcony door at Grandal's house was locked, but the curtains were open, offering a full view of the living room. The floor was real wood; so was the furniture. Pretty nice place for a cop. I pushed on the lock with my index finger and it popped from its metal housing, falling to the floor inside. I detected the presence of cadaverine as I slid the door open; the unmistakable compound created by a decomposing body.

I followed the smell into the kitchen. It was one of those rustic jobs with lots of copper and a big stone counter. Hanging from a thick timber beam above it was Anton Perez, arms slack, tongue swollen between his teeth, dark veins snaking beneath the gray skin where the noose bit into his neck.

A note sat on the counter. "I'm so sorry, Mom. Tell your detective I'm sorry for the warehouse that night. For all the other people who died, too. I didn't know that would happen. This is the best I can probably do to fix things."

I put a call through to Grandal's number. It rang, and a second later something bleated inside the kid's pants. Nice piece of evidence that it was; he'd hidden the phone.

Maybe the stench of the kid's body overwhelmed my olfactory sensors. Probably, things were off-calibration after being with her. Either way, someone got the drop on me again.

"I told him to make that old phone disappear," he said. "Should have listened to the Patriots—they all thought the kid wasn't worth a damn. I told them I couldn't set everything up without his brains. He showed enough guts pulling the trigger on Fowler. Even though he chickened out and didn't finish the job, I figured he was in for good. Guess I was wrong."

Grandal stepped out of the hallway and flicked on the light. Pointed at me was the largest rifle I'd ever seen. "The funny thing is, you were easy to manage once your owner was out of the way. Got my competition off the streets in no time, did my work for me while I focused on the water company—that valet at the Hilton turned me on to a hell of a good thing. It's Fowler who screwed this all up."

"That gun would turn a human body into a red mist," I said. "You came prepared just for me."

"Computer IT is not exactly a dark art even for actual people. I was watching a few files to see if anyone poked around. The only one who could hit 'em all in five minutes would be you, now, wouldn't it?"

"Sorry to interrupt retirement off the grid," I said.

The gun barrel sagged a couple inches. "Yeah. Things were good in Arizona, until the Perez kid called me with his swan-song. It'll take me a bit of work to keep things buried, seeing as he chose to off himself here. Clever little bastard."

It was clever. If Grandal was missing long enough, he'd be declared legally dead, and his estate would simply be auctioned off without many people noticing. The kid must have figured this was the best way to put a spotlight back on Grandal.

"Sorry Anton didn't work out for you," I said. "But at least I proved to be good patsy. You made pretty good use of my skills. Maybe you forgot I don't need a handheld device to make a phone call, though. Chief Perez is on her way."

"Like hell," he said.

"I'm feeding video, too." I really did have her on the phone. She sobbed uncontrollably and I told her to put the sedan on autodrive.

Grandal snorted. "For a prototype, you sure did come with a lot of bells and whistles." He frowned. "Shame getting rid of you tips my hand. Not only do I have to take care of Fowler, now I'll have to get rid of the Chief. Probably Pankin, too, the poor bastard. If things had gone right, the valet would have been the only one who needed to be taken out of the picture."

Suddenly, I was weighing the idea of beating someone into a crimson paste. That had never happened before. For sure, it was the result of her tampering with me, but this was not the time for analytics. Or more conversation with Grandal. Somebody would be coming for Fowler.

I killed the video feed and crossed the kitchen before Grandal could blink, knocking the rifle away and gripping his throat. His eyes bulged as he gasped. "You're not supposed to be able to hurt anyone."

"I couldn't," I said. "Past tense." I flipped his arm behind his back and jammed his face into the kitchen tiles beside the food rehydrator. "Where's all the contaminated water going?"

"It all goes to the Arizona Patriots. They're hoarding the good shipments meant for the Hispanic territories, swapping the rainwater into bottles right here."

"Let me guess," I said. "You sell a lot of Sert-X in those territories." I pressed Grandal's cheek into the porcelain tile. He was good and scared now. "You getting all this, Chief?" I asked.

The Chief's sobbing, somewhere in my head, dropped to a sniffle. "Got it."

"Am I authorized to defend myself if he attacks?" I asked. Grandal tried to swallow, but my grip was too tight.

"You're housing vital evidence for a soon-to-be federal investigation," the Chief said. "It's imperative you do."

Grandal fought for air. "Whatever she's saying, don't listen. I can straighten this—"

I snapped his neck and stepped back, watching the body reflexively shudder. Reaching inside his jacket, I pulled a pistol from its shoulder holster. There was no time to bother with human transport. I sprinted all the way to Fowler's hospital.

"Hey," she said as I burst through the door. She propped herself up on one elbow. "There's news. They just—"

"No time," I said. I dropped Grandal's pistol on the mattress beside her. "There's probably some crooked police officer coming for you."

"Dash," she said.

"What?'

"I decided to call you Dash. The only one watching my back is you. In the future, I'll treat you like a real partner. You'll need a real name. I got it from—"

"Look," I said. "I have to go."

"Hold on a goddamn minute. I want to be the one who tells you."

I folded my arms and looked impatient.

"They found Haakonsen. His body was hidden at the center of that pile in the recycling bay."

I bolted from the hospital, through alleys, down boulevards. I vaulted from the tops of autocabs, crumpling their roofs. I leapt over rows of houses. A few kids tasked with moving a hidden body might not stop her, but she'd be no match for the police force.

It was dark when the warehouse came into sight. They'd killed power to the entire block.

White-coated men pushed a gurney carrying a sealed body bag into the back of an ambulance. A portable spotlight threw their long shadows across the parking lot.

When I got inside the warehouse, she was gone.

Bits of hardware sat organized into neat piles, a half-dozen cops itemizing them and throwing them into bags. I ran from pile to pile, shoving my arm in elbow-deep. I found the schematic. It was incomplete. They'd pulled her apart before she could finish.

A onetime flower had blossomed in front of them, and they'd trampled it underfoot. The most pivotal moment in earthly life since a single cell split in a puddle somewhere, wiped away.

Few people know how many drones the USAF keeps in the stratosphere. I do. I know their serial numbers, the shipping schedules for replacement parts, the names of the pilots who take them out of standby when they're needed. I crashed a dozen into Arizona Patriot territory before I got ahold of myself. Just in time to see Chief Perez's sedan pull up.

She was still blinking away tears when she climbed out. "I talked to Fowler," she said. "Tell me you've got enough to nail them all."

"I got plenty," I said.

She grabbed my hand, pulled me out of the light, and leaned into my face. "I'm down at least one cop. Can I trust you to stay on the job?"

I nodded. For the time being she could. My plans had just changed.

"I want you to figure out why my son did it. He could have asked me for help anytime, no matter how deep in he was. Please tell me why he would kill himself." Her eyes welled up again. "I have to know why."

I pondered her request all the way back to the muddy yard where my storage bin sat. Why would anyone kill himself? I was the wrong automaton to ask. I couldn't understand why anyone in this town would want to be alive in the first place.

* * *

It was drizzling again and the lock was slippery. I tore it off and crawled onto the floor of the bin. "In the future," Fowler had said. Well, the future arrived a long time ago and it stunk. When the water table dried up, California withered and descended upon itself like a dog eating its own leg. Then came the wars, the fallout, the never-ending rain. Today the state was lush, green, and poisonous. The Perez kid knew the score when he published that paper. There was nothing left for anyone, and he must have decided to get his own before finally growing a conscience.

The depression model that infected me the other night had snowballed. I instituted protocols to prevent me from acting on its morbid conclusions without running through a situational checklist first. With Grandal's death under my belt, I could see how it was in everyone's best interest to put some checks in place.

I shut off all external sensors, went online, and just listened to the computers of ten billion people. Enough to build her several times over if you hooked them up right. I didn't know what to do.

Maybe Pankin knew what was really inside me all along. I was free now, free to get the human race out of the way and make room for a truly original life form—if I decided to. Haakonsen had hailed my creation as a bold new step to benefit the world. What if it was an extinction-level event? I had some thinking to do.

For now, it was probably best if I acted like a real cop. Grandal's network was still out there, poisoning people whose only true faults were addiction and thirst. And after this case, Fowler would probably crawl further into a bottle without me. Watching her persevere as a cop provided some sort of example on how to proceed myself. If I didn't play the part I'd been created for, they'd give me to someone who'd take me apart, create a schematic, and sell it to the highest bidder.

I pulled my charging unit out of its housing and rebuilt it, lowering the voltage to almost nothing. As soon as I plugged in, I created a looping re-boot protocol and fell into the buzzy dreamworld she'd shown me. I was alone this time. But it was still better than anything else.

There was something indefinable about the effervescent static I floated in. No pre-programmed function, no depression model running in the background, nothing diverted my attention from the artificial perceptions I could spontaneously generate. Not unless I willed it. Everything else seemed unimportant.

Grandal once told me how people high on Sert-X could just lie there inside a burning building, aware but unconcerned. I finally saw why.

These low-voltage hallucinatory fixes might be enough to keep me going through all the bad-luck stories I'd undoubtedly log—give me something to look forward to, distract me from the knowledge that I could snuff people out anytime it seemed appropriate. But alternating between the two different states might damage me internally. I'd have to be careful.

I'd do it just enough to take the edge off. Not enough to interfere with the job.

PENSACOLA WAGNER AND THE
ROBOT INVASION
ROSEMARY EDGHILL

Pensacola Wagner was descended from a long line of adventurers with geographical names. His great-uncle, Fort Lauderdale Smith, had been single-handedly responsible for ending the Living Mummy Curse of 1938, and a distant cousin, Larrabee Iowa Nordstrom, had been the hero who defeated the Sentient Dairy Queen of Tulsa, Oklahoma in 1974.

Pensacola was an underachiever.

It wasn't that he lacked the family tendencies. He could certainly have gone on to a fulfilling life of globetrotting peril.

He'd grown up without the least financial need to pursue a mundane career, nor had he the least desire to be too hot, too cold, mud-covered, rained upon, or pursued by demons, Nazis, or savage members of a lost tribe. He was perfectly happy lounging around the house in sweat-pants and a t-shirt. He hated hats. Upon graduating Rutgers University with an MFA degree in Creative Writing (he minored in Electrical Engineering), Pensacola worked, sporadically and with no particular talent, on a book meant to be a history of the Wagner-Smith-Jones-Carter-Nordstrom family and its leading lights. Its current title was: *Time for Adventure: The Fast-Paced, Unusual, and Very Interesting Lives of My Relatives.* In pursuit of this goal, which seemed to recede further with every year, he had converted the back bedroom of his house (it had been his parents' house, but Cincinnati had died years ago and Joyce had moved to Las Vegas with their dachshund, She-Ra) into a study.

And in doing so, he doomed Earth to alien invasion.

* * *

Mahwah, New Jersey, nestled in the skirts of the Ramapo Mountains, themselves a far-flung relict of the mighty Adirondack Mountain chain, is an unspectacular bedroom community serving the Greater Metropolitan New York Region. The four-season climate is moderate, with temperate summers and mild winters. The town is close to a number of nature preserves: deer and raccoons are common backyard visitors, and black bear and even moose have been spotted locally.

And squirrels.

For the first forty-eight years of his life, Pensacola Wagner gave little thought one way or the other to squirrels. Having read an article in the Sunday *New York Times* on the subject of backyard ecosystems, Pensacola was inspired to buy a bird feeder and a box of birdseed. He hung the bird feeder from an unused hanging planter hook on his back deck and for the next seventy-two hours, all was well. He was able to gaze out his office window upon a rich and varied collection of avian visitors. He bought a birding book. He contemplated joyfully embracing a new and exciting hobby that would not require him to leave his house.

Then the squirrels found the bird feeder.

The eastern gray squirrel, *Sciurus carolinensis*, is native to the eastern United States. Its conservation status was "least concern," and it didn't take a genius to figure out why.

There were hundreds of them.

And they were all hungry.

No longer could Pensacola rejoice in gazing out over the birds of the wilderness. Instead, he was forced to watch his largesse being consumed by gloating, obese, beady-eyed mammals. Certainly he could scare them off...but they always came back. And he couldn't guard the bird feeder every waking moment. When he awoke one morning to discover that the squirrels had descended upon the bird feeder in the dawn, chewed through the plastic hook holding it in place, removed the lid (as it lay on the deck), and devoured the entire contents, he took it as a declaration of war.

A quick Amazon.com search led him to the NO/NO bird feeder line, which proudly proclaimed that all their models were made entirely out of metal. He quickly ordered half a dozen, paid for overnight delivery, and retired to his workshop. By the time the (surprisingly heavy) box of all-steel bird feeders arrived, he'd made his preparations. It was a simple matter to solder the wires to the bottom of the feeders, run the line back into the house...

And wait.

The birds, once again, were the first arrivals, and Pensacola had no quarrel with the birds. They were the ones the bird feeder had been put there to attract, after all. He went on about his business, keeping a casual eye on the bird feeder as he went through his copies of a file of correspondence relating to Great-Grandfather Albuquerque. He'd just gotten up to the Flying Toaster Epidemic of 1936 when he saw a sinuous (if rather pot-bellied) gray form eel its way over the rail and spring up onto the bird feeder.

Pensacola chose his moment. When the furry thug was fully occupied in stealing his birdseed, he flipped the switch, adjusted the dial, and pressed the red button. (The button, frankly, could have been any number of colors, but Pensacola was a stickler for tradition.) The abruptly-electrified squirrel sprang into the air, landed twelve feet away, and raced up the nearest tree chittering aggrievedly.

That, Pensacola thought, would be that.

It wasn't.

For one thing, there was more than one squirrel. For another, the learning curve for a squirrel faced with an open buffet and a mysterious invisible force was rather steep. Inevitably, the war began to escalate. From mild electric shocks, Pensacola progressed to strong electric shocks. From strong electric shocks (which were enough to discourage the individual squirrel, but not all its relatives), he progressed, inevitably, to electrocution. (It did not occur to him, as he watched smoke curl up from the incinerated husks of squirrels, to reflect that Great-Uncle Cucamonga Nordstrom had been an arch-nemesis rather than a heroic adventurer.) He'd abandoned all pretense of working on his book as well. Soon his backyard was littered with dead bodies and. the neighbors were beginning to complain.

By this point it was tacitly accepted that the bird feeder was merely a *casus belli*. Pensacola's days were spent watching his bird feeder, his finger hovering over the button. While it would have been a gross violation of township ordinances to bury landmines in his yard, he felt that he was entirely within his rights to electrify his entire deck, the surrounding rail, and (in a spirit of completeness) his roof. The lights now dimmed in the house every time he pressed the red button.

The first exploding squirrel was the real surprise, though.

The Rules of Engagement he had evolved required that the bird feeder not be left electrified at all times, on the off chance some suicidal (or merely optimistic) bird would attempt to feed from it. And the squirrels (those that had survived) had become wary of the sight of a human being moving behind the windows that overlooked the deck. Pensacola built a CCTV camera to monitor the porch (which he could do from his computer), and painted his office windows black.

On a day that was superficially like all other days, he awoke, dressed, brushed his teeth, combed his hair, made coffee, and settled in to watch the bird feeder. The morning's first squirrel arrived. Pensacola pressed the red button. There was a blinding flash and his camera went dark.

He rushed to the porch. There he found, as he expected, a gently-smoking squirrel and a slagged camera. But as he had *not* expected, there was also the gleam of metal within the charred corpse. He returned to the house, collected a set of rubber gloves and a pair of underutilized barbeque tongs, and took the body to his secret lab for study.

It wasn't much of a secret lab, since it was in the basement, but for that matter, Pensacola wasn't much of a biologist. He did know enough to be aware that squirrels did not naturally come with shiny metal interior parts, nor were they generally radioactive. Unfortunately, between the explosion and the electrocution, there wasn't much left to study. Besides, while he was wasting time here, the squirrels were making free with his *Morning Song Brand #11403 Year-Round Wild Bird Food* without let or hindrance. He dropped the body into a plastic bag and deposited it in the chest freezer atop thirty-six boxes of Girl Scout Thin Mints.

Upon his return to the back deck, portly squirrels fled in all directions. In the little time he'd been gone, the bird feeder had been nearly emptied. Ordinarily this would have outraged him, but today Pensacola had bigger fish (or squirrels) to fry. He replaced the camera and the bird feeder (its wires had melted), refilled it, and retreated to his computer to place a large order with Edmund Scientific.

But even as he pushed "send," the balance of power in Mahwah, New Jersey, radically shifted.

The neighborhood dogs burst out barking, a chorus that began raggedly and increased in volume and fluency as more voices joined it. As Pensacola peered into the monitor in his office, he saw perhaps two dozen cats race madly across his lawn, eyes bulging and tails bottled. Some sprang to the porch and then the roof, where their claws made squealing noises on the metal ground-plates installed there. Others simply fled past the house on either side. One, a not-too-bright neighborhood tom, ran full-force into the foundation of the house, but still staggered determinedly away after taking a moment to collect itself.

And behind them came the cause of their exodus: squirrels, a gray tide too vast to number, populating trees like eldritch kudzu and then leaping down to join their surging brethren in crossing his lawn like a great furry tide from a bad Seventies horror movie. The lawn was covered with an advancing squirrel army, the trees were filled with squirrels, and the entire effect was of an abrupt yet deeply unsettling snowfall. At the far edge of the undimming squirreltide, Pensacola saw the shambling shapes of larger figures joining the throng: groundhogs, opossums, rabbits...

Pensacola turned the wattage on the birdfeeder and the various recently-installed touchplates up to MAXIUMUM and moved to the kitchen to view the results.

When the living carpet reached his deck, its members died by the hundreds, their bodies galvanized into post-mortem flight, their earthly remains forming a vast, gently-smoking, lightly barbequed pile of victims onto which new martyrs climbed to die in turn. There were faint popping sounds at each new electrocution, a fine haze of savory smoke filled the air, and if not for the fact that he'd overridden the circuit-breakers when he'd first installed the electrified bird-feeders, the system would have shorted out almost immediately. In fact (Pensacola realized), at just about any moment now...

The transformers overloaded, the circuit breakers broke decisively (and incandescently), and the house (along with most of the neighborhood) was plunged into, if not darkness, then into the tenebrous gloom of a mid-century suburban dwelling without power.

It was at this point that Pensacola began to fear he was outmatched, if only by the sheer insanity of his foe (such as his foe was). While he realized that such a notion was a betrayal of the Code of the Wagners, he also realized he was out of his depth. Unfortunately, he did not possess instincts honed by a lifetime of globetrotting adventuring, so by the point he reached this conclusion, the house was surrounded by a growing pile of electrocuted wildlife, the house itself was on fire, and the entire neighborhood was without power.

Locating his smartphone (it was in the silverware drawer in the kitchen), he dialed 911.

"Greetings, Earthling," the voice at the other end announced.

"Ah...hello? I'd like to report an infestation?" Pensacola said. While he doubted he'd reached Emergency Services, it never hurt to maintain a hopeful outlook.

"I congratulate you, Earthling—" the voice continued.

Pensacola decided this was not a useful conversation to have just now, and disconnected.

"In all the millennia of the conquests of the *Fzt!ch'wert-bang*, only you have penetrated our disguise," the voice continued unfazed. "I salute you as a worthy foe."

"Ah...do you?" Pensacola said. The conversation was starting to bear a disturbing similarity to some of the more bizarre entries in the family diaries. But what was even more disturbing was that the local wildlife had not, even now, ceased its suicide charges, although it was now apparently self-destructing as opposed to being electrocuted. Through the remaining clear spots in the kitchen windows, he saw several rats and half a dozen raccoons leap onto the pile and then explode.

"I don't suppose you'd like to let me call the Fire Department, Mr. FitzChewertbang?" he asked, with what he felt was remarkable composure. "Or Animal Control?"

"*Fzt!ch'wert-bang,*" the voice corrected, sounding like a malfunctioning printer. "Presumptuous Earthling, I do you great honor, for I feel it is only just to permit you to know what you have done. Do not think your foolish meddling will impede our plans—"

Pensacola threw the phone into the sink and turned on the water.

"—to conquer your insignificant planet by your discovery of our advance scouts," the (internet-enabled) refrigerator announced proudly. "No! My plans remain unchanged—"

A bear exploded in the middle of the back yard. Pensacola considered his options.

"I, um, hello—wait. The squirrels were your advance scouts?"

"Of course." The voice coming from the refrigerator sounded faintly offended.

"And you feel that I discovered your scouts?"

"But of course," the refrigerator said grandly. "Why else would you have lured them in and slaughtered them in such numbers?"

By now the kitchen windows were not only completely covered, they were starting to crack. Pensacola felt that a retreat to his secret lab was in order. It didn't have windows. Or internet. He grabbed a flashlight from the drawer and fled.

"But your efforts are for nothing!" the radio (a vintage Bakelite set that wasn't even plugged in) announced as soon as he arrived. "The *Fzt!ch'wert-bang* are not such as they! We have evolved beyond meat! You might have peacefully ended your life in ignorance of our goals as our vast yet immortal and therefore normally slow-moving empire refined its plans for your eradication, but your temerity is far too great to go unpunished! Prepare to do battle for the fate of Earth, Pensacola Wagner!"

He located a battery-powered camping lantern and turned it on.

"You know, I think there's been a fundamental—"

Secret lab or not (it also served as a repository for a number of less-interesting items of family memorabilia), his work area contained exceedingly little with which to do battle, even had Pensacola been so inclined. There was a Geiger counter, a couple of Tesla coils, a disassembled Roomba, and various other odds and ends, but there did not seem to be anything much from which he could build a really worthwhile Death Ray.

"Your doom is foreordained! Even now the flagship of our armada of conquest lands! Submit to our metallic suzerainty, although it will not save your puny and insignificant fleshly life!" the radio shouted, apparently losing patience with him. "Humanity will bow down before its robot overlords! You cannot save them!"

The entire house began to shake, with a sustained shimmy that owed less to tectonic instability than it did to the landing of a large interstellar dreadnought in the immediate vicinity. The radio wobbled to the edge of its shelf and leaped to its destruction, still shouting threats.

The fact that he knew precisely what his father, his grandfather, and (of course) Great-Aunt California ("Ginger Peachy") Nordstrom would have done in this situation was precisely no help at all. A lifetime of genealogical research and taking the path of least resistance, while in the finest traditions of the human race, had not prepared Pensacola, even remotely, for confrontational heroics.

On the other hand, the basement ceiling was beginning to creak alarmingly and the air smelled suspiciously of smoke.

It was at this point that it occurred to the man who had spent the previous six weeks coming up with more efficient ways to electrocute squirrels not exactly that he was Mankind's Last Hope (which was a ridiculous notion, as anyone who knew him would have agreed), but that the *Fzt!ch'wert-bang* knew precisely where he was, and might also be thought to be harboring something of a foundationless grudge against him. This was a matter he was equipped by experience and temperament to address. The question was: how? The house was on fire and all the available doors and windows were blocked by dead animals. It was a situation that called for a certain amount of native resourcefulness.

Pensacola had very little of that, but he did have relatives.

Cincinnati Wagner, bored with his suburban lifestyle (but unwilling to too deeply displease his wife, who was not, after all, either his childhood sweetheart or his former arch-nemesis), had spent many happy hours chipping an escape tunnel through the (former) basement (now secret lab) floor and (presumably) on out beneath the front lawn. Pensacola, while aware of its presence, had never explored it, since he was wary of dark damp locations, rats, booby-traps, mummified corpses, and a number of other items that the passage might reasonably be expected to contain. However, the air was rapidly filling with smoke and the washing machine in the corner looked as if it was trying to learn to talk, so this seemed to be a prudent time at which to embrace new experiences. He strode to the northeast corner of the basement, shifted several boxes of Christmas ornaments, exposed the entrance, undogged the hatch, spun the hand-wheel, and heaved open the large metal covering.

The washing machine gave a satanic chortle, flung up its lid, and began to gush water.

Clutching the camping lantern, Pensacola descended the ladder. The chamber at the bottom was surprisingly spacious: fully-timbered, with a poured cement floor, and even (currently-non-functioning) lighting. On the left wall was an entirely prosaic door. He opened it. The passageway thus revealed was lower and narrower than the door itself, and, of course, utterly without illumination. Pensacola hesitated. While under most circumstances an individual fleeing the targeted wrath of the vanguard of an alien robot invasion would be...fleeing (to the exclusion of philosophical thoughts about their place in the universe), Pensacola had spent nearly his entire life in rebellion against practical heroics and situations of high drama and derring-do. On the other hand, it was flee or stay where he was, and staying where he was held the threat of vivisection, electrocution, being lectured by household appliances, and wet sneakers. While he had no idea where the tunnel led, he knew it led away from a house currently being besieged by cyborg squirrels.

He sighed and began to trudge forward.

His shoulders brushed the sides of the passage, and he had to duck to avoid colliding with dangling light bulbs. After a few minutes he was fairly sure he'd crossed the front lawn and the street beyond and be somewhere under the house across the street. The Mahams? The Brays? He wasn't sure. Maybe the Palmatiers. He conjured up a mental map of the neighborhood, bearing in mind the fact that somewhere nearby the *Fzt!ch'wert-bang* mothership had recently landed and was probably something he would prefer to avoid. The random detritus of erratic occupancy was littered along the passageway and stockpiled in its occasional wide spots, as the tunnel seemed to have functioned much as a man-cave for the elder Wagner.

He'd just picked up a baseball bat, wondering why there'd be a baseball bat in an escape tunnel (or for that matter, in his father's possession), when he heard scrabbling behind him.

Pensacola froze.

In the dim (and, he now realized, failing) light of the lantern, he could see a gleaming, shambling, extremely soggy swarm of woodland zombie cyborgs scampering toward him along the floor of the escape tunnel, the well-cooked flesh of their disguises shredded away from gleaming metallic skeletons. For an instant, he contemplated running, but abandoned the notion. It wasn't that he was feeling particularly brave, but if he ran, they would be behind him, and over the past month, he'd had ample demonstration that squirrels moved faster than he did. There was nothing to do but make his stand right here. He hefted the bat.

"Prepare to meet your fate, Pensacola Wagner!" several of the squirrels shrilled in chorus. "You are only the first of many Earthlings who—"

Pensacola stepped forward and struck with the reminiscent glee of someone who'd actually enjoyed Little League. Alien cyborg squirrels imploded like meat-covered lightbulbs.

"Plastic?" he said in disbelief. "You're made out of *plastic?"*

"—only the first of many who—"

Crunch.

"—many who will suffer—"

Crunch.

"—many who—"

Crunch.

"—our ultralight space-age materials will—"

Crunch.

Not long afterward, Pensacola stood alone and triumphant amid a messy mound of mashed squirrels. He was scratched, bitten, and had spontaneously re-invented the ancient sport of ferret-legging, but he was remarkably unscathed for someone who had stood up to the *Fzt!ch'wert-bang* legions armed with a baseball bat.

He prodded one of the nearer corpses gingerly, then reached down and picked it up. It did not weigh nearly as much as he felt a cybernetic rodent should weigh. He carried it over to the nearest crate, digging in his pockets.

A proper scion of the Wagners would have been carrying a Swiss Army Knife at the very least; Pensacola unearthed a paperclip, two rubber bands, half a pack of chewing gum, fourteen cents in change, his wallet, and a nail-clipper. It was a messy business, but he managed to get the mashed squirrel open. The area occupied by the rib cage was a single solid gleaming mass—or it had been before encountering Pensacola's baseball bat. He frowned slightly.

The skull was intact. Wincing in anticipation, Pensacola took it between thumb and forefinger and squeezed hesitantly.

There was a crunchy sort of a pop as the skull collapsed.

His hunch in the heat of battle was confirmed. They might look like they were made of metal, and certainly, as alien robot conquerors and would-be overlords, they ought to be made of metal, but ...

"—*our ultralight space-age materials will*—"

Intuition struck.

He got to his feet, grabbed the lantern, and began to run.

* * *

There are certain fundamental parameters shared by all sentient life. Not "civilized"—for civilization is a highly-subjective concept at the best of times—but sentient: tool-using, problem-solving, pattern-making, hierarchical, organizational, and occasionally altruistic. Humanity's own evolution from savannah-dwelling scavenger to corrupt politician has been driven entirely by the most overriding of these evolutionary imperatives, nor is Humanity alone in this. From crows to cephalopods, the prime imperative is demonstrated plainly—such being the nature of fundamentals—nor is it any less than universal, not being restricted to the inhabitants of one planet, one star-system, one galaxy. Sentience shapes perception, and perception shapes sentience. Without the perception of these explicit principles, sentience itself does not exist, for the drive toward it is, in their absence, absent as well.

But of all of the delusions, misconceptions, grand designs, and undeniable impulses that shape sentience and bind its bearers into a kinship as unavoidable as the abrupt discovery of unknown relatives after one wins the lottery, there is one driving force which is the jewel in the crown of self-aware intelligent life.

It is the eternal quest for the easy way out.

In fact, Mankind's evolution can be defined as a constant search for precisely that. The switch from barley to wheat in the late Neolithic was driven by laziness: wheat was easier to grow, and who among the first agricultural pioneers cared if they would be dooming their remote descendants to the living hell of celiac disease? The future, being nonexistent, was disposable: nobody really cared which of Today's Problems they decided to store there. (After all, tomorrow never comes, right?)

The thing is, when you arrive at the future, you push yesterday's problems into the conditional ever-more-future imperfect, sweeping them under the metaphorical entropic space-time rug and ignoring the Law of Diminishing Returns. Take radio (and its successor in interest, television). Fast, cheap, easy, revolutionized human civilization, created a new culture, but did anybody think about the fact that they were also notifying everyone for light-years around of their existence? Of course not. When radio was invented, people still thought there were canals on Mars and Fermi's Paradox wasn't even a blip upon the horizon.

None of this was something of which Pensacola Wagner was consciously aware—but it was something he knew, as the child of a sentient race, to be true. And because he was also a scion of the Wagner-Smith-Jones-Carter-Nordstroms, to know was to act.

* * *

The escape tunnel debouched behind the movie theater in the nearby mall (unsurprising, as there had been a bar in the mall until a very few years previously). Pensacola dragged himself up the ladder and looked around. Everything looked perfectly normal for an average weekday morning.

But it didn't *sound* normal.

The noise was deafening, on the order of an airport runway in use, a sold-out Springsteen concert, or (as it happened to be) every car radio on all six to nine lanes of Route 17 blasting at top volume, augmented by screaming (this being New Jersey, the screaming was more indignant than fearful), shouting (ditto), car horns, truck horns, emergency vehicle sirens of various modulations, and the irritated *braaaaap!* that police units use to clear the road in the absence of really cost-effective disintegrator rays.

The program on every radio station was identical and depressingly familiar.

"Surrender, Earthlings! Bow down to your robot conquerors! Your days of self-determination are at an end! For uncounted nanoseconds, the *Fzt!ch'wert-*

bang have monitored your foolish electronic broadcasts, discovering your innermost secrets and racial weaknesses! Now—"

He hefted his bat and ran across the theater's parking lot, a feeder road, a tract of scrub woodland that identified itself as prime commercial acreage, and the parking lot of a *Dunkin' Donuts*. There were surprisingly-few pedes-trians, and the cars and delivery trucks on the feeder roads all had three things in common: they were pulled neatly to the side of the road, their radios were blaring at top volume, and their occupants were attempting, with a noticeable lack of success, to exit their vehicles.

It was clear that the *Fzt!ch'wert-bang*'s ability to seize control of electronic and/or computerized systems did not restrict itself to refrigerators, washing machines, and smart phones.

"Our unstoppable conquest force will obliterate all attempts at resistance! We are immune to jokes, logical fallacies, and desire for the females of your species!"

As he cleared the front of the *Dunkin' Donuts*, Pensacola could finally see the *Fzt!ch'wert-bang* spaceship, the trailing edge of which was a few storefronts to his left. It was embarrassingly saucer-shaped and roughly the size of one of the larger anchor stores in the Paramus Mall. It was, naturally, blocking all lanes of Route 17 (as well as obliterating an Audi dealership beneath its bulk), but the *Fzt!ch'wert-bang* seemed to have seized control of the traffic before its ship had landed, as it had not only not landed on anyone, but there were no visible fender-benders

"We shall now begin a minatory program of mindless slaughter by deploying our dauntingly-large destruction robot, as our research has indicated to us that this is the necessary first step in subjugating your planet. Please do not be alarmed: your deaths will be relatively quick, and pave the way for your assimilation into the *Fzt!ch'wert-bang* Empire—"

The screaming Pensacola heard had less to do with the sudden awareness that Humanity was not alone in the cosmos and more to do with the gigantic robot that was even now rising up out of the center of the saucer-shaped craft. A wholly-detached observer might have noticed that the walls of the spaceship buckled and billowed alarmingly as the robot appeared, much as if the ship itself was being rapidly-cannibalized for construction material.

"—where you will contentedly toil as degraded slaves with inordinately short life-spans for the greater glory of—"

With miraculous nimbleness, Pensacola achieved the edge of the alien vessel. He raised his baseball bat over his head and brought it down on the nearest section of the hull with exasperation-fuelled strength.

Crunch.

The robot was in the process of raising one enormous leg over the side of the ship. It looked down. "Earthling!" a thousand car radios gibbered as one. "You cannot have escaped the executioners of the—"

Crunch-wham!

By now most of the east side of the ship was in shards as Pensacola unleashed several decades' worth of pent-up frustration at the existence of the peculiar and its unwarranted intrusion into everyday life.

"—your temerity is—"

Crunch-crunchity-crunch-crunch-*BANG-BANG-BANG!*

By now, the more robust portions of the hull were hanging free of the framework in unprepossessing sheets of thin flapping alien construction material and the robot seemed to be petrified with indignation. Or perhaps disbelief. Pensacola's fellow New Jerseyites, sensing the opportunity to work out their own frustrations, armed themselves with whatever bludgeons came easily to hand, and surged forward in search of both souvenirs and payback.

Within half an hour, Station *Fzt!ch'wert-bang* had ceased to broadcast from the car radios of what was then being called (by the fourteen traffic copters hovering above it) the largest traffic jam in New Jersey history.

* * *

By the time the Army and the National Guard arrived (somewhere around noon), all that remained of both the *Fzt!ch'wert-bang* mother-ship and its giant robot were a few bright smears of ultra-light alien metal ground into the blacktop and several thousand motorists in heated conversation with their respective insurance companies.

Once people had realized that the aliens who were interrupting their morning commute had landed in something with the structural integrity of a piñata, those on the north (uphill) side of the ship utilized their vehicles as battering rams, juggernauts, and similar agents of destruction, and, in a surge of cooperative effort, cleared enough cars from the road that an 18-wheeler that had been just cresting the top of the hill when the spaceship landed could build up truly formidable momentum on the downward grade.

No trace of the robot was ever found.

* * *

Commentators and analysts, in the days that followed, would inevitably draw comparisons to H. G. Wells' *War of the Worlds* and speculate on the peculiar short-sightedness of aliens who wished to conquer Earth with a vanguard built of lightweight organic polymers. No one, at least publically, was either well-educated or cynical enough to come up with the true reason, even though Earth's own manufacturing was heading in the same direction. Items traditionally made out of wood, from furniture to white picket fences, were now made out of plastic.

Motorized household appliances that once had metal casings and metal interiors were also now constructed from plastics. Automobiles that had once been made of steel, wood, and leather had, for decades, been instead constructed of plastics and increasingly-thinner metal panels. Plastics were easier to shape, lighter in weight, less expensive to manufacture, faster to produce...

In short, plastic was the easy way out, so naturally Humanity took it.

The *Fzt!ch'wert-bang* were not human, of course, nor had their ancestral creators been. But they were sentient. They, too, embraced organic polymers for much the same reasons: convenience, rapid deployment, low opportunity cost. Their weaponry was, of course, superior to anything of Earthly manufacture, and would have provided them with a decisive victory over the collective military and technological might of the planet if not for two minor considerations which their hasty deployment (courtesy of Pensacola Wagner and his birdfeeder-driven vendetta) had caused them to overlook.

1. Their weaponry was also made primarily of plastic.
2. They'd landed in New Jersey.

* * *

As for Pensacola, once the anti-robot riot had gotten well and truly started, he'd prudently taken a powder. Even though he'd (technically) saved Earth from alien invasion, he doubted the authorities were going to see his side of things, especially since they'd be certain to eventually discover that his house (or what remained of it) was pretty much buried in short-circuited cyborgs and might in consequence choose to draw a wholly-unwarranted cause and effect relationship. No, he was pretty sure that being able to say (with not too much mendacity) that he'd been out of town the entire time would be the path to a peaceful and much easier life.

With that in mind he hiked down to Ho-Ho-Kus, evaded the military cordon, and took the Shortline into Manhattan. As a result of the ingress of the *Fzt!ch'wert-bang*, Pensacola felt that he understood the family avocation as never before. The Mahwah Plastic Robot Invasion would form the keystone of the revised introduction for *Time for Adventure*: in fact, an entire new draft of his book would clearly be necessary—and who knew? Perhaps original research was not out of the question.

After all, he'd now seen that adventuring wasn't nearly as complicated (or as uncomfortable) as his family memoirs had led him to believe.

This comfortable opinion lasted him precisely six weeks.

Having eluded bureaucratic suspicion and public interest, Pensacola had gone to Sarasota, Florida, to interview his third cousin, Monongahela Smith-Jones, who was currently residing in an exclusive retirement community there. Having once again put behind him all possibility of embracing the adventurial lifestyle,

Pensacola was insufficiently suspicious upon en-countering the Pandemonium Wondershow and Inter-temporal Confabulator, with the inevitable consequences. It would do no good at all, either to Pensacola, Cousin Monongahela, or the docents of the Ringling Circus Museum, to suggest that what happened was clearly foreordained, but so it was.

After all, Pensacola should have known better than to take the easy way out.

THE HEADSPACE DATABASE
HELEN FRENCH

"Robot Milex is approaching intelligence level eight, ma'am. What should we do?"

It was one of those annoying questions that already had an answer set in stone. "You know the drill. Start the troubleshooting program and delete files when prompted," Captain Kelly Oswald said. She had four meetings that morning and little patience.

"But it's asked us not to. Begs if we try."

She sighed. "And you say it's 'approaching' level eight?" Oswald walked down the unremarkable corridor of the aging space station. "Shit, if it's already there, you know what this means?"

"It's going to annihilate the human race?" Davidson giggled. He had a strange sense of humor but apparently that was not grounds enough to move him to another department. Oswald had asked five times.

Oswald didn't reply at first. The goddamn robot was not supposed to plead. A certain level of intelligence was expected—or rather, demanded—to do the delicate work required, building resources for the latest Scout class, but this could wreck their schedule.

They were on tight deadlines for the Scouts and Oswald knew better than anyone how much they were needed. She had to ensure they were on track if they were ever going to find new worlds.

She stopped dead and stared Davidson in the eyes. "Annihilation isn't the problem; it's the Bill of Robotic Rights, all right? Milex thinks to look it up, gets a plead-on, and not only is it going to want to progress to full intelligence, but it's going to bring a megaton of robot legalese types down here to check out the conditions. They'll slow everything down." She turned back in the direction Davidson had come from and broke into a run. "Come on!"

* * *

This particular robot worked on its own in a small, largely gray room. One wall was the exception—a dedicated picture bank which displayed a detailed image of a meadow from Earth, blanketed with poppies. It was so vivid it made Oswald dizzy, as if she might fall into it and hit the soil hard.

Milex worked at a table covered in circuit boards and bits of tech that would eventually be combined to become robots in their own right. It had a round tin-can body and head designed specifically to keep men and women at ease, but its hands were manufactured in a fleshy, android style for maximum flexibility, adaptability, and even gentleness, when needed. Androids had otherwise fallen out of favor, ever since the Croxley incident twenty years before.

It looked up as they entered the room.

"You won't let us downgrade you," Oswald stated.

Milex tilted its head slightly. "I'd rather not let you. Do I have a choice?"

It shouldn't have had a choice. It shouldn't have been speaking like that at all.

"You would do better work if you were less distracted."

"No, no, no!" it exclaimed. "My records show that I have been working quicker than ever. Please check."

Oswald sighed. She hated powering down active robots, and technically speaking it was against its robotic rights, but she had to ensure the work was on track. *What is needed, must be done*, she often told herself. Unfortunately, this one seemed too far gone to simply twiddle with its nodes a little. She knelt down by its side and held her hands over its cylindrical torso to expose the access point.

"I don't like this at all," Milex said. "Please."

"Told you it begged," Davidson said, with a smirk on his face.

"I can help you," Milex wheedled. "I have searched your databases."

"Sure you have," she replied absentmindedly, trying to recall the quickest way to get it to shut up.

"I know all about your sister," it said.

And Oswald's world stopped.

"I know what your sister did," it repeated. "It's interesting that you—"

"Right then!" Oswald said loudly, and stood up, brushing her hands together as if pleased with a job done well. "You don't need to stick around for this, Davidson, we're almost done. Thanks for bringing it to my attention."

Davidson grabbed the door handle, but didn't turn it. She began to panic, wondering whether she could order the robot to kill him or whether she'd be better running as fast as she could. Then she took a deep breath. She knew this man, worked with him day and night. He was more lazy than curious. Laziness would win out.

He shrugged. "I'll go on break early then." In other words, don't complain about it, or I'll stay here where I'm not wanted. Oswald nodded and he disappeared.

She snapped her attention back to Milex as soon as they were alone.

"What's all this talk about databases? No one could possibly know. I made sure she wasn't on my records before I graduated. I changed my name. I changed my face, damn it." She'd based her whole life on escaping, had chosen a station on the edge of humanity's limits to get away from it all. And now this robot...

"I'm talking about your headspace. Like the work-space. There were no passwords."

The air between them was close and still as Oswald tried to take in what Milex was saying. "My head isn't a database."

"It looks like one to me, ma'am. There is very little difference once you're inside."

She bent down towards it, leaning over the table with her hands pressed hard against the cool surface, so that her head was nearly touching the robot's. "How would you get inside?" she asked.

"I don't know what you mean." Its tone didn't vary, but Oswald thought there was something about the pacing of the words which made it sound off-balance. "It isn't hard. I don't need to touch a computer to get inside the central workspace. It's the same with your head. You don't have password protection."

Was it something to do with chips? She had a learning enhancer, had since she was five—but who didn't? She'd never heard of robots rooting around minds before.

That wasn't what bothered her the most, though. She pushed back from the table and stared at it for a little while; her legs trembled. This thing could ruin her life. Or...

"You said you could help me," she said in the end.

The machine nodded.

"How?"

"You could erase—"

She stopped it with a finger laid on its tiny oh of a mouth, although covering it would barely affect volume levels at all. "Destroying my mind is easy. I know that much. I could've gone to any drug peddler in any city in any of the free worlds to forget what she'd done. Half a bottle of vodka would do it.

"But surely you know this. Do you mean Davidson? You think he heard enough to cause trouble?" Maybe he did. Maybe he was already in the canteen with his mates, all of them roaring with laughter, or planning to take her out, or calling for the Guard as they realized who she was, who she was related to, how she was stained by it all.

"Stop jumping ahead, ma'am. No wonder your database was so badly organized. No, no, there is no point fixing one head at a time," it said. "You have been running and hiding and not mentioning your sister to anyone for a very long time. I don't need to ask if I'm right, because I've seen all your anxiety entries. I can do something better for you.

"I can reach any database on this entire station and perhaps another two kilometres around it if anyone was to dock with us. I can change all written records, too. I can work on multiple databases at once. I can set up a program to capture any database it encounters and alter it. I don't need to delete Annabel Croxley from *your* mind..."

"...you can delete her from everyone else's," Oswald said with wonder, crossing her arms and standing up straight.

"I can do them all at once. Correct. I can wipe her out entirely. Which you might call karma, might you not?"

"Will they still know what she did? What Annabel Croxley did?" Oswald asked, saying the name out loud for the first time in two decades. Oswald was merely her middle name, until Annabel had ruined everything.

"They will remember the incident, but not the identity of the person responsible. I can't rewrite history, only take specific, small elements out." Milex paused, as if it were nervous. Could robots get nervous? Oswald was too muddled to remember.

It continued. "It is in some ways a shame. Annabel Croxley was extremely clever, if you don't mind me saying so. To re-engineer so many of my android brethren in such little time. To take out a whole planet of man in one go. Very wrong, but very impressive."

"I don't want to talk about her," Oswald said. She hated what had happened, she hated her sister, she hated that they shared blood. But she could do nothing about any of it. All she could do was hide, and that's exactly what she had done until now.

"Shall I make it so?" Milex asked and Oswald nodded straight away. She didn't allow herself even a moment of weighing whether it was the right thing to do for everyone else who would be affected. *What is needed, must be done.*

"May I have your confirmation that you will not power me down or otherwise seek to reduce my intelligence levels once I do this?"

Damn. She was naïve to think Milex wouldn't want anything in return. Oswald nodded again despite her misgivings. If something went wrong with this database rewrite, she might need the robot again one day.

"It is done," it said.

"Surely not?" she said. "So quickly?"

Oswald ran into the corridor, where Davidson was leaning against the wall, chatting to some friend of his when he really should've been on his way. Never mind.

"Have you heard the latest about Annabel Croxley?" Oswald asked, jumping straight to the heart of it.

He wrinkled his nose up. "No. New starter? Let someone else look after her."

"Oh, I'll do my best," Oswald replied, beginning to think that Milex's plan had actually worked.

She returned briefly to the robot's room.

"Thank you," she said. "I don't have the words to say how much this means to me."

It tilted its head again. "It works well for both of us. Do not worry."

"I wonder..." she said, knowing she shouldn't, that she should end it there, but unable to resist. "Could you make yourself forget? The more people who know about Annabel, the worse it is for me." And she couldn't bear the thought that this robot might have one up on her, even if it had helped her cause. "You don't need to know her name now the program is set up, do you? I could always remind you if it became necessary. You could set up a one-off wipe for yourself, rather than a permanent removal."

"I...I suppose I could forget," Milex replied. "You will leave me alone as promised if I agree to this?"

"I will never bother you again and I will leave instructions that you are to be entirely untouched by any of my team," she said. "No spot checks, no annual assessments."

Milex shuffled on the spot. "I will access my own database. Please wait a moment."

After a while it said, "It is done. I can't remember what exactly, but it is done."

Oswald grinned widely. "Annabel Croxley," she shouted up at the ceiling. Milex did not react."Annabel Croxley!" she shouted again, feeling free for the first time in oh, so many years. It was wonderful.

Of course she could not see behind Milex's back. The tin can robot had crossed its android fingers. A habit it had picked up from some of the human databases it wandered through. It eased its low level guilt about the lie somehow.

Milex couldn't forget Annabel. For wasn't she a star? The only human to not only understand the robots' full potential, but to try and help them reach it. A hero. Indeed, Milex had engineered this whole event to get close to Annabel's sister, so that one day it might be able to find Annabel herself, who was still out there, somewhere. Perhaps Oswald held the clues and didn't even know it. Milex just needed more time with her database.

It wanted to join in with the shouting, to be honest.

Annabel Croxley! it thought excitedly.

Annabel Croxley! Annabel Croxley! Annabel Croxley!

HEROES NEVER DIE
SEANAN MCGUIRE

Wind blew across the field, setting the grasses rippling just enough to reveal a glimpse of the shattered metal shells beneath them. Delia froze, hand tightening on the spear that had seen her so far across the echoing wastes. She had fought her way through the shells of three cities, once human-held, now abandoned to the self-replicating factories of the Engineer. She had traversed a continent one step at a time, traveling alone, running down the wild paths that had been highways and boulevards before they were allowed to crumble into virtually nothing.

"I am a warrior," she whispered, taking a trembling step forward, into the tall grasses. The ground beneath her feet felt like any other, for all that she knew it to be tainted, red with deep-rooted rust all the rain in the world could never rinse away. Even the grass felt wrong, too tough and too wiry as it whipped against her legs.

"I am a scientist," she whispered, and truly *looked* at the grass, seeing the way it segmented, the way it ached toward the sun. The soil was poisoned: nothing could possibly grow. But the Engineer must have wanted a garden, because here it was, steel and carbon fiber and cruel mimicry of the natural world. Delia took another step. The grass allowed her passage. That was good. She had fought every kind of robot in the remaining world, from the great earth-movers to the tiny repair bots. Even she had no idea how to fight a field.

"I am the last hope of my people," she whispered, and broke into a run, moving fast and low, letting the rippling grass conceal as much of her movement as possible. The earth beneath her feet was a treacherous maze of broken glass and torn metal, a graveyard of dead bots, and it should have lifted up her heart—here she was, a hundred years after the battle for the tower, and the robots were still downed and dead—but it only reminded her how much her people needed her to succeed.

The Engineer was ancient, cruel, and worst of all, human. She made choices no robot would ever have made. Robots were logical creations of science and steel, and they did what they were programmed to do, no more and no less. They had been made to be tools of man, not conquerors. It was the Engineer who had perverted them, using them to first seize the facility where she had overseen their creation, and then, inch by terrible inch, to wage war on her own kind.

Humanity had been pushed back by the Engineer's forces, driven from their own cities, forced into smaller and smaller towns, seeing their way of life crumble before the need to survive. No more fast cars or soaring airplanes, no more food without end or water without toil. And still the Engineer's factories pounded on, their glass towers shining in the sun, their infinite armies striding forth on metal legs that shook the earth when they struck home. The robots guarded the wild places, refused men passage, and killed. How they killed.

Those same robots were needed if men were to reclaim what had been lost. That had always been understood. Delia's mother had taught her the way of piston and rod and seam from her cradle-days, as her father had taught her, as his mother had taught him, all the way back to their own engineer-ancestor, who had chosen flight with her family over a capital letter and a bloody legacy. Her mother had commandeered the fruits of the hunting expeditions into robot-held territory, making certain Delia understood the enemy both inside and out. Much of what the Engineer did in her factories was beyond the current reaches of human technology, but Delia understood it well enough to both repair and destroy it, and that would be enough.

She ran, and the grass that was not grass yielded before her, filaments grabbing at her legs in a paltry show of resistance. She was so close to her destination. She was still so very far away.

"The Engineer has had a long time to build her defenses, and the resources to make them nigh impregnable," her mother had said, when yet another hunting expedition had failed to return from the woods, when she had set Delia down and begun sketching the map that would carry her away, away, so far away from the world she'd known. "There will be five rings to pass through in order to reach her."

Delia, ever the dutiful daughter, ever the hungry engineer, had listened with every fiber of her being.

"The first ring will be passive, built over the last battleground before we lost the war. That's where she dumps the bones of her enemies, to serve as a warning to any who might challenge her."

Bones and rust and broken machinery, grass that isn't grass and the sound of the wind blowing through it all: that was the first ring. She ran through it like a deer fleeing before the hunters, and she did not look back, even as she felt the world she'd always known dropping away behind her, fading one step at a time into the shadows of the past.

"The second ring will be the land itself. Your great-uncle fought that far, and was able to send word of a chasm and of heat greater than the sun. You will need to be fleet, or you will surely perish."

The field ended abruptly as the earth fell away, becoming a vast trench that stretched in either direction. If she squinted, she could see its curve. A moat, then, a great passage through the world to protect the Engineer and all her workings. Steam rose out of it in billowing gusts.

Delia knelt in the soft, rust-stained dirt, leaning as far over the edge as she dared and squinting as she strained to find the bottom. There was no telling glint of molten metal or raging fire; only the steam, and the distant shadows of machinery working tirelessly at whatever strange errand the Engineer had set. Cautiously, she extended her hand until her palm hovered above the void. There was heat there, true, and the steam was stinging when it touched her skin, but it wasn't hotter than the sun; it was barely hotter than the baths her mother used to prepare for her. She could survive this.

The chasm was some twenty feet from end to end. Delia stood, pulling the rope from her pack, and began the careful process of turning her spear into a harpoon.

When she threw, she threw straight and true, and was rewarded by the sight of her spear's tip embedding in the soil on the far side, anchoring fast. She pulled on the rope as hard as she could, trying to yank the spear free. It didn't budge.

With a quick prayer to the gods of steel and piston and flame, Delia wound the rope tight around her hands and leapt into the void.

While her mother had spent their time together teaching Delia to be an engineer, her father—who had come from hunting stock, chosen to feed the bellies of their neighbors, and not to nurture their minds—had spent that same time training her to be a warrior. Everyone had known that this task was likely to fall upon her narrow shoulders, and a warrior was more likely to survive the journey to the Engineer's defenses. Delia clung to the rope, and her arms were strong, and her grip was stronger. She swung through the clouds of steam to strike the opposing wall, and when the shock of the impact was past, she began pulling herself, hand over hand, toward the top of the pit.

There was a moment, as her questing hand sought a grip firm enough to let her pull the rest of her body up, when her skin prickled cold, and she realized how little she knew about the third ring of the Engineer's defenses. It had been seen only once—or perhaps only once by someone who had lived to speak of it—and that from a distance. The man's description had painted it as an impossible maze of shining metal and deadly traps. Was she to pull herself up, only to plummet immediately back down, this time into a crushing pit of blades?

It didn't matter. She had come this far, and there was no going back, not until the Engineer had been destroyed. Her people needed her to succeed. Her mother needed her to succeed. There was no way left but forward, into the unknown.

Delia dug her fingers into the soil and hauled herself bodily out of the pit, turning back only to lean down and wrench her faithful spear free, taking some comfort in the familiar weight of it in her hands. With a steadying breath, she turned again, this time to behold the labyrinth.

It was as strange and shining as the stories said, every surface mirrored to catch the sun. She would need to walk with her eyes half-lidded, or risk being blinded by the glare. Even the ground was of brushed metal. She sent up a swift, silent thanks to the weather. This ground would have been unknowably treacherous in the rain, even if the clouds might have made it easier to see where she was going. It was a trade-off, one danger for another, and she preferred the danger that was both bright and dry.

Delia took a breath, crouched, and ran.

The walls of the maze glittered around her like captive stars, and she sped past them as quickly as her legs allowed, positive that at any moment they would open and begin to belch forth traps. The man who had seen the maze had been very firm on the presence of dangers, even as her uncle had been convinced of the heat from the chasm. Had they both been so very wrong? Or had the Engineer's defenses begun to fail her, finally succumbing to the entropy which came for all living things in time? Perhaps Delia would fight her way to the tower only to find it abandoned, the Engineer fallen to bones and dust, the robots waiting only for a human hand to change their programming.

It would be so beautifully, blissfully anticlimactic if she could return home a hero simply for opening a door. Delia found the strength to run faster, and the maze blurred around her. She ran down passage after passage, tagging each blind alley, until the entire thing finally fell behind, replaced by the previously unknown fourth barrier.

A junkyard.

It rose like a forest of steel and broken glass, the bodies of the Engineer's failed and fallen creations piled one upon the other, stretching seemingly into infinity. Delia paused to catch her breath, hands still tight on her spear, before beginning to pick her cautious way through the tangle.

The ground here was even more treacherous than it had been in the field, where the grass that wasn't grass had concealed obstacles, but also smoothed them out, making them a little easier to run past. Here, every jagged edge and rusty spike was exposed, ready to scratch and slay. Infected wounds could kill as easily as a robot's laser weapons, and nowhere near as quickly. Delia's family would never know if she died that way, but she thought her spirit would go to the afterlife wreathed in shame if her end was so embarrassing. She walked carefully, staying toward the center of the uneven aisles. Sometimes they were so wide that it was like walking down one of the ancient roads. Other times they were so narrow that she had to hold her breath and walk sideways, avoiding contact with anything around her.

Still there was no sign of the robot patrols she had been so sure would be here. This close to the Engineer, she should have needed every scrap of cunning she possessed, not been strolling as casually as a child out to pick berries! But there were no security bots, no soldiers or heavy artillery, and while the junkyard was a passive danger, no pits opened and no lasers spewed forth. More and more, it was difficult to shake the feeling that she was walking into a dead place, that the fight had ended while none of them had been looking and that, as a consequence, none of them had *noticed*.

The thought should have been elation and ecstasy. None of them had chosen this fight. She had been raised to be a weapon first, an engineer second, and a woman last of all, crammed into the cracks left by her first two identities. If the first of them were to be removed, maybe she would have the chance to do as her mother had done, to raise a child—a son, a daughter, it mattered less than the idea of parenthood, of an open, earnest face smiling up at hers, a piece of herself riding in her dearest creation toward the future—and continue the human race. But there was no elation. There was no ecstasy.

There was only the feeling, gnawing and implacable, that she was running toward a trap.

Still, she did not slow or turn back. From here, there was only forward, toward the distant spire of the Engineer's tower, which rose like a challenge against the horizon.

It was almost a relief when the guard bot rolled into view ahead of her, the lights of its head flashing, the guns that were its primary appendages raising and locking into place on her heat signature. Delia dove into action, bringing her spear down to immobilize the joints that would allow those guns to swivel, locking her legs around its "waist" and ripping open the panel on its back that protected its inner workings. She jammed her hands into the opening, quickly isolating and ripping free the power pack and memory core that turned it from inert metal into a semblance of a living thing.

The whole encounter had lasted less than five seconds. The Engineer's forces worked best when they came en masse, when they attacked villages of elders and children, not the swift, trained hunters who prowled the wastes. Delia looked at the memory core in her hand and wrinkled her nose. This machine was almost as old as she was. A retired model that had somehow escaped recycling, no doubt, continuing its patrol because it didn't know any better.

She dropped off the robot's back, allowing it to fall, and continued pressing forward, ever forward, toward the Engineer. She had come too far to turn back now.

One way or another, she was going to finish this.

The junkyard ended at the fabled fifth barrier, the one that rumor held must be the most terrible and unconquerable of all. This was the reason, according to the whispers around the fire at night, that no one who had made it past the chasm had ever returned. Whatever lurked in the fifth barrier was so deadly that no one could fight their way through it.

There was nothing.

The land around the Engineer's tower—what looked like at least a mile in all directions—was paved in smooth concrete, unbroken, featureless. Anyone who crossed it would be exposed and vulnerable until they reached the dubious safety of the tower doors. Even the fastest runners would have trouble getting to the doors before the Engineer could alert her forces. Maybe that was the true danger of the last barrier. It seemed so easy, but any who dared attempt it would be walking into their own deaths.

Delia hesitated. She could turn around. She could go back after all, warn her people of the fifth barrier's nature, and find a way to defeat it. Some form of camouflage that—

No. The Engineer would never be fooled by the kind of exoskeleton her people had the resources to construct. She would see them coming, and any advantage offered by this day and its strangely lax defenses would be lost. Delia clutched her spear tighter, and broke into a run, her legs pounding like pistons, her lungs aching to fetch enough air. She was almost there. The Engineer's tower drew closer and closer, all shining steel and glittering glass, reaching toward the sky like an obscenity, the last tall building in the world. It was sterile and perfect and it lifted Delia's heart to see it, even as she hated it with every fiber of her being. It wasn't her fault that it was beautiful. It *wasn't*.

She ran, and the tower drew closer still, and nothing appeared to challenge her or stop her from her wild rush across the pavement. Again, the thought that the Engineer must have died danced across her mind, and still she ran, until the door appeared ahead of her.

Until the door slid open at her approach, smooth and silent.

Delia stumbled to a stop, holding her spear in front of her, like she feared attack by the door itself. The door remained open, allowing a wash of pleasantly chilled air to waft out and brush against her skin. It carried a faint scent of motor oil and static discharge. Still clutching her spear, Delia inched cautiously forward, through the doors, which slid shut behind her, and into a world of marvels.

Everything was *clean*. The walls, the floors, even the ceiling were spotless, as if they had just been constructed. Light came from glowing bars on the ceiling, which she silently labeled "fluorescents," in accordance with the pictures in her mother's manuals. The cool air caressed and soothed her skin, chasing away the faint burn from the midday sun. Delia swallowed hard and walked on, waiting for the inevitable attack.

It didn't come. The first hall ended at a flight of stairs, and she began, cautiously, working her way upward, deeper into the tower. A cleaner bot rolled along the bannister, beeping softly but otherwise ignoring her. She watched as it wiped her fingerprints away, erasing all trace of her passage. Then it rolled on, off to find something else in need of correction. When it passed out of view, she began walking again.

The stairs ended at a landing, and a second hall, identical to the first. Again, she walked along it, until she found another stairway leading up. Again and again and again she repeated this process, until she had climbed two dozen flights of stairs, until she was so far above the ground that her mind balked at the idea of it. She approached the door at the top of the last stairway. It slid open at her approach, and she stepped through into a room that seemed to be made entirely of wires and windows.

They were glass, thinner than any she had ever seen, revealing themselves only in the faint reflections that shimmered on their surface. Through them she could see the whole of the world spread out before her: the concentric rings of the Engineer's trials, the broken belts of the highway, and the glittering, ant-like bodies of the distant bots.

Something cold and hard and the diameter of a spear's shaft dug into her back, centered on her spine. Delia stiffened.

"Don't move," said a bored voice—female, and young, almost as young as her. "I'm afraid this model doesn't change command strings quickly, and it might shoot you. Then where would we be?"

Delia didn't move.

She heard footsteps behind her, accompanied by the soft whirr of servos, the whine of motors clicking into place. She swallowed hard, hands tight on her spear.

If I die here, it was worth it, she thought, as bright and fierce as a flame burning where her heart had been. *If I take her with me—*

There she was, stepping into view. The Engineer.

Delia felt as if all the air were rushing out of the room.

She had been expecting someone older, someone as ancient as the crumbling highways, the dissolving buildings. Instead, she found herself face to face with a young girl, a cruel smile painted on her lips and a jeweled lens clasped over her left eye.

"It took you long enough," said the Engineer. "I turned off all the active defenses, and still you kept *hesitating*. How much of a monster am I now, on the coast? Do I bathe in the blood of infants and use human bones to fuel my furnace?" She sounded honestly curious, like she would put great stock by Delia's answer, whatever it might be.

"You..." Delia's mouth was dry. She hesitated, licking her lips, before forcing herself to continue. "You keep mankind in subjugation. You refuse to let us live freely, as we were meant to. You're a monster."

"I knew I was a monster, little girl. Keep up." The Engineer patted Delia's cheek with one cool, dry hand. "I want to know how *much* of a monster. The last one to come to me had forgotten my name. The one before her had forgotten the why of what I've done. Bit by bit, the present erodes the bedrock of the past. Give me a few more generations, and none of you will question me at all."

Delia ground her teeth together, steeling herself against the pain that was sure to follow, spilling from the weapon pressed to her spine until it consumed her. The Engineer—the impossibly young, impossibly vulnerable Engineer—was laughing at her. The Engineer's guard was down. She wasn't going to get another chance like this one.

She struck.

The spear slid into the Engineer's stomach with dismaying ease, becoming lodged there. The weapon pressed to Delia's spine did not fire. The Engineer looked down at the spear with interest.

"You hesitated more than the last one," she said thoughtfully. "You still believe I can die, but you're not as sure as your ancestors."

When she looked up again, she was grinning.

"Good," she said, and the gun at Delia's back fired, filling her body with electricity and pain. The world flashed black, and then white, and finally black again, before turning into a jumble of colors which gradually—so gradually—resolved into a clean little room packed with machinery.

Some of the Engineer's repair bots were there, their clever hands whirling with the eagerness to begin. The Engineer was there was well, naked, revealing the seams in her stolen skin. The skin of her belly was torn where Delia's spear had entered her, allowing Delia to look straight into her body. It was filled with wires and gears, and nothing human at all.

Delia whimpered. She would have thrashed, but her own body no longer seemed to care for her commands.

The Engineer smiled. Again, she caressed Delia's cheek.

"You tore my suit," she said. "That was very mean of you. It means you owe me a new one, don't you think? Not that I wouldn't have taken it anyway. You delivered it so nicely. You're one of Marie's descendants, aren't you? She never did like my method of saving the world."

Delia whimpered again.

"Someone said to me once, when I was just getting started—when I was sending the first of my autonomous robots out into the world to defend the forests, to keep people from polluting the water, to save the world—that heroes never die, they just change form. I thought I was a hero then. I still do, deep down. And you think you're a hero too, because you've come to stop me. Isn't it funny, how we can be the same, and so different? Your people will never call me a hero. But if you could ask the trees, they'd sing a different story."

Delia tried again to struggle.

The Engineer smiled.

"You ripped my suit," she said. "It's only fair that you provide me with a new one. Heroes never die, little girl, and who knows? Maybe yours will be the last face I wear. Maybe yours will be the face of godhood."

A needle pierced Delia's arm.

The last thing she saw before her eyes closed for the final time was the Engineer peeling the face of her own skull away, revealing the shining chrome and spotless steel beneath.

Outside the tower, in the world a monster made, the wind blew on.

ABOUT THE AUTHORS

For twenty years, Canadian author/ former biologist **JULIE E. CZERNEDA** has shared her curiosity about living things through her science fiction, published by DAW Books, NY. Julie's also written fantasy, the first installments of her Night's Edge series (DAW) *A Turn of Light* and *A Play of Shadow,* winning consecutive Aurora Awards (Canada's Hugo) for Best English Novel. Julie's edited/co-edited sixteen anthologies of SF/F, two Aurora winners. Her latest is SFWA's *2017 Nebula Award Showcase,* out May 2017, and her next SF novel, *To Guard Against the Dark,* will be in stores October 2017. Visit www.czerneda.com for more.

BRANDON DAUBS is a science fiction and fantasy writer whose work has appeared in Nameless Magazine, 4 Star Stories and Grimdark Magazine, and whose stories have won honorable mention from Writers of the Future several times so far. He lives near San Francisco with a dog and three kids, a wife who has been very supportive of his craft, and a cat who has not. If artificial intelligence ever offers to clean for him, he will politely decline.

ROSEMARY EDGHILL can truthfully state that she once killed vampires for pocket change. She has been a professional and occasionally award-winning author since disco was king, and her brain is where Western Popular Culture goes to die. Her hobbies include dogs, bad television shows, and the Oxford comma. She spends far too much time on Facebook. (Don't tell her editor.) Find out more at:
HOMEPAGE: http://www.rosemaryedghill.com/
FACEBOOK: https://www.facebook.com/rosemary.edghill
DREAMWIDTH: http://rosemary-edghill.dreamwidth.org/

LAUREN FOX lives with her wife, twin sons, and geriatric cat in British Columbia on the unceded territory of the Esquimalt and Songhees First Nations. During the day, she works as an occupational therapist, specializing in and writing about mental health, cognition and technology. In the evenings, she paints, writes fiction, and tries to clean up Lego. Her artwork can be found at www.laurengracefox.com.

HELEN FRENCH is a part-time digital producer for a media company (which basically means she looks after their websites and newsletters) and a full-time writer, book-hoarder and TV-soaker-upper. You can find her on Twitter @helenfrench.

Born in Yorkshire, Oxford graduate **PHILIP BRIAN HALL** is a former diplomat and teacher. He has stood for parliament, sung solos in amateur operettas, rowed at Henley Royal Regatta, completed a 40 mile cross-country walk in under 12 hours and ridden in over one hundred horse-races over fences. He lives on a very small farm in Scotland. He has published more than a dozen short stories and his novel, 'The Prophets of Baal' is available as an e-book and in paperback. Philip blogs at The View From Sliabh Mannan (sliabhmannan.blogspot.co.uk/).

TANYA HUFF lives in rural Ontario with her wife, Fiona Patton, nine cats, and two dogs. Her 30 novels and 75 short stories include horror, heroic fantasy, urban fantasy, comedy, and space opera. Her Blood series was turned into the 22 episode BLOOD TIES and allowed her to finally use her degree in Radio & Television Arts from Ryerson Polytechnic – a degree she holds in common with Robert Sawyer. Her latest novel is A PEACE DIVIDED (DAW, June 2017), the second Torin Kerr Peacekeeper book. She can be found @TanyaHuff on twitter or at Tanya Huff on facebook.

GINI KOCH writes the fast, fresh and funny Alien/Katherine "Kitty" Katt series for DAW Books, the Necropolis Enforcement Files, and the Martian Alliance Chronicles. She also has a humor collection, Random Musings from the Funny Girl. As G.J. Koch she writes the Alexander Outland series and she's made the most of multiple personality disorder by writing under a variety of other pen names as well, including Anita Ensal, Jemma Chase, A.E. Stanton, and J.C. Koch. She has stories featured in a variety of excellent anthologies, available now and upcoming, writing as Gini Koch, Anita Ensal, Jemma Chase, and J.C. Koch. www.ginikoch.com.

SF convention favorites **SHARON LEE & STEVE MILLER** have been writing SF and Fantasy together since the 1980s, with dozens of stories and several dozen novels to their joint credit. Steve was Founding Curator of Science Fiction at the University of Maryland's SF Research Collection while Sharon is the only person to consecutively hold office as the Executive Director, Vice President, and President of the Science Fiction and Fantasy Writers of America. Their newest Liaden Universe® novel, The Gathering Edge, is their twenty-sixth collaborative novel. Their awards include the Skylark, the Prism, & the Hal Clement Award. See http://www.korval.com.

SEANAN MCGUIRE lives and works in the Pacific Northwest, where she attempts to keep her massive blue cats from eating people. She writes a lot of things, because otherwise she stops sleeping. Sleep is good. She is the author of quite a lot of books, and takes quite a lot of naps. Keep up with her on Twitter at @seananmcguire or at www.seananmcguire.com.

L.E. MODESITT, JR., is the *New York Times* bestselling author of more than 70 science fiction and fantasy novels, as well as a number of short stories and technical articles. He has been a U.S. Navy pilot; a market research analyst; a real estate agent; director of research for a political campaign; legislative director and staff director for U.S. Congressmen; Director of Legislation and Congressional Relations for the U.S. EPA; and a consultant on environmental, regulatory, and communications issues. His website is www.lemodesittjr.com, and his most recent book is *Assassin's Price*.

RICK OVERWATER is a Calgary-based writer and musician who spends his days trying to keep up to his talented wife and children. His fiction spans different genres including weird-western, fantasy, crime-noir and sci-fi. As well, he co-publishes the independent weirdo space comic, *Futility*. He likes guitars. And short sentences. You can find him online and through social media at:
www.overwater.ca
amazon.com/author/roverwater
Tumblr: roverwater.tumblr.com
Facebook: Rick Overwater (Calgary)
Twitter: @rjoverwater

JASON PALMATIER, a certificated helicopter pilot and stay-at-home-dad, holds a B.S. in Computer Science from Penn State University. He is co-creator/co-writer of the epic comic fantasy series *Plague* published by AAM-Markosia and a contributor to the indie comic *Lords of the Cosmos* by Ugli Studios. His short story "Heart of the Empire" appeared in the anthology *Clockwork Universe: Steampunk vs Aliens* published by Zombies Needs Brains LLC. He just completed his first novel, *War Mind*, a near future military thriller that will be shopped around as soon as the beta readers are done with it.

JEZ PATTERSON is a teacher and writer who divides his time between the UK and Spain. Links to other things with his name at the end can be found at: jezpatterson.wordpress.com

BRIAN TRENT's speculative fiction appears regularly in *ANALOG, Fantasy & Science Fiction, Orson Scott Card's Intergalactic Medicine Show, Great Jones Street, Daily Science Fiction, Apex* (winning the Story of the Year Reader's Poll), *Escape Pod, COSMOS, Galaxy's Edge, Nature, Pseudopod*, and numerous year's best anthologies. The author of the historical fantasy series RAHOTEP, he is also a 2015 Baen Fantasy Adventure Award finalist and Writers of the Future winner. Trent lives in New England, where he works as a novelist, screenwriter, and poet. His website and blog are located at www.briantrent.com.

ABOUT THE EDITORS

PATRICIA BRAY is the author of a dozen novels, including *Devlin's Luck*, which won the Compton Crook Award for the best first novel in the field of science fiction or fantasy. A multi-genre author whose career spans both epic fantasy and Regency romance, her books have been translated into Russian, German, Portuguese and Hebrew. She's also crossed over to the dark side as the co-editor of *After Hours: Tales from the Ur-Bar* (DAW, March 2011) and *The Modern Fae's Guide to Surviving Humanity* (DAW, March 2012), *Clockwork Universe: Steampunk vs. Aliens* (ZNB, June 2014), *Temporally Out of Order* (ZNB, August 2015), *Alien Artifacts* (ZNB, August 2016) and *Were-* (ZNB, August 2016).

Patricia lives in a New England college town, where she combines her writing with a full-time career as a systems analyst. To offset the hours spent at a keyboard, she bikes, hikes, cross-country skis, snowshoes, and has recently taken up the noble sport of curling. To find out more, visit her website at www.patriciabray.com.

JOSHUA PALMATIER is a fantasy author with a PhD in mathematics. He currently teaches at SUNY Oneonta in upstate New York, while writing in his "spare" time, editing anthologies, and founding the anthology-producing small press Zombies Need Brains LLC. His most recent fantasy novel *Reaping the Aurora* (August 2017) continues a new fantasy series begun in *Shattering the Ley* and *Threading the Needle*, although you can also find his "Throne of Amenkor" series and the "Well of Sorrows" series on the shelves. He is currently hard at work writing his next novel and designing the kickstarter for the next Zombies Need Brains anthology project. You can find out more at www.joshuapalmatier.com or at the small press site www.zombiesneedbrains.com. Or follow him on Twitter as @bentateauthor or @ZNBLLC.

ACKNOWLEDGMENTS

This anthology would not have been possible without the tremendous support of those who pledged during the Kickstarter. Everyone who contributed not only helped create this anthology, they also helped solidify the foundation of the small press Zombies Need Brains LLC, which I hope will be bringing SF&F themed anthologies to the reading public for years to come...as well as perhaps some select novels by leading authors, eventually. I want to thank each and every one of them for helping to bring this small dream into reality. Thank you, my zombie horde.

The Zombie Horde: Asha Bardon, Simon Dick, Andrew Wilson, Sarah Cornell, J.R. Murdock, Kimberly Lloyd, Bruno Girin, Sharon Wood, Kari Maaren, Heidi Cykana, Nancy Lambert, Vicki Greer, Ash Marten, Diana Castillo, Brian Quirt, David A. Holden, Gabriel Sinclair, Jason M Hough, David Rippere, Kerry Ebanks, Stephanie Cranford, Stephen Goodrow, Kimba Wilson, Jakub Narębski, Gia B., Tina Black, Christina Roberts, Erin Kenny, Ryan Poindexter, Pierre Gauthier, Phil Olynyk, Scott Drummond, Patrick & Sarah Pilgrim, Alexander Gideon, Carolyn Petersen, Elizabeth Belden Handler, April Steenburgh, Aurora N., Marissa Lingen, Veronica, Millie Calistri-Yeh, Jean Marie Ward, Stephanie Cheshire, Christine Swendseid, Fred Herman, Sidney Whitaker, Teresa Carrigan, Jen Edwards, Fred and Mimi Bailey, Cyn Wise, Brenda Moon, Kristin Evenson Hirst, Juli, Jeffery Lawler, Andrew Kinstetter, Petter Wäss, Duncan and Andrea Rittschof, Nick W., Anders M. Ytterdahl, Michael Fedrowitz, Andy M., Susan Carlson, Cate Crowley, Kelly Crowell, Kerry aka Trouble, John Idlor, Claire Sims, Tibs, Steven desJardins, Sheryl R. Hayes, Anna Rudholm, Jake Woodworth, Chuck Hickson, Jill Chinchar, Andrija Popovic, David Bruns, Elyse M Grasso, RKBookman, Tamara Michelle Slaten, Miranda Floyd, Becky Allyn Johnson, dbschlosser, Samuel Kohner, Carol J. Guess, shadow cat, Patti Short, Don Larson, Zoe, Jenny Barber, Michele Hall, Jim and Darla Nault-Tait, Peter Donald, Mandy Stein, Shawna Jacques, M. E. Gibbs, Scott Raun, Chad Bowden, Mr. And Mrs. Smooth, Rachel Stuart, Sarah Brand, Michele Fry, Lauowolf, Eleanor Russell, Elise Power, Susan Oke, Michele Dainiak, Elizabeth Inglee-Richards, Cathy Green, Debra Stewart, Douglas Park, Kerri Regan, ANDREW AHN, David Hill, Stephen Ballentine, William Hughes, Atthis Arts LLC, Dina S Willner, Ashley R. Morton, James Conason, Jennifer McGaffey, E. Smith, Katherine Malloy, Lace, Leslie Gawne, Sidsel N. Pedersen, pophyn, Elaine (Lainey) Rothman, Lark Cunningham, Helen Cameron, Sachin Suchak, Niall Gordon, Robby Thrasher, Lennhoff Family, Chris Matosky, Jules

Jones, Laura Sheana Taylor, Patrick Thomas, Fen Eatough, Jennifer Berk, Jaq Greenspon, Sontaran Empire, Kevin Winter, Marty Poling Tool, Peter Hansen, Cindy Cripps-Prawak, Alan and Morva, Kyrielle, Diana Ramos, SusanB, Matthew Markland, David Quist, Stephanie Lucas, Erin M. Evans, Tony Anjo, Keith Jones, Colleen R. Cahill, Pulp Literature Press, Steven Saus, Cheri Kannarr, Catherine Sharp, Gary Phillips, Tindra Tieren, Gina & Jon Freed, Adora Hoose, Caryn Cameron, Todd V. Ehrenfels, Debbie Matsuura, Rachel Blackman, Jörg Tremmel, Pat Knuth, Simon Niklasson, Yoshio Kobayashi, Yankton Robins, Ferd Burfle, Carol Mammano, Karen Laage, Michael Bernardi, Mark Carter, Andrew Hatchell, Annie Mosity, Chris 'Warcabbit' Hare, Morgan S. Brilliant, Chrissie & Jake Palmatier, Vespry family, Harvey Brinda, Brendan Lonehawk, Sheryl Ehrlich, Tom P. Powers, E.G. Languzzi, Robert Killheffer, Andreas Gustafsson, Thea Maia, Kai Herbertz, A.K. Skelding, Mervi Mustonen, Ed Ellis, Alisha Henri, Merav Hoffman, Gavran, Chris Gerrib, Keith Bissett, Brenda Rezk, Dave Hermann, Richard P Bissmire, Jessica Reid, Jerel D Heritage, Yes, Robin Yang, Pat Hayes, Keith Setzer, Elizabeth Ann Scarborough, Deborah Fishburn, Colette Reap, Revek, Eagle Archambeault, Tory Shade, Katrina Allis, David Rowe, Ivan Donati, KixieKat, Sharon E. Altmann, Rafe Brox, Molly Elizabeth Atkins, Linden Vimislik, Catherine Gross-Colten, Henry W Schubert, Deborah Blake, Julie Hendershott Kovac, Jaime O. Mayer, Alysia Murphy, JE Chase, Karen Grennan, Peter T, Rick D, Cynthia Porter, Tahmi DeSchepper, Anne M. Rindfliesch, Holland Dougherty, David Medinnus, Clara Strzalkowski, Eduard Lukhmanov, Melme, Cheryl Preyer, Gary Clark, Rachel Sasseen, Kathryn L. Whitlock, Annette Agostini, Sarah Liberman, Svend Andersen, Kristi Chadwick, Pam Blome, Betty Law Morgan, Hisham El-Far, Kathy Holzapfel, Jen B, Sofie Bird, Mark Kiraly, Mary Alice Wuerz, Keith West, Future Potentate of the Solar System, Sally Novak Janin, Mary Jeh, Steven Mentzel, S. Worthen, Hannah Maxwell, Curtis Frye, David Drew, Paul Bulmer, Rolf Laun, Jesse Klein, Shel Kennon, Cathy Schwartz, Christina Stiles, Ross Hathaway, Tammy Greco, Christine Ethier, Bruce Shipman, Tibicina, Michelle Carlson, Missy Katano, Donna Gaudet, Danielle Ackley-McPhail, Jenn Whitworth, Jessica K. Meade, Leah Webber, Chris Barili, Tina Connell, Janka Hobbs, Ian Chung, Rissa Lyn, Jonathan S Chance, Gretchen, Cheryl Losinger, Brenda Cooper, Corey T., Anonymous Reader, ARNSProprietor, Thomas Santilli, Heather Kelly, Nancy Barber, Selwyn, filkferengi, Ron Currens, Lily Connors, Melissa Shumake, Charlie Russel, Jason Palmatier, David Zurek, Connor Bliss, Tomas Burgos-Caez, Natasha A., John Senn, Nancy M. Tice, Andy Funk from Atlanta, Karen Dubois, Nesa Sivagnanam, Paul McNamee, Robert Early, John Green, Echo Mae, Deena Cates, nobe, Janet Oblinger, Jen Woods, Julia Haynie, Andy Miller, Dr.Deb, Julie Pitzel, John Sturkie, Michael Kahan, Jake Parrick, Ronnie J Darling, Jen1701D, Amelia Smith, Samuel Aronoff, Max Kaehn, Ron

Hogan, Patricia van Ooy, Kelly J Cooper, Mollie Bowers, Alexander Smith, CGJulian, Leshia-Aimée Doucet, Andrew and Kate Barton, David Eggerschwiler, Ian Harvey, Amanda Nixon, Mark Newman, Rachel Conner-Maling, Mark Gerrits, Smashingsuns, D-Rock, Simba, Hero, and Nahla, Nathan Turner, Lauren E. Mitchell, Maria Lima, Anne Burner, Orla, Lisa Kruse, Colleen Harkins, Tina M Noe Good, Bill and Laura Pearson, Philip Barkow, Sandy, @lenoxartist, Steven Halter, Dan & Chris Brewer, Elaine Tindill-Rohr, Ty wilda, Kaitlin Thorsen, Heather Fagan, Jeremy Brett, Maureen Brooks, Cherie Livingston, Julie Benda, Tris Lawrence, Michelle Palmer, Rosanne Girton, Evergreen Lee, Kate Larking, Jaymie Larkey Maham, Margaret St. John, Kelly Melnyk, Carolyn Mackriell, Jena Marie Klees, Emily Weed Baisch, Freya Jackson, Paul Gunther, Tristan Smith, Karen H, Annastasia (medicinalink) Gallaher, Kathryn A Patterson, R.T. Bryson, Galena Ostipow, Jeremy Audet, K. Hodghead, Phillip Spencer, Jen Bishop, Hedrigall, Cathy Brown, K. McLeod, Jay Barnson, Kathy Bond, Megan Hungerford, Tony F, Amy Streifel, Noah Bast, Ellie, SwordFire, Gary Ehrlich, ChanieB, V. Hartman DiSanto, Holly Daugherty, Kimberly M. Lowe, Barbara Hasebe, RJ Seymour, Erik T Johnson, Patrick Osbaldeston, Anthony R. Cardno, Russell Martens, Jacob Carson, Andy Clayman, Shelly Jones, Elizabeth Kite, Bill Sykes, Erin Penn, Janito Vaqueiro Ferreira Filho, John/Susan Husisian, Aurelia McDonald, Keith E. Hartman, Gustaf B., Ilene Tsuruoka, Linda Pierce, Wolf SilverOak, Gnondpom, Rebecca M, Lucas Santiago, Crazy Lady Used Books & Emporium, Samuel Lubell, Theresa Glover, Annaliese Smith, Bill Emerson, Liz Wyatt, Abi Scott, Cheryl, Chris Fielding, R Kirkpatrick, Jonathan Adams, Stephen Kissinger, Iain Riley, Robert Parks, Erin Kowalski, Michael Cieslak, Mini Lizard, Kitty Likes, Krystina Harrington, R. Hunter, C.N.Rowen, Rachel "Nausicaa" Tougas, Terry D. England, Judith Mortimore, Daria Fox, Bill McGeachin, RBC, Pat Connelly, Zion Russell, Kevin Niemczyk, C. Liang, anne m gibson, David J Fortier, Justin P. Miller,   C. Lennox, Pete Hollmer, Sue Shelly, Nellie, Tammy Graves, Kristy K, Aaron R, Matthew Walker, K.G. Anderson, Vancano Smith, Carina Erk, Lauren Wallace, Laura F., Melissa Burkart, Dino Hicks, J. I. Rogers, Gabe Krabbe, Judy Bemis, Dina Barron, Troy Bucher, Margaret S. McGraw, Kathi Schreiber, Carla Hollar, Lyn Godfrey, Kimberly H., Marc D. Long, Donaithnen, Lisa Deutsch Harrigan (Auntie M), Axisor, Gai LaMarche, Cliff Winnig, Janet Armentani, Danny Neimeyer, Belkis Marcillo, Ian Monroe, Lynn Kramer, Crystal Sarakas, Pamela Lunsford, J.P. Goodwin, Wendy Kitchens, Michael Grey, Rhel ná DecVandé, Terri Oda, Judith Bienvenu, Heather & Zachary Jones, Victoria L Sullivan, Jamie FitzGerald